HOW NOT TO MURDER
YOUR EX

KATIE MARSH

Boldwood

First published in Great Britain in 2023 by Boldwood Books Ltd.

Copyright © Katie Marsh, 2023

Cover Design by Head Design Ltd

Cover Illustration: Shutterstock

A CIP catalogue record for this book is available from the British Library.

Paperback ISBN 978-1-78513-881-2

Large Print ISBN 978-1-78513-877-5

Hardback ISBN 978-1-78513-876-8

Ebook ISBN 978-1-78513-874-4

Kindle ISBN 978-1-78513-875-1

Audio CD ISBN 978-1-78513-882-9

MP3 CD ISBN 978-1-78513-879-9

Digital audio download ISBN 978-1-78513-873-7

Boldwood Books Ltd
23 Bowerdean Street
London SW6 3TN
www.boldwoodbooks.com

To Isabelle Broom, with thanks for killer Post-its and so much more.

1

CLIO

On the many occasions Clio had imagined murdering her husband, it had never been anything like this. Her mind's eye had always turned away from what came next – avoiding the gore that would accompany the click of a trigger or the scream that might follow his flailing body after it was pushed from a cliff. She had never been serious, anyway. Everyone knew that. It was just Clio saying her piece, moaning about Gary the way she always did. People thought it was funny – last week her darts team had even stuck his picture over the bullseye for their Friday night match. Clio's ensuing scores had led to the Raging Bullseye's first victory over the Dart Vaders for well over a year. It was amazing what a little motivation could do.

But Clio hadn't seriously wanted to kill him. She had simply craved justice: her house back; the company they had founded together to be half hers again; every penny he had taken repaid in full. But not this. Not even Gary deserved this ending. She forced herself to look down at him, so still in the wind that raged around the clifftop static caravan that Clio had been forced to call home. As her PVC windows rattled, there he lay, his face turned to one side, his arms outstretched across her bottom step. In the dim glow of the security light above her flimsy front door she could see the salt and pepper hair, the thick neck emerging from his checked shirt, the broad shoulders beneath the leather jacket he misguidedly believed made him look like a *Top Gun* recruit. His blood pooled thickly around him, a macabre halo, staining the brown step red.

Clio knew what she had to do. When she had been a jobbing actress in her early twenties she had played a runner discovering a body in an episode of *Casualty*, and she repeated the motions she had gone through on camera, forcing her unwilling limbs to move. She knelt, ignoring the loud clicking of her knee, stretching out her freezing fingers, pushing his gold chain aside to place them on his neck.

Hope rose, despite all the evidence in front of her. 'Gary?' She found the spot where his pulse should be. She felt – nothing. No rhythm. No life.

He was gone.

Unable to believe it, she pushed harder, her wrist connecting with his chin, forcing it sideways so his head turned against the step, his face angling away from hers. She gasped as she saw that the back of his skull was caked in blood, the bone smashed and gaping, splinters of white visible against the wood.

She took one more look, checking, praying, just in case this was another anxiety dream, one of the ones she woke from at 'Just Kill Me o'clock', swearing, terrified and hotter than the earth's core. But the chill of his skin told her that it was not a dream. It was 5.30 a.m. on her forty-fifth birthday and the husband she had hated was lying dead on her doorstep. Even worse, this was no accident. Someone had killed him. Someone had murdered him and brought him here.

Clio's stomach was churning now, shock starting to set in. She backed away from the body, leaning against the caravan, her mind whirling. When she had tottered back here, she had never expected to find this. For a moment she wondered if perhaps she could have killed him. Maybe Amber's lethal margaritas had tipped her over the edge – cocktails mixed by someone doing the Macarena were always going to be a risk.

Clio licked her salty lips and tried to remember. She knew she had left the caravan during Jeanie's screeching rendition of 'Wuthering Heights', driven as much by an urgent need for air as by her friend's terminal inability to carry a tune. She had aimed for the beach, wanting to feel the sea spray on her burning face, hoping to reach the waves before she went up in flames. But then her mind went blank, as it had so often of late, leaving her with a black hole where a memory should be.

The only thing Clio knew for sure was that she must have reached her destination, as she had woken up half an hour ago face down in a sand dune with an empty carton of chips at her side. It was a miracle, really. Despite the gale, the darkness and a new high in blood-alcohol levels, she had managed to make her way along the narrow pathway that ran along the edge of the cliff, somehow navigating Death's Drop, which revelled in the dubious honour of being the number one seaside suicide spot in the south of England.

To have survived all that, only to find herself here, was beyond belief. Here, with her dead husband's body at her feet. Clio had thought that slipping a disc while doing up her bra would go down in history as her worst birthday ever, but it appeared that life always had new treats in store.

She shivered, dimly aware that *Little Miss Trouble* pyjamas were not the ideal attire for the discovery of a dead body on a stormy February morning. Inside her caravan her friends were wearing them too. It was one of their birthday traditions, like karaoke and the neon cheese puffs from the corner shop that made their finger-tips glow in the dark. Clio wanted to time travel back, to stay in her caravan, to be just the birthday 'girl' listening to an unspeakable performance of a Kate Bush classic. Back then she was a wronged woman, rebuilding her life one terrible temp job at a time. Now, she was a potential killer standing over the corpse of the man who had taken everything from her. It would take the police about ten seconds to put her in handcuffs and lock her away.

Could she have done it? Despite her brain fog, surely Clio would remember if she had. She checked her hands, but found no marks, no bruises, no blood. She looked around but couldn't see a weapon. But she wanted to be sure – to have her story ready for the inevitable police interview in some hellish room with the kind of lighting that would make her look like she belonged in a nursing home. She put her head in her hands, listening to the crash of the waves far below her and searched her mind, hoping for a clue, a moment – a flicker of something that would absolve her.

Her mind was as empty as her bank account. She might as well get a T-shirt saying PRIME SUSPECT. To the police it would be such a simple story: an embittered wife discovers the body of her husband and says she can't remember where she was when he was killed. They would throw away the key.

Clio could almost hear the clang of prison gates. She fought to breathe, but the nausea was rising. She stood up and retched, sharing the majority of last night's margaritas with the tub of early daffodils that Jeanie had brought round to 'brighten things up'. Even when she had nothing left inside her, Clio stayed bent over, hands grasping her knees. Something strange was happening. In all those nights spent hating him and slating him, Clio had never imagined how she might actually feel if Gary died. How her eyes might fill with tears. How her mind would scroll through the good times, pushing the bad aside.

For a second she trembled, about to cry. But then she heard a crunch that could have been a footstep on the gravel path that ran through the centre of the caravan park. Clio stared into the darkness, hairs prickling at the back of her neck. She couldn't see anyone, but as she didn't have her glasses on this didn't mean much. She had taken the wrong bottle in the shower yesterday and accidentally exfoliated her hair.

Her pulse spiralled. She had to do something before someone saw the body. Even though she was at the far end of the caravan site, hidden away behind the bin store, someone could come along at any minute. You never knew with this lot. Last week the woman in number nine had started rooting through the recycling at 6 a.m., apparently searching for her passport. So, Clio couldn't just stand here – she had to do something fast, before someone found her with the body and called the police. She would never get out of prison. She would die in there, toothless and wailing and alone. '*My mum the murderer,*' her teenage daughter Nina would say, while selling her body on the streets to fund her spiralling drug habit. '*I never had a chance.*'

Of course Clio knew that she should go into the caravan, find her phone and dial 999. But her mind alighted on another option – one that would give her the time to work out what she had been doing for the past few hours. Time to prove – to herself and to the world – that she hadn't murdered Gary Goode.

Because that was the problem. Gary was dead on *her* doorstep. Given that she had been MIA when the body appeared and given everything that had happened between them, who on earth was going to believe that Clio hadn't put him there?

The rain chose this moment to begin pouring down. Perfect.

Clio stood up. 'Happy bloody birthday to me, eh, Gary?'

She swayed for a second, blood rushing to her head. She had a plan, but even at her best she would struggle to carry it out. Reluctant though she was to drag her friends into this, she needed backup. She needed companions at the top of their game. She needed James Bond, Luther and a whole pack of Avengers too.

Instead, she had two hammered forty-something women snoring on her living room floor. She had Amber and Jeanie.

They would have to do.

Stepping over her dead husband on the doorstep, Clio went inside to wake her friends.

2

GARY

8.30 a.m.: Death minus nineteen hours

On the day that he was going to die, Gary Goode woke up feeling even more pleased with himself than usual. He waited a moment before opening his eyes, appreciating the kiss of silk sheets against his skin and the scent of lilies from the majestic bronze vase in the centre of the stone fireplace to his left. He had come such a long way. He had bounced back as he always did, and now he had landed in a four-poster bed in a country hotel so luxurious that it was about to star in its own fly-on-the-wall documentary. He had always known that the world was his for the taking. What more proof did he need?

He stretched, wishing he could brag more openly about where he found himself right now. But he had to keep it a secret, so instead he stared in satisfaction at the thick, honey-coloured hair of the woman lying beside him. Cherie was the stuff of fantasies, all five-foot-nine of her, all curves, long legs and tan, and he had known at their first meeting six months ago that he had to have her. Never mind that her husband, Marshall Fernandez, was by far his most affluent client. Never mind that Gary had a live-in girlfriend, Denise, nor that he was still married to Clio, aka his biggest ever mistake, because she wouldn't agree to the terms of their perfectly reasonable divorce settlement. He was Gary Goode. He would have Cherie soon enough.

As ever, he was right. One of the many plus sides of having wealthy clients was the amount of time they spent quaffing champagne in first class. Soon Marshall was off overseas on business, leaving Gary to drop in on Cherie with some updated designs for the rebuild he was project-managing at their home. Within an hour he was taking full advantage of the businessman's absence to bed his wife on top of their ten grand kitchen table.

Naturally, Cherie had come back for more. They all did. And Gary was happy to indulge them. Now, he ran an exploratory finger down her cheek and checked the ornate clock on the wall, embossed with trails of golden ivy and cherubs. Thirty minutes until he had to leave for his first appointment of the day. Plenty of time. It would be a shame to waste this opportunity. Criminal, even.

Cherie's eyes remained closed, so he tried again, his hand tracing the curve of her hip until it reached her thigh. He leant down and kissed it.

That got her attention.

'Morning, you.' That sleepy smile. Wide lips, pink tongue peeping through dazzling white teeth.

'Morning, *Chérie*.' He pronounced her name the French way. He liked showing her his cosmopolitan side.

She gazed at him, wide green eyes soft. Even her yawns were sexy as hell.

Gary's hand was still stroking her silky thigh. All those gold-topped lotions in her Chanel washbag clearly did the trick. Clio had never taken that much trouble, no matter how many times he had thoughtfully let her know she was letting herself slide. As Cherie arched towards him, he wondered idly how much her beauty regime set her back. She could afford it, mind – a leading sportswear designer, married to her childhood sweetheart who just happened to have built a successful sportswear label, Printz, from scratch. Their mansion was worth ten million and then there were the coach houses, cottages and stables scattered around the estate as well. When he had landed his first meeting with Marshall, Gary had known that getting the job could be his passport to the kind of clientele he wanted. At last, he could be who he was born to be. Design guru to the rich until – one day – he would become one of their number.

Clio still insisted that she had won the contract, that it was her ideas that had swung it, but then she had always tried to put Gary down. In truth, Gary had been planning this for years. Sitting there in his tiny teenage bedroom, staring at that awful navy and white charity shop duvet, he had always known that he would hit the heights. He had understood that the mouldy semi his parents so happily called home was merely a launch pad for the man he would become. Something to keep secret. Something to escape.

It had taken him a while to find his way, to be sure – but that was his parents' fault. They were always so bloody happy – content with their life of hard graft and a fish and chip tea on Fridays. They liked blending in, being 'normal', doing the kind of jobs absolutely no one noticed. His dad had swept roads. His mum had cut hair in a salon where nobody tipped. When they had died, within six months of each other, Gary hadn't even cried. He had nothing in common with them, after all. They were his past.

Women like Cherie were his future.

'Babes?'

He was back in the present – silk sheets and sunlight and a

woman who was currently starring in her own swimwear commercial.

'Yes?' His hand was against her now, fingers moving in a steady rhythm – he was doing his finest work here if he did say so himself. Last night she had proved herself more than capable of giving the same treatment in return, and had shared some juicy gossip too. Her indiscretion had proved very useful over the past few months – she had told him of dissatisfied friends seeking new designers and perspectives, enabling Gary to undercut his rivals and swoop in with his ideas. Loss leaders, sure, but worth it in the long run, whatever Clio said.

'Gary.' Cherie's voice was tiny, her back arched. She was close, he could tell.

'Yes?' His middle finger was starting to ache, but he was man enough to handle it.

There should be gym machines for this. Little weights, to build up stamina. He might look into that. His next empire. What would he call it though? *Magic Touch*? Yes, something along those lines. Even now in the midst of pleasuring a beautiful woman, he just couldn't switch off his entrepreneurial flair.

'Gary?'

'Yes?' He wished she would stop talking. The clock was ticking. He was all for equality, but a man needed his turn too.

She kissed him. 'I think we should get an aquarium built in. Behind the hob? Beneath the Sicilian tiles. I'd love to see the little fish swimming around while I cook.'

Gary sighed inwardly. All that effort and she just wanted to talk shop. He removed his finger and circled it in the air, trying to get rid of the pins and needles.

'That's a great idea.' It wasn't. Fish next to a hob? They would die the first time anyone attempted a stir fry. But maybe he could put them somewhere else. He struggled to remember what was in the current plans. He had five projects on the go at the moment, all rich clients with endless wish lists. One was even importing a marble countertop from Asia, where it had been blessed by the Dalai Lama or some such shit.

Gary checked the clock again. He was running out of time, and he really couldn't miss this meeting. Another day, another new millionaire client – this time Marshall's brother Johnny, looking for a sweeping extension and extensive internal redesign on his new property. Initial discussions had proved positive, and Gary had every reason to believe that he was going to get this gig. He needed it – without Johnny's deposit, the turnaround plan he had put together last week would collapse. But Gary knew he could do it. His company, Looking Goode, was going places. Take that, Clio.

His companion sighed, twirling a strand of her hair around a glossy pink nail that he had rather been hoping would be digging into his back by now. Still, needs must. Business first, pleasure second. He had an empire to build.

'You like it? I knew you would.' Her husky voice belonged on a sex line. Gary should know – from the years he had spent in the wilderness with Clio and her begrudging once-a-week regime. It was hardly his fault that he had looked elsewhere.

'I love it.' He would work something out. 'I'll add it in to the plans when I get to the office.' He gave her one last look, but she was staring at the ceiling, lost in contemplation of little fish swimming nowhere. Oh well. No accounting for taste – he had learnt that long ago.

Gary worked out that he wasn't going to get what he wanted, so he pushed himself up, ready to swing his legs out of bed. A shower and some of the hotel's excellent Turkish coffee would do the trick. Almost the perfect start to the day.

But then there they were. The hands pulling him down again, wanting him, needing him. He could fit in a quickie. He was flexible, he could duck and dive. Give him a problem and he would fix it. Give him a challenge and he would find a solution. Nothing kept Gary Goode down for long.

He kissed her deeply. Pulling away he saw that smile. *Come to me* and *yes* and *now, now, now,* all rolled into one. Fingertips against his skin. Hips opening for him as he lowered himself. He nuzzled her neck in a semblance of foreplay, pleasure prickling through him as he heard her gasp.

Gary was so busy thinking of his own pleasure that he didn't hear the rustle of curtains behind him as a phone was pointed in his direction, the camera set to record. A minute later, he didn't see the figure quietly disappearing behind the heavy silk, before climbing out and descending a drainpipe to the rose beds below.

Gary Goode was too busy ruling his world to notice anything. He had a beautiful woman moaning his name. He had a thriving business. He had come back from the kind of financial setback that would make other men throw in the towel for good. And so he carried on thrusting his way to glory, unaware of the person creeping quietly towards a waiting car, scrolling through their camera roll, smiling.

Gary Goode was going to die today, but he was too busy starring in his own story to be able to see the writing on the wall.

3

JEANIE

'Jeanie.'

Jeanie turned over. Just a few more hours of shut-eye. Or days. That was all she needed to become human again.

'Jeanie.' The voice was low and rushed – nothing like the piercing cries of her twins. They must be OK for once, meaning she could just turn over and go back to slee...

'JEANIE. I NEED YOU.'

'YeswhatisithowcanIhelpwhatcanIdo?' Jeanie sprang straight up to a sitting position, wondering why she was cuddling a sparkly karaoke mic. She had dim memories of belting out 'Reach', of doing her Vanilla Ice routine, of eating microwave chips and cackling over teenage hairdos in an ancient school yearbook.

And then there had been... tequila? Jeanie groaned. No wonder she felt as if she was made of doom. Once, she had drunk her friends under the table, but now she was the kind of woman who slept underneath said table while the party raged above her.

More sleep. She lay down again.

'JEANIE.'

A hand was jostling her now. She opened her eyes, taking in the expression on Clio's face. Instantly, she took her friend's hand, ignoring the nausea churning in her gut, the fact that her head was screaming for mercy.

'What's wrong?'

'It's Gary.' She had never seen Clio look this pale: not when Gary got together with Denise, the nubile journalist who had been sent to interview them both for the local paper; not when Clio had realised that Gary had remortgaged their house without telling her; not even when Gary had got the board to fire her from Looking Goode, the company Clio's money had enabled them to set up together.

Jeanie pressed Clio's cold fingers in hers. Her friend was dripping wet and shivering.

'Why are you so cold?'

Clio shook her head, her blue eyes glistening with tears.

'Oh lovely, what is it?'

Silence. This was a bad sign. Clio could always say anything. She specialised in speaking her truth, no matter how unwilling the world was to hear it.

Jeanie tucked a strand of Clio's scarlet hair behind her ear. The blue tips were black with rain. 'OK.' She was waking up now. The twins had got her used to going from sleep to hysteria in sixty seconds flat. 'How about you show me what he's done, then?'

'I...' Clio tailed off.

Jeanie heaved herself up to standing, grasping Clio's shoulder as the room swayed. 'God. How much did we drink last night?'

'Too much.'

'True.' Jeanie pressed her hands to her temples. 'And it's outside? Whatever Gary's done?'

'Yes, but...'

Jeanie hesitated. 'It's not down on the beach, is it? Because the wind sounds mad and I'm not sure I'll make it down...'

Clio shook her head. 'No. It's on the doorstep. I mean he's on the...'

'OK, I'll have a look.' Jeanie staggered to the door.

Clio was trying to pull her back, her chunky gold rings digging into Jeanie's fingers. 'No. It'll be too much for you. I need to—'

'It's fine.' Jeanie was sure she could handle whatever lay ahead. Clio did have a tendency to be dramatic – a legacy of her years playing bit parts in TV soaps and leads in pub theatre pantos.

'But...'

'Just show me, Clio.' Jeanie's stomach was starting to roil. She saw the empty bottles lying in the sink and wanted to hurl. Judging by the state of her spine she had done a lot of dancing last night, and her neck was so sore she was struggling to look down.

She stopped. 'Where's Amber?'

'Dunno.' Clio shrugged. 'Maybe she left?'

'I doubt it.' Jeanie put her hand on the doorknob. 'She sang "Wired for Sound" after you went outside. She only does that when she's really wasted. Maybe she's gone for a walk?' She opened the door, only for the wind to push her back inside.

She tried again, making it onto the top step. All she could see was darkness. 'What am I looking at?' The rain was lashing down so hard she could barely see the end of her own nose.

Clio stood next to her, pointing downwards. 'There. Look.'

'What? Where?'

'Down there!'

Jeanie followed her finger. Her sore neck meant that she had to bend at the waist in order to see what lay on the bottom step. She rapidly wished she hadn't.

'Oh my God.' Now she really was going to be sick. 'That's...'

'Yes.' Clio jumped off the steps and started pacing as Jeanie mentally apologised to the daffodils and hurled. Clio seemed oblivious to the rain pouring down around her.

Jeanie wiped her mouth. 'It's Gary.'

'Yes.'

Jeanie shuddered. 'And he's...' She couldn't look again.

'Dead. Yes.'

'Oh my God.'

'Yes.'

'But who...?' Jeanie tried to stand up straight but her head was swimming. Gary was so still. So covered in blood. 'How? Who...?'

'Who did it? I don't know. Maybe it was me?' Clio's laugh was high-pitched. Hysterical. 'I have no idea. I can't remember a thing.'

'Ssssh. Don't say that.' Jeanie slid down against the step, her back to his body, trying to get some semblance of control. 'Someone might hear you.'

'But it could have been me, Jeanie. I'm serious.'

She could hear the panic in Clio's voice and wanted to calm her. She must ignore her neck, ignore her hangover. She must help. Jeanie levered her way to a vertical position and put her hand on Clio's shoulder. 'You didn't do this, Clio.'

'How do you know that? *I* don't even know that.' Panic gleamed in Clio's eyes. 'I can't remember where I was, Jeanie. And he's right here. Where I live. So maybe...'

Jeanie hugged her. It was all she could think of. To be honest she needed the support too. Arms around her. Human contact. Normality.

When she pulled away Clio was biting her lip the same way she always had, nibbling voraciously, a squirrel with a fresh nut. Jeanie knew all her mannerisms. The three of them – Clio, Amber and Jeanie – had been friends since spending hours together at school not being picked in PE. Five years of standing in the freezing cold feeling invisible. Five years of pretending that they didn't care what the world thought of them and of only seeing the best in each other – the kind of trio that nothing could ever break.

After school finished, they had somehow all returned to Sunshine Sands, which had the depressing distinction of having the highest rainfall of any small seaside town in the UK. After loud teenage proclamations that they would move to America and lead the glossy lives depicted in the TV shows they devoured on E4, somehow they had never quite managed it. They had not moved to LA, bumped into Leonardo DiCaprio and married him as they had intended. *His loss*, they would giggle over chips and tea from the beach café as their twenties became their thirties, and their thirties became decades they would rather not name. *He could have had us, and all he got was a string of supermodels and an Oscar. Poor Leo.*

'Jeanie, I'm serious. I could have done it.'

Jeanie looked down at the mess of bone and blood. She didn't know much, but she knew that Clio wasn't capable of murder. 'No. I know you, Clio. There is no way you did this.'

Clio leant into her. 'Are you sure?'

'Yes.' Jeanie thought for a second. 'I mean, you were so hammered you could barely sing, let alone manage to do that.' Jeanie gestured towards the body at their feet. 'And then there's who you are. You pick up spiders and put them outside. You recycle. You run a free Zumba class at the community centre. You're no killer.'

'But I was outside when it happened. I must have passed out. So it'll look like I did it.' Clio was pacing now.

'No. We'll call 999, the police will come and they'll figure out what happened.' Jeanie reached for her phone, only to discover it wasn't there.

'No.' Clio shook her head, the rain running in rivulets down her cheeks. 'Don't call yet.'

'Why not?'

'Because...' Clio's face was alight with desperation. It reminded Jeanie of the time Clio had got all dolled up for the lower sixth disco, only to see the boy she fancied sticking his hand up a supply teacher's dress during the first song. 'Because I need to hide the body.'

'What?' Jeanie cupped a hand around her ear. She must have misheard.

Clio yelled. 'I need to hide the body.'

So she had heard correctly the first time. 'Why?'

'Because they'll lock me up, Jeanie. I need time to prove it wasn't me. And yesterday I—'

'No.' Jeanie had to stop this. 'We can't hide him, Clio. We'd be breaking the law.' Jeanie had to convince her. 'Look, I get that this is a shock, but hiding the body would be madness.'

Clio was taut, breathing fast. Jeanie tried again. 'Let's call it in, Clio. Now.'

Clio shook her head. 'I can't. I need more time.'

'No.' Jeanie hated refusing her friends – she was always the one who stayed for one more drink she didn't want or who drove miles to see a movie she knew she wouldn't enjoy. But this was too much. 'Clio, we can't. We'd be in all kinds of trouble. And I have the twins so—'

'And I have Nina!' Clio threw her head back, as theatrical as the time she played Éponine in a college production of 'Les Misérables', still singing as the flimsy barricades literally collapsed beneath her. 'That's why, Jeanie! I mean, Nina needs me. I can't leave her. Not after what Gary's done to her.'

Jeanie's brain struggled to keep up. As far as she was aware Clio's daughter Nina had no contact with her stepfather Gary any more. 'To Nina? What has he done?'

'Yesterday I found out that he'd...' Clio shook her head. She started pulling up her soggy pyjama sleeves, readying herself for action. 'Are you going to help me or not?'

Jeanie looked at her friend and felt a fierce pang of love shoot through her. Clio was a one-woman miniseries, but she was also fearless, loyal and absolutely always there when Jeanie needed her. It was Clio who had driven Jeanie to that last IVF appointment, the only person to believe that it would finally work this time. And it was Clio who had lost her savings, house and livelihood thanks to – Jeanie mentally apologised for thinking ill of the dead – that git Gary. Now Clio might lose her freedom as well.

'I...'

'I'm moving him now.' Clio stood over the body. 'Are you in?'

Jeanie stalled. 'What do we need to do?'

'I don't know. I've never done this before! My car? Let's get him in there.'

Jeanie frowned. 'Is he going to fit though? He's a bit big for a Fiat 500.' Her stomach spiked with an adrenaline she normally reserved for her twins' unintentional flights down the stairs. She couldn't do this.

'We'll have to make him fit. Please, Jeanie?' Clio's voice shook.

The fear in her eyes. That was what swung it. Jeanie had never seen Clio scared before. She held up her hands. 'OK. OK.'

She had to help. Clio and Amber were her people. They had shared hangovers, birthdays, teenage escapades, hot flushes and tears over boyfriends, parents, arrogant bosses, boobs drooping and bums spreading. They had eaten together, puked together, Inter-railed together, shared changing rooms, screw-ups, painkillers and hangover cures. The three of them were a team. A family.

And Gary Goode wasn't going to ruin Clio's life again. Not on Jeanie's watch.

'Right then. I'll take the...' She looked at the head and balked. 'I'll take the legs.' She tottered to the south end of Gary, wondering if she might faint. The rain plastered her hair over her eyes which was probably for the best.

'OK.' Clio positioned herself above his shattered head. 'Thank you.'

'You're welcome.' Jeanie lowered her hands towards his ankles, suddenly wishing she had drunk more. She was trembling and her mind was swirling with horror. But she had given birth, for God's sake. Twice. In a lay-by. She could do anything.

Thunder rumbled in the distance. How appropriate.

Clio bent down. 'On my count. One. Two...'

'STOP!'

They both froze. They knew that voice.

They waited, heads hanging, as Amber came outside to join them.

4

GARY

Blissfully unaware of the picture that had just been taken of his backside in full flagrante, Gary, showered, dressed and doused in Boss, was right on time for his appointment with Johnny Fernandez. As he passed through the wrought iron gates he stopped his car, tapping a message into the small grey phone in his hand, before turning it off and putting it back in its hiding place. He smiled, satisfied. The money should land today. It wasn't even 10 a.m. and already he was well on his way to being a winner.

The wheels of his red MG crunched on the white gravel of the winding drive as he passed a life-size topiary elephant and swept up to 'The Magisterium', a vast seventeenth-century vicarage just begging for Gary to bring it up to date. It was a crumbling canvas: ivy spread across the eastern corner, green leaves against honey-coloured walls, and trails of winter roses climbed the tapering pillars that stood on either side of the imposing front steps. Gary's first move would be to rip the plants out to create the clear clean lines he preferred. Maybe he would go glass-fronted too, just to maximise impact. He could explore that further when the owner Johnny signed on the dotted line today.

Gary checked his reflection in the rear-view mirror before getting out of his car, proud of what he saw. Since entering his forties longer ago than he would choose to admit, he had been careful to preserve his good looks. They were even more important now that he was sole CEO of Looking Goode, without Clio to drag him down with her embarrassing small talk, wild hair and dramatic taste in scarves. Gary straightened his collar. His image helped him to make his mark, like the fleet of company vans he had yet to pay for and the staff he had hired to design virtual tours like the one he was about to deliver. Only the best for the firm now Clio was out of the way. It would all pay off in the end.

He strode up the wide stone steps, feeling powerful in his favourite navy suit, until he was standing in front of the heavy black front door. As he lifted the brass knocker he had a feeling he was being watched and turned, hoping to catch his observer by surprise. A tabby cat was walking across his bonnet, claws skittering across the paintwork that Gary waxed himself every Sunday after-noon – his own form of religion.

Gary swore under his breath. No one touched that bonnet except him. It was hallowed territory, like Wembley stadium or Wimbledon Centre Court. 'Get away!' he hissed at the cat, which steadfastly refused to move. Gary strode down the steps and had just grabbed the bloody animal by the scruff of its neck when he heard a voice.

'Gary. Hi.' The last word was at least ten syllables long. Public school twat, check.

Gary turned, switching on his biggest smile. 'Hi Johnny.'

'What are you doing to my cat?' Johnny folded his arms, his eyes hidden behind aviator shades.

He was so different to his brother Marshall. Johnny was wiry where Marshall was bodybuilder broad; Johnny wore a tight white T-shirt while Marshall was always dressed in extravagantly patterned shirts. But there were similarities: the cheekbones; the Fernandez signet ring on his little finger; the way he oozed money, right down to his expensive brogues and ostentatious Carrera watch. It must be nice, having an inheritance. All Gary's dad had left him were freckles and an allergy to freshly cut grass.

To be fair Johnny had experienced downs as well as ups. He had run his father's shipping business into the ground, only to rise again as the inventor of the Fernandez chip, now used in smartphones across the globe. His company Fernandez Tech was about to float on the stock exchange and the shares were priced high. Johnny was the kind of client Gary needed. The kind of client Looking Goode deserved.

Gary became aware that Johnny was waiting for an answer, his eyebrow arched.

'I was just saying hello to him.' Gary tried to stroke Jerry, but the animal yowled so loudly that Gary jumped despite himself. He tripped, falling to his knees behind his car, out of sight of Johnny. He was about to give the animal a good clout when he heard a voice.

'Dad. I—'

Johnny cut in. 'Not now, Christian.'

Gary froze, his knees pressing into the gravel, listening. You never knew what might come in useful.

Christian spoke again. 'I took—'

'Later, OK?'

'But I just want to tell you...' Christian's voice rose to a whine.

'Christian.' Johnny's voice was as final as a descending guillotine. 'Later. Haven't you got a job to go to, or have you been fired already?'

'No. I mean yes. I do have a job. But...'

'So go. Whatever it is, it can wait. I'll see you later.'

Gary stood up to see Christian's slicked-back brown hair and sloping shoulders disappearing reluctantly towards the row of cars that were parked around the side of the house. He knew all about Johnny's eighteen-year-old son, despite his absence from Johnny's carefully curated Instagram grid, which was full of #blessed pictures of Johnny, his second wife and their one-year-old girl. But Gary had done his research. He knew that Christian had just been expelled from one of England's most prestigious schools, and he knew that it wasn't the first time.

'Gary.' Johnny beckoned. 'Are you coming in, then?' He picked up the cat, now angelic and purring, and stepped back to let Gary come inside. The hallway was cavernous, with a dark, mahogany floor and green floral wallpaper that belonged in a Jane Austen remake. Wide stairs spiralled upwards on both sides, and Gary knew from the plans that they led to a floor featuring five bedrooms, with five more in the south wing.

Gary's plans for the Fernandez home were ambitious; he would knock down all the walls downstairs – creating a huge living space the likes of which would get his firm featured in *Ideal Home*. It was solely Gary's design, after their architect Angus had walked out in misguided loyalty to Clio. Not that Gary missed him. He had found his calling – he had always been more than a brickie and without Clio there was no one to hold him back. Soon, the whole country would be Looking Goode.

'This way.' Gary followed Johnny, past imposing mirrors and doors leading into rooms with cream sofas, dark tables and huge floral displays. Finally, they arrived at the kitchen, where Gary saw Johnny's wife, Vivienne, standing in the corner staring at her phone, one hand playing with her hair. She spoke without turning round, her words rushed and impatient.

'Darling, he's just called *again*. It's the third time this week. It's like...' She shook her head, eyes still trained on her phone. 'We have to do something about him.'

Johnny coughed, walking across and kissing her, as if to quieten her.

'Baby, Gary's here.'

'Oh.' She turned. Was that a flicker of dislike on her face? Gary shook the thought away. She and Johnny couldn't know what he had been up to. He had covered his tracks too well.

A moment later she was smiling. 'Sorry about that. I was just talking about our gardener. You know how they can be.'

'Of course.' Gary didn't. Waste of money, gardeners. Just lay concrete and be done with it.

'I'm Vivienne.' She wafted towards him, all fragrance and legs in tight black jeans and a crisp white shirt. A necklace sparkled at her throat, and Gary knew that he was looking at genuine diamonds. Her long hair tumbled down her back, just the way Gary liked it. He gave her one of his humblest smiles, running a hand over his salt and pepper crew cut.

'Nice to meet you, Vivienne. Thank you for inviting me here.'

'Of course.' Her red lips curved upwards. 'We can't wait to hear the final plans.'

Her dark eyes glittered, and he suddenly had the sense that he was trapped – that if he turned towards the kitchen door it would slam shut, leaving him alone with vipers or spiders or – God forbid – his soon to be ex-wife. He must be more nervous than he had realised – a lot rode on today, after all. If Johnny didn't transfer the deposit, then... Well. Gary stopped himself. He had this in the bag.

'Come and sit down and I'll get you a coffee.' Vivienne's husky voice made it sound like she was inviting him into a private booth for show and tell. Gary pulled a chair up to the long oak table, complete with orange Fernandez Tech mugs and the kind of biscuits that were so pricey you couldn't even get them in Waitrose. He looked at the curve of Vivienne's hips as she flicked the Quooker tap on to fill up the cafetière and wondered if some day he might end up in her bed too. He would certainly enjoy that. He would enjoy that very much indeed.

He got out his iPad – ready to sell the bold, innovative design that would rewrite their lives. His pitch was pure gold, if he did say so himself, demonstrating how, if they chose him, their parties would be the stuff of *Hello!* magazine double spreads. How every single day would be golden because of his vision.

'OK. We're listening.' Johnny and Vivienne sat opposite him, a baby monitor on the table beside them, the screen showing a small figure spread-eagled in a cot.

'Bear.' Vivienne followed Gary's eyes. 'Our little one.'

'Cute.' Gary couldn't stand toddlers. Loud, dumb and demanding. His limited experience of step-parenting Clio's daughter Nina had shown him that he didn't like teenagers much either.

The two of them gazed soppily at the monitor for so long that Gary began to wonder if they were going to give it a cuddle. He forced a smile. 'So... Shall I start now?'

'OK.' Johnny's eyes met his.

Gary took a breath. 'When Bear grows up, I bet she's going to want to live in a house that reflects your ambitions for her.' A seamless link. God, he was good. 'Let me show you what I've got in mind.'

He started talking, fast and loud. And they watched him – their faces blank. Too blank. As Gary shared his vision of skylights and snugs, of underfloor heating and cornices, he knew something was wrong. They were giving him nothing. He tried harder, raising his voice as he reached the end. 'So there you have it. Modern, yet classic. Luxurious, yet in keeping with history. The new Magisterium, just for you.'

'I'm not sure.' Johnny leant back in his chair, yawning. 'It's a bit basic, isn't it?'

Gary clenched his fists. 'No, it isn't.' His design was brilliant – his girlfriend Denise had told him so. 'No, these plans are ambitious, in keeping with the way you live. You'll have an infinity pool overlooking the Downs, a solarium, two towers and a 360-degree deck.' He leant forwards, still smiling, while inside panic was starting to pulse. He needed the deposit today. He had wages to pay, and more.

Johnny shrugged. 'I don't know. It all seems a bit Ikea.'

Gary nearly spilt his coffee. 'You what?'

Johnny sighed. 'We just expected a bit more from you.'

Gary fought to keep his voice even. 'But you approved the initial designs I sent through. I thought you were going to pay the deposit today, so we can get things moving. I've got builders on standby.'

'We can't decide now.' Vivienne had picked up her phone, already scrolling. 'Maybe when we're back?'

'Back from...?'

'From London. We have a black-tie event tonight.'

'But...' Gary had to salvage this. 'I've spent...' He stopped himself. For a moment he wished Clio was with him. She could always get anyone on side.

No. The last thing he needed was that bloody woman. He licked his dry lips. 'How about I come back at the end of the day? Once you've thought about it?'

'We told you, we're going away.' Johnny stood up. 'We'll be in touch.'

'When?' Gary sounded like a needy teenager asking for a date.

'When we're ready.' Johnny finished his coffee and walked to the door.

Gary swallowed, reminding himself that he was the one with power here. Gary knew Johnny's secret – he could bring him down with one phone call. But that was the nuclear option. He wasn't there yet. Instead, he needed a Plan B.

Without the deposit he was under pressure. The company accounts were empty, he had no money to pay the staff today and he was being pursued by various contractors whose invoices were long overdue. The gap was about a hundred grand in total, peanuts to a man like Johnny, and this deposit would have kept things going until Gary could get some other clients on board.

But now he had a hole. Now he had a problem.

'Well, thank you for your time.' He tucked his iPad under his arm. 'And – do let me know.' He had a sudden image of Marg, whose grey hair and cashmere cardigans belied her reputation for relentlessly punishing anyone foolish enough not to pay her back on time. Last week she had granted Gary a loan at an eye-watering interest rate of fifty per cent. The first repayment was due at 6 p.m. tonight. Ten thousand pounds he absolutely didn't have.

Yet.

He had work to do. 'I'll see myself out.'

'Goodbye, Gary.' Vivienne had picked up a magazine and was flicking through the pages. Clearly it was another tough day at the coalface for her. 'Oh look, it's BooBoo!' she squealed at Johnny. 'I did *Vogue* with her once.'

Gary strode down the hall, his heart beating fast. This was a setback, but he held his head high. He was Gary Goode. He could figure this out if he moved fast. He got into his car and drove out of the gates, stopping for an obligatory Instagram snap for his feed, tapping out some text about new opportunities before posting it to his 350 followers. Soon he would have more. Thousands more. It was only a matter of time.

Then he revved the accelerator and rounded the corner in a

flurry of dust, so lost in thought he didn't even see the battered red mini approaching, nor the dark-haired driver hunched over the wheel. The car swerved to avoid him, but Gary didn't care that he was on the wrong side of the road. He didn't care about anything but how he was going to get the money he needed.

Without even braking, he flicked the other driver a V-sign and sped on. He was Gary Goode and it was time that the whole world got out of his way.

5

AMBER

Amber frequently felt as if the world fell apart if she dared to switch off for more than a nanosecond. This morning was proving to be no exception.

Having just spent several hours locked in the loo in Clio's caravan, she was not in the best of moods. That her two friends had failed to hear her was nearly as incredible as the fact that Jeanie's pelvic floor hadn't propelled her into the bathroom for all that time. Eventually Amber had fallen asleep, but now, after finally managing to break the lock and escape, she found herself wiping the rain from her eyes, checking that she wasn't still drunk. Or rather, checking that she wasn't so drunk that she was seeing things.

No. They really were about to be that stupid.

'STOP!'

Jeanie and Clio froze, hands perilously close to what looked like a dead body. Amber curled her hands into fists and made a silent vow never to drink again. She couldn't leave these two on their own. Not for a second.

'Step away, people!' They both shuffled backwards, heads hanging, shoulders slumped.

Amber leant down to see who the corpse had been. 'Shit.' Her hand flew to her mouth. 'Gary?! Oh my God. What the hell happened?' She reached into the pocket of her hoodie and pulled out a pair of latex gloves.

Jeanie gasped. 'Why do you have those? You left the police weeks ago.'

'Just in case I fancy a one-night stand.' For a second Amber allowed herself a smile.

'Really?' Jeanie's blue eyes widened.

'No.' Amber snapped them on, bending down to examine the body, though the rain was doing its best to stop her. 'I'm still a detective, whatever they say. Now tell me what happened.'

That set them off. Both together. Same as ever. 'Clio wanted to move the body and I couldn't say no. But I knew it was wrong. I knew...' And 'I think it might have been me. And I just wanted some time to prove it wasn't. And I can't die in prison, Amber. There's Nina and...'

'Wait.' Amber took in the blood, the fractured bone, the position of the body. She needed to commit as much as she could to memory before the rain and wind made mincemeat of the crime scene. She tucked the images away in her memory, ready to process later.

Thoughts came quickly, as did questions. This didn't seem like a premeditated crime – too messy, too much blood. But why was he here at Clio's caravan? Surely the killer had done it to set Clio up? Why was he on his back when he it looked like he had been hit from behind? Had anything else been involved? A spiked drink? A text message luring him here? Where was his phone? She scanned the ground. Nothing. She investigated his pockets. No phone to be found.

'I checked his pulse. He's definitely...' Clio petered out. Amber glanced at her face. She saw shock. Panic. She overcame a lifelong aversion to hugging and opened her arms.

Within a second they were nestling next to her, the two of them, her family.

She took deep breaths as they pressed even closer. Proximity. She could do this.

'How are you both doing?'

Clio was shivering in her sopping wet pyjamas and Jeanie was crying.

'I'm...' Clio's teeth were chattering. 'I'm fine.' The way she was clinging to Amber told her otherwise.

'Me too', Jeanie lied, wiping her eyes.

'It's OK. I've got you.' Amber's head throbbed. She had vague memories of dancing like an Egyptian. Dear God. 'I'll look after you.'

She gave them a final squeeze, stepped away and refocused on Gary. There was nothing in his hands, and no weapon in the vicinity. She scanned the ground for footprints, but the rain was so ferocious it had evidently already washed them away. She needed to know who he had talked to in his final few days – needed to see his bank accounts, his messages, his diary. She could get out to his house today and start asking questions. She could set up the incident room as she had a thousand times before, start the suspects board, brief the team.

Except... The realisation hit her. She wasn't a detective any more. She had just been fired. Not just fired, but humiliated: her pass and warrant card taken away in full view of the team she had worked with for years. Marco had made an example of her, just because she had never played the game, because she always said her piece, even when the top brass didn't like it. They had pretended it was that other thing – but the gross misconduct accusation was laughable given what she had been trying to do. Amber knew they had just seen an excuse to get rid of her and made it fit. Bastards.

'Amber?' Clio's eyes were huge.

Amber dragged herself back to the present. 'Clio, you can't move the body.'

'But...' Clio's chest heaved. Things were going to get operatic if Amber didn't act fast. She put her hands on her hips. 'What happens next? If you two move it? Have you thought about that?'

Clio started to stutter, but Amber cut in. 'Wherever you manage to put him, you'd be tied to that body for ever, terrified every time a jogger goes anywhere near it. Plus, Jeanie can't dig with her dodgy back, you know that. It's a no-go.'

Clio pouted. 'But if we don't hide it, I'll...'

Enough. Amber abandoned logic and decided to appeal to Clio's innate dislike of hassle of any kind. 'Remember when you moved house in the Mini?'

'Yes.'

'This'll be so much worse. He's big. And heavy. And your car is tiny.'

'Oh.' Clio took this in. That move had taken two days, a hundred coffees and the help of the local fire brigade when Clio had reversed her car into a wall. 'Then what do I do?'

Amber knelt down, examining the ground around Gary, inwardly cursing the rain. It was exactly what the killer would want – removing all trace of them, whoever they were. 'We call it in, Clio. We'll all be taken in for questioning. And you tell the truth. No lying, OK?'

'I never lie.'

'Um...' Amber stood up again.

'I don't. I exaggerate.'

Amber let it go. She had bigger fish to fry.

Clio's hand pressed into Amber's arm. 'So I tell them I can't remember where I was when he was killed?'

'If that's the truth, then yes.' Amber knew Clio needed certainty. 'And they'll realise there's no evidence against you and they'll find the real killer.'

'They will?'

'Yes.' Amber met her eyes.

'But you said Marco – the DCI, you said he's...' Clio screwed up her eyes in thought. 'An egotistical prick with zero detective skills.'

Amber winced. 'I didn't mean it. That was before I went on HRT.' Once again she felt the kick of having to give up the job she loved thanks to a man she regarded as an idiot. Now, she was sitting on her arse, useless – helpless. As someone who had been nearby when the murder happened, her face might even be on the suspects board, making her toxic professional reputation even worse.

She refocused on her friend. 'They'll follow the clues, Clio. And they won't lead to you.'

'Are you sure?'

Amber squeezed Clio's arm. 'Yes, I'm sure. Look. It's not just Marco, is it? He's not working alone. There's a whole team. And if they can't find the real culprit right away, they'll probably draft in extra people for this too – extra detectives, forensics – the works. There's bound to be something on CCTV, or a witness who's seen whoever did it. There's no such thing as the perfect murder – there's always a slip up, every time.'

'I hope so.' Clio stared miserably at the body. 'So I just say that I went for a walk, passed out, and found him when I came back?'

'Exactly.' Amber tried to organise the questions now flooding her mind. 'So, you didn't hear a car?'

Clio shook her head.

'You didn't speak to Gary?'

'No. He was dead. Already. So I came inside and woke Jeanie. Where were you?'

'Locked in the loo.'

Clio nodded. 'Oh yes, the lock's a bit dodgy, isn't it? You should have woken Jeanie up.'

'Funnily enough I did try.' Amber gritted her teeth. 'I'll call it in now.'

Clio's face fell. 'No!'

'Yes.' Amber grasped Clio by the shoulders. 'You're innocent. I know it. Jeanie knows it. And deep down, you know it too.'

Clio shook her head, tears rolling down her face. 'But what if the police get it wrong? Like they did with you? Kicking you out when you hadn't done anything bad?'

Amber sighed. The clock was ticking. 'That's different.'

'It's not. You lost your job. You loved that job.'

Amber had to get her back on track. 'I'm calling them now, Clio. Every second lost is a second the murderer can cover their tracks. And I don't want that to happen. Why don't you go inside and get warm and I can call it in?'

Clio screwed up her face. 'But there's something I...'

'Please?' Amber held her gaze. 'Trust me. I've got this. I've got *you*.' She had to get Clio inside – away from Gary. Away from his blood dripping down the steps.

'Oh... OK.' Clio reluctantly turned to go inside.

Amber turned back to the body. Her brain was coming alive. These past weeks of unemployment had felt endless. But this was a puzzle – one she could surely solve. One she had to crack to save her friend. She crouched down, using her phone torch to see if there was something – anything – lying nearby. A scrap of paper. A cigarette butt. A clue.

Nothing. She turned her phone over, but as she tapped the final

'9' she heard Clio's voice again, and turned, blinking the rain out of her eyes.

'Amber. I really need to tell you something. So you've got the full picture. Before the police get here.'

Amber frowned. 'Right now, Clio?'

'Yes.' Clio nodded. 'It's really important.'

Amber sighed. 'Just be quick, OK?' She walked up the steps and back inside the caravan. The pounding in her head wasn't improved by the smell inside: a heavy mix of crisps, booze and body heat. The air was thick with hangover, and Clio's belongings were scattered far and wide. A bra hung from the white lampshade above the bright red coffee table and a sparkly rucksack spewed old scripts, books and bills onto the floor.

Amber wiped the water from her face and picked up a note that was propped against the kettle.

When are you going to sail away with me, my amazing Nina? x

'From DJ.' Clio had followed Amber's eyes. 'They've only been together five minutes, but already they're in love and he wants to whisk her away from me. He worships the ground she walks on. Young love, eh?'

Amber stopped short. 'Wait. Where *is* Nina? She's not going to come back and see the body, is she?'

'No, thank God. She's at DJ's and said she won't be back till after lunch.' Clio flung herself down on the leather corner sofa that ran around the edge of the living room, her arms spread wide along the cushions. 'Everything hurts. I need tea.'

'I'm doing my best, Clio.' Jeanie was rifling through the cupboards, her long blonde hair dripping down her back, her pink pyjamas nearly black with water. 'I'm just trying to find the kettle.'

'It broke and I haven't got a new one yet.' Amber could tell Clio was about to cry. 'Oh God, we can't even make tea.'

Amber tried again. 'Clio. Tell me. I need to...'

Clio bit her lip. 'I need a kettle. And now I'm broke till payday. Divorce lawyers are so expensive.' Her face fell even further. 'Wait. Oh God. That's *another* reason everyone will think I killed him. To get what I'm owed.' She slumped back despairingly. 'I'm doomed. DOOMED.'

At least melodramatic Clio was still in there somewhere. Jeanie quietly walked over and handed her a jar of Nutella and a spoon. Clio dug feverishly into the jar, and put the loaded spoon in her mouth.

'Ahhhhhh.' She met Amber's eyes. 'That's better.'

Amber raised an eyebrow, waiting.

Clio swallowed. 'Something happened yesterday.'

'With Gary?'

'Yes.' Clio nodded. 'I found out he had done something really bad. And...'

'And what?' Amber felt a trickle of dread as she noticed something now the rain had washed Clio's make-up away. 'Is that why you've got that scratch on your face?'

'Yes.' Clio stuck her chin out. 'He hurt Nina. It was the final straw.'

Amber exhaled, trying to stave off a looming sense of disaster. Clio was never exactly stable, but she was particularly unhinged when it came to her daughter. She had always been this way: strong words at the primary school gates when a girl had dared to eat Nina's packed lunch by mistake; teachers reported for being too strict if they politely requested that Nina hand her homework in on time; Nina's first boyfriend reduced to tears when Clio had spotted him in town with another girl (his sister, as it turned out). Clio was a

Mama bear. If Gary had hurt Nina, who knew what Clio would have done?

Amber put her phone down, needing to hear this before the squad cars arrived.

'Just tell us, Clio.'

And, in a faltering voice, Clio started to talk.

6

GARY

11.30 a.m.: Death minus sixteen hours

The main reason Gary had asked Denise to move in with him was the fact that she made him feel like a king. He loved the way her eyes lit up at the sight of him, the frenzy with which she unbuckled his trousers, her rapt expression when she asked about his day. She always had time to listen, to sympathise and she was proud to be at his side at networking events or client dinners. She put him first, which was just the way Gary liked it.

Take today, for example. One text and here she was meeting him for coffee in the Copper Kettle on the market square. She worked at the local paper, where she was paid a pittance to cover local 'news', which meant a flexible schedule perfect for daytime meet-ups. He could still remember the day she had come to interview him and Clio in this very café just over two years ago, when Looking Goode's work had been nominated for a design award. They had lost out to that smug cow who imported her supposedly eco-friendly fittings all the way from bloody Thailand, but Denise had been the true prize. Clio had left early to pick up Nina, but Gary had remained: an afternoon coffee becoming prosecco becoming a whole lot more.

He searched for her as he pushed his way into the soupy heat of the café.

'Babe.' She waved a hand. 'Over here.'

The sight of her made him stand a little taller, unlike when he had been with Clio and her ever-expanding backside. Denise's blonde ponytail stretched down to her waist, and her slender legs were sheathed in shiny black leggings, tapering to stacked white trainers. The words 'I would' blazed across the front of her tight pink hoodie in diamanté, a sentiment Gary knew most of the men in here would agree with.

Gary made his way towards her, past grumblers queuing for their sad little pots of tea, market day shoppers with windblown hair, wet macs and dripping shoes. Gary passed baristas sweating in a sea of steam as they worked the silver coffee machines, swerved around a woman failing to choose between red velvet cake or lemon drizzle, until finally Denise was wrapping her arms around him. At her touch, his money worries receded. He would get the cash, he was sure of it. He reached a hand down and squeezed her bum, so firm, so perfect. What a girl she was, his Denise. He kissed her, king of the world again.

'How was the trip, babe? I missed you.' Denise sat back down on a brown leather chair, twirling the straw in her iced coffee. She had ordered him his favourite – a double espresso with steamed milk on the side.

'It was great.' He took a sip before adding the milk.

She leant forwards, long pink nails resting on his thigh. 'I couldn't get hold of you. I tried loads of times. Where were you?'

For a moment he couldn't remember what lie he had told to

enable him to spend the night with Cherie. 'Sorry. I went to the hotel bar after the site meeting. I got chatting with some clients and then it was too late to call. You know how it is.'

'Not really.' She wrapped her fingers around his. 'I was at a local planning meeting – loads of pensioners moaning on about bins.' She hissed air between her neat white teeth. 'I swear my boss has got it in for me. She gives me all the shit stuff. I just want a story I can get my teeth into, you know?'

Her almond eyes blazed with the injustice of a twenty-something denied. Gary made sympathetic noises, hoping they could get back to talking about him soon. 'I'm sure you'll be writing for *The Times* by the end of the year.'

'Nah.' She shook her head. 'Nobody reads that shit. *Mail Online*, that's where it's at. And socials, of course.'

'Of course.' Gary saw the hands on the hideous yellow kettle-shaped clock on the wall. Was it that time already? He pulled out his phone and checked his PayPal account.

No payment yet. He felt a punch of panic.

Denise leant forward. 'Babe?'

'Yeah?'

'Did you get it, then? Johnny's business? The rebuild?'

'Um. Sure.' He nodded confidently. 'He's playing hard to get but we're nearly there.'

'Great. That's big money then, yeah?'

Oblivious to the elderly couple in matching stripy red and white jumpers sharing a slice of cake at the next table, Denise started to run her hand along Gary's thigh. Then she came round to his side of the table and sat beside him on the banquette, her mouth warm as she kissed him. He was just starting to enjoy himself when she pulled away, a challenge in her eyes.

'What's that smell?' She sniffed his neck.

Shit. He thought he had showered Cherie off.

'Smells like...' She inhaled. 'Smells like La Vie.'

'What's La Vie?'

Mr and Mrs Stripy were watching them, forks hovering over their Victoria sponge.

'Clio wears La Vie.' Denise's voice was ominously quiet. 'Why do you smell of Clio's perfume, Gary?'

Stripy and Stripy weren't even pretending not to listen. Their eyes went from Denise to Gary, spectators at a Wimbledon rally.

Denise frowned. 'You're not cheating on me with *her*, are you?

'With Clio? God, no.' This, at least, was true.

Her eyes raked his face. 'You'd better not be lying to me.'

'I'm not.' He held his arms wide, palms up. 'I haven't heard from her in weeks.'

'Really?'

Stripy and Stripy appeared to have stopped breathing. Gary would bloody well take their cake in a minute, as payment for giving them such a good show.

He folded his arms decisively. 'Really.'

'Then why is she heading towards us right now?'

'What?' Gary turned around, wondering for a wild second if he could hide. 'Where?'

Mr Stripy was now looking at him with something like sympathy.

Gary could see Clio now. His bloody wife, wearing one of those garish curtain dresses he hated. And what the hell had she done to her hair this time? Red? And blue? For fuck's sake.

She was next to him now, bright red lips drawn into a sneer. 'You bastard.'

Gary had a feeling he might know what this was about. 'How did you know I was here?'

Clio placed a hand melodramatically across her chest. 'I track you, obviously. Constantly. Can't stop myself.' She put a hand to her brow. 'There's just no getting over you, Gary Goode.'

'Really?' Gary couldn't help smiling.

'God, no.' Clio shook her head. 'Your PA said you were here.'

That bloody woman. He would have to fire her.

He folded his arms. 'Well, what do you want?'

'Where's Nina's money?'

'What money?' Gary shifted in his seat.

'You know what money.' Clio's knuckles were white, fingers balled into fists, her heavy rings flashing in the lights. 'The account with Nina's university money – the one I opened when she was born?' She took a step closer and Mr and Mrs Stripy sensibly decided to try to blend in to the wall. 'The one with all her tips from waitressing, with what was left of my inheritance money, with all my savings, with Bez's top-ups. The one with about twenty-five grand in it?'

Gary stalled for time. 'Why are you asking me?'

'Because the account's empty, Gary. And you are the only person who would have done it. I forgot you had access to it, more fool me.' Her lip curled. Gary would need more than a teaspoon to defend himself, judging by her expression. 'And you know what, Gary? It turns out I have a red line. And you have just crossed it.'

Her ponytail was starting to unravel. He could see the lines on her forehead as she loomed over him – she was really letting herself go. 'You've hurt me, you've taken my money and used it to build a company you've now had me fired from, you've locked me out of our home and moved *her* in.' A dismissive flick of the hand towards Denise. 'All of these things I have survived. But this? Taking away Nina's future? Her dreams of being a doctor? You have officially gone too far.'

Gary stared at the floor – anything to avoid looking her in the eye. He had felt a twinge of guilt on the day he had emptied that account. It had been over a month ago – typical of Clio's chaos not to notice until now. Her flurry and her increasing forgetfulness had proved useful – not that he had taken advantage of course. It was her look out if she didn't ask questions, wasn't it?

And he wasn't to blame, of course. He had been forced into taking the money. The monthly wage bill had been looming and he hadn't been able to pay it, and his advertising budget was spiralling off the charts as he pushed to expand the firm now Clio was gone. He had remembered the savings account in the nick of time. It was a stroke of genius, really.

'I'll pay it back, Clio. Soon.' He couldn't meet her eyes. Instead, he finished his coffee, thinking briefly of the girl who used to be his stepdaughter, her wide cheekbones, curly black hair, her raucous laugh.

Clio held out a trembling hand, palm upwards, as if expecting cash. 'I won't let you do this. Give the money back now or I will—'

Denise piped up. 'Or you'll what?'

Team Stripy were enthralled. This was better than *EastEnders*.

Clio blinked. 'Or I'll take it back.'

Denise laughed. 'Oh yeah. How?'

Clio's eyes flashed. In a weird way he almost fancied her like this.

She leant down, speaking only to him. Behind them a small child started to wail – Gary could relate. 'Give it back, Gary.'

Gary swallowed. 'I can't. Not today. Soon, though.'

'Give it back now.' Clio's face was pure rage, nostrils flaring, jaw set. She picked up a knife from the Stripy table and held it high. Her cheeks were postbox red and Gary wondered if she was suffering from some kind of cardiac condition.

'You're embarrassing yourself, Clio.'

Clio waved the knife in his face, spit landing on his face. 'You will pay it back right now, or I swear I'll kill you.'

Gary stood up, trying to assert himself. 'You'll what?'

Denise joined him. 'You'll kill him? With a blunt knife?' She was laughing now. 'Great plan, Clio.'

'Oh shut up.' Clio flung the knife down and it clanged against the floor. 'He'll ruin your life too, you know. I bet he's already got a bit on the side. Found any burner phones yet? That's where the trail starts.'

'As if!' Denise flicked her ponytail back theatrically, thrusting out her chest.

Clio was shaking now. She was living proof that yoga didn't work. Inner peace. What a joke. 'Gary. This is my girl we're talking about. This is her future – her dream. You know how much this means to her.' Her teeth were so clenched she could barely get the words out. 'Please? I will say yes to everything – all those shitty things you want in the divorce. I'll sign anything. But please. Give Nina's money back.'

'I can't.'

And then she was on him, clawing, yelling. 'You bastard. You total bastard.' She was half sobbing now. 'You've gone too far this time.'

Gary bent over, trying to shield himself, as she scratched and yelled. Then his body took a renewed blow as Denise threw herself into the fray. His hip clicked out. How he hated middle age.

'Get off him.' Denise's nails raked Clio's face.

'This isn't about you, Denise.' Clio's voice came in bursts as the two of them grappled with each other. 'This is about my girl.'

Denise grabbed at Clio's scarf. 'Nobody hurts my Gary.'

Part of Gary was enjoying this situation, but the other part was aware that this wasn't exactly solving his problem. Moreover, his phone was buzzing. As the women wrestled, he checked it, still bent over, hoping PayPal was notifying him that a payment had arrived.

But it was not PayPal. It was Adam, his site manager, a man who only ever texted with bad news. He was right on form here.

No one's been paid. Again. WTF?

Shit.

Another buzz. Withheld number. This message was even worse.

See you at 6. You know what for. Your place not mine.

Gary's stomach lurched as hands and arms attacked each other above him. He was dimly aware of a waitress leaping into the fray, bravely trying to part the two women. All she got for her pains was a punch in the face. Gary felt panic rising as Clio's rings came dangerously close to his face. He had to get out of here. He had to fix this.

And then his lightbulb moment came. The idea was perfect. Brilliant. The ideal solution.

Now he knew what to do – how to get out of this mess and back on the road to glory. As the two women scratched and tore at each other, Gary Goode gave a slow satisfied smile. He was only hours from death, but he had never felt more alive, more daring, more deserving of a place in history.

7

CLIO

Clio had often wondered whether anything would ever truly worry Amber. As a police officer for twenty years and counting, she had seen it all – dead bodies, fights, newborns left in bus shelters. No matter what she had dealt with, Amber's cool exterior had always remained intact.

Until now.

Amber was sitting on the sofa, head in her hands. 'Clio. Seriously? You threatened to kill him while holding a weapon?'

'Um...' Clio reached for a positive spin. 'It was blunt, so...'

'And you fought his girlfriend?'

'Well, wrestled, really. And she attacked me first.'

Amber shook her head. 'That's hardly the point.'

'Isn't it?' Clio squirmed.

'No.' Amber's expression was decidedly at odds with *Little Miss Trouble*'s cheeky pyjama beam. 'And you did all this in front of a full house at the Copper Kettle?'

Clio squirmed. 'Um...' She tried to think of another way of putting it but came up with nothing. 'Yes? That's why I thought you should know. In case it changes your mind?' She edged towards the door. 'About hiding the body?'

'We are not hiding the body.'

Amber's voice of no return. That was that then.

'What were you thinking, Clio?' Amber ran her hands despairingly through her short dark hair.

'Gary took Nina's money.' Anger smouldered inside her. 'Of course I was angry. What was I meant to do?'

Amber groaned. 'I don't know, Clio. I mean...' She stood up and started to pace. There wasn't exactly a lot of room in the caravan so she turned every four steps, every inch of her exuding disapproval. 'What happened to taking a breath? What happened to yoga?!'

'Gary happened.' Clio hung her head. 'I know I was wrong, but I couldn't see straight. I had to try to get the money back. I didn't want Nina paying for my mistake. I mean, I'm the reason he was still a signatory – I forgot to take him off the account.' Tears were in her eyes and she let them fall. 'I'm sorry.'

Jeanie was there in a second and Clio snuggled into her. Jeanie's shoulder was a reliable place in an unreliable world – a place to hide when teenage boyfriends told everyone you were rubbish in bed, or when your mum said it wasn't surprising you didn't get into drama school as you'd always been a bit lacking in imagination. Jeanie's shoulder was home.

She spoke into the sopping pink material, her voice choked. 'I'm just so ragey at the moment. I can't stop myself.'

Amber had stopped pacing now. Her hand rested briefly on Clio's head. 'Menopause. It's a nightmare. The sooner you stop being in denial and get some help, the better.'

Clio sobbed. 'Oh God, menopause? And I thought today couldn't get any worse.'

'There, there.' Jeanie rocked her back and forth. 'More Nutella?'

'Yes please.'

'Here you go.' Jeanie held out another full spoon. Clio was just closing her mouth around the chocolatey heaven when she heard Amber say 'Police.'

'No.' Clio's head whipped up to see Amber speaking into her phone. The end was nigh. Her time was running out. Soon her life would be handcuffs and strip searches from terrifying women with blackened teeth and tattoos.

Jeanie leant towards her. 'You're spiralling, aren't you?'

'How did you know?'

'You're not breathing, Clio. Bit of a give-away.' Jeanie took the spoon and dug it deep into the jar. 'More.'

Clio obediently took her medicine.

Amber's voice was calm. 'Yes. Male, in his forties, lying outside number 15 at the Sunshine Sands Caravan Park on Beach Road. Killed by a blow to the head, by the look of things. Found ten minutes ago by my friend – we couldn't find our phones to call until now – we'd made a bit of a night of it.'

Outside the wind howled, and the caravan was shuddering as if it was about to collapse – a perfect metaphor for Clio's life. For a moment she wanted her mum – a capricious free spirit who smelt of roses, didn't believe in shoes, and who now roamed the hills on the Greek island of Zakynthos finding flowers to use in the perfumes she sold on Etsy. Her mum had never tried to hide the fact that she hated Gary. She would probably applaud the fact that he was dead.

But, as usual, she wasn't here. Still, her friends were with her – that was all that mattered. Clio looked at Amber. 'So what do we do now?'

'We wait. They won't be long.' Amber took in the state of the three of them. 'And maybe we get changed?'

'Good thinking.' Jeanie bustled out, aiming towards the bathroom. She emerged seconds later, flinging towels their way. Clio peeled her pyjamas off and got to work. Jeanie headed into the bedroom, towelling her long hair as she went, and threw a cluster of clothes in their direction – the outfits they had been wearing last night, aka a hundred years ago. Clio was just pulling her green dress over her head when she heard wheels on the gravel and a squeal of brakes. A car must have pulled up around the corner on the main path.

They had come for her. 'Amber. I'm scared.'

'I know.' Amber smiled. 'Just tell the truth. It's all you need to do.'

'Are you sure? I mean, I could tell them that something else. Like...' Clio's imagination began to fire.

Amber held up a hand. 'No. Lying bad. Truth good. OK? Same goes for you Jeanie.'

'For me?' Jeanie's hand flew to her mouth. 'But I was asleep, so they won't want to talk to me.'

'Yes they will.' Amber nodded. 'You'll be a suspect too, at first. Until they rule you out.'

'I will?' Now it was Jeanie's turn to hyperventilate.

'Yes. You were here. When he died. So...' Amber peered out of the window. 'Hang on...'

'What?'

Amber was struggling to see. 'It's not the police.'

Jeanie was now circling the tiny coffee table on repeat, twisting the karaoke mic in her hands. 'Oh God. A suspect. Me?'

Amber raised her eyes to the heavens. 'A suspect who will rapidly be ruled out, Jeanie. Christ! The police aren't total idiots, you know.'

Clio found she had finished the Nutella. She put the spoon back down. 'Who's outside, Amber?'

'I'm trying to see. Let's all just play it cool, shall we?' Amber moved towards the front door and pulled it open. She peered out. 'It's... Shit.'

Clio's chest was so tight she wondered if a heart attack was going to be her next birthday surprise.

'It's...'

Jeanie lost any pretence of calm. 'WHO IS IT, AMBER?' She frowned. 'WHY AM I TALKING SO LOUD?'

'Maybe switch the karaoke mic off, Jeanie.' Clio took it and put it gently on the sofa.

Amber turned. 'It's Denise.'

'WHAT?' Clio actually believed she was going to explode. 'What on earth is she doing here?'

They all watched as Denise marched across the gravel and saw the man she was living with lying dead on the step. She stopped, shock etched on her face, and then dropped to her knees, giving the kind of scream that belonged in a horror movie.

Despite everything, Clio wanted to comfort her.

'I should...' She started to move, but Amber got in front of her, throwing the door wide. 'No. I will.'

Denise's wail cut across the wind. 'Oh my God.' She put her hand to her mouth. 'Oh my GOD. Gary?' She knelt down next to the body. 'Gary? Babe?'

She reached for his hand but Amber stopped her, crouching down, gently trying to pull her away. Clio watched from the doorway, Jeanie's hand on her shoulder.

Amber's raised her voice to be heard over the wind and rain. 'I'm sorry but you can't touch him. This is a crime scene.'

'But...' Tears rolled down Denise's face. Clio hadn't realised her replacement actually cared about Gary – she had thought it was all about the big house and the status that Gary brought with him.

Denise pulled away from Amber, her hand outstretched again. 'But he's my Gary. I want to touch him, to hold him, to—'

Amber held her back. 'I'm sorry, Denise. You can't.'

Rain was drenching Denise's hair and yet she still looked like she belonged on the front cover of a magazine. 'I came to find him.' Her words were interrupted by sobs. 'He smelt of her perfume earlier, yeah? So I came here. He was meant to be at home with me last night, but he disappeared around six. I fell asleep in the end, and when I woke up his phone was off.' She pushed up to her knees, black lingerie clearly visible through her soaking white T-shirt. 'And I thought he'd be here. With...' Her voice became a snarl. 'With *her*.' She collapsed forwards, sobbing. 'I can't believe he's gone.'

Amber stayed with her, awkwardly patting her on the back as she cried, until Denise suddenly sat up, her face wet with tears and rain, pointing towards Clio.

'It was you, wasn't it?'

Inside the caravan Jeanie pulled Clio backwards and stepped in front of her. 'Get down. I've got you.'

Clio felt a pulse of gratitude and did as she was told.

Denise scrambled to her feet. 'Clio? You can't hide from me.'

She was coming towards the caravan and as she peered round Jeanie, Clio saw that there was murder in her eyes. 'Clio? Don't think you're going to get away with this. I heard what you said in the café. I saw you threaten him with a knife. Half the town did.'

Clio dropped her head again. She could see that Jeanie's leg was trembling, but her friend didn't budge.

Amber was trying to get ahead of Denise, to stop her getting to Clio, but Denise was a woman possessed. 'Come out, you spineless cow.'

Enough. Clio stood up. 'It wasn't me, Denise.' She wanted to explain, to make everything OK. She moved right. So did Jeanie. Clio moved left. So did her friend. The two of them must look like they were bloody line dancing.

Fine. Clio would shout instead. 'I didn't kill him, Denise!'

'Yes, you did.'

'No, I didn't.'

Denise pointed at Gary. 'Well, how come he's lying here then?'

'I don't know.' Clio flung her arms wide. 'I came back and he was just – here.'

'Back from where?'

'I don't know.'

'You don't know?' Denise's voice would shatter glass. 'Is that the best you can do?'

'It's the truth.' Clio could hear how pathetic she sounded. How guilty. But Amber had told her what to do and following her advice had generally worked out in the past. And not listening to Amber was what had got Clio into this mess in the first place. Amber, who had stood there on Clio's wedding day and begged her to reconsider.

Denise was now nose-to-nose with Jeanie.

She jabbed a finger. 'I'll get you, Clio. I'll make them see it was you.'

'And I'll make them see it was *you*. Maybe...' Clio knew she was flailing. 'Maybe you're here to cover your tracks. Maybe you killed him to set me up. Maybe...'

'Shut up, Clio!' Amber indicated the area outside, where a uniformed officer was approaching the caravan. An ambulance pulled up, and two paramedics got out and walked towards Gary. Denise turned back to his body, sinking to her knees again, her hands covering her face, the ring on her middle finger catching the light. Seeing it gave Clio an idea. One thing that might save Nina's future.

She ran across and pulled open the cupboard beneath the TV, reaching to the back, past DVDs of TV shows from the nineties that she would never watch again: *The OC, Beverley Hills 90210, One Tree*

Hill. Relief flooded her as she found what she was looking for and turned to Jeanie.

'Can you hide this? In the hut?' She pressed the battered blue box into her friend's hand. 'Please?'

'Is this...?'

'The real one? Yes.'

Jeanie blinked. 'Why me?'

'Because they might search me, and the caravan too. They're obviously going to think I did it. And this is all I have left to give Nina – to get her to uni. And you have all that mum stuff in your handbag – maybe...' Her mind raced. 'Maybe you can hide it in that tub of nappy cream you always carry. They might not look in there.' Her heart was thudding. 'Can you do it for me, Jeanie?' She held the ring out to her friend, tiny diamonds gleaming.

'Of course.' Jeanie grabbed her bag and took the pot of cream. She opened it and plunged the ring deep, smoothing over the top like pastry over apple in a pie. 'There.' She dropped it back into her bag.

'Thank you.' Clio squeezed her shoulder. She might be about to meet her first pair of handcuffs, but at least she had good friends.

'Get ready girls, the cavalry's arriving.' Clio heard brisk footsteps climbing the steps. A moment later they were face to face with Marco, the man who had fired her best friend. Clio felt rage rising again. If anyone deserved to be dead on the doorstep it was him.

'Evening. I'm Detective Chief Inspector Marco Santini.' His navy coat dripped onto the floor, his wavy black hair wild from the storm. His brown eyes searched the caravan, missing nothing. He looked lean, alert – everything the three of them were not.

He didn't bother with small talk. 'Who found the body?' He took in Amber, standing next to Clio in her tight black jeans and red shirt. 'Oh, it's you.'

Amber widened her stance and folded her arms. 'Did you miss me?'

'Not really.' Marco examined the chaos in the living room, his eyes widening as he saw the bra hanging off the lampshade.

He averted his eyes. 'Who found the body?'

Clio raised her hand, a little child at the back of the class. 'Me.' She tried to walk towards him, her legs jelly. She nearly nosedived onto the floor. Amber and Jeanie came and walked beside her, arms laced behind her back, helping her forwards.

'Clio.' His eyes gleamed. She had met him once at the pub, back when he and Amber had actually got on. He had regaled her with his training stories and, later, had cried on her shoulder about how much he missed his two boys now his ex-wife had moved them up to Scotland. She wished she hadn't let him ruin that silk shirt now. It had been one of her favourites. 'You found the body?'

'Yes.'

'I see.' She could practically see the cogs whirring inside his head and she knew what conclusions he would draw. Next stop: prison.

He turned. 'Can you come outside please? I just need to ask you a few questions.'

She looked at Amber, full of panic, needing to lie, needing to escape.

But Amber just mouthed 'Tell the truth.'

Clio had no choice but to trust her. So she stepped out, towards the body, trying to steel herself for whatever came next.

8

AMBER

As Clio went outside with Marco, Amber raised her middle finger at his back.

'Amber!' Jeanie spoke in a panicked whisper. 'Stop it. He might see you.'

'I don't care.' Amber walked to the steps, trying to hear what Marco was asking over the roar of the storm, keeping an eye on Clio as she answered his questions, her hands arcing through the air.

Jeanie came and stood beside her. 'I know you two have history, but...'

Amber snorted. 'You could call it that. If you mean he fired me for no reason, then yes, we have serious history.' She felt a beat of hesitation, aware that she wasn't quite telling the whole story.

Jeanie's hand was on her arm now. 'But Clio found her ex's body. Maybe it's best not to antagonise Marco right now?'

Amber took a breath. She must dig deep, find the strength to keep her cool, to look after Jeanie and Clio. Amber didn't need any support. She was used to taking care of herself – her childhood had seen to that. 'You're right. I'll try.'

A young officer approached them, high-vis jacket half zipped up, his black police hat keeping the rain off his pale face. 'Stand apart, please. No conferring.'

Jeanie leapt forwards onto the gravel, holding her hands up. She had always followed the rules. Amber stepped towards her. 'It's OK, Jeanie. He hasn't got a gun.'

Jeanie squealed. 'A gun? Oh God.'

The officer frowned. 'I said no conferring.' Officious prick. 'No talking until we've interviewed you. So you...' He indicated Jeanie. 'Go over there. Next to the wall. And you.' It was Amber's turn. 'Over there, next to the bins.'

Amber's heart twisted as a tear rolled down Jeanie's face. She didn't move. 'Come on, Rylan. You can't be serious.' Only eight weeks ago she had been signing off his overtime slips. Rylan Redwood. A detective constable who had transferred from Bristol last summer. Young, hungry and an absolute jobsworth. 'You're not really going to do this?'

He scratched his laughable attempt at a beard. 'Yes. I am. Now move, please.'

Jeanie gave her a shaky thumbs up, mouthing 'Think of Clio.'

Amber swallowed down her anger and went and stood in her assigned spot by the bin store, seeing Denise being led away by a female officer, a blanket around her shoulders. Marco left Clio with Rylan and stood silently, assessing the scene, every detail important in the hunt to find the killer. Amber felt a jab of envy so acute it took her breath away.

Water dripped down her neck from the gutter above and she glared indignantly at the sky. The rain would be deleting so much evidence with every minute that passed: footprints, tyre tracks, DNA. If Amber was in charge she would be running a much tighter ship. Already, a forensics tent would be up, protecting the scene and hiding the body from the cluster of onlookers who were already gathering, summoned by the ambulance siren and the flash of the blues and twos. On Amber's watch, crime scene tape would already have pushed them back, and...

'Amber.' Marco had appeared at her side, and she got a faint whiff of Tetley as he leant close to speak into her ear. 'What happened?'

His tone was formal and it stung – vinegar in an open wound. This man knew her. He had worked with her for twenty years – he had mentored her, for God's sake. He had taught Amber all he knew, and in return she had solved more cases than anyone else on the squad. She had been at his wedding and she had brought him beers and listened to his drunken rambling when he divorced. And then, one little blip and he had fired her. He should have had her back. He should have looked after his own.

Well, screw him.

She spoke through gritted teeth. 'I got locked in the loo in Clio's caravan, I fell asleep and when I woke up and finally managed to bust my way out – you can check the lock if you like – I found Clio and Jeanie outside with the body. I called it in. The End.'

'Nothing else?' His eyes searched her face. He knew that she would have followed her instincts, that she would have looked, examined, checked the scene.

'Nothing else.' She folded her arms.

'If you say so.' Marco called across to the officers now cordoning off the scene. 'Get SOCO out here and forensics. And we need to get a tent set up and get fingertip searches underway.'

The officers scurried off, black caps pulled low, shoulders hunched against the rain.

Marco turned back to her. 'We're going to interview the three of you under caution. Leaving in five. OK?'

Amber shook her head. 'Why under caution? We were asleep. This has nothing to do with us.'

'So you say.' Marco lifted his chin. 'But it's a bit too much of a coincidence, isn't it? Given what Denise has just told us about what Clio did yesterday at the Copper Kettle. Threatening to kill him? With a knife in her hand?'

Shit. It was like they were thirteen again, Clio being followed to school by a pack of girls intent on stealing her lunch money. But Amber was waiting behind the post office, accompanied by her latest foster brother, who was six foot two with biceps and every intention of teaching the thieves a lesson.

Amber would protect her this time too. 'Clio didn't mean what she said. Her hormones are all over the place. A lot of what she says is total bollocks.'

'That's no excuse to threaten murder.'

Amber tried again. 'She was having a bad day.'

'So was the killer, wouldn't you say?' He gestured to the state of Gary's head.

Amber could see the case through his eyes. An angry wife drunkenly hitting her husband over the head. Case closed. She thought of Clio behind bars. Clio in the dock. Clio forever defeated by one mistake: falling in love with the kind of man who takes everything and then gets dumped on your doorstep to die.

For Clio, she would try to build some bridges.

She tried a placatory smile. Marco looked terrified and stepped back. Amber put a hand on his arm but he jerked it away. She really needed to work on her people skills. 'Marco, she didn't do it. I promise you.'

'We need to follow the evidence, Amber. I know you're her friend, but...'

Amber tried again. 'If you like I can help out? With the investigation? Just informally, of course. I just know it wasn't her, and...'

'No.' He pulled his notebook from his pocket, not even bothering to look her in the face.

Anger bubbled up again. He needed her. She was the best.

'But—'

'No, Amber. You can't help us. You know why. You've been fired.' Behind him Clio was being led to a squad car, her face pale and terrified as she ducked inside. Amber wanted to run to her friend, to tell her everything would be OK. 'And you're biased, Amber. You've already dismissed a key suspect.' Marco checked his watch. 'Now, wait here. An officer will take you to the station.'

'In a squad car? Seriously?' Amber frowned. 'Marco, come on. I'll get there on my own. I used to work there. Please don't do this to me. It's…'

He shook his head. 'It's what we do with any murder suspect. We question them under caution. It's procedure. And I can't treat you any differently, you know that. If the roles were reversed, you'd do exactly the same.'

She opened her mouth to argue, but knew he was right.

'Amber? Where's Mum?'

It couldn't be. She whirled around to see Nina's dark curls and pink DM boots making their way towards her. Amber stepped forward. Clio's daughter did not need to see this.

'Amber. Stay here.' Marco moved to stop her, but Amber was too fast. She dodged him and ran towards Nina, blocking her way to the body. 'Have some heart, Marco.' She threw the words over her shoulder. 'Just give us a minute.'

She held up a hand and Nina and her boyfriend DJ came to a halt. They were sharing a poncho, their bodies close inside the white plastic. Nina was clinging tight to DJ's hand.

Amber spoke gently. 'Don't go any further.'

'What's happening?' DJ peered over her shoulder towards the crime scene. 'Are they shooting a TV show?' He nudged Nina. 'This is mint. We can make a brew and settle in.'

Amber chose her words carefully. 'I'm afraid this is real.'

'No way. That's never a real body?' DJ pulled Nina closer, protective, his long hair falling around his face. He reached underneath the poncho into his trademark shorts, ever present even when it was minus three outside. He passed Nina a tissue. 'It's OK, love. It's OK. I'll look after you.'

Nina's only answer was a sob.

Amber took Nina's hand. 'I don't have much time. But you need to know that...'

'What?' Nina's mouth trembled.

Amber steeled herself. 'It's Gary. He's dead.'

'What?' DJ blinked. 'Gary? Clio's ex?'

'Oh God.' Nina tottered on her long legs, a Bambi in boots. DJ caught her and started rubbing her back in long slow motions as he held her tight. 'It's OK, I've got you.'

Despite the poncho, Nina's exuberant black hair was starting to flatten in the rain. Amber wondered what she was doing here. Wasn't she meant to be at DJ's place till lunchtime? It was way too early for them to be awake – normally they didn't appear until noon.

'I can't believe this.' Nina's voice was a husk. 'Gary is...dead?'

'Yes.' Amber had no idea how to do this. *Needs to work on her soft skills* was always the feedback she got in her annual review. 'And it looks like he was killed.'

'What?' Nina's mouth dropped open.

'Shiiiiiiit.' DJ shook his head. 'That's mad, that is.'

Nina stumbled and she and DJ nearly fell. Amber grabbed them, her fingers slipping on the soaking poncho.

She turned her head to see Marco tapping his watch officiously.

Amber spoke fast. 'Nina, because his body is here, outside your mum's caravan, and we were all here last night, the three of us have got to go and answer some questions.'

'What? They think it was Mum?' Panic flickered across Nina's face and she was chewing the inside of her cheek like it was gum.

'It won't take long.' Amber hoped she was right.

'But I only—' Nina stopped, winding a curl around her finger.

'You only what?' Amber stared at her, curiosity starting to spark.

DJ pulled Nina close. 'She just wanted to get back to make her mam her birthday breakfast. She woke up me up mad early. We weren't expecting all this.'

'That's enough now, Amber.' Marco stepped forward. 'Come with me, please.'

Nina spoke up. 'Mum didn't do it. You can't arrest her. You...'

Amber wished Clio could hear the fierce love in her daughter's voice.

Marco didn't answer, his dark eyes hooded, so Amber filled the gap. 'It's OK, Nina. This is just a formality.'

'No.' Nina was shaking her head now. Her voice rose to a wail as Marco steered Amber away. 'No.'

DJ pulled her in, arms wrapping around her, her face disappearing into his shoulder. 'Ssshhhhh. It's OK, love. I'm here.'

Amber would have to leave them to it. There was nothing more she could do.

'Amber, go with Rylan please.' Amber glared at Marco, but knew she had no choice. All around them officers were fanning out across the area, starting to talk to the onlookers standing in pyjamas and hoodies, nudging each other and craning to get a better view.

Amber's face burned with humiliation as she got into the car. The door slammed, trapping her inside. But as she stared out of the window, she knew one thing. She would save her friend and she would show everyone on the force how stupid they had been to fire her.

She would solve this case before Marco.

That would bloody show him.

9

GARY

1.30 p.m.: Death minus fourteen hours

After Denise had left to cover a story at the local hospital, Gary headed to the dilapidated caravan park that Clio now called home. On the way he fielded several irate calls from a multi-millionaire who was having the south wing of his mansion redesigned, complaining that no one from Looking Goode was on-site. Gary had made his excuses while firing a one-handed text to Adam telling him to get focused and get someone out there pronto. Adam had replied saying that they were focusing on sitting in the pub until the wages came in, and Gary had written back using multiple swear words, wondering if anyone but him could see the bigger picture here.

He would pay his staff, they all knew that. He always came through. And now Clio had left the Copper Kettle with her tail between her legs and gone back to her latest temp job, it was time to pull his rabbit out of the hat. He parked up outside the static caravan which she now called home, thinking that it wasn't surprising she was so bloody miserable. The place was a dump – its green paint faded, the white plastic windows covered in mould, the front steps disintegrating and spattered with offerings from the seagulls wheeling through the grey skies above.

Well, that was what happened when you walked out on Gary Goode. Trust Clio to make a dramatic exit. He had loved her once – back in 2018 when they met and she was mad for him. Then she had come into money and marriage had been the obvious thing to do. But she was just like all the rest – asking too much, wanting all of him. Gary wasn't designed for fidelity. He had too much to give.

Gary locked his car door even though he was only going a few metres. He didn't like this place. Among the rows of dilapidated caravans there were some shady characters hanging around – a man in an Amnesty T-shirt who seemed to be plaiting his long grey beard while listening to heavy metal, and a woman wearing some kind of lace dressing gown, taping lost cat posters to every available surface. What a shithole. He would almost feel sorry for Clio if she hadn't just threatened him with a knife.

He pulled out his phone and pretended to take a call as he leant against his bonnet, waiting for the coast to clear. Once it had, he crunched across the gravel and approached Clio's caravan. He stood on tiptoe to peer inside. The windows were grimy and he saw big grey pants drying on the storage heater in what Clio might ambitiously call the living room. She had been here since July – over six months now – and the place was still a tip. He could see the remains of a microwave meal on the coffee table, a pile of washing up in the sink, an empty bottle of wine balanced on top of the biscuit tin.

God, was there no middle-aged female cliché that Clio was leaving untouched? Gary shook his head – it was clear she was lost without him. He got his credit card out of his pocket, ready to slide it into the door and jimmy it open, a skill he had learnt from a fellow builder at the beginning of his career.

'Clio's out.' Gary spun round. A tall man in a green polo shirt and jeans walked towards him, a hammer in his hand.

'Bez. Hi.' Gary slid the credit card back into his pocket, extending a hand to Clio's other ex, Nina's father.

Bez didn't return the favour.

Gary tried again. 'How are you?'

Bez didn't even crack a smile. 'Why are you trying to break into Clio's van?' His biceps were big when he folded his arms across his chest.

'I...' Gary tried to think of something. 'I'm just here to drop something off.'

'Yeah? What?'

Gary pretended to pat his pockets. 'Do you know what, mate?' He gave his best rueful grin. 'I must have left it behind.'

'I'm not your mate.' A muscle flickered in Bez's cheek. 'Especially since you stole my daughter's money.' He took a step closer, and Gary could see his eyes glinting behind his glasses.

Gary shifted from foot to foot. Bez was right in front of him now, blocking out the light. He was bigger than Gary remembered. Had he been working out?

Bez slung the hammer from one hand to the other. 'By rights I should punch the living daylights out of you for stealing from my Nina.'

Gary swallowed. Normally he would take Bez on, of course, but he was having a bit of a day so it probably wasn't the right time. 'I'll pay it back.'

'You'd better.' Bez really did have a very hard stare. 'Because I still do kick-boxing and I'd hate my foot to accidentally collide with your skull.'

Gary was sweating now. He prayed for his phone to ring. For a police siren to sound. For anything to get him out of here.

Bez put his head on one side. 'So... Are you going to pretend you have something to do here, or are you going to get the hell off my land?'

'BEZ!' A high-pitched voice cut into their conversation. 'I need you. NOW! The water's gone again and I need to wash my smalls.'

Bez sagged. He was no longer a man with a hammer and a six-pack; he was the owner of a shit caravan site on an eroding cliff, boasting fantastic views of the rusting cargo ships that were permanently moored at sea.

Bez pointed the hammer at Gary. 'Get out of here. OK? Before I do something I'll regret.'

'I'll do what I want, thanks.' Gary was rallying now. 'Go on. The smalls are waiting.'

Bez clenched his fists but then the urgent cry was heard again. 'BEZ! I need you NOW!'

Bez went. As soon as he had rounded the corner, Gary got out his credit card. Bez was a threat, but Marg loomed larger. He knew her reputation. He didn't want to lose a limb. He was in the caravan in seconds, swallowing down his revulsion at the smell of feet and damp washing. He needed to find the ring. The one ring Clio owned that was worth something – worth quite a lot, actually. If she could wave a knife in his face, he felt perfectly entitled to take it. It was made of silver with inset stones that Gary had assumed were fake until an old jeweller mate had spotted it on a night out a couple of years back. He had told Gary that it was actually platinum, that the diamonds were real, and that the ring was in fact worth about twenty thousand pounds.

Twenty grand Gary could do with right now. A short-term fix. A cash injection. Gary had noticed in the café that Clio wasn't wearing it, so here he was. It would get him through another day. Problem – solution. That was how Gary rolled.

He started in the kitchen, knowing that Clio always put anything important in her 'drawer of boring', where unused spatulas and meat thermometers jostled with oven instructions and Weight Watchers rules Clio would never follow. He found a tenner on his travels and put it in his pocket, but no ring was to be found. He spied a self-help book called *Inner Calm* and laughed. As if. Clio was about as calm as an erupting volcano.

Then he went into her bedroom, shuddering at the state of it – clothes covering the bed, the floor, the wobbly chair, the tiny dressing table squeezed into the corner. A tampon lay on the pillow, still in its wrapper, thank God. Gary checked out of the window but Bez was nowhere to be seen. He started to go through Clio's chest of drawers, holding his breath as he touched her clothes, her garish kaftans and enormous bras. He had no idea what he had ever seen in her, he really didn't. And then, when he thought he might have to start digging around underneath her pants, he found it. The ring. At last. Tucked away inside an old tights box from M&S. He pulled it out of its velvety black box and held it up to the light, marvelling at the way the stones shone.

This was it. His ticket out of trouble. His way back.

And so Gary Goode tucked the box away in his pocket, crept out of the caravan and closed the front door behind him. He saw nobody, and soon he was back in his car, on his way to turn his life around. Just one more visit to make and he was home free. And, of course, his PayPal money might arrive at any minute – he just needed to exert some more pressure. He pulled over, took out the little grey phone from its hiding place, switched it on and typed.

He smiled as he pressed send. That should do it. Then he turned up the radio as 'We are the Champions' came on. He threw his head back and sang along, his foot on the accelerator, delighted yet again by his own genius and by how skilfully he was carving out a long and prosperous future.

10

RECORDED INTERVIEW

06.31 5 February 2023

Location:– Promenade Police Station, Sunshine Sands
Conducted by: – DCI Marco Santini and DC Selena Hayes

MS: – Ms Martin? Hello?

JM: – Zzzzzzz. Yes? What? Sorry, I must have dropped off. That's embarrassing.

MS: – Please state your name.

JM: – Jeanie Martin.

MS: – Thank you. And your full address?

JM: – 16A, The Rise, Sunshine Sands. That's 16A, the little pink house? Not 16 the big one with the Grecian pillars. So silly, the addresses on our road. You know—

MS: – And what was your relationship to the victim?

JM: – I don't have one, really. I mean, I'm best friends with his wife, Clio. Is that what you mean? God, I feel like I'm back in school again, getting everything wrong, and—

MS: – That's fine, thank you. Could you tell us exactly where you were last night between the hours of 2.30 a.m. and 5.30 a.m.?

JM: – I would love to tell you all about that, but I just have a little problem.

MS: – If you could just answer the question?

JM: – Yes, but first I really need you to bring me my—

MS: – Where were you last night, Jeanie?

JM: – Oh no. Look what's happening. My top, it's... I can't stop it. It's time for their feed, you see. I hate to be rude, but can you please bring me my breast pump?

MS: – ?!?Your what?

JM: – Now? Please? Then I'll answer all your questions, I promise.

MS: – *Sigh.*

Interview suspended at 06.35.

11

JEANIE

When Jeanie had set out to celebrate Clio's birthday, she would never have predicted that only hours later she would be leaving a police station on her way to break into a beach hut. She owned an electric mop. She did her pelvic floor exercises. She was way too unexciting for this kind of thing.

She stopped at the zebra crossing on the high street, checking behind her in case the police were following, although after she had accidentally fired some breast milk at the ceiling in the custody suite, they presumably deemed her too incompetent to be a killer. The street was deserted except for a cleaner wearily hosing vomit off the pavement outside Sandy's, the town's one and only night-club. As she watched him, a man with wild hair and no coat shuffled into view and started digging into an overflowing bin as relentlessly as a seagull taking a picnic basket apart.

Jeanie walked over and gave him the change in her pocket before continuing down the road towards the beach. She heard the roar of the waves and panic started to prickle. Since that awful day at the pool, she started to hyperventilate as soon as she approached any expanse of water bigger than a bath.

She wasn't cut out for this. Jeanie liked to live between the lines, safe within the rules. Rebellion had never ended well for her. Once, for a dare, she had taken a can of Fanta from the corner shop, only to drop it as she tried to make a sneaky exit. The inappropriately named shopkeeper, Joy, had delighted in forcing her to clean the floors for the rest of the year as punishment. Lying wasn't her forte either: she could barely maintain the pretence when she told her partner Tan that everything was going fine with the twins, when only minutes before she had been googling nannies and weeping.

She had felt constantly guilty during that police interview, despite having done absolutely nothing wrong. Marco and his side-kick had sat there, both unsmiling (where was a good cop when you needed one?), asking what had happened – getting her to repeat, to give more detail, to remember – when all Jeanie had wanted to do was to lie face down in a mountain spring until her hangover was over.

She could do so once she had hidden the ring – once Clio's last remaining asset was safe. Jeanie shook her head, remembering how Clio had poured every penny of her inheritance into Looking Goode, back in the first flush of her Gary love (or her Gary coma, as Jeanie and Amber secretly called it). They had both urged caution when her gran had left Clio £100,000 and Gary had suddenly proposed two days later. But Clio's nightmare taste in men held strong – she had always fallen for anyone with a leather jacket or the ability to play a few chords on a guitar. Gary ticked both boxes, so the entire world had to start throwing rose petals and singing 'I Will Always Love You' on repeat.

At least Clio hadn't taken his surname, Jeanie reflected, as she turned off the high street by the bookies which, as usual, had one of its windows smashed. She headed past bins and graffiti down the narrow alleyway that cut through to the promenade. As she came to the end, she caught a glimpse of herself in the darkened window of

The Frying Squad, which boasted 'the best batter in town'. She did not like what she saw: a chubby ghost in a sensible beige mum raincoat (lots of pockets), curls exploding around her face, her skin ghostly in the glass. In the historical thrillers she had devoured so constantly before having children, people involved with murder inevitably looked gorgeous, inhabiting a world of handsome scoundrels and diamanté tiaras, of tapping fans and arched eyebrows. In reality, Jeanie was staggering along dimly lit roads in a lashing gale, looking and feeling like a duck's arse.

She took one more dispiriting glance. A year ago she had been glowing, skin bright, hair thick, her hand clutching the bump she had waited so many desperate years for. Bus conductors had smiled at her, baristas had offered her free cake, women had asked when she was due and given up their seats on the train. But now she was invisible. Just another exhausted midlife mum on her way to nobody cared where.

She shook her head and started on her way again. She must stop being so negative. It was just as well no one was looking at her, given what she was doing right now. And it was good to have a clear sense of purpose for once: to have a goal, something to tick off her list. She couldn't remember when she had last felt this certain about how to be a mum to Yumi and Jack.

She wondered what her partner Tan would make of this when she told him later – if she got the chance to speak to him at all. He was so adept at leaving the house when she wanted to talk – always another call, another case, another emergency that only he could solve. It was hard to argue when your other half worked for a housing charity, literally helping people off the streets, and much of her maternity leave had been spent talking to the front door as it closed, tears glazing her eyes as *In the Night Garden* played on in the bomb-site that had once been their living room.

She sighed as she crossed the road. She loved being a mum, of course, but she was so *bad* at it. Yumi and Jack hadn't yet slept through, despite being nearly one, and every time she made it to a baby group, she shrank into herself as other mums talked about how little Jonty was already running marathons, while her own twins sat in the corner chewing toy cars. And then there was the crying. The constant crying. Before they were fed, after they were fed, before she changed them, and then afterwards too. Every day a little bit more of Jeanie died at her total inability to stop them – to be the mum they needed, one who would inspire smiles and giggles rather than puke and wailing.

If Jeanie was honest, she loved her twins most when they slept – the wrinkled challenge of them smoothed over like the covers keeping them warm. When they were asleep, she was the best mum in the world. It was only when they were awake that she lost her footing.

Jeanie picked up speed as she headed for the beach, the smell of salt and seaweed catching in her throat. It was further than she remembered. Sunshine Sands had recently started to expand, and a housing estate was being built on the eastern side, under the cliffs, with five hundred starter homes the first to go up. Jeanie trotted past the barbed wire fences that surrounded the building site, past silent diggers and huge holes in the ground, wondering at every moment if a hand was about to land on her shoulder.

She was nearly at the beach now. She practically sprinted round the corner, past the bus stop where she had had her first kiss with Tony from Year 9, which had resulted in a cut on her tongue that had lasted for weeks. Then she took a right at the old cinema, now a bingo hall in the summer and a place to shoot up in winter, down the stone steps and onto the pebbly beach.

Jeanie looked nervously at the grey-peaked waves, before crunching determinedly across the top of the beach, past driftwood and clumps of browning seaweed, towards the colourful row of beach huts set into the brown earth and wiry bushes of the cliffs. She aimed for Clio's hut, as she had so many times before. In their teens this haven, with its rainbow stripes and fairy lights was where the three of them had met Bez and his mates to drink the cheap spirits Clio's mum never seemed to miss. In their twenties they had gathered here to gossip on summer evenings as they ate chips and necked white wine so cheap you could get three bottles for a tenner. And then, in their thirties, it was where they sipped cocktails and moaned about their jobs or their love lives or discussed important issues like their top three pop songs of all time.

Since the twins had arrived nearly a year ago, Jeanie had barely been here, but reassuringly it hadn't changed a bit. The door handle was still smudged with pink paint, and white splatters told Jeanie that the seagulls were still using the roof as a toilet. She remembered that the key had always been buried beneath the red pottery owl that sat to the right of the door, and she dug down with chilly fingers, praying that this hadn't changed.

It hadn't. Her hands closed around the key, still attached to the Eiffel Tower key fob that Jeanie had bought for Clio on that terrible French exchange where her host had shrunk all her underwear. She smiled as she stood up, remembering the ridiculous bloomers she had been forced to wear instead, courtesy of her host's gran.

The smile disappeared when she noticed that that the padlock was hanging open. Adrenaline spiked inside her. Was someone here? She unhooked it, keeping its weight in her hand, just in case she needed a weapon. There was a killer on the loose, after all.

The door creaked as she pushed it open. She took a step and tripped on some plastic buckets, falling into the hammock where Clio had lost her virginity to Bez, recoiling, even though that event had taken place many years before. Jeanie groped around for the torch that was always kept on the windowsill, before falling over her own feet and landing on the spikes of what felt like a garden fork.

'Ow.' Her whole body hated her now. What a morning. Jeanie sat back against the wall, inhaling the familiar musty smell, the scent of summers gone, wondering how the hell life had taken this turn. Yesterday morning she had been worried about naps and feeds and whether she would ever have time to wash her hair, while now Gary was dead and here she was stashing a ring that was all that was left of Clio's future. She flicked on the torch and saw cobwebs and dust motes, old bits of rope and a charred barbecue that had probably last been used before Nina was born. She remembered Clio bringing it out into the sun, her bump shiny with suntan lotion beneath a tiny red bikini, laughing as she fired it up to cook sausages and burgers. Amber had put together a salad and they had all sung along as Bez had played 'Yesterday' on his guitar. They had been young. Free.

A tear rolled down Jeanie's cheek as she thought of what a narrow tunnel her life had now become. But she mustn't get melancholy. There was no time for that. She reached into her bag and took out the jar of cream. She dug inside, finding the ring and wiping it off on her sleeve. Then she slid it under the loose floorboard where once they had hidden packets of Marlboro Lights and cans of cider. As she dropped the wood back into place her hand knocked against something in the corner. She felt cold metal under her fingers and pointed the torch downwards. The light danced across a silver surface. It was a trophy, silver, a cup rising from a square pine base, the two handles curving outwards.

Jeanie swore quietly as she saw something else.

It couldn't be.

She peered more closely and yes – she had been right. Fear stopped her breath. There, in the light of the torch, she saw a dark red stain colouring the light wood of the base. She stared, paralysed. Was there a scattering of salt and pepper hair in the red?

Gary's hair?

'No!' Jeanie leapt to the other side of the hut, nearly garrotting herself on the hammock. She fell back against the rickety wall, whimpering as her mind whirled. She wanted Amber, but she was still at the station. Jeanie was on her own. What should she do?

'OhGodohGodohGod.' Beneath the panic, a chill was growing inside her. She knew who had been at the hut yesterday and she knew they hated Gary. It was obvious what must have happened. Jeanie might be terminally incapable of following the plot of *Line of Duty* but even she could work this one out.

She whimpered, her hand to her mouth. It all made sense now.

Jeanie knew who the murderer was.

12

RECORDED INTERVIEW

07.45 5 February 2023

Location:– Promenade Police Station, Sunshine Sands
Conducted by: DI Marco Santini and DC Sian Hayes

MS:– Please state your name for the tape.

AN:– You know my name.

MS:– Please?

AN:– Amber Nagra.

MS:– And your full address?

AN:– You know my full address.

MS:– Again, please say it for the tape.

AN:– 15 Pebble Drive, Sunshine Sands.

MS:– And what was your relationship to the victim?

AN:– Really?

MS:– Yes, really.

AN:– His wife Clio is one of my best friends.

MS:– And where were you last night?

AN:– I don't have time for this.

MS:– Could you please answer the question?

AN:– I was in Clio's caravan celebrating her birthday. I sang, I mixed margaritas, I attempted a Conga. Then later on I accidentally got locked in the toilet in Clio's caravan and fell asleep.

MS:– Thank you. And could you tell us about the events of the evening preceding Mr Goode's death?

AN:– Oh dear God.

MS:– Please answer the question.

AN:– No comment.

MS:– Ms Nagra, don't play this game. You're better than that.

AN:– No comment.

MS:– Come on.

AN:– No comment.

MS:– *Sigh.*

Interview suspended at 07.52.

13

@SUNSHINESANDSONLINE
Followers: 1200
NEWS BLAST: Caravan park killing

Today a brutal murder has shattered our quiet and contented community. A high-profile local designer, whose firm was recently featured in House and Home magazine, was found dead today on the doorstep of his wife's home, his skull smashed to pieces. The couple are in the middle of an acrimonious divorce, and the wife has now been taken in for questioning by local police. 'I saw her threatening him with a knife', a witness told us. 'She looked capable of anything.'
Detective Chief Inspector Santini was tight-lipped as he began the investigation. More to follow soon. Like and follow for updates.
Comments
@ BarryWhiteNotThatOne: That'll show those losers at The Guardian that we're not the country's most boring seaside town, eh?!

Shares: 500
Likes: 1650

14

CLIO

After what felt like years of being interviewed by Marco, Clio was really homing in on the things that she didn't like about him. There was the way that he sat – legs wide, crotch out, hands planted on both knees despite there being a perfectly good table available. There was his voice – low and monotone, more suited to a meditation app than a police interrogation, meaning that she was genuinely struggling to stay awake, which was ridiculous given the circumstances. And then there was his tendency to lean forward, so that her face was regularly dampened by flecks of his spit. It felt like he was marking his territory, reminding her of the way her mum's ancient spaniel had peed on her leg during their Sunday walks, only even less fun. She inhaled and regretted it. No wonder his wife had left him given he had breath like that.

'So, run me through it again, Clio.'

Clio resisted the urge to cry. The more she talked, the more Amber's strategy of telling the truth wasn't proving a winner. Clio's memory was starting to play tricks on her now – muddying the already confusing waters caused by alcohol and brain fog. She now thought she could remember snatches of conversation last night, and maybe a hand reaching for hers. Had it been Gary? Oh God, she hoped not.

'I don't know what more to say, really.' She pressed her fingers to her aching temples, which made no difference whatsoever. She needed an IV and a decent pillow. 'As I've already said, I was drunk, I woke up, I went down to the beach, and I can't remember what happened there at all. Then I found his body when I came back to my caravan.'

Marco stayed silent, steepling his fingers like one of the many pretentious directors she had auditioned for in her youth. Beside him DC Sian Hayes bent over her notebook, red hair falling around her face.

Clio's mouth was arid but the water had run out ages ago and she didn't dare ask for more. 'Look, I know it looks bad. I mean, *everyone* knew I hated him. And then there was what happened yesterday, when I was really upset about my daughter – he had stolen her money, you know.'

'You mentioned that.' Marco folded his arms. 'Several times.'

'Well, it was a terrible thing to do.' Clio flung her hands wide. 'And I had just found out, and...'

'But it wasn't stealing, was it?' Marco's expression would freeze lava. 'He had access to the account.'

Clio closed her eyes, trying to find words that would help him to see how to her, as a mum, it was the worst crime ever committed. He would never understand how primal her reaction had been when she had seen the zero on the screen where thousands of pounds should have been – how raw she had felt when she had gone inside the bank and discovered what Gary had done. Even on her best day she could never find the words to show him.

She had to try. 'Maybe it wasn't technically a crime, but morally Gary was way out of line. Nina had been paying for years into that account, saving as much as she could for medical school, and he just took it all without asking.'

'And you were so angry you wanted to kill him?'

'No.' Clio shook her head. 'I told you.'

'But you *said* you wanted to kill him, didn't you?'

Here they were again, back at the café, the noose around her neck. 'Yes, but...'

Marco's brown eyes lit up. 'So you did plan to kill him?'

'No. I've told you that.' Tears were threatening now. Clio dug her nails into her palms to stop them.

'So do you often say things you don't mean?' He leant back, thick eyebrows arched.

'Yes. I mean no. I...'

'And do you mean it now when you say you didn't kill him?'

'Yes.' Fear pierced Clio. She had known this would happen. She had known she would be suspect number one. Maybe she should ignore Amber. Come up with a new story.

'Are you sure, Clio?'

She was opening her mouth to answer when Marco moved on, pivoting with the speed of a man who had not spent the previous night glued to a jug of margaritas. 'And how long were you alone out there? With him?'

'I don't know.' Clio was aware she sounded defensive. 'Five minutes, maybe?'

'And you're sure he was already dead when you found him?'

'Yes.' Clio had told him this so many times. 'His eyes were wide and staring. There was blood everywhere. He was definitely dead. But I felt his pulse, to make sure. There was nothing.'

'I see. And why didn't you call an ambulance? Or the police?'

'I don't know. I must have panicked – I can't remember really. I'm sorry. I just don't know.' Her voice was rising and any minute now she would confess just to get this horrible experience over with.

Fortunately, there was a knock at the door. Somehow, Clio knew that it wouldn't be a waiter with a fried breakfast and vat of coffee to refresh her flagging brain. This small room with its scuffed floors and battered chairs was fast becoming home, it seemed. She looked up at the camera set high in the wall opposite her. Not quite the vision she had cherished of her return to the small screen. She pressed the heels of her hands into her eyes and sagged back as a young male officer came in, red socks sticking out beneath his uniform trousers, his Adam's apple bobbing as he got up the courage to speak to his boss.

'The first results are in. Fingerprints. I got them fast-tracked.' He smiled, pleased with himself, a dog who had fetched a ball.

Marco didn't even look at him. 'I'll come and look. Interview paused at 11.35 a.m.' He heaved himself out of his chair and went to the door. It clunked behind him, leaving Clio with the personality vacuum that was DC Sian Hayes. Did she ever speak? Apparently not. Clio wasn't going to tempt her. Marco would probably be gone a while, so maybe she could lay her head down on the table and have a kip. She was just closing her eyes when the door opened again.

Marco was back.

'Interview recommenced at 11.42 a.m.' He looked almost cheerful now. This couldn't be good.

'Clio. You said earlier in the interview that Gary Goode had never set foot in your caravan?'

Clio nodded. The one thing she was sure of. 'I did.'

'You're certain that's true?'

'Yes.' She nodded. 'The caravan was mine. Shit, but mine. Bez – my daughter's dad – rented it to me on mate's rates when I left Gary. Obviously, I thought I'd get a lawyer and walk straight back into the house again, but it turned out Gary had put it in his name without me knowing.' She felt the kick of failure yet again. 'Anyway, he definitely hasn't been in the caravan. I would never have let him inside.'

'I see.' Marco seemed to mull this over, his head on one side. He coughed. 'It's just that we've just had some preliminary results from our searches on your caravan.'

'Yes?'

'And his prints are all over the place.'

'What?' Her mouth fell open. There was only one reason Gary would be poking around in there. The bastard. 'He must have been looking for the...' Just in time she stopped herself.

Marco raised his eyebrows. 'Looking for the what, Clio?'

She shook her head. 'For something else to ruin my life with, I suppose.' She couldn't believe that Gary had come to her caravan, to the one place that was hers, to try to take her one remaining asset. Because that was the only reason he would have come in. To take her ring.

Her jaw was so tight it might crack. Her friends were right. She had terrible taste in men. If she hadn't lost the ring once on the beach and had a copy made once she had found it, Gary would have got hold of the real one. Then she would be totally penniless. As it was, he must have found the fake.

Well, that served him bloody well right. 'What a total and utter git.'

Oh no. She had said that out loud. She saw the corner of Marco's mouth rising upwards, and realised that these weren't quite the right words to say given her current circumstances. 'Well, if he's been there, it wasn't because I invited him, Marco. He must have broken in.'

Marco gave a small smile that made her want to slap him. 'We even found traces of his DNA on your underwear.'

'Gross.' Clio's rage was well and truly bubbling now. 'That's disgusting.'

'Disgusting enough to make you want to kill him?'

'No. But disgusting enough to make me want to wash all my pants as soon as I get out of here.'

Was that a suppressed smile from the inscrutable Sian? It was hard to tell.

Marco leant forward. 'Are you sure you didn't invite him? And forget to mention it?'

'Of course not.' Clio shook her head. 'I hated him. I didn't want him anywhere near me.'

'Except in the café yesterday, which you went to with the express purpose of finding him.' Marco played with his pen, spinning it round and round in a way that made Clio want to snatch it away. 'It doesn't really add up, does it? Are you sure you two didn't meet? Is there something going on you don't want to admit to, even to your friends?'

'No. Absolutely not.'

'Did something rekindle between you?'

Clio couldn't help it. She laughed.

'That's crazy.'

'Then why was he in your caravan, Clio?'

'I already told you – I have no idea. How am I supposed to know why Gary did what he did? I didn't really know him, apparently even when we were married, so...'

As she talked she could see Nina's face receding in a rear-view window as Clio was driven away to prison. No more Amber and Jeanie. No more tea and temp jobs. No more Sunshine Sands.

Marco was talking again. 'It's just that – given your history it all seems to stack up one way. You were getting divorced. You were shouting at each other all over town. You were in legal dispute with him over the company you built together and over the house too.

His DNA is in your caravan when you swore to me it wouldn't be. You told half the town you wanted to kill him only the day before he died, and you have a scratch on your face from your subsequent fight with his fiancée, so you say, but it could also have come from Gary, couldn't it?'

'No. Ask Denise. I bet she's proud of that scratch.'

Marco waved her objection away. 'And finally, he died on your doorstep and you can't remember where you were before you found him.'

Clio had to admit this did sound bad. 'Forgetting things isn't a crime, is it?'

'Of course not. But it does all seem to point one way, wouldn't you say?'

Clio felt nausea rising again. She put her hand to her mouth as sweat prickled across her brow. She inhaled the stale air of the interview room, wondering how she had ever complained when the freezing sea breeze hit her face in the morning. If only she could remember where she had been when she left the caravan. If only she could recall a single thing that had happened. A witness. A moment. Anything.

She faced up to the man across the table. 'Marco, I realise that it seems like it must have been me that killed him, when you list everything out like that. But I really don't think I did.'

'You don't think you did? Not very convincing, is it?' Marco's face was a gauntlet. But Clio kept talking, carried on telling her story. Words were all she had in here and she knew that if she stopped talking he would fill the gap with the sentence she had been dreading. He would read Clio her rights. He would tell her that she was no longer free to leave.

He would tell her that she was under arrest.

15

GARY

3.30 p.m.: Death minus twelve hours

Gary's trip to the jeweller did not go as planned.

'It's a copy.' Julius leant his elbows on the glass counter. He indicated the stone at the heart of the setting. 'There's a circular reflection inside the stone. You can see against the paper. Here?' He pointed. 'It means it's a fake.'

He flicked off his microscope and pushed the ring over to Gary. 'Bad luck.'

This had to be a joke. Gary stood up and walked over to the shop window, looking out at the Southampton crowds outside. A young couple paused, hand in hand, exclaiming over the rows of engagement rings cushioned on red velvet stands in the window. Gary pitied them. They would learn, soon enough, that marriage wasn't all it was cracked up to be. Gary turned back to Julius, who hadn't changed a bit in the twenty years Gary had known him. His old pal peered again at the ring, his eyes bright behind gold-rimmed glasses. He was just having Gary on. He always did this. He was constantly trying to lead Gary down the garden path – to make a few quid on top of the bloody great piles of cash he was making already. This was just part of the game. No bother. Gary could take it.

'Yeah, right. It's fake.' Gary smiled conspiratorially, as he walked back to the counter, indicating a diamond necklace locked inside a glass case to his left. 'Just like this is, yeah?'

Julius's face flickered. 'That's worth a tenner. The Southampton Players just used it in their production of *The Importance of Being Earnest*.'

'Oh. Well. Yes.' Gary shifted from foot to foot. 'I mean, obviously. I knew that. Just testing, eh...?'

Julius smiled. 'Just kidding. It's worth half a million.'

Inside, Gary started to smoulder. But he needed cash, so he would have to play nice. 'You got me. Again.'

'Yes I did.' Julius pushed the ring dismissively at Gary. 'Now off you go. Go con some other bugger.'

'But...' Gary hadn't seen Julius acting like this before. When he had brought the engagement ring Clio had flung at him when she had caught him with Denise, Julius had haggled a bit, but he had given Gary the money he deserved.

Maybe his friend was losing his touch. Maybe he no longer knew a good thing when he saw it. Gary would have to help him.

He pushed the ring back. 'But it's real. It's a hundred years old.' He decided not to share that Clio's gran had left it to her. 'It's worth at least twenty grand. Or maybe even more.' He faltered. Julius's expression hadn't changed. He stood, blue shirt buttoned too high, grey hair neatly brushed, face unusually set. No smile twitching at the corner of his mouth. No lightening of the eyes.

He looked deadly serious.

The ring lay in front of Gary, twinkling in the overhead lights. He picked it up, twirling it in his fingers, seeing the tiny diamonds sparkling.

He knew what this ring was worth.

A memory came to him. One that made him shiver. Clio had made a copy. She had bloody made a copy, that summer when she had lost the damn thing.

He couldn't have accidentally taken the copy, could he? It looked real enough. Panic started to swirl inside him. He didn't have time to find the real one. He barely had time to have a slash, given the fact that Marg's deadline was approaching and everyone knew what happened if you kept her waiting. Where the hell was the payment he had been expecting? He turned and took another walk across the thick grey carpet, examining the wall of expensive watches as he got himself under control. He was Gary Goode. He could do anything.

Couldn't he?

'What's wrong, Gary?'

There was nothing to do but bluff it out. Gary turned towards Julius, who was watching him, head on one side, his bright eyes not missing a thing.

Gary had to make this work. He needed the money. He needed it so badly that he could hear the clock ticking down to doom in his head. He was suddenly mortal, vulnerable, a man who might not last the week. First Johnny, now Clio and the damn ring. The whole world was out to get him, when all he was trying to do was spread some beauty, some inspiration, to make the world a better place.

God it was hard, being an innovator. Gary took a breath and stood tall, preparing a speech in his head that would sound incredible. The one that would win Julius over. 'Mate. This ring. It's been in my family for generations...'

Julius begrudgingly listened, and Gary could see the silver flecks in his eyebrows. His old friend should watch out – his new lady wouldn't stick around if Julius let himself go. Gary took a breath. He must focus. He needed cash, and he needed it now.

'Look. It's the real deal. Diamonds, platinum. The works.' He lowered his voice, deliberately dropping his Ts like Julius did. Connection was the key. 'Come on. Stop playing around and give me what it's worth. We're old mates. I'm just asking you to be fair.'

Julius shrugged and Gary felt a glimmer of triumph.

'Just give you what it's worth?'

'Yeah.' Triumph beat a tattoo in Gary's heart.

'And then you'll go?'

Gary nodded. 'Yeah. Of course.'

'OK then.'

Julius reached into his back pocket, bringing out a roll of notes.

That was more like it. Gary always made the magic happen.

Julius peeled one off and put it into Gary's hand. Then he tucked the rest back into his pocket. 'Here you go.'

Gary blinked. 'Come on, mate.'

'Oh, all right then.' Julius sighed dramatically. 'Make it twenty.' Another note landed in Gary's palm.

Gary had three hours to go and the ring had been his last hope. His heart rate doubled and he had to fight to breathe.

'Julius. Mate...'

'I'm not your mate.' Julius calmly went back to cleaning the watch that was lying on the counter. He bent to his task, absorbed in the tiny cogs and wheels.

'Mate, but...'

'You stopped being my mate when you shagged my girlfriend at Christmas.'

Gary opened his mouth to deny it.

Julius held up his hand. 'Don't lie to me, Gary. That bloody aftershave. Boss, isn't it? All over my pillow. You're like a dog pissing on a tree.'

'I...' Gary swallowed. 'It was only once.'

'And that makes it better, does it?'

'Yes. No...?' Gary looked around frantically. He was suddenly a man without a plan. A man who was going to be at the wrong end of a baseball bat by nightfall. Gary was suddenly very scared indeed.

'Take the money and piss the hell off.' Julius's eyes met his. They were stone.

Even Gary knew he was beaten this time.

'OK, OK.' Gary knew it would be more dignified to leave the notes, but he was a desperate man so he stuffed them in his pocket and left.

As he strode past mums dragging unwilling toddlers and women dragging dawdling men he thought about Clio and felt murder pumping through his veins. Without her, his life would be simple. He conveniently skipped over the fact that he had stolen her property: without her, he would have twenty grand in his pocket right now. Without her, he would be home free.

He turned the corner, scattering a group of teenagers, his hands curling into fists. Clio would have her bloody friends round tonight, like she always did. They gathered every year on her birthday, starting with tea and finishing with Spice Girls songs at full volume. But he would sort her out. He would head round there when they were nice and pissed and he could get what he needed. They were no match for him.

His phone buzzed. One message. Words that made his blood run cold.

6 p.m. No excuses.

Gary swore, feeling his heart beating faster. He needed a plan, an idea, a way forward. He needed a bloody miracle. There was only one thing he could think of.

It was time to go nuclear. He ripped the parking ticket off his car, got inside, and drove.

16

Amber Admin @WorkoutGoddesses NAME CHANGE to @SaveClio
Icon change from 1980s Nike trainers to a magnifying glass

Jeanie: – Amber? You out yet? Need to talk to you.

Jeanie:– Hello?

Jeanie:– About to get home and feel even worse than I look. Selfie incoming. See?

Amber:– Sorry. In car. Looking now.

Amber:– 💀 Very Walking Dead.

Jeanie:– Told you. Need to talk in person. Now.

Amber:– Can't. About to meet a contact who can help us solve this.

Jeanie:– May already have done that.

Amber:– Can see her now. See you at Rainbow café? 12?

Jeanie:– I know who did it.

Amber: –You do? WHO?

Jeanie:– In person only. Can you come here now?

Amber:– Going to miss contact if I don't go now. Café at 12?

Jeanie:– Will have twins. Here better.

Amber:– Need fry up.

Jeanie–: Um. OK. If you can handle them, then café might be OK.

Amber:– No probs, unless you're bringing yoghurt again.

Jeanie:– Of course I am. Am middle class parent. Got carrot sticks too.

Amber:– 😖

Jeanie–: Still drunk, btw.

Amber:– Wild child.

Jeanie:– 🍸😖

Amber:– Got to go.

Jeanie:– Wait. Your contact. It's not Freya, is it?

Amber:– No.

Jeanie:– It is, isn't it?!? AMBER. You said things are weird between you.

Amber:– It's not her.

Jeanie:– Are you crossing your fingers behind your back?

Amber:– No.

Jeanie:– Really?

Amber:– Maybe.

Jeanie:– 🫣

Amber:– 👍 See you at 12.

17

AMBER

'Hello, Freya.'

'Oh God no.' The woman she was here to see turned and stalked off in the opposite direction. Amber followed her. It wasn't a good start, but at least Freya hadn't screamed at her, which was a step up from their last encounter.

'Freya?' Amber followed the tall figure down the soggy pathway that circled the gym they had joined together, way back before the internet was invented.

Her old colleague didn't slow down. 'Go away. I don't want to talk to you.'

'Please?' Amber was shivering. She had left her coat in the car and February was out to get her.

Freya kept moving. 'You look like crap.'

'I do.' Amber nodded. At this pace they would be back at the entrance in under a minute. 'I've been up all night. But then you probably know that.'

'Well, you clearly can't handle it at your age.' Freya shook her head, the thin gold chain at her neck catching the light. 'Anyway, I couldn't talk to you even if I wanted to.'

'That's why I came here – so no one would see us.'

'Alright, Freya?' A man in a blue hoodie grinned as he passed them. 'Hi Amber.'

'Hi Stu.' Amber raised a hand and dropped it again.

Freya rolled her eyes. 'So, the whole incognito plan is going well, then?'

Amber let the challenge slide. At least Freya had stopped walking now, if only to stare at Amber in a distinctly aggressive fashion. Her bracelets jangled as she folded her arms. 'What do you want, Amber?'

'I...' Amber fixed her eyes somewhere to the left of Freya's ear. 'I need your help.'

'I'm sorry?' Freya's voice dripped sarcasm. 'Was that Amber Nagra asking for help?'

Amber had known this would be bad. Freya was still angry. Angry enough to forget their shared history, their time spent training together in Hendon, two women in a class full of over-competitive men, the months spent doing bleep tests and memo-rising by-laws and of course their first arrest: a woman stealing a pork chop from M&S. Back then they had been each other's back-up, each other's champion, a team.

'I...'

Freya held up a hand.

'Look, Amber. I guessed you might come and try to find me and I guessed why. You and your friends are in trouble. You need me to save Clio's arse. I get it.'

'That's not quite how I'd have put it, but yes. Please?' Amber tried a smile. Freya would never understand what Amber had done, no matter how many times she tried to explain it, so all she could do was smile and wait this out for Clio's sake.

Freya continued. 'So following absolutely no apology from you, you want me to forget how close you came to blowing my life apart and you want me to risk my job to feed you information from the investigation into Gary Goode's murder. Am I right?'

Amber exhaled. It was so much more than that. Yes, she needed information – to have all the pieces of the puzzle at her fingertips. Whatever Jeanie thought she knew about the killer, Amber would need proof. Evidence. But she also needed Freya herself – her sounding board in all the cases they had ever worked. She needed her cool head and her ability to extract information no matter how tough the source.

Freya was waiting for an answer, hands on hips. Amber nodded. 'Yes. I do need your help. And—'

Freya held up a hand. 'Well, the answer's no. No bloody way.'

Amber forced her lips upwards. 'But you're the best, Freya. You always know—'

Freya shook her head. 'If this is you trying to win me over, then no wonder no one misses you at the station. You're trying to charm me and you look like you're facing off in a courtroom battle. No wonder everyone was so happy to see you leave.'

Amber was horrified to feel tears in her eyes. She bit fiercely on her cheek to hold them in. She had known that she wasn't popular, but she had never heard it stated quite so brutally before. She had sensed her colleagues' dislike in the silence when she entered a room; in the reluctance to work a shift with her; in the space around her in the canteen. Amber had spent her life trying to escape the loneliness of her chaotic childhood only to create a whole new solitude of her own.

At least she had always had Jeanie and Clio. They were why she was here. They were why she had to try again. 'Freya. Please. I'm begging you. I need someone on the inside. Someone who can give me more intel on Gary – what he did the week before he died, who he called, where he went.'

'Why, Amber? There is a team on this. Of *real* police. A murder squad, for God's sake. Officers with warrant cards and evidence bags and access to criminal records. We don't need you.'

Amber put her hand on Freya's arm. 'You know why. Clio's my family. I have to help her.'

Freya shook her off, twisting the tip of her trainer into the ground in a movement Amber had seen on a thousand shifts, back when they were on the beat together, two rookies with dreams of cleaning up crime. Now they had multivitamins, mortgages and the knowledge that however hard they tried, the bad guys would always reappear, as inevitable as mould on a shower curtain.

'You're sure Clio didn't do it?' Freya put her head on one side.

'Of course I'm sure. She was so drunk she couldn't even open a packet of crisps. And besides – she just couldn't. She has a temper but it never goes anywhere. Just a lot of words and then she collapses and binges on junk food. She didn't do it.'

'Really?'

'Yes.' Amber was practically begging now but she no longer cared. 'Please help? I know you're angry with me. I know I went too far.' She hadn't. She really hadn't.

Freya arched an eyebrow. 'Wow. That's almost an apology. You must really want my help, hey?'

'I do.' Amber wrapped her arms around herself, trying to get warm. 'Gary was such a bastard, Freya. He made Clio feel so small. He took everything she had.'

'And now he's dead. And Clio was right there when it happened.'

'I know.' Amber wished she still smoked. Anything to take this terrible anxiety away. 'But she didn't do it, Freya.'

'If you say so.'

One final try. 'Freya, don't you see? Without our help, Clio is going to get taken down. She's going to get blamed, the way women always get blamed. She's going to get beaten by Gary. Again. He took everything else from her when he was alive – let's not allow him to take her freedom too.'

'Silence.

'Please?'

Freya shifted her gym bag higher up her shoulder. 'Why should I?'

'Because deep down you know I'm right. And you know Marco isn't going to look hard enough to find anyone else, is he? He likes the obvious answers. That's why he needs people like us.'

Amber had played the only card she had left.

She waited, holding her breath.

Freya gave a curt nod. 'Maybe.'

'Thank you, Freya, I...'

Freya shook her head. 'I haven't said yes yet.'

'OK, OK. Thank you – for thinking about it.'

Freya rolled her eyes. 'Well, don't hassle me, OK? No calls, no visits to my house, nothing. I can't lose this job – Dev's taken a loan out and my mum's managed to...' Freya tailed off. 'Doesn't matter.' She was already moving off towards the entrance. 'If I help you, I'm doing it my way.'

'OK.' Amber nodded.

'Which means you have no control.'

Amber held up her hands. 'I'll have therapy. It'll be OK.'

'Good. Now, we never met. I still hate you. Goodbye.' Freya strode off towards the doors. She stopped. Turned. 'And whatever you do, don't let Marco even suspect you're working this case. It'll make him crazy.'

'I wouldn't dream of it.' Amber nodded.

Wait until she solved it. That would *really* drive him nuts.

18

GARY

5.30 p.m.: Death minus ten hours

The bloody cat detected Gary's arrival as soon as his tyres hit the long drive, and it was all he could do to resist running it over as he zoomed up to the house, gravel splattering beneath his wheels. He was now feeling desperate enough for anything, and the animal could take its chances if it got in his way again. He opened his car door and began to storm up the steps.

He paused, hearing footsteps from behind him and a voice shouting into a phone. 'Well, get rid of him. We paid him off, for Christ's sake.' Johnny appeared from the garden, shades resting on the top of his head.

'Oh God.' He spotted Gary and halted. 'I've got a visitor. Can I call you back?'

He crunched towards Gary, his mouth set in a hard line, regarding him as dismissively as if he were there to clean the drains. His disdain made Gary's temper flare.

'We need to talk.' Gary squared up to him, fists clenched.

'You again?' Johnny folded his arms. He was in a red V-neck jumper, a crisp white collar showing beneath. 'What are you doing here? I told you we'd get back to you.' He glanced down the drive. 'I must get the gates fixed. We can't let just anyone in, can we?'

Gary took a step towards him. How he would love to land his fist in the middle of that entitled face. 'Thought I'd pop by – see if I could catch you before you go to London. Or was that just another one of your lies?' He had nothing to lose now. Thirty minutes until he would have the living daylights kicked out of him by Marg or one of her many sidekicks. It was time to tell Johnny what he knew.

Johnny's eyes narrowed. 'I'm no liar, Gary.'

Gary felt the power glowing inside him. He was taller than Johnny, broader than Johnny and he definitely had a better right hook than Johnny. The man in front of him was brought up amongst ivory towers. Gary's childhood was spent at the back end of a dodgy housing estate. He had nothing to fear from him.

'Aren't you?'

Johnny folded his arms. 'No.'

'Really?' Gary didn't have time to savour the moment as much as he might like. 'So, tell me what happened to Rajiv, then?'

Gary saw a flicker of discomfort before Johnny rallied. 'Who's Rajiv?'

'You know who he is.'

'Do I, Gary?' Gary felt a beat of doubt as Johnny held his gaze, ice in his eyes. But there was no time for hesitation. Gary took a step forward. They were nose to nose now.

'You know exactly who Rajiv is.'

'No.' Johnny shook his head. 'I don't. But I'll tell you what I do know.' Johnny circled Gary, face set in stone. 'I know that you are trying to make a fool of me.' He inhaled. 'I know that you are the fucking blackmailer who's been taking my money, while having the cheek to call me The Devil. That you are the lowlife piece of shit who thinks they're too clever to be caught. Isn't that right, Mr oh-so bloody original X?'

Shock was slowing Gary down. He had set the scheme up so well. Separate email address, phone number, a burner phone kept hidden beneath his passenger seat. Payments to a fake PayPal business account. He had covered his back. So how had Johnny found him out?

Fuck it. It didn't matter now. 'So what if it was me?'

He didn't like Johnny's laugh, nor the look in his eyes. It had been far easier doing this anonymously. Threats issued via text – payments delivered – an income stream to prop up Looking Goode so he could sort out the mess Clio had left behind. No matter that blackmail was illegal. Given Johnny's secret, he deserved everything that was coming to him.

He stood his ground. 'You can't say no to me, Johnny.'

'I think you'll find I can.' Johnny checked his watch, yawning. 'And I just have.'

'That's a mistake.'

'I don't think so.' Johnny flicked a tiny piece of dirt from his sleeve. 'You are not getting one more penny from me. Not for whatever secret you think you know.' That shrug again. That casual, moneyed shrug.

'Listen to me.' Gary stood tall. He had power, he did, whatever this rich bastard thought of him.

'No.'

'I know what you did.' Gary heard the front door open behind him, but he didn't care who was listening now. Let them hear. Let the whole world hear. 'I know that you're a fraud. A fake.'

Somebody swore behind him, but Gary barely cared. He would make Johnny see – would make him understand that he couldn't say no.

Johnny sighed. 'What an imagination you have.'

Gary took a step towards him. 'Rajiv told me everything.' Gary could still remember the buzz when he had seen the papers lying on a bookshelf – well, OK, when he had been nosing through a filing cabinet as he always did, just in case. He had got the whole story eventually, overcoming Rajiv's reluctance by spiking the teetotaller's Cokes with vodka and loosening his tongue.

So, Gary knew everything. 'Johnny, you're a fake. And I'm going to tell the whole world all about it unless you pay me now – and the price has just gone up. If I talk, it's goodbye big house. Goodbye company. Goodbye floating on the London Stock Exchange. Goodbye reputation. So just pay me, Johnny. Now. A hundred grand.'

Johnny looked at him, death in his eyes.

'No.'

Gary shrugged. 'Then I'll tell everyone what I know.'

Johnny's voice was sharper now. 'No you won't.'

'But...'

'You see, Gary, I was on to you pretty fast.' Johnny rolled his eyes. 'It was too easy. I tracked your IP address, and then I got you working on those pitiful plans so I could have a good look at you – see if you were a real problem or not. But you're not, are you? You're still just a builder, a man laying bricks in the mud. You might have dressed yourself up to look all fancy, nice car, a suit you probably think is stylish...'

This was too much. This suit was from Ted Baker, for fuck's sake. 'But I can ruin you, Johnny—'

'No. You can't.' Johnny looked infuriatingly sure of himself. 'Because if you do share anything you think you know, I'll show my brother Marshall this video. It came through from a source this morning. I don't think Marshall would be very happy, do you? Your number one client?' He held out his phone.

Gary stared at the video. His first thought was that his butt was in pretty good shape. His second thought was far more prosaic.

'Fuck.' He couldn't keep the word in. 'Fuck, fuck, fuck.'

'Well, quite. Fuck is the operative word, isn't it?' Johnny nodded. 'You must be more careful when you're sowing your wild oats – Marshall's got some pretty unpleasant friends. Maybe I should just pay one of them to get rid of you, but it would be way more fun if Marshall took the lead. He's always had a temper. I just hope the fragrant Cherie was worth it. Look – you can see her face so clearly here and it's so helpful that she's moaning your name.'

'Dad?' A figure appeared from behind Gary in a tight white T-shirt and black skinny jeans, hair gelled back. It must have been him who swore a moment ago. 'Dad. Do you want me to get rid of him?'

Johnny's eyes didn't leave Gary's face. 'I've got this covered, Christian. And we all know even Gary would be more than a match for you.'

'That's not fair, Dad. I've been going to the gym, and...'

'To use the sauna, from what I've heard.'

Christian's mouth turned downwards. 'No. I've been doing weights, and...'

'Weights?' Johnny sneered. 'I don't think so. Now go back to your flat. I don't know why you're always hanging around here.'

'But I can help, Dad.'

'I've got this, Christian.' Johnny folded his arms. 'So, Gary. Now you've seen the video, I think it's time you pissed off, don't you?'

Gary thought about Marg; about the deadline he was about to miss and the ten grand he didn't have.

He found he didn't give a flying one about the video.

'Christian, your dad's a lying bastard, and I'm about to tell the whole world why.' He pointed at Johnny. 'You have one more night.

If you don't get me a hundred grand by 9 a.m. tomorrow, I'm going public, whatever you do with that video.'

Johnny sighed. 'I thought you were stupid, but I didn't know you were this stupid. Honestly, I wish someone would just get rid of you, you little prick.'

'Dad—' Christian's knuckles were white. A muscle flickered in his pale cheek.

'No.' Johnny ignored him, speaking only to Gary. 'You're not getting a penny from me. Not one.'

Gary made one last stand.

'I know what you did, Johnny. Money by 9 a.m. or you're history.'

He turned and got into his car, landing heavily behind the wheel, hands shaking as he started the engine. The two of them were standing on the steps as he drove away, Christian gesticulating wildly, still trying to get his dad's attention. Pathetic.

Gary had only fifteen minutes until he had to pay ten grand to a female loan shark who was famous for owning the town's largest collection of guns. But he would come up with something – he always did.

He was Gary Goode, and he was going to live forever.

Wasn't he?

19

JEANIE

'Where have you been? I was worried about you.'

Jeanie looked into her partner's big brown eyes. He certainly didn't look worried. He looked like a man who had just spent half an hour in the loo scrolling sports headlines on his phone.

She opened her mouth to answer him, her own phone ready in her hand so he could see the news blast about Gary's death. She wanted him to put his arms around her, to sit down, to listen. Instead he neatly sidestepped the large pile of washing that he appeared to think was physically attached to the bottom step before sprinting up and retrieving his battered Adidas trainers from the landing.

Then he bounced back down, stepping over the Tesco bag spewing baby bottles, muslins and nappies that she had dumped in the doorway yesterday after a disastrous trip to the local soft play centre. He just left the bag where it was, apparently seeing it as another obstacle in the ever-increasing assault course that their home had become since the twins' arrival. As a charity caseworker, Tan had been trained to stay calm in all situations and their descent into mayhem was apparently no exception. Sometimes Jeanie wished that he would lose his temper just *once*, if only to make her feel less psychotic. Here she was, two hours late home, and all she had sent him was a minimal text to explain: *Got caught up, sorry.* If it had been the other way around, she would have been all passive aggressive monosyllables and clattering saucepans. But here he was, sliding his trainers on, not commenting. It was infuriating.

She would tell him the whole story now. 'We had a bit of a night.' Jeanie tried to kiss him at the precise moment he bent over to tie his shoelaces, leaving her embracing the banister.

'Oh yeah?' He was up now, staring at his phone. Lately, his eyes were always elsewhere: his phone or the TV or his plate or the twins, of course.

'Yeah. You see...' She swallowed, wondering where to start. She needed to tell him everything. The sticky table in the police station. The blotchy cream walls. The blood on the trophy. Her fears about who had put it there. She needed them to curl up on their battered red sofa together, as they had done so often, sharing pizzas and stories, laughing over the memes his friends had sent over from Japan or about how many extra hours Jeanie's then boss had asked her to work that weekend.

He cut in before she could collect her thoughts. 'Did the three of you have too many cocktails?' His phone was out and he was typing, thumbs moving fast. 'Have you overdosed on ABBA?'

'No. Well, yes.' Jeanie wished he would look at her. Surely he would see that something huge had happened – surely he would see her distress?

'Well.' He put his phone back in the pocket of the black jeans that were his daily uniform. 'I took the twins to the park, when you said you were running late.'

'Great.'

'But I've got a busy day, so...'

She wanted his arms around her – to keep him here.

'Can't you stay?'

She needed him to agree. She had to meet Amber, and taking the twins anywhere felt so perilous, so fraught with disaster and embarrassment. She was hoping she could leave them with him.

'Sorry.' Tan pulled his coat on. Easy. Methodical. That was Tan through and through. The product of a wandering English language teacher and a Japanese singer, he was incapable of getting worked up about anything, apart from the Yomiuri Giants and their persistent failure to top the League.

Jeanie wanted to reach out and hug him, but didn't know how. 'Please? I was hoping we could talk. And I need to leave the twins with you for a bit. A lot has happened, and...'

'I can't.' He kissed her cheek. 'I'm on call this weekend. We need a placement for a vulnerable eighteen-year-old. I have to go in and see how I can help.'

Jeanie sagged. Tan did such good work. It was impossible to believe that her needs should come first, even on a day like today.

'You can tell me everything tonight.' He stepped away, giving her a clear view of the damp patch that was blooming by the front door. 'Have fun with the twins.'

She put her hand on his arm to stop him, wanting to tell him everything as she always used to do. But then she realised something. The house was quiet.

Too quiet.

'Where are they? The twins?' She looked around, scanning the narrow stairs, the tangle of coats at the door, the door to the cupboard under the stairs. Yumi and Jack had just started moving, jolting her out of her holding pattern of feed, feed, rest, feed, feed, rest into a new nightmare of basically trying to imprison them long enough for Jeanie to be able to drink a cup of tea. Not for the first time she envied Tan his ability to leave the house and not think about parenting again until he returned. Jeanie's current dream was to have a wee on her own. It showed absolutely no sign of coming true.

'They're in the living room.' Tan gave her a perfunctory kiss on the cheek. 'I put the telly on. *Night Garden*. Macapaca is polishing people's faces with that disgusting sponge of his. It's a trip, that show.'

He was by the front door, hooking keys from underneath a pile of bills.

'I...' Jeanie hesitated, measuring her words. *Tan, I've just been interviewed by the police under caution* seemed a little blunt. She tried again. 'It's...' If only her brain was working, but instead it appeared to be in storage with the rest of their adult things, stashed away to make room for bright Bumbos and plastic cutlery emblazoned with Thomas the Tank Engine's face.

'Yeah?'

He was already halfway out of the door.

She redirected. She couldn't tell him now. Not in a rush.

Tonight. She would tell him tonight.

Shame clouded in again as she realised the car was still at Clio's. 'You'll have to get the bus. I'm so sorry.'

'Oh. OK.' Even now he wasn't angry. Even now when she had made him even later for work. 'Where is it?'

'It's a long story. I...'

A shrug. A half-smile. That dimple in his cheek. A hand running through his thick dark fringe. 'It's OK. Big night, hey? Glad you got to let your hair down. I'll get the bus.'

And he was gone.

He reappeared, catching the door just before it shut. Her heart lifted.

'You must go out more often, Jean Jeanie.'

His old nickname for her, from one of his mum's favourite songs. Something in Jeanie relaxed as she waved a farewell.

The door opened for a third time. 'I paid the gas bill.'

'Great.'

He hovered a second. 'When... are you going back to work, by the way?'

And just like that her happiness ebbed away. 'I don't know, Tan. The twins aren't even one yet. Give me time.' The words fired from her far more aggressively than she had intended.

'OK.' She wanted him to fight, to stand up to her unreasonableness, to care. But instead, she heard that sing-song tone again. '*Sayonara.*' A peck on the cheek and he was gone.

'Bye.' Jeanie flung her hands over her exhausted eyes, before kicking off her boots and sliding down to the floor. She wondered how the two of them had become like this. Once they had looked into each other's eyes, marvelled in each other, been intertwined. They had met during the three months she had spent teaching English in Tokyo, buoyed by a spirit of adventure that had rapidly disappeared when she realised how much she missed home. She had met Tan in the cinema, watching that most English of movies *Four Weddings and a Funeral*. She had lost her ticket as she was going in – he had bought her a new one. They were meant to be.

Within days they were spending every spare second together, wandering Tokyo fish markets, seeing golden temples at dawn, standing at the huge pedestrian crossing in Shibuya letting the crowds ebb and flow around them. When she went back to the UK he followed. And while they had never got engaged, she had always known that it didn't matter – that they would be together forever.

Until now. She laid her head back against the wall. Maybe it was IVF that had started the decline – the months of injections and paper cups and failure. Or maybe it was the twins themselves – the small, all-consuming creatures who were so funny yet so relentless, so joyful yet so draining. All those years dreaming of them and she and Tan had not had a clue about what it would really be like to become parents. She sighed. She felt so alone now, even when he was right there. She could handle the exhaustion and the military schedule required to keep two small people in clean nappies, fresh clothes and pureed vegetables, but it was her self-doubt that really put a wall between them. The anxiety that woke her at 2.30 a.m. when she ran into their rooms to see if they were still breathing.

As a PA at a marketing company, Jeanie had once felt in control of her days. She was the one people turned to in a crisis – the one who always knew where to find the keys or the spreadsheet or the biscuit tin. Now she could barely get her pants on without an existential crisis. With every day that passed she felt more and more useless – just another sweaty mum on the bus, bent over her double buggy, stuffing breadsticks into her children's mouths to try to keep them quiet. So she went out less – her world getting smaller while his remained exactly the same.

She checked the clock on the wall, and saw that she didn't have long enough for a shower if she wanted to meet Amber on time. She forced herself to stand up, still leaning against the wall, about to test her theory that she was so tired that she could actually sleep standing up. She was just drifting off – a minute or two might make all the difference – when she heard the crying.

Instantly, she snapped awake, already moving towards her children. She walked down the stained carpet of the hall, where the once-white walls had become a map of her children's childhoods so far. A bowl of blueberries had been mashed into the paint by the kitchen door, creating a shape that closely resembled Italy, while just by the downstairs loo there were indistinct stains from the night that Yumi and Jack had taken their commitment to projectile vomiting to new and horrifying heights.

She followed the crying, and found her children. There they were, sitting together in front of the TV in matching navy and white sailor suits sent by their proud grandmother in Japan. Yumi and

Jack, chubby fists full of the strawberries she had warned Tan never to give them in the living room, were screeching in displeasure. Jeanie couldn't blame them. Macapaca looked terrifying in HD.

Yumi raised her hand. 'Oh no.' Jeanie ran forward as the strawberries fell towards the white carpet. She caught one, two, three only for the wailing to increase. Jack was on the move, crawling his way towards the nirvana of the living room door. Tan had forgotten to put the baby gate across and her boy was halfway to freedom before Jeanie could catch him.

She kissed his soft black hair and placed him down gently by the TV. She was just congratulating herself when she tripped head first over the huge toy Olaf that was lying by the sofa, landing face first in Yumi's bowl of berries.

This, apparently, was hilarious. The twins threw their heads back, throaty chuckles roaring from their warm, compact bodies. For a second Jeanie considered staying where she was, face down in a pile of fruit. It was nice here. Soft. And the twins would probably be OK for a half hour or so. The front door was locked. The telly was on. They would be fine. And it was easy here – no one could see them, there was no one to worry about. If she was honest she had spent most of her maternity leave here in the house, too tired and anxious to attempt the trips that she had so long dreamt of making: to the park, the steam train, the local farm.

Jeanie's eyelids closed, sleep nearly overcoming her, and she was almost in the promised land when the image of Gary Goode's prone body inserted itself in between her and unconsciousness.

She pushed herself up, wiping a pip from her cheek. How was it still only 11.45 a.m.?

'Time to go.' She scrambled up, readying herself to start the laborious process of getting the children out of the front door. Their laughter stopped. Jack's brown eyes widened and his cheeks started to redden. Yumi already had a fat tear seeping down her cheek and a suspicious smell was coming from her rear end.

Jeanie sighed. A classic start.

Bribery was the only answer.

A record ten minutes later nappies had been changed, bobble hats pulled down over wispy black hair, straps had been tied, snow-suits had been put on and dried fruit was being consumed with gusto by the twins. Jeanie would pay for it later, but for now she felt an unusual beat of pride. She had got the job done.

As she shut the front door she caught sight of a photo stuck halfway up the stairs. A seashell frame around two of the happiest faces Jeanie had ever seen, heads flung back, the sunset painting the sky red. For years she had barely noticed the picture, but now the sight of it sliced through her like a guillotine through paper. The murderer was on her wall. Gary Goode's killer was hanging on her stairs.

Jeanie clasped the door handle, worried she might faint.

Then she forced herself forwards. Amber. She needed Amber.

Amber would make everything OK.

20

AMBER

Amber twisted a packet of sugar between her fingers, sniffing the air appreciatively. She hoped those were her eggs being fried, and her slices of toast being buttered.

She sipped her coffee, seeing a lady in a smart navy scarf looking up from her Sudoku, melting like ice cream on a sunny windowsill as she spotted Yumi and Jack. The children were sleeping, both heads lolling to the right, Yumi's tiny pink tongue poking through her pearly white teeth. Amber saw the lady mouthing 'Oh, bless' before turning back to the numbered squares on the page in front of her.

Amber gestured to the waitress for another coffee as Jeanie made her way through the café tables in a clatter of dislodged cutlery. She turned back, reaching down to pick up the spoons she had sent flying, flinging words over her shoulder.

'Amber. I know who did it.'

'And hello Jeanie.' Amber blinked as Jeanie straightened, only to push her double buggy into the next table. Jeanie's face turned a blotchy red as she mumbled apologies, and part of Amber felt bad for dragging her here, out of her comfort zone. Since the twins had arrived it had started to feel as if Jeanie was on her own personal lockdown. She was scared of taking them out, scared of the unknown, scared of getting the buggy onto a bus.

'So, I was at the beach hut? Hiding Clio's ring like she asked me to...' Jeanie knocked over a pot plant in her final push to join Amber at their favourite corner table. It overlooked the beach and had a lone daffodil at its centre, with a rainbow tablecloth trailing down to the floor. Outside, the storm had quietened for now, the waves calm and grey.

Jeanie righted the plant and checked on her children, who were bound as tightly as criminals on their way to the dock, zipped into red snowsuits so warm that their little faces were flushed. Amber could only tell them apart because of the comforters that they held – Yumi's a bright yellow bunny and Jack's a once-white trainer sock that he had clung to no matter what Jeanie had offered instead.

'Do you think they'll be OK?' Jeanie's fingers anxiously pleated her coat.

'They're asleep. Of course they will. Sit down. Relax.' Amber saw the exhaustion on Jeanie's face. Deep hollows were carved out beneath her blue eyes and her skin was so pale it was almost transparent. Only her curls were in party mood, cascading around her shoulders, as effervescent as the prosecco that had marked the beginning of the night before.

The server delivered Amber's second coffee and looked at Jeanie, iPad at the ready. The notebooks and pens had disappeared six months ago, as had the owner with the purple hair who had always made tea no matter what you had actually ordered. Now the Rainbow Café was lighter, brighter, with coloured tea pots and sparkling walls, serving pancakes as thick as toast and salads to die for.

The girl smiled down at Jeanie. 'Would you like anything?'

'Oh. I don't know.' Jeanie had her confused maths GCSE expression on, and Amber hadn't missed it one bit.

The server was new, with long dark hair pulled back into a tight ponytail and silver rings glinting in her ears. 'Oh my God, they're so cute!' She gazed at the twins.

'Thank you. You won't be saying that once they wake up.' Jeanie twisted a paper napkin in her fingers.

'How about a cappuccino?' Amber suggested.

'Sure.' Jeanie stared at the waves below them, seemingly lost.

'Coming right up.' The server moved towards the coffee machine.

'Jeanie?'

Nothing. Amber would have to take charge. 'So, you were at the hut.'

Jeanie nodded. 'Yes. And when I was there I saw—' She stopped. Seconds ticked by. 'I saw something with blood on it. The murder weapon, I think.'

'What?' Amber sat back as the waitress brought over Jeanie's cappuccino, white and fluffy in a red cup.

Jeanie waited until the girl had gone. 'It was a trophy. Stashed in a corner, in the dark, like someone had tried to hide it.' Jeanie sipped her drink and a foam moustache appeared on her upper lip. Amber reached out to wipe it away. Honestly, some things never changed. 'And I didn't want to touch it, of course, in case I left prints. But I saw that the base was covered in blood. And...' She leant even further forward. 'Hair.'

Amber's mind whirred. 'Gary's hair?'

'Salt and pepper hair, yes.'

Amber's mind grappled with this new information. The hut meant Clio. Or Bez. But actually, also anyone who knew that the key was kept under the pottery owl, which was probably half the bloody town, given Clio's tendency to overshare after a few drinks. 'With blood on it? You're sure?'

'Yes.' Jeanie's eyes darted to her son as his long eyelashes fluttered open. 'Oh no.' Her whole body tensed. 'I've got ten minutes max until he kicks off.' She undid her coat and started to lift up her top and unclip straps in an operation that seemed as complicated as Houdini escaping an underwater chamber. 'It's time for his feed. It'll buy me some time.'

It occurred to Amber, not for the first time, that for Jeanie parenting seemed to be one long mission to stop your child actually doing anything: anything noisy, anything dangerous, anything at all.

Jeanie unstrapped Jack, pulling him close. He relaxed back, sucking happily. What a life, Amber thought as she emptied two packets of sugar into her coffee. If only children knew how lucky they were.

Jeanie stroked his hair with her spare hand, a faraway look on her face.

Her next words were a surprise. 'So Bez must have done it. He must have killed Gary.'

Amber nearly laughed. 'Why Bez? He can barely be bothered to do up his shoes. I can't imagine him bothering to smash someone's skull in.'

Jeanie's eyes were alight. 'But he was at the hut yesterday, fixing the roof. Clio told me. And he and Gary have history, don't they? Over Clio? And Gary did just take all Nina's money too. Bez must be furious, his daughter being stolen from like that.'

'True.' Amber frowned. Something didn't fit here. 'I just... can't imagine it. He's not a killer.'

Jeanie drank her entire coffee in one. 'Well, who else could it be? It's too bloody cold for anyone else to want to be at the hut. Maybe Gary went there for some reason – looking for the ring, maybe? Yes...' She clicked her fingers the way she had when she had known the answers when they watched *Blockbusters* after school. 'He was hunting for the ring because he needed money and he was a thieving git.' She looked downwards. 'Sorry, Jack. And Bez was there, and...'

'But then how did Gary get up to Clio's place? His body, I mean?'

'Oh.' Jeanie's face fell. Then her fingers clicked into life once more. 'Maybe Bez hit him outside Clio's van and then hid the trophy in the hut?'

'Maybe.' Amber sipped her coffee. 'But wouldn't he have just thrown it into the sea? Or at least washed it clean?'

'I don't know.' Jeanie lifted Jack so that his head was over her shoulder, her hand massaging his back. 'Maybe he panicked?'

Amber considered this. 'Maybe. You know, you're good at this, Jeanie.'

Jeanie blushed. 'Just some stupid guesses – I got lucky.'

Amber felt a needle of frustration. Jeanie had never exactly been confident, but now she appeared surprised if she knew where her front door keys were.

Amber clapped her hands together.

'OK, this is what we're going to do—'

'We?' Jeanie settled Jack back into the buggy and unclipped Yumi for her turn.

Amber nodded decisively. 'Yes, Jeanie. We. *We* have to solve this case.'

'But I don't know how.' Jeanie shook her head. 'Besides, won't the police be doing that?'

'No. They're going to think Clio did it.'

'Oh.' Jeanie inserted her boob into Yumi's mouth and started delivering her second lunch of the day. 'But you said she would be OK.'

'I said what Clio needed to hear.' Amber shrugged. She had done the best she could – she didn't have time to make things pretty. 'But the fact is that Marco is going to uncover a whole load of circumstantial evidence that will make him want to charge Clio. And he's not very clever, so he'll do what's obvious. It's how he is.' She remembered the last case they had worked together – how long it had taken to prove to him that it wasn't always the wife that did it. Sometimes it could be the next-door neighbour. 'It's who he is.'

'That's terrible.' Jeanie blinked. 'Poor Clio.' Her big blue eyes could fill at an alarming rate.

'Don't get upset.' Jeanie was all she had – Amber had to get her to focus. 'Because we're going to find who really did it. OK? You and me. The dream team.' Sitting in a deserted café on a hangover, this didn't quite have the verve that Amber was going for.

'But we've already solved it. It's Bez.' Jeanie tried to pin down a struggling Yumi.

'It might be, yes. But we don't know that for sure yet.'

Jeanie removed a piece of lint from her daughter's cheek. 'But it's too dangerous. I don't want to die.'

Jeanie was anxiety in action. Amber had to remember this. 'You won't die. No one wants to kill *us*.'

'But they might. If we get in the way.'

Amber had never missed Freya more. Freya who would leap into any fight without a second thought. Freya who had no fear.

But Jeanie was her team-mate now. 'We'll be too clever for the killer.' Amber smiled reassuringly. 'Won't we?'

'How will we be too clever, Amber? You might be, but I...'

Amber suppressed a sigh. She flashed back to Jeanie's hand up in chemistry classes, painstakingly asking every possible question about a simple experiment involving a magnet and some iron filings. 'I'm crap at puzzles, Amber. I can't even do the simple cross-word in the *Herald*. So...'

'So we're going to divide and conquer.' Amber pushed a napkin across the table. 'Here's a map of the crime scene – we'll embellish it as we go along, obviously. It's just a starter – where the body was, possible entry routes, caravans etc.'

Jeanie sniffed. 'OK.'

'And we can do a suspects board. Do you have anything with you we could use now?' Amber looked at the juggernaut of a buggy which had enough pockets, trays and hooks to store the entire contents of the local Cash and Carry.

'Um....' Jeanie chewed her lip. 'I've got a Teletubbies black-board. I got it from a charity shop last week.'

Amber poked around, finding a Mr Man cushion, an open packet of rice cakes and a used tissue that really did belong in a bin.

'Got it!' She waved it in the air. 'This is perfect. It's even got chalk tucked into the bottom.' She started to write. *Clio. Jeanie. Amber. Bez. Denise.*

'Why are you and I on there?' Jeanie watched her, open-mouthed. 'We know we didn't do it.'

'Just being thorough.' Amber rubbed out their names, her hand colliding with Dipsy's hat. 'And we need motives.'

Jeanie frowned. 'How are we meant to know what they are?'

Amber sighed. 'Well, Denise – jealousy. Bez – rage and/or jeal-ousy. You see? We're building up a picture of the reasons people might want to kill Gary.'

'But...' Jeanie chewed her lip.

'Yes?'

'Is this how real investigations work?'

'What do you mean?'

'Well, if you were on the force now, would you be doing this?'

'Yes.' Amber sat back. 'Just with the help of the police national computer—' she saw Jeanie's mouth opening to ask a new question '—which has details of anyone ever arrested ever, their history, vehicle registrations – that kind of thing.'

'Wow.' Jeanie bounced a restless Yumi on her knee.

'Yeah.' If Jeanie was going to be on her team, Amber might as well talk her through the basics. 'Look. In a nutshell, a good detective finds out how someone lived. If you know that, you'll find out how they died and who had means, motive and opportunity to kill them. You see?'

Jeanie stroked Yumi's cheek. 'So if you're not very nice, like Gary, then you might have a long list of suspects?'

'Exactly.' Amber nodded. 'The police team will be building a picture of everything now – victimology, it's called. They'll be finding out about his lifestyle, his relationships, his finances – the lot. They'll be using CCTV, bank statements, witness statements, his diary. His phone will be key, if they can find it, though I reckon it's probably at the bottom of the ocean by now. And they'll be doing other things – crime scene officers will be posted at the scene, seeing who comes and goes. Forensic officers will be combing the site for DNA or clues and of course there's the post mortem too. There'll be daily briefings and a big team of detective constables doing the grunt work – door to doors, background checks – that kind of thing.'

She looked up, surprised to find Jeanie's hand on hers. 'I'm sorry, Amber. I know how much you miss it.'

'I'm fine.' Amber prickled. 'I'm just telling you what happens in a murder investigation.'

'The look on your face when you were talking about it, though.' Now Jeanie lifted Yumi up on her shoulder. 'It was like when you had that crush on Skylar in our GCSE maths class and she asked you to share her Sunny Delight one lunchtime. Your smile.'

'I wasn't smiling.' Amber realised she had just split a sugar packet in two.

Jeanie's cheeks reddened again. 'Sorry.' She turned towards her little girl, curls covering her face.

Amber pushed on. 'We need to get working, Jeanie.'

'But how are we going to get all that information?' Jeanie kissed her little girl and placed her back in the buggy.

Amber smiled. 'We're going to go undercover.'

'We are?' Jeanie was clipping straps again.

Amber summarised. 'Here's what we know. Gary landed on the doorstep between 2.30 a.m. when Clio left, and 5.30 a.m. when she came back. As far as we know he was killed by a blow to the head. We know there is a trophy in the beach hut with blood on it, but we don't know whose it is. His fiancée suspected him of shagging Clio. And he was in such financial shit that he had to steal from a teenager's bank account. There's a lot to go on.'

'Um. OK.' Jeanie nodded. 'But what do we do first?'

'I'm not sure.' Amber smiled. This was the fun bit. Assessing, prioritising. 'But it might be worth starting with Johnny Fernandez. I've had a quick trawl of Gary's social media and his last Insta post shows he was at Johnny's house yesterday – I recognise the hideous gold wanker gates from a case I was on when I was a DC.'

'Johnny Fernandez?' Jeanie flinched as Yumi started to cry. She took hold of the handlebars of the buggy with all the enthusiasm of a warhorse heading into battle.

'Yes. He's CEO of Fernandez Tech.'

'I used to work with them, back when I had a brain. Make coffee for them, I mean, while they had their big ideas.' Jeanie started half-heartedly jiggling the buggy up and down. 'And I know his wife Vivienne.'

'You do?' Amber looked at her, surprised.

'Not through work – I was far too lowly for that. Johnny wouldn't even remember me. But their baby just started nursery with the twins. Bear. That's her name. She and Yumi were in the sandpit together on their first day.'

'That's perfect!'

'Is it?' Jeanie bit her lip. 'I mean, we don't know each other well.

Not really. She's far too glamorous for me.'

'Not any more she's not. It's a connection and we need to use it. You can find out what happened when Gary went there.'

Now Jack was crying too. The friendly server was looking far less enamoured now.

Jeanie's forehead creased in an all-too familiar way. 'She's organised a spa day tomorrow – a mixer for new parents. At Thrive – that new spa near Southampton? So I guess she'll be there. I wasn't going to go. Tan and I were planning a lunch together and…'

'Well, you're going now. For Clio.' Amber felt a beat of satisfaction.

'But…'

'Jeanie, we have to help Clio.'

Jeanie gave a tiny nod. 'OK. But, I don't know if I'll be any good at this, Amber. So don't rely on me.'

'You'll be great.' Amber patted her hand, keen to get out of here now the twins were really kicking off. It was time to start work – to start the process of sifting through facts and motives and people until the puzzle was solved. God, she loved this.

'What are you going to do, then? While I'm spying at the spa?'

Amber's phone rang and she reached into her bag. 'I'll talk to Bez and see what's what with that trophy. Then I'll start figuring out Gary's movements over the past week and making a timeline. I think Freya's going to help us too.'

'Really?' Jeanie's surprise was stamped all over her face. 'But I thought things were weird between you since you left the police?'

'It was fine. Stop worrying.' Amber answered her phone.

She heard a breathless voice. 'They let me out.'

'Clio?'

'Yes. I'm out. Can you come?'

Amber stood up.

'Let's go get our girl.'

21

CLIO

'Clio?'

Clio froze.

'Yes?' She turned around, fully expecting handcuffs to click around her wrists. She knew they hadn't meant to let her go. She knew they had just been toying with her.

She braced herself as Marco marched down the steps outside the police station. It was new evidence, no doubt. An eyewitness who had seen her doing something even more ominous than waving a blunt knife in her husband's face. She held out her wrists. It had been a great five minutes of freedom.

He had something in his hand. 'You forgot your wallet.'

'Oh.' Clio took it, relief starting to seep through her. 'Sorry.'

She turned away.

'Clio?'

What now? She turned.

'Remember, you can't go anywhere. No leaving town, OK? We may need to ask you further questions at any time. No disappearing.'

As if. Her car would probably break down before she reached

the bypass. And all she wanted to do was have a bath and hug Nina, quite possibly forever. 'Don't worry, I'm not going anywhere.'

'I hope not.' There wasn't a flicker of humour in his face. 'Because we'll find you.'

He turned and stalked back into the station. Divorce really hadn't brought out the best in him. Clio stretched out her arms, breathing in the outside world. She smelt the lunchtime pies being served in the Fisherman's Friend pub, valiantly battling with her own armpits which were giving a nearby bin a run for its money. But to Clio, each inhalation felt like a gift, direct from heaven itself. She had no idea why Marco had let her out, but she knew that she was happy about it. She was going to enjoy every single second.

The time she had spent in the custody suite had proved to her, once and for all, that she would never survive incarceration. She massaged her aching back with her thumbs, her head pounding. Then she reached for her phone. She needed to hear Nina's voice. Yesterday her daughter had been furious with Clio about letting Gary take her money – asking why she hadn't taken him off the account, why she had been so stupid.

But however much Nina hated her, Clio hated herself more. She felt betrayed by the way this detail had escaped her, by the way her brain was constantly letting her down: cash vanishing, keys disappearing – a thousand small betrayals that led her to wake at 3 a.m. and spend the rest of the night googling online dementia tests and then being too scared to take them.

She closed her eyes and swore to herself that she would not let this divide with Nina widen. They had always been so close – even when Clio had met Gary and fallen head over heels, even when they had been forced to move into the caravan – it had always been Clio and Nina against the world, the Gilmore Girls of Sunshine Sands. Nina was going to be a doctor and Clio was going to be married to Gary for ever.

Now, only one of those things would ever be true again. Clio's phone buzzed and she eagerly checked the screen, swearing when she saw it was just another message from her temping agency asking where she was, and could she please warn them as per the terms of her contract if she wasn't going to turn up for work?

Well, no she couldn't as it turned out. With shaking hands Clio deleted the message. She heard a car pulling up and saw a familiar blue Skoda with Jeanie peering over the wheel. The passenger door was still battered from a scrape with a gatepost last summer, and Clio watched as Jeanie's lack of spatial awareness led to a very close encounter with a bin.

'Risking life and limb.' Amber was out of the car in seconds and Clio found tears were rolling down her cheeks. She really had felt like she might never taste freedom again – never get to hug her friends without being strip-searched first by a sinister screw with a vendetta against her. Amber reached out a finger and wiped a tear away. 'Alright, Clio. It's alright. They've let you out. That means they don't have enough evidence to charge you, OK?'

It wasn't really OK, but then Jeanie was beside her, her arms tight around Clio's shoulders. Jeanie let Clio cry for a minute or two before pulling away. 'Monster Munch?'

'Yes please.'

Amber looked her up and down. 'Man, you look like crap.'

'Thanks, friend. You sure know how to make a prime suspect feel good.' Clio took a shuddering breath. 'What took you so long, anyway?'

'We came as quickly as we could. Oh no, Jack's escaped again.' Jeanie stuck her head into the passenger window, grappling with little limbs.

Amber spoke in a whisper. 'The buggy wouldn't fold up. There were tears.'

Clio ripped open the Monster Munch. 'Jeanie or the twins?'

'Guess.' Amber arched an eyebrow.

Clio crunched her first crisp. 'God, these are good.'

'Only the best for you.' Amber squeezed her arm. 'You OK?'

'No.' Clio ate another. 'Marco was vile. But I'm hoping you've already worked out who did it, so I can go in and tell him it wasn't me.'

'Not quite yet.' Amber ran her hand through her hair. 'But we're on the case. We were just making a plan when you called.'

Clio ate eagerly. 'I knew you would be.'

Jeanie spoke over her shoulder, still wrestling with her son. 'We've got our first lead, too. I found a trophy with blood on it in the hut. Blood and Gary's hair too. So, maybe Bez hit Gary with it? I mean, they don't like each other, so...'

It took a second for Clio to take this in.

'What?'

'A trophy.' Jeanie's face became a grimace. 'Oh my God that smells disgusting, Yumi. Why now? Why never at home when I have everything I need?' She disappeared again and was soon seen pinning her daughter to the back seat, the little legs flailing and screams piercing the air.

Clio stuck her head into the car to talk to Jeanie. The smell was so thick it caught the back of her throat. She held her sleeve over her nose. 'What did it look like? The trophy?'

Jeanie's hair was flying around her face. 'Like a trophy. You know. Handles. Silver.'

'In the hut?' Clio could practically feel her blood pressure rising. 'What shape?'

'Um. Round?' Jeanie was wringing her hands. 'I was so shocked by the blood I didn't notice that much, I'm sorry. But you said Bez was down there yesterday, so I assumed it was him.'

'Oh God.' Clio escaped the smell and stood up straight again.

Her head was reeling, and this time not from hangover or hormones.

Because she knew more than Jeanie. She knew that Bez had not been at the hut yesterday after all. At the last minute he had been forced to head to Brighton to pick up a new extractor fan for the woman at number nine. Instead, Clio had sent someone else to check on the roof. Someone who had every reason to be very angry with Gary.

Her friends continued talking, oblivious to Clio's turmoil. Amber was shaking her head at Jeanie. 'I'm still not convinced.'

In the car, Jack giggled as he escaped his straps again. Clio remembered Nina doing things like that. One day she had pulled a windscreen wiper off and used it as a sword. Then there were the trails she had left around the house – paths of crumbs and toys and Lego – every drawer completed with a tiny doll or a pine cone. Her little girl, now seventeen and all grown up on the outside, but still needing so much love, still needing to find the way towards the amazing woman she was going to be.

Before she knew it Clio's eyes had filled with tears again, and she turned away from her friends. Her suspicion was growing, unstoppable and terrifying. The trophy. The blood. The money. It all made a horrible kind of sense. Nina had been different yesterday. Her usual mellow calm had become fury when Clio had told her what Gary had done.

Could the girl who once sang herself to sleep have really done this?

Clio had to find out.

'Hey. No need to cry. We're here. We can get you to a shower. To coffee. To anything you need.' She heard a smile in Amber's voice. 'We can't sort out that terrible outfit you're wearing, but we'll do what we can on everything else. And most of all, we're going to find who did this. We're going to solve this case. Together.'

But Clio didn't want them to solve it any more. She just wanted to look her girl in the eye. To ask her what had happened. To help. For Nina, she would step in front of a bus. For Nina, she would take a bullet.

Her voice was tiny. 'Can you take me home, please?'

'Sure.' Amber held the passenger door open and Jeanie climbed into the front and started the engine.

'Let's go.'

22

@SUNSHINESANDSONLINE
Followers: 1800
NEWS BLAST: Caravan Park Killing

With the surprise release today of the chief suspect in the Gary Goode murder, the town is holding its breath. With over fifteen per cent of murderers caught in the first twenty-four hours, time is ticking on for DCI Santini and his team. The town is fearful today, as police start a fingertip search of the area and door-to-door questioning continues.
Will they catch the killer before they strike again? Keep following and liking us if you want to stay safe.

Shares: 1150
Likes: 2000

23

CLIO

Her caravan appeared to have become a tourist attraction.

'What the...?' Clio drew up short, Amber and Jeanie beside her. Her home was fenced off with yellow crime scene tape, but this wasn't deterring the onlookers jostling to take the perfect selfie in front of the white forensics tent where Gary's body had been. After months of seeing nothing but flaws in her place of exile, so tiny compared to her old house on the clifftops, Clio now felt a rush of nostalgia for what the caravan had been. A safe place to land. A haven.

'How do they all know what happened?' Some onlookers had flasks and cool boxes, and were setting out camping chairs as if settling in for the foreseeable future. A man whose eyes were barely visible above his beard saw Clio and nudged the woman next to him. Her head turned, eyes widening as if Clio was some kind of celebrity, before she elbowed the woman beside her, passing word down the line. On the many occasions Clio had imagined becoming famous it had never been like this: unwashed, starving and a prime suspect.

Clio turned to her friends. 'How did they know to come here?'

'Um...' Jeanie blinked frantically at Amber.

'There's just been a bit of chat online.' Amber shrugged. 'Nothing major, but still...' She peered off into the crowd, distracted. 'Hang on, what's Marg doing here?'

'Who's Marg?' Clio tried to ignore the stares, searching for Nina.

Amber frowned. 'An old... *acquaintance*. Dresses like she's off to a tea dance with her pensioner friends, but actually she's the local loan shark and criminal queen bee.'

'She sounds delightful.' Clio flushed, feeling too many eyes upon her.

'Is that her?' A red-haired woman turned, her knitting needles clicking as she worked on a scarf that was clearly going to be just as bright as her voluminous yellow cardigan. 'Is that the Clifftop Killer?' Her voice was loud enough to be audible in the Isle of Wight. She frowned, turning to her friend. 'She looks rough, doesn't she? No wonder, after doing a thing like that. Maybe I should get her autograph.'

'Nah.' Her friend threw a chocolate wrapper into a Tesco carrier bag, looking Clio up and down, brown eyes bored. 'I hear Zoe Ball's just bought a place round the corner. Let's get her instead.'

Clio felt too exposed. She needed a hat. Or a scarf. Or a bodyguard.

Her throat was dry. 'Get me out of here.'

Amber took her hand. For a woman who didn't do physical proximity, she was really stepping up. 'I thought you always wanted to be famous?'

'Not this kind of famous!' Clio felt the glances like knives on her skin.

Amber shrugged. 'It's a small town and nothing exciting has happened for years. If ever.' She sighed. 'And Denise is on the warpath. She's "reporting" the story online for the *Sunshine Sands Extra*. She's staying the right side of the libel laws, but only just.'

Clio bristled. 'I'll bloody sue her.'

Amber squeezed her fingers. 'Take a breath. Murder charge first, libel second. OK?'

'Fine.' Clio turned and walked back to the main path towards the entrance. 'I just need to find Nina.'

'She's probably at Bez's place.' Jeanie took her other hand. 'Let's talk to him about the trophy.'

'I'll do it.' Clio spoke quickly. 'It should be me.'

She could feel her heart rate start to rise as she approached Bez's van. He had lived in it since time began, staying there when his parents passed and taking over the management of the site his dad had founded thirty years ago. The caravan was painted pink, green and blue and had decking running along three sides, home to dilapidated chairs, decaying guitars and one half-empty paddling pool. Fraying strings of fairy lights fluttered in the breeze, suspended above the front door. Clio spotted a familiar figure through the window.

'Stop.' She held up a hand and her two friends came to a halt. 'Nina's tidying.' She stared through the open red curtains, seeing her daughter spraying and wiping her room with unusual energy. 'The last time she did that she had just crashed Bez's car. Bad sign.'

Clio's breath was catching in her chest, as she watched her girl bend and polish. Nina's normal style involved leaving trails of clothes, make-up and mugs wherever she went. Snakes of used teabags wound across kitchen surfaces and wherever Nina landed she left apple cores, sandwich crusts or rings from the cups of tea she made but rarely finished. Once she had buried a packet of Wotsits under a sofa cushion with distinctly unpleasant results for Gary's favourite suit. Another time Clio had surprised a mouse under her daughter's bed, gorging on a packet of popcorn that could well have been opened a year before.

Something was up. Clio could feel it as strongly as she had felt

Nina's presence in her womb before she saw two lines on the pregnancy test. Clio turned to her friends. 'I need to talk to her alone.'

Jeanie let go of the buggy handlebars, flicking her long blonde curls out of her eyes. 'Are you sure?'

'Yes.' Clio nodded, resisting the urge to cling to the two of them, to have them at her side. 'I'll call you. When we're done.' She knew already that she would not. They would try to talk her out of the plan she had come up with in the car, and knowing her powers of resistance, they would probably succeed.

'OK. If you're sure. We'll get on with finding out who did this. OK?' Amber kissed Clio on the cheek.

'OK.' Clio squared her shoulders, enjoying the final moments before her suspicion became truth. Then she walked up the steps and entered the caravan.

It smelt of polish and perfume: a new fragrance, almost bitter, that DJ had given Nina for Christmas and she now wore every day.

'Nina?'

Her daughter didn't hear her. She had left her room now and was engrossed in wrestling with the contents of the crockery cupboard. Clio knew this caravan so well – it had been her home for years and Bez hadn't moved a thing since Clio had left him when Nina was five. He still kept the tea towels in the drawer Clio had chosen, and she knew that his bed would be covered by the sunrise duvet that they had bought from BHS the day before Clio gave birth.

Nina pulled out a mug, only for it to shatter on the floor.

'Shit.'

Clio was about to step forward, but DJ was there before her. He rose up from the sofa in the living room, his bare feet slapping against the floor.

'It's alright, love. I've got this.'

Clio saw the way Nina leant into him, a sunflower finding the light. She turned away, trying to give them a moment, spotting his iPad on the sofa. Normally he was surgically attached to it, always online, planning the round the world sailing trip that he was determined to embark on next year, once he had saved up enough money.

Clio glanced at the screen, surprised to see a site called The A to Z of Northern Slang. She peered closer. So that was what 'scran' meant.

'Clio.' DJ crossed the room and closed the tab. It was replaced by a boating app with charts, weather and tides – one his mum had told him about, one he had shown Clio so many times that she felt like she might be able to captain a yacht herself.

'Hi DJ. Are you writing websites now?'

'Yes.' He laughed. 'Helping out some mates, as it happens. It's good to see you.' He kissed her on the cheek.

'You too.' She watched as he went back to Nina, looping his arms around her, resting his chin on her head.

'Mum.' Nina's voice quivered.

'Nina.' She stepped forward. Once, she had known how to hug her daughter, but not today. Today she was all angles and hesitation. Her girl's beautiful face was streaked with tears and Clio's heart contracted. 'Are you OK?'

'No.'

'I thought not.' Clio held her arms open. 'Whatever it is, I can help. I love you.'

'Oh, Mum.' Nina broke away from DJ and ran into her arms. Clio greedily inhaled her girl. There was no way she could ever get close enough.

'I love you.' Clio realised hadn't said these words for far too long. They were too big for the snatches of time they spent together. Her daughter was always so busy, so independent. She had started walking herself to school at nine, cooking her own tea at ten, taken on the washing at eleven, chosen medical schools at twelve. UCL was top of her list.

Now, as Nina's tears soaked her cardigan, Clio's heart seemed to be growing inside her, threatening to burst out of her body.

'I was so worried, Mum.'

'I know.' Clio forced herself to pull away. They didn't have much time. If the police even got a whiff of what was in the hut, Clio's plan would fail.

'Is there something you want to tell me, Nina?'

'What?' Nina folded her arms defensively, her green hoodie riding up at the back. 'No.'

'Go on. Sit down and talk. I'll make you a brew.' DJ flashed a smile at Clio. He picked up the kettle, turning on the tap to fill it. 'I think you should tell her, Nina.'

'What?' Nina stared at him, mouth open. 'But I thought we agreed to—'

'We need help, love.' He flipped the lid of the kettle back down, pushing his floppy hair out of his eyes. 'You know we do.'

'I can't.' Nina sank down against the kitchen cabinet.

This was Clio's opening, but suddenly she didn't want to take it. She didn't want to see the guilt on Nina's face, or to imagine the future that was heading their way.

But she had no choice.

'Nina. I know what happened.'

'No, you don't.' Nina shook her head. 'You can't. I...'

DJ crouched down next to Nina, his hand on her shoulder. 'Just tell her.'

Nina swallowed. 'Mum. I...'

'It's OK, Nina. It was you, wasn't it? You hurt Gary?'

With every fibre of her being she wanted Nina to laugh, to accuse her of going crazy, to tell Clio she was wrong. But Clio knew she had been at the hut yesterday checking the roof. And Clio knew that the trophy Jeanie had found belonged to Nina.

'Go on, love.' DJ kissed Nina's cheek.

Nina collapsed forwards. 'I didn't mean to, Mum.'

Clio nodded. She had known it, deep down inside, a spiky unavoidable truth, like the knowledge that she was losing her memory or that Gary wasn't even pretending to live up to his wedding vows.

'It was awful.' Nina's head was in her hands.

'Can you tell me what happened?'

'No.' Nina's shoulders shook with sobs.

Clio gave her a squeeze. She needed to know everything. Every detail. Every event. She stood up. 'OK, then we'll have to find some biscuits and see if that helps.' Clio walked into the kitchen, not wanting her girl to see her face. This time, she would protect Nina. She would finally get something right.

She leant against the bright red counter top, thinking of little Nina toddling around with a spade, staring into rock pools, always trying to understand the world around her. She saw Bez piggy-backing her up the cliff path and tucking her into her bed, where she would curl around the plastic stethoscope that was her favourite toy.

'I want to help.' Clio emptied an entire pack of chocolate Hobnobs onto a plate and sat down at Nina's side. And gradually, hesitantly, her daughter started to talk.

24

GARY

6.30 p.m.: Death minus nine hours

At two minutes to six, all Gary had managed to find in his trawl of the house were a pair of silver candlesticks and an early Agent Provocateur gift for Denise that was worth a couple of hundred, if he remembered rightly. Marg and the truncheon she was rumoured to carry sewn into the sleeve of her smart navy coat would definitely not be happy with that. But it was OK, because Gary had just worked out where the real ring must be.

He left the house without explaining where he was going to Denise – no time – focused simply on getting the damn thing into his hand. He practically ran down the high street, past teenagers downing cider and beer, who were laughing as they revved up for a night out, the lucky bastards. He turned left at The Codfather and ran down an alley, past bins smelling of rotting fish, heading towards the beach.

He sprinted onto the pebbles, his boots crunching, aiming for the row of bright huts halfway up the cliff. There was Clio's, complete with its annoying rainbow motif and the bloody fairy lights she hadn't grown out of yet. Gary ran towards it, breath rasping. Then he thought he heard footsteps behind him, someone pursuing him, and he dropped to his knees behind a ragged tree, fear pounding. He peered out, only to see a middle-aged couple ambling along the beach in matching cagoules, hands tucked in each other's pockets, braced against the wind.

Gary exhaled and continued towards the hut, where he lifted up the pottery owl to find the key that Clio insisted on leaving outside, despite these huts now being worth a few quid. Since millionaires had started to colonise the southern side of the town, they couldn't get enough of these mouldy cubes with no heating and a sea view. Clio could perfectly well sell it – that would solve Nina's money problem and get her to uni to study whatever pointless subject she had in mind. Instead, Clio banged on about sentimental value and kept hold of it, while having the front to berate *Gary* for ruining Nina's life. He sighed. If only everyone was as pragmatic as him, the world would be a much better place.

He lifted the final pot. The key wasn't there.

'Fuck.' Gary put his hands to his head. Was nothing going to go right today? He leant against the door, eyes scanning the darkness for Marg and her sidekick, whose biceps were bigger than Gary's head.

The door gave way. Thank God. Gary staggered inside, his eyes slowly adjusting to the gloom. The hut was bigger than he remembered and he was just getting his bearings when a figure loomed out of the darkness.

'Shit!' Gary grabbed the nearest thing he could find – the giant flamingo inflatable that Clio had insisted on bringing home from their honeymoon and predictably never picked up again. He brandished it as menacingly as he could.

'Don't move. I've got a gun.'

'Gary?' Someone stepped forward. Dark hair. Heart-shaped face. Attitude.

'Nina?' Gary dropped the flamingo, impatience rushing through him. 'I'm in a hurry, OK?' He kept searching, looking for the bloody ring. It was now past six, and Marg would be coming for him. She had seemed so harmless when she had agreed to lend him the money – back when he was sure he could repay it, when it was just a temporary fix. But now he remembered the fierce glint of her grey eyes, the thin line of her bright red lips as she outlined her terms. Her casual references to what horrors would happen if he let her down.

He had heard stories, of course. Everyone knew Marg. Gary had heard tell of what she did to people foolish enough not to pay up. Broken legs were a win. One man had an arm full of cigarette burns. Marg was vaping now, though. Could you burn someone with one of those things? Marg probably could.

Gary might be about to find out. His hands were shaking. Bloody Clio. Trust her to put the ring in a mouldering shack rather than in a drawer like a normal person. He dropped to his knees, hands scrabbling, eyes searching. There had been a loose floor-board in here, hadn't there?

'Don't you know you're trespassing?' Nina had a half-empty vodka bottle in her hand. She swayed slightly in her heavy black boots. She was pissed. He had always known that she would go off the rails – how could she help it with a mum like Clio? Now she picked up the torch that had been kept here since time began and shone it in Gary's face. He raised a hand to shield his eyes, seeing the heavy rings on her fingers as she swigged from the bottle. She was so full of aggression she had practically grown spikes. She had her mum's eyes – all rage and blame. Thank God Gary had got away from them.

She spoke again. 'What are you doing, Gary?'

'I'm looking for something, obviously.' Somebody laughed outside the hut and he felt a clutch of terror. He had to get a grip. It couldn't be Marg. She didn't know how to laugh.

'Looking for what?' Nina's chin jutted forwards. 'Those terrible Speedos you used to wear?'

'No.' God, couldn't he ever have any peace?

'That Mexican sombrero you used to think was cool?'

'No.' Gary kept looking, hunting. He considered taking up prayer but that ship had well and truly sailed.

'Or perhaps that horrible bikini you got Mum – the one you told her she looked fat in?' Nina folded her arms.

'She did look fat.'

'Christ, Gary, have you no shame?'

'Christ, Nina, do you ever shut the hell up?'

Another tip of the bottle, another swallow.

'No.' She put her head on one side. 'Not when someone like you is trying to steal from my mum.'

'I'm not stealing.'

'Only because you can't find what you're looking for.' She smiled, clearly proud of her devastating repartee.

He didn't bother answering.

'Oh my God.' Her voice went up a note. 'You're here for the ring, aren't you? For Mum's ring? It's not even here.' She started to laugh.

'You don't know that.' He turned and pushed his way past a deflated beach ball into the far corner. It had to be here. The alternative was too terrible to contemplate. He opened a carrier bag only for an old plastic croquet set to fall out. He was running out of time.

She spoke again. 'You really are a total shit, aren't you?'

He deflected. 'And you're a drunk.'

'I'm here to fix the roof, Gary. And I just happened to find Mum's secret stash of vodka.' She hiccupped. 'And if I am a drunk,

I've got good reason. Someone stole all my money.' Nina came round in front of him planting her hands on her hips, stooping to avoid hitting her head on the low beam of the hut. She had got even taller since he had last seen her. Her shoulders were broader too. There was something raw about her today – something desperate.

Gary was running out of options now. Marg would find him here, he knew that. She had people. Someone would have tracked him.

'Nina, get out of my way. If I don't find it, I'll...'

She pointed a finger. 'You don't get to order me around.' She hiccupped. 'Not after what you've done.'

'What do you mean?' He had learnt to always feign ignorance – it gave him the chance to feign innocence later on.

'Cut the bullshit. You know what you did.'

'Nina, just go.' He pulled out his phone to check the time. Three missed calls, all the same anonymous number. He started listening to the first voicemail, in case it was Marg relenting, giving him more time. 'Gary. What the fuck are you up to? Johnny's coming after me and...'

Gary cut the call. No time. The clock was ticking and he was seriously in the shit. Where was the bloody ring? He looked around, seeing cobwebs and clutter and buckets and an ancient tea towel telling him that 'Life's a Beach.'

No it bloody wasn't. He stood up, only to see Nina right in his face, so close he could smell the vodka on her breath. 'You stole my money, Gary.' She raised the bottle again. 'You know how much I want to be a doctor – how hard I've studied. And you just didn't give a shit, did you?'

The way she was watching him, head on one side, dark curls framing her face, reminded him of Clio. Nina was trying to keep him down too. But he would rise up. He would show them all. One day books would be written about him. One day he would be a hashtag.

That would show them.

'I didn't do it, Nina. Your mum is...'

'Don't lie to me.' Her breath was coming in gasps. 'How could you do it, Gary?' Her voice was rising. Mascara streaked her cheeks. He had to force himself not to push her aside. Her hormones were clearly on the rise again. He looked around, wildly. Where the hell was the ring?

'Give it back, Gary.' Nina's eyes flashed. 'Now.'

Gary had never noticed how shrill her voice could be.

Time to take control. 'Nina. Enough. I had no choice, OK? Clio left things in a mess at Looking Goode. She never was very good with numbers.'

'Don't you dare blame Mum.'

'Why not? It's her fault.'

'It's your fault for being a selfish prick.'

Gary found the floorboard. He dropped down, tugging it upwards.

'Give my money back, Gary!'

She was clearly unstable. He slid his hand into the compartment beneath the floorboards, expecting to find a small box. Nothing. He groped around some more. 'Why are you here, anyway? Meeting a boy?'

'No.' There was a slight hesitation and he knew he had hit a nerve. Jackpot. 'I told you. Mum sent me to check the roof.'

'Vodka helps, does it?'

'No, but it helps everything else – like having all my money stolen.'

He checked under the floorboard again, shining his phone torch into the hole.

Nothing.

The ring wasn't bloody here.

He was screwed.

He stayed low, his brain trying to find one more idea, one more solution. Maybe the flamingo was worth a few quid?

He sat back down on the floor, head in hands. God knew what Marg would do when she got hold of him. He could feel his rage building, all the tension of this endless shitty day getting the better of him. Bloody Nina. Bloody life. Bloody hell.

'Do you know what, Nina? You don't have a clue about the pressure I'm under. I'm just trying to keep Looking Goode afloat. Borrowing money, tapping up old mates, finding new clients, even borrowing off a loan shark. I've done them all. I'm working my arse off here. It's tough.'

'Really?' She shook her head. 'So tough you had to steal from a teenager?'

Fuck this. She was too stupid to understand. As he stood up, his back went into spasm.

'FUCK.'

'Poor Gary.' Nina's voice mocked him.

He turned on her. 'Shut up, Nina. Just bloody shut up.'

'No, you shut up.' She was shaking now, her breath a rasp. Her hatred was so thick you could serve it up with gravy for Sunday lunch. 'Mum told me you'd be like this. That you never take responsibility for anything.'

Something in him snapped. All he did was take responsibility for things, not that anyone gave him credit for it – not Nina, not bloody Johnny, not Clio, not anyone. Bollocks to the lot of them, that's what he wanted to say. I'm Gary Goode and if you would only let me I can change the world.

'I am Mr Responsible!' His voice was a roar. Seeing her shrinking from him made him feel powerful. He moved towards her. 'It's on me. Everything. The contracts. The employees. The house. You, for years, even though you weren't even mine.'

She squared up to him. 'If you mean buying fish and chips on a Friday night and chucking the odd fiver my way then yeah, you did a great job, *stepdad*.'

'You were bloody lucky you got that.' He was damned if he was going to waste his energy making her feel better. 'And I did a better job than your real dad.'

The fury on her face made his heart sing.

'My dad is amazing.' Her voice shook.

'Bez?' He laughed. 'Amazing? Is that why he can't pay for uni then?'

'That's not fair. He's got the caravan site, and...'

'A site he's running into the ground.'

She was baring her teeth now. 'You don't know him. Don't you dare—'

'Oh for God's sake, Bez hasn't got a smart bone in his body.' Gary sneered. 'Always stupid, always will be. That's why he's got no money, whatever he may have told you.'

'That's not true. Stop saying that about my dad. You don't get to talk about him like that.' She bent down. She had something in her hands now – something silver.

But Gary didn't care. He was a man with nothing more to lose. Unleashed. Free. 'Your dad is lazy and your mum is useless. That's why you've got no money.'

'It's not. They're...'

'Useless. Both of them. Total wastes of space.'

Her flinch gave him a savage pleasure. 'Don't say that.'

'I'll say whatever the hell I like. And you take after them, don't you? A sad teenager alone in a beach hut with a bottle of shit vodka. It's just as well you can't go to uni, Nina – they wouldn't want you anyway. You'll never be a doctor – you're not good enough. You're nothing, Nina. Nothing. Just like your parents!'

He turned away and moved towards the door. Maybe he could run. Steal a boat? Get to France, somehow? Swim?

He had to try, but he had barely reached the door when something stopped him. Something crunched against his head – landing so hard it propelled him forward, slamming him down onto the sandy path outside. So hard he couldn't even see. He didn't hear the gasp of horror from Nina. He just felt a searing pain as he fell.

'Fuck.' Gary's eyes closed and the world went black.

25

CLIO

'So you see, Mum. It was me. I killed Gary.'

Hearing these words was even worse than Clio had imagined – the slam of a truck into her soul. Her mind ran an unhelpful showreel of *Moments with Nina*: at five, rolling around the floor with her hamster, James Bond, a consolation gift when Clio had left Bez; at eight, tongue protruding as she iced Amber's birthday cake into oblivion. And then all the Ninas that came next – cuddling, thinking, nestling, raging, studying, snacking, questioning, twirling a strand of hair around her fingers.

'It's OK, Nina.' Clio held her tight. 'It's OK.'

'I'm sorry, Mum.' The beanbag rustled as Nina snuggled even closer. 'I was so off my face and angry and he was so vile about you and Dad. I don't really remember throwing the trophy at him, but it must have been me, because one minute I'd picked it up and the next he fell, right there in front of me. I was the only one there. DJ was caught up at work, and…' She started sobbing again. 'Oh God, what am I going to do?'

DJ dropped down beside her. 'It's alright, love. I just wish I'd come sooner. I got stuck pressure washing the pontoons just as I

was leaving, and then there were the fenders and lines to check....'
He shook his head. 'Sorry. None of that matters.' He stroked her
hair. 'I just wish I'd been there.'

'Me too.' Nina's lips trembled as she turned her head towards
his for a kiss. Clio did her best to disappear. Tricky, at this proxim-
ity. Then Nina pulled away, burying her face in Clio's shoulder. 'It's
all over, isn't it? My life? They don't do A levels in prison. I'll never
be a doctor now.'

'Nothing's over.' Clio stroked Nina's hair, trying to tuck the feel
of it away in her memory to sustain her through the separation
ahead. 'It's not over. I promise.'

'How do you know?' Nina stared at her.

'I just do.' Clio shrugged, unable to share her plan. She kissed
the top of Nina's head. 'I know you'll be a doctor – the best doctor
there's ever been.'

'Really?' Nina hugged her close.

'Really.' Clio would show Nina – show her how much she was
loved. 'You're my best surprise – my sunrise. I'll make sure your
dreams come true. And this wasn't your fault, OK?'

'But I killed him.' Nina was trembling now. 'What am I going to
do, Mum?'

There it was: the question Clio had been dreading.

DJ's phone rang and he dug it out of his pocket, checking the
screen. 'I'd better get this – it's my boss.' He walked to the window,
listening to the caller, shifting from foot to foot, barely saying a
word. When he hung up his face was as dark as the clouds outside.
'I'm really sorry but I've got to get to work – someone's called in
sick.' A brief smile. 'Don't let her go anywhere, Clio. There has to be
another way.' He knelt down next to Nina. 'I'll be as quick as I can.
How's that sound?'

'Mint.' Nina gave a small smile. 'It sounds mint.'

'That's right.' DJ smiled, bending to kiss her. 'We'll make a Manchester girl out of you yet.'

Nina gave a noise that was a cross between a sob and a giggle as he walked out. She nestled into Clio, her head on her shoulder. 'He works so hard. He's so...' Her voice rose. 'Oh God, I'm never going to see him again, am I?'

Clio shook her head. 'Nothing's going to happen to you, Nina. Not on my watch.'

Nina sniffed into Clio's shoulder. 'Well, you must have a magic wand, then.'

'Maybe I do.' Clio kissed Nina's temple, her mind racing.

'Do you think you could tell me a story, Mum? Like you used to? I'd like to hear one, before...' Nina took a shuddering breath. 'Before they take me away.'

'That's not going to happen.' Clio shook her head. 'I promise. Besides...' She wanted to stop Nina shaking, to paint her world technicolour again. 'Besides you probably didn't kill Gary. I mean, he ended up here, didn't he?'

Nina wiped her beautiful big brown eyes on her long blue skirt. Her hands fluttered to the necklace that Clio had made for her tenth birthday, twisting the red and blue beads round and round on the plaited black string. She sat up straighter, leaning her head back against the wall behind them.

'DJ and I talked about how Gary got up here. We think he must have passed out for a bit and then staggered up here and just – collapsed.'

Clio frowned. 'But why would he come here?'

'We thought he must have been coming to find me.' Nina swallowed. 'To get his own back for what I did.' She was shaking even more violently now. 'But he never got the chance.'

She stared up at Clio, needing certainty, needing a way out.

'But...' Clio stopped herself. She couldn't let Nina know what she had decided to do. 'But you didn't mean to do it. It was self-defence.'

'I still killed him!'

Clio's heart contracted. Distraction. That was what Nina needed. 'So, a story?'

'Yes please.' A corner of Nina's mouth curved upwards. 'About Superhero Nina.'

Clio laughed. 'A classic. Here goes. Once upon a time...'

She knew this could well be the last story she ever told Nina. As her daughter's breathing slowed she talked on, spinning tales of Superhero Nina saving the world until she was sure her girl was deeply asleep. Then she breathed her in, her seventeen-year-old superstar, before going to stand by the window staring down at the sea below.

It was time.

'Clio.' Bez put a hand on her shoulder.

'Oh, hi.' She hadn't heard him come in.

She started, puzzled, as he pulled her close as if to kiss her, brushing her cheek with his hand. He smelt of spice and WD40 as he always did. He gazed at her intently, and she could see the tiny scar on his chin, a gift from a close encounter with an Alsatian the day before Nina was born. Behind his thick black glasses, his eyes were full of something both new and familiar.

'Clio, I feel so...' He took a step forward.

She stepped backwards, indicating the sleeping Nina.

'Clio.' He reached out, running a thumb gently down her cheek-bone. What on earth had got into him? 'It's so good to see you. Are you OK?'

'Yes. I'm fine.' The lie was automatic. She wasn't fine, nowhere near. She was full of the kind of fear that would paralyse her if she let it take hold. She needed to act now, fast, before she could talk herself out of it. She pressed a hand to her forehead, feeling her temples tightening, a warning of the migraine to come.

'Thank God they let you out.' Bez hesitated, before pulling her close in a move that brought back memories of teenage discos with sticky floors and even stickier kisses; the smell of rum and coke; his hand in hers. He held her face in his strong hands and gazed into her eyes, almost as if he was going to press his lips to hers.

Something flared in her memory, disappearing before she could catch it.

'Do I have something on my face?'

'No.' He smiled and leant in again.

What the hell was happening? They hadn't been nose to nose like this in well over a decade.

Clio needed an out. 'I could murder some food.'

'Food?' His face sagged.

Her last meal. 'Yeah. I'm starving.'

'Oh. Right.' He turned away from her, his hand to his forehead.

She talked into his silence. 'I can't get into my van, you see.' She gestured towards the crime scene behind her, to the tape, the onlookers, the police in dark uniforms searching the site on hands and knees. 'So I wondered if—'

'Sure.' He waved towards a carrier bag he had left by the door and she saw their beloved Codfather logo. 'Chips?'

'Oh you bloody superstar.' She pulled the bag open and reached eagerly for the Styrofoam tray, fumbling in her eagerness to get the food into her mouth. 'Oh my God. Heaven.' She took more and leant against the windowsill, relishing every salty, soft, vinegary bite.

When she had finished she let out a breath that had been a long time coming.

'Thank you.'

He stood next to her. Too close. Too expectant, again.

He nudged her. 'You always loved chips.'

'Yes.' She glanced up at him. Another fragment came back to her, of laughter over the waves, of hands clasped.

She had no time to pursue it. She needed to find out if he knew what their daughter had done. 'Bez…'

'Clio…'

They both laughed. 'You go first, Bez.'

'OK.' He ate his final chip. 'I had fun last night.'

'Why?' She looked up at him. 'What did you do?'

'You know what I did.' He stopped, pushing his glasses up his nose as he always did when caught off guard. 'I…'

'Yes?'

'You don't remember?'

'Remember what?' She licked salt from her fingers.

'Seriously?' He was staring at her, a peculiar expression on his face, a balloon losing air. 'You don't remember anything?'

She felt defensiveness start to prickle. She didn't need him going on about her forgetfulness too. 'About what?'

'Oh.' His eyelids fluttered. 'Oh wow. Nothing?'

'Nope.' She shrugged. 'Sorry if I did something annoying. I was hammered. I left the caravan to get some air but then I've got a total blank.'

'But…'

'Bez, stop.' Clio held up a hand. She needed to tell him. Now. 'Nina just told me something.'

'Nina?'

'She's…'

'Yes?'

Clio thought of the trophy, lying there just waiting to be discovered. The clock was ticking. She forced the words out. 'She was with Gary. When he was hurt. In the hut?'

'The beach hut?' He was twisting a napkin in his fingers now.

'What? But he was here, wasn't he?' He hesitated. 'Gary was found here?'

'Yes. But Nina – she threw her trophy at him. The one she left at the hut because it was so hideous but she was secretly proud of winning it. The maths one?'

'What?' He blinked. 'Back up. You're telling me she killed him? Are you crazy?'

'I wish I was. She told me everything.'

'But Nina wouldn't do something like that.' He shook his head. 'No way.'

'Not normally, no. But Jeanie found the trophy there and so I asked Nina what had happened. And she just told me everything. She threw the trophy. She hit Gary, and now he's dead.'

'No.' Bez was pacing now.

'Yes.' Clio needed him to speed up. 'And Bez? The trophy's still there, with his blood on it, and you need to get rid of it. Clean it up. Hide it. Throw it in the sea if you have to. OK? So no one ever finds out what our girl did.'

'But...' His voice was rising, his panic clear to see.

'Bez.' Clio kept her voice even. 'This is one of those times where you just need to do something. Like when I was about to give birth in that burger place and you got me to the hospital? Remember?'

'Covering up a murder is a bit different, isn't it, Clio?'

'No.' Clio shook her head. 'Well, yes. But we're looking after Nina. That's what we have to do. And it can't wait, Bez. You have to go now. Bleach the hut. Lose the trophy. Chuck it way out at sea. That way, Nina will be safe. OK?'

He was still stuck in shock. 'But that's – the police – how did this happen?'

'Gary was at the hut, looking for my gran's ring – he wanted to sell it, the bastard. Nina was there and she was drunk. Very drunk and very angry. And of course Gary got in her face. It's what he did best, isn't it?'

Bez's face darkened. 'That bloody man. I'll...'

'It's a bit late for that, isn't it?' Clio stood right in front of him, giving him no choice but to listen. 'Bez, it's happened now. And we can't let her life be ruined. She deserves more. She deserves *everything*. So, you'll do that, right, Bez? You'll get rid of the evidence? For Nina?'

Silence. Classic Bez. Where other people screamed, Bez very slowly made a cup of tea. When anyone else would be dialling 999, Bez would be vaguely searching the cupboards for a thermometer.

Eventually his words came. 'And what will you be doing?'

'Me?' Clio felt her resolve hardening. 'Don't you worry about me. I'll be busy doing what I need to do.'

She was starting to shake. His arms closed around her, and she inhaled his warmth and his strength. She breathed in and out. One more moment. One more.

Then she looked up at him, at the man who loved Nina just as much as she did. She took in his big brown eyes, his short black hair, the tattoo of a treble clef curving around the base of his neck, his skin dark against his white polo shirt.

She nudged him. 'You know the funniest thing? Jeanie convinced herself you were the killer.'

And there it was. Bez's deep rumbling laugh, the one that started in his belly and then took the whole world with it.

'Me?'

'Yes.'

A glint. 'If I'd done it, I wouldn't have left any clues.'

'Good point.' It was time for her to go. She forced herself to stand up but his hand shot out, and held hers.

'Where are you going, Clio?'

'I've just got an errand to run.' She squeezed his fingers. 'You'll look after her, won't you? Our girl?'

He leant close and placed his lips on hers. She surprised herself by kissing him back, leaning in, losing herself. Then she turned and walked away, knowing what was coming next, knowing she had no choice.

She had to protect Nina.

She had to hand herself in.

26

4.30 P.M.: 5 FEBRUARY 2023

@Clio to @Nina I love you, Nina girl. Don't worry about me. Sell the ring and off you go to uni, just like you planned. Love you, Mum xxx

* * *

5.30 p.m.: 5 February 2023

@SaveClio

Amber:– She's confessed. Clio. She's bloody confessed. WHY?!

Amber:– Why aren't you answering your phone? Jeanie?

Jeanie:– 🦆 🦩 🦢

Amber:– WTF?

Jeanie:– ⚽⚽⚽💩💩💩💩💩 fffffjjjjjjjTTTTTTT

Amber:– Have you invented a secret code and not bloody told me? IS THERE
ANYONE OUT THERE??

Amber:– Why the hell didn't she talk to us first? And she's refused a lawyer too. AAARRRGGGGHHHH.

Amber:– Jeanie?

Amber:– JEANIE

Jeanie:– 😊😊😊😊😊😊😊😊😊😊😊😊😊😊😊😊😊😊😊😊😊😊
😊😊

Amber:– Oh God it's the twins, isn't it? Jeanie THEY'VE HIJACKED YOUR PHONE.

Amber:– FFS

Jeanie:– 😊 🐎 xxxxxxxxxjjjjjjjjllllllll

Amber:– Sweet Jesus. We're trying to solve a murder here.

Jeanie:– Sorry, sorry. They swiped the phone. What are we going to do?

Amber:– Talk to Nina. Find out what actually happened. Find real killer. Easy.

Jeanie:– If you say so.

Amber:– We'll be done by teatime.

Jeanie:– Or bedtime tonight. Call me later?

Amber:– Will do. 🔥💪

27

AMBER

Amber was absolutely fuming, but now was not the time to show it. This was just typical of Clio: always thinking she had to make the dramatic move, even when her choices made absolutely no bloody sense whatsoever. Rather than coming to Amber – an actual detective with actual experience – before going in and confessing to a crime she hadn't done, she had instead chosen to go it alone. No sharing, no discussion, just Clio following her heart, despite the fact that it had got her absolutely nowhere good for the past forty-five years.

'I can't believe she's done that.' Nina had wept all over Amber's favourite leather jacket, until Amber had been forced to get up and dry some dishes in a belated attempt to save it. 'For me.'

But Amber could believe it all too well. This move was one hundred per cent Clio, like leaving the caring father of her child for a succession of men who treated her like dirt.

She finished the dishes and started on Bez's sink. She hunted for bleach in the jostle of bottles in the cupboard underneath, but found only vinegar. It would have to do. She poured it liberally around the stained enamel surface and started to scrub.

'This is all my fault.' Nina couldn't stop talking. 'I was so drunk and I just lost it.' She closed her eyes, hands shaking as she raised a slice of toast to her mouth. 'He was trying to get me to feel sorry for him, giving it all that about how Mum had left the company in a mess, saying he'd even had to borrow money from a loan shark.'

Amber stopped, sponge in hand, the vinegar stinging a paper cut on her thumb. 'A loan shark?'

'Yes.'

Interesting. 'Did he mention a name?'

'No.'

Amber went back to cleaning. She bet he had borrowed from Marg. It was always Marg. She drove a camper van, she was the over seventies surfing champion of southern England, she collected guinea pigs named after Simpsons characters (Amber had been bitten by Lisa III during one particularly lengthy investigation). She was the hub of the Sunshine Sands criminal scene, yet her charitable donations were so prolific she had recently won an award for Charity Fundraiser of the Year. The chief of police had been so incandescent he had actually used the gym membership his wife had bought him several years before and had injured himself over-doing it on the treadmill. Amber gave a final polish to the plughole. Marg had been at the crime scene, now she came to think of it. This gave her rather a good idea. A lead. Her first solid lead.

'How are we going to help Mum?' Nina was already through the box of Kleenex that Amber had brought with her.

'I don't know, sweet pea.' Bez held tight to Nina's hand, and Amber wished again that he and Clio had stayed together. Clio had been so happy with him. So sure of herself. But, of course, she had needed more drama, and had been seduced by a theatre director with an extreme taste in shirts and an unmatched ability to sing falsetto. 'But it's her choice. She wanted you to be protected.'

'But I don't want her to take the blame.' Nina's voice was choked with sobs. 'I should go to the police station. Now.' She stood up and grabbed her denim jacket. Mascara ran down her cheeks. She looked about thirteen. 'I'll turn myself in.'

'No.' Bez and Amber spoke in unison.

Amber shook her head. 'That's the last thing you should do now, Nina. Just lie low, OK?' She dried her hands on one of Bez's many Bob Marley tea towels. 'Bez, you got rid of the evidence, didn't you?' She found to her surprise that she enjoyed saying these words. It felt good to be outside the rules, to behave badly, to rebel.

'Yes.' He nodded. 'Nobody's going to find that trophy again.'

'Good.' Amber inhaled. 'So now you just need to wait, Nina. Wait for me and Jeanie to solve this and get Clio out. I just have one more question, OK? Then I'll leave you to – um… to the rest of your evening.'

'OK.' Nina looked like she might never relax again. 'What do you want to know?'

Amber folded her arms. 'Did you move the body?'

Nina looked blank. 'No.'

'So you left him there? At the hut?'

'Yes.' Nina twisted a multi-coloured bracelet around her wrist. 'Well, just outside it. That was where he fell.'

'OK.' Amber inhaled. 'So how did he get up here?' The question was more to herself than to anyone else.'

'I assumed he must have got up again. And walked to find me.' Nina reached for the tissues again.

'That he walked to your Mum's and landed nine hours later?' Amber was feeling a rush of something like joy. Nina hadn't killed him. No way. 'It seems a bit unlikely.'

'But… I definitely hit him. And he's dead now. So it must have been me.'

Amber wasn't at all sure about that. Her gut told her that there was a second assailant. She wished Freya would get in touch –

Amber needed to see the post mortem. The results might be in by now. They would rush it through for a case like this.

'So you...' Amber searched for the right words. 'You left him at the hut. Around – what? 6.30 p.m.?'

'I guess so. A bit after, maybe.' Nina held her palms wide. 'I don't know, really. I just panicked, shoved the trophy in the corner and ran.'

'OK.' Amber ran a hand through her hair.

'So can I go to the police now?' Nina sighed, shakily. 'I have to tell them. Please let me tell them.'

'No.'

'But I can't let her take the blame for me. It's not right.' Nina threw her arms wide. 'I can't live with myself if I don't say anything.'

Amber had to stop her. 'It's not forever. It's just until we solve the case. Because I don't think it was you. We now have a window – a window in which a second person might have killed him.' Her brain was up and running now. It had never left her – the need to interrogate, to sift, to solve. 'An opportunist, maybe? Someone with a grudge...'

'Who?' Nina's nose-blow made the caravan shudder.

'That's what we need to find out, isn't it?' Amber kept her voice gentle. 'And of course Clio has gone steaming off to the police station to take the blame. But—'

'But what?'

'Just give us a bit of time. OK? To get the full story, Nina.'

Nina wiped her eyes. 'I don't know...'

'Just hold fire. Please? And remember, Clio won't be charged unless they get substantial evidence against her. Which isn't going to happen.'

Bez shifted in his seat. 'Um. Amber. Can I have a word?'

Amber nodded and walked with him to the door.

The two of them stood outside at the top of the step, keeping their voices low. 'Yes?'

'I know where Clio was.' He pushed his glasses up his nose. 'Last night.'

'You do? Why didn't you say so?'

'Well. It's complicated. Because...' He kicked the tattered door mat for no apparent reason. 'I was – I'm her alibi.' He stared steadily at the floor.

'You were with her?'

Bez fiddled with the pocket of his jeans. 'Yes.'

'No way.' Amber put her hand to her mouth. '*With her*, with her?'

'Yes.' Bez looked embarrassed. 'With her with her. I was coming back from the pub. She came out of her van and... we headed down to the beach.'

'What time?'

'Around 1 a.m. – that's when we bumped into each other. And we were in the dunes – kissing and stuff – you know. Nothing more than that – she was off her face.' He shifted from foot to foot.

'Oh, Bez.' Amber felt a pang of sympathy. 'I take it she doesn't remember?'

'No.' He looked so crestfallen, a child with a dropped ice cream. 'And I didn't know how to tell her. And then she went to the police, and it was too late.'

Amber thought fast. 'Well, given what she's decided to do, don't tell anyone for now. Just pretend you've forgotten what happened too.'

'Lie, you mean?' His brow was furrowed.

'Absolutely.' Amber patted him awkwardly on the shoulder. 'Because it's what Clio wants, isn't it? And if you give her an alibi, then...' She glanced through the door to Nina, crying in Jeanie's arms. 'You know what happens to Nina. And we need to find the real killer first.'

'OK.' He sighed. She knew she should hug him, reassure him. But other people provided shoulders to cry on – Amber did things to help.

And in this case, she would find the killer, and set Clio free.

28

JEANIE

'The pot plants are beautiful, aren't they?' Jeanie cringed inwardly. Her small talk really needed some work. After nearly a year of conversing with babbles and squawks she had nothing for adult surroundings as luxurious as the Thrive spa. She scoured her mind for a fresh topic but found only nursery rhymes and the weather. She had known this spa trip was a bad idea – finding things out meant asking questions, conversing, and right now she had all the conversational skills of a potty.

'Yu-uh.' Vivienne examined one of her elegant Shellacs, before draining her cleansing juice until only ice was left. 'I must go and get another drink. Excuse me.' She swayed her way across to the cluster of nursery mums with actual things to talk about, leaving only a waft of perfume in her wake.

Jeanie sagged back onto her lounger. Here she was, alone again, a blight on the turquoise perfection of the infinity pool. Framed in green tiles and trailing vines it boasted two whirlpools at either end and a wide white swing dangling above the water. She edged her lounger further away from the edge. The pool looked serene, peaceful even, but there was no way Jeanie was going to get in and test it.

She looked away, through the huge windows that opened onto the sundeck, up to the postcard-blue sky. If ever there was a place to relax, this was it, but instead Jeanie was taut with tension. Without the twins to busy herself with she felt horribly exposed for the non-event she had become. Maybe Yumi and Jack hadn't made her invisible all these months – maybe she had been using them as a shield.

She looked at the other mums, envying their sculpted waistlines, their glossy hair, their laughter. Her phone beeped and she checked it, almost praying for an emergency to give her an excuse to get out of here.

It was Amber.

Have you tapped Vivienne up yet or are you too busy drinking papaya juice and cuddling hot stones?

Jeanie tapped out a reply.

Just got here. Fluffy robe in place. About to launch.

Her phone buzzed again.

Good luck, Miss Spa-ple. G post mortem due any minute. Will update you. x

Post mortem. Jeanie shivered. She had preferred it when they messaged about who was bringing the wine or about whose childhood crush was most embarrassing (Jeanie's was Jon Bon Jovi while Clio had plumped for Henry from *Neighbours*). She checked her messages but there was nothing from Tan. He was probably still smarting from the argument that had kicked off just before she left, beautifully timed to coincide with her emptying cupboard after cupboard, trying to find the swimming costume she kept for her annual birthday trip to her mum's health club.

Tan had frowned. 'But how does going to a spa help Clio?'

If Jeanie had been clearer on this herself, the conversation might have gone better. But she was tired and worried and dreading what lay ahead. 'Because I'm meant to be finding out who might have wanted Gary dead.'

'At a spa?' He took his glasses off and cleaned them with his T-shirt.

'Yes, at a spa. I told you that.' Jeanie had stuffed her swimming costume into her bag. She would have to figure out how to fit into it when she got there. 'I know you're working, but you just need to drop the twins at nursery and I'll be back by lunchtime. Their bags are packed so it's easy, isn't it?'

She had grumped her way out of the front door, aware that she was going to have to show her breastfeeding body to some of the chicest ladies in town. After getting changed she had looked at herself in the long oval mirrors, nervously tugging at her ancient floral swimming costume, sticking in breast pads to make sure she didn't leak. Folds of fat had appeared on her back, and green veins stood out in her milk-white thighs. Thank God for the towelling robe. She had closed it around herself, tying it securely with the kind of knot that wouldn't be out of place on a Mount Everest rock face.

As a man started doing a splashy front crawl down the pool Jeanie finished her own drink and assessed the mums sitting around the hot tub. All she had to do was talk to them – to ask a few questions. She stood up, still hesitating, as a pair of older women high on massage and essential oils wandered past her. 'Do you really think I should? But he's only fifty-five,' one of them squealed, before they both dissolved into giggles.

Their laughter summoned a memory of Clio, her hands arcing through the air as she told a story about drama school, her multi-coloured hair glinting in the pub lights.

She missed her friend. And there was only one way to get her back.

Jeanie approached the group. 'Can I join you?'

Before they could answer she had taken off her robe, hung it on a wicker peg on the tiled wall, and sat down on the edge of the whirlpool, water frothing around her. Instantly the bubbles stopped, leaving only clear water and several sets of legs that were a lot more shaven than hers.

'Jeanie.' Vivienne's eyebrow lifted. 'I think you might be sitting on the "on" switch?'

Oh God. Jeanie lifted one wobbly buttock and saw the silver button, so obvious now that she was looking properly.

'Sorry.' She tried a laugh, which dwindled when absolutely no one else joined in.

'Don't worry about it.' Cherie, Vivienne's sister-in-law, was kind enough to smile. Jeanie recognised her from a magazine cover she had seen in the dentist's reception a few months ago, when Cherie had been talking about her new range of running gear, modelling her designs herself. She was even better-looking in person – her long blonde hair twisted on top of her head, a dimple dancing in her cheek.

'Hello. I'm Cherie. Not a nursery mum, just here for the spa.'

'Hi.' Jeanie tried to suck her stomach in as she pressed the button, but suspected she only succeeded in looking like she had wind. She slid nervously into the warm water, which started to swirl around her. She sat on the top step, clinging to the silver rail as it grew stronger, bubbling and foaming around her, drops flicking her face.

Vivienne spoke above the roar. 'We're just chatting about the nursery sports day.'

'Oh yes?' Jeanie closed her eyes as the water roiled and spat. Despite herself, her panic was increasing and she was back in that pool, the water closing over her head, her body dropping to the bottom.

She needed to get this over with and get out. There was no time for subtlety. 'Did you hear about the clifftop killing? The local builder?' She watched Vivienne and Cherie carefully. 'It's terrible, isn't it?'

There was a moment of silence.

'Well, he had it coming, if you ask me.' Vivienne rolled her eyes, a perfect flick of eyeliner in the corner of each lid.

Jeanie leant forward, only to be splashed in the face. She straightened. 'How do you mean?'

'He had his fingers in all kinds of pies.'

'Did he?' Jeanie noticed that Cherie was silent, staring downwards.

Vivienne nodded, stretching perfectly tanned legs. 'He had money troubles, let's put it that way. He was desperate for cash. His staff weren't paid last week. And he was such a chancer!' She wrinkled her button nose.

Jeanie nodded her on. 'What do you mean?'

'Well...' Vivienne paused for dramatic effect. 'Johnny and I had a meeting with him the day he died.' She was met with a flattering range of gasps. 'And he was really trying it on.' She flicked a strand of her fringe out of her eyes. 'Trying to charge us through the nose, to get us to pay him a deposit before we'd even signed anything.' She shook her head. 'We said no, of course. But it was clear he was broke. Debts everywhere, Johnny thinks. It's no wonder somebody killed him.'

Cherie stood up suddenly, splashing water, moving fast.

'Where are you going, babe?' Vivienne pouted. 'We...'

'I've got a massage soon. I'll see you all later.' Cherie's honey hair trailed down her back as she walked up the steps, holding onto the handrail with knuckles that were as white as her bikini. She took a towel from the fragrant stack near the loungers and flung it around her shoulders as she strode away.

Jeanie turned back to see Vivienne, all eyes and secrets. 'Well, we all know why she's so upset, don't we?'

'Do we?' Jeanie blinked. 'Why's that?'

'Her and Gary had a bit of a thing going on. Since Gary did that job for them.'

Jeanie's jaw dropped. Gary's success with women would never fail to amaze her. 'What?'

'Yes.' Vivienne clapped her hands together. 'They were having an affair. Cherie told me, of course. She knows she can trust me.'

'Of course she can, babe.' This from Trudy, the only mum with the kind of eye bags Jeanie could relate to. 'Did Marshall know?'

Vivienne shrugged. 'Maybe. Maybe not? You can't really tell with those two.'

Trudy frowned. 'But maybe he did know. Maybe he didn't like it.' Her voice rose. 'Maybe *he* killed Gary. Do you think he might have done?'

Vivienne threw her head back and laughed. 'Marshall? No way.' She shook her head. 'Besides, everyone says Gary's wife did it. Jealous, apparently.'

Her tone was so disparaging it made Jeanie want to hold her head under the water. Instead, she gritted her teeth and nodded along.

'It's shocking, of course, knowing there was a killer on the loose, but hopefully it's all in the past now.' Vivienne inhaled sanctimoniously. 'I'm having the body cocoon today. Got to look after ourselves, haven't we? Happy mum, happy baby, after all.' She smiled. 'Anyone up for a cocktail?'

Jeanie had heard enough. Job done. She felt a tiny prick of pride. She had found something out – she had been useful. She had not screwed up or run away. She got out and put her robe on again, her phone buzzing as she was tying the belt. She put her hand into her pocket while trying to slide her feet into her towelling slippers, which had the word Thrive emblazoned across the toes in silver. Her foot slipped, tipping her off balance and the next thing she knew she had fallen forwards, landing face first in one of the pot plants she had been admiring earlier.

She tasted earth and leaf. Slowly, cheeks burning, she lifted her head. Six pairs of eyes were trained on her. She felt a familiar rush of heat and shame as she wondered how on earth to make an exit. Black-clad staff rushed over, clearly far more concerned about the plant than about her.

'I'm so sorry.' Jeanie tried to set it upright again, only to realise she was inevitably making things worse. Instead, she waved pathetically at the other mums and ran, brushing mud off her face and onto her no longer pristine robe.

Gary and Cherie. That was a surprise. And risky, given Cherie was married to Gary's biggest client. Even Jeanie had heard of Marshall Fernandez, Johnny's brother, who had gone out on his own and founded his own sportswear label, Printz, from scratch. Every garment had a tiny fingerprint on it in gold – each one unique, apparently. And with Cherie as its lead designer, it had gone from strength to strength. Marshall was a man with money and connections. A man to respect. A man who could make anything happen.

Jeanie sat on the bench in the changing room, took out her phone and began to type.

Gary sleeping with Cherie Fernandez. Marshall might have found out?
Done something about it?

Amber was typing.

Nice work, Miss Spa-ple. Anything else?

Jeanie sent Amber another update.

Johnny turned down Gary's design the day G died. Gary was broke,
apparently.

Amber fired back a quick reply.

OK. Get in that pool. You can do it.

As a rule, Jeanie always followed Amber's advice, but not this
time. She couldn't get in the pool. Not today. Not ever.
Not after what had happened last time.

29

AMBER

Amber drove as fast as Bez's bulky pick-up would allow, windows down despite the freezing weather, bumping around corners and enjoying the roar of the engine. In the cars she passed she saw people huddled in scarves and coats, their windows starting to steam up, but Amber wanted the air on her face – to feel the power of the antique truck as it ate up the road.

Amber had always moved at speed. The files she had finally been allowed to read at eighteen had told her that she had walked at eight months and ever since then she had – according to the various foster families who had hosted her and then ejected her – been absolutely impossible to keep track of. She was always escaping down drainpipes or clambering up pylons, more to entertain herself than with any kind of criminal intent. The police, however, didn't see it that way, and it was only Jeanie's dad William, a family lawyer with a heart of gold, who managed to prevent her from getting a criminal record by the age of eighteen. It was thanks to him that she had joined the police rather than being pursued by them, and ever since she had been on the force Amber had done her best to follow the rules, to fit in with what was expected of her.

But now? Now she could break every damn rule in the book if she wanted to. Now, she could be bad.

She drummed her fingers on the wheel as she came to a halt at the traffic lights. There were advantages to operating outside the law. No more red tape. No one to sign things off, no one to tell her that she wasn't allowed to follow her gut. After Jeanie's discovery, Amber knew she needed to find out more about Marshall and Cherie. A few calls to local catering companies revealed that they were having a party this week to celebrate Cherie's birthday. One more conversation had seen Amber taking the place of a poorly member of the gardening team which was spending today preparing the grounds for the festivities.

As she turned into the gravelled waiting area in front of the sleek black gates she checked her phone for the fiftieth time, but the screen remained stubbornly blank. Freya had not been in touch with any information, and any hope that she would was starting to drain away. Amber gripped the wheel as frustration pulsed through her. The post mortem results must be in by now, and Amber needed to see them.

The intercom crackled a greeting and Amber leant over and stated her business. Another second and the truck was making its way up the drive, passing neat rows of daffodils and pale winter roses and perfectly arching willow trees. Amber went over everything she knew about Marshall Fernandez, Johnny's younger brother. Rumour had it he was a grafter, building his sportswear business Printz up from a seaside market stall to a globally recognised brand sported by A-listers and influencers.

Amber's internet research in the sleepless small hours had showed that Marshall was ruthless and charismatic while his wife Cherie, Printz's lead designer, was innovative and original with teeth so perfect they had a dedicated Instagram fan page all of their own. She and Marshall had first got married in their school playground aged seven (Love Hearts were exchanged), and now here they were, King and Queen of Hampshire. Gary may well have been a fly in their very successful ointment. Could it be that his affair with Cherie had led to his murder?

A skeletal man in a black shirt waved the truck over. 'You part of the gardening team?'

'Yes.'

He jerked his thumb towards the side of the house.

'Park round the back.'

'Sure.' She bumped across the gravel, driving down a narrow lane edged by the magnificent house on one side and deep green hedges on the other. Marshall and Cherie had knocked down the old mill that once stood here and installed an eco-palace, built from golden stone topped with wood that had all been bought within a ten-mile radius. Huge windows gleamed to her left, reaching up to a red roof with a curved edge, designed to hide the solar panels that powered the whole place, according to the *Grand Designs* episode in which it had featured. It was Gary's favourite TV show of all time after that.

Around the house, the garden spread out to every side, hugging its hexagonal shape like a lover. Amber turned the corner and passed a rainbow fleet of sports cars – she would love to get behind the wheel of that Triumph Spitfire – and parked up by the green-houses at the top of the lawn. As long as no one spoke to her, she would be fine. She had a convincing bag of gardening gear, borrowed from Jeanie's loft, where it had languished since her eldest and most righteous sister had given it to her for Christmas three years ago. Amber was no gardener, but knew that Marshall and Cherie would look straight through a slightly sweaty middle-aged woman with a pair of secateurs.

Amber walked purposefully around to the rose bushes by the side of the house. She had found plans of the property online, submitted when the old mill was first demolished. She ignored the team of gardeners fanning out below her, on what looked like a croquet lawn, and snuck into the winter rose bushes that grew beneath Marshall's office. She would loiter, pretending to care for the pink and white blooms that filled the air with their perfume, until she got an opportunity to climb up and have a look around. Anything she found could be significant – the key to the mystery of who had really killed Gary Goode.

Even the thought of him and of the damage he had done to Clio made the anger boil up inside her. Seeking an outlet, she took out some chunky secateurs from her gardening bag and viciously snipped the roses around her.

'What are you doing?'

Shit. Expensive perfume and the swish of silk. Cherie had appeared, standing on the path by the rose bushes, her hand raised to keep her long blonde hair off her face. She was so tall Amber had to crane her neck to see properly, her eyes level with the words 'Sweat it Out' written in leopard print across Cherie's silver hoodie. Cherie's phone was tucked into a pocket in her pink leggings, which tapered to a matching leopard print trim.

'I'm gardening.' Amber felt sweat start to prickle. An interrogation about roses was really not going to be her forte.

'I can see that. But we're not doing this bed, I told Rory that.' Cherie pouted. 'Does he never listen?'

Amber put the secateurs away. 'Sorry. He did tell me. I forgot.'

'Well, that's not good enough, is it?' Cherie grimaced. 'Now. I dropped a glass back there. Pick it up, will you?'

'I...' Amber swallowed her reply. She was undercover. Blending in was the aim, not starting an argument. 'Of course.'

Cherie hesitated – her unnaturally smooth forehead doing its best to frown.

'You're new, aren't you?'

'Yes.' Amber tensed. Please, no gardening questions. Please.

Cherie shook her head as if in despair. 'Try to dress a bit better next time, won't you?'

'Yes.' Amber spoke through gritted teeth. She was wearing her best jeans, for goodness' sake.

'Good.' Cherie wafted off towards the swimming pool that Amber knew was discreetly hidden in a copse to the west of the grounds. 'Don't forget that glass.' These words were thrown over her shoulder as she walked away.

Amber muttered a few swear words at her departing back. Cherie definitely wasn't exuding grief for her lover, that was for sure. Amber wondered what she had seen in Gary. A bit of rough? A boy from the other side of the tracks? He had been handsome, Amber supposed, and relentless when he wanted something or someone. Poor Clio.

Amber turned back to the roses, only to hear a familiar voice coming from a window above her. She leapt sideways, landing in a particularly thorny rose bush.

'Shit!' She tried to extract herself from its clutches, scratching her arms and only managing to entangle herself more completely.

'Listen, Marshall. I'm not going to mess about.'

Denise. Why was she here? Amber was pretty sure a thorn was trying to burst her ear drum, but stayed still, straining to hear.

'I can see that.' A deep voice with a faint trace of mockney. Amber had watched enough of Marshall's Insta reels to know it was him. Footsteps moved across a wooden floor above her. Amber's heart rate spiralled and she turned her head, only for the thorns to get an even stronger hold on her hair.

'I'll be straight with you Marshall, I'm not happy.' Amber heard heels pacing up and down. She could see Denise in her mind's eye – dressed in something tight no doubt, stalking the room, thinking she was owed something.

'And what has that got to do with me?' Amber could imagine him too, head down, broad shoulders hunched. He was big, bulky, made for a rugby scrum.

Denise was talking again. 'I've been doing some digging. I'm a journalist, you know. On *The Extra*.'

'So?'

'So, I've been going through Gary's things. His papers. Every-thing.' Amber trained her ears even more carefully. 'And you owed him money, didn't you? I found it in his tax return. On his laptop? So I know that you owe him a hundred grand.'

Amber froze. If this were true, it could change everything.

'You think I owe him money?' Marshall's laugh was a slap. 'As if.'

'You do.' Denise's voice had gone up a tone. 'Like I said, I found it. On his laptop. There's a spreadsheet, see, and there's a gap where your payment should be. From the work he did for you. Look, I'll show you.'

'Your Gary is a liar, I'm afraid.' Marshall spoke slowly, over-enunciating, as if to an idiot. 'That row on the spreadsheet – the one with my name on it – that's total crap. Gary was cooking the books, Denise. And he did it a lot, see, because I know for a fact that I paid him for his latest designs last November. He's switched income and outgoings around – probably trying to dodge tax. You see? I paid him that much, to do the work he did for me. But he has made it a minus – see?'

'No. You're lying.' Denise was nearly shouting now. Amber almost felt sorry for her. Almost. 'He wouldn't do that.'

'He *has* done that.' Marshall's heavier footsteps moved away again. 'He was hiding stuff from the tax man.'

'No.'

Marshall again. 'Look, Denise. Your Gary – he liked the high life. He was always wanting me to take him to Monaco or to my box at the Champions League final, you know? He wanted flash but he didn't have the cash. So he cheated. I've been running my business for years now – I know every trick in the book. And he was playing the system. OK? You should show these accounts to the police, yeah?'

'You're wrong.' Denise's heels followed his voice. 'I'll prove it. I will. You can't take my money from me. Gary's money. It's not—'

Marshall's voice cut in, impatient now. 'Denise. I don't have time for this.'

'I don't care if you've got time. I want my money.'

'His money.'

'Whatever.'

Marshall sighed. 'You know, I didn't want to have to tell you this.'

'Tell me what?'

'Your Gary. He wasn't just yours.'

'You shut up.'

'No, Denise, it's true. Did you know that Gary was having an affair with my wife, Cherie?'

Amber stiffened. So Marshall did know about the affair. Hello, motive.

'He wouldn't do that.'

'No?' Footsteps again. 'I can show you a video if you like. Here. From a couple of days ago, as it happens.'

'Liar!' Denise's voice spiralled. 'My Gary wouldn't do that to me. He…'

'Look.' Marshall's heavy footsteps moved towards Denise. 'Here. The two of them together. Someone was kind enough to send this over this morning. Now, I'm not bothered – Cherie and I have always had an open marriage. That's what happens when you meet your wife in the school playground. But I'm guessing, from your reaction, that you and Gary weren't like that?'

'No.' A sob. 'He wouldn't have...'

'See? He did. And, if he betrayed you like that, then he probably betrayed you in other ways too. Like actually being broke while telling you he was loaded?'

'No.' Quieter this time. Amber could imagine Denise, head down, blonde hair falling around her face.

Marshall's voice was quieter now.

'Shall I get you a drink?'

No answer. Amber wondered what he was doing up there. Whether he was placing a hand on her shoulders, leaning down.

'Get off me, you creep!'

Well, that answered that one. Amber heard heels running and a door opened and slammed shut.

Marshall's heavy footsteps came back to the window, just as Amber was hoping to escape the rose bush's embrace. She stood immobile, powerless to do anything but wait, as she heard the click of a lighter as he lit a cigar.

Her mind was racing. However much Marshall claimed an open marriage, Amber wasn't sure she believed him. As she knew herself, jealousy was a fire that could easily flare out of control. Maybe the video had tipped him over the edge. Maybe he had needed to get rid of him. To kill him.

All Amber and Jeanie had to do was prove it.

30

CLIO

Clio was struggling to remember her lines.

Here she was, back at the same table, blinking in the neon glow of the custody suite. Marco was in position, leaning forwards, eyes raking her face. And here was his silent sidekick, complete with notebook and nods. The stage was set. Clio the murderer was in the spotlight.

All she had to do was stop fluffing her cues.

Marco leant forward into his favourite position. 'Clio, you keep changing your story. One minute you're out cold on the beach, the next you're throwing stones into the water. So which is it?'

Brain fog swirled. 'Stones?'

Marco exhaled impatiently. 'Look, it would be better if you didn't answer as if you're asking a question. You're confessing to a murder. Details matter.'

Clio rubbed her exhausted eyes. 'I'm sorry. It's just – I must have blanked a lot of it out.' *Come on, Clio. For Nina.* She thought of her daughter's face glazed in tears back at the caravan, of the tiny clay handprints in a frame on her living room wall, of the thumbprint on the silver necklace that had been around Clio's neck until it was taken away from her when she had arrived. Now it was in a plastic evidence bag, together with her rings, her earrings, her clothes, her shoes and a packet of Dulcolax she wished she had disposed of beforehand. She looked down at the scratchy grey tracksuit she had been given. This was her costume now. She was wearing a murderer's clothes.

She sat up straighter, lacing her fingers in her lap. She would pass this audition. For her girl.

'I just feel so terrible, Marco.' She summoned tears. It wasn't difficult. Her daughter had mortally injured someone. It was enough to make any mum cry. 'I can't believe I killed him.'

'I know.' That patronising steepling of his fingers again. How had Amber managed to work with him for so long? He was the kind of person who enjoyed reading instruction manuals. Out loud. 'But could you just go through your confession one more time?'

Confession. The very word filled Clio with dread. Confession meant barred windows and locked doors. It meant that she would be powerless, that her life would be over. But anything was better than Nina being in here. Her little girl, climber of trees, teller of knock-knock jokes. She couldn't be shut away for ever. Anything was better than that. If Nina was happy, Clio could handle clanging doors and sleeping next to an open loo. She could.

Couldn't she?

Marco rustled through the papers in front of him. 'So, we just need to go over your meeting with Gary that morning.'

'OK.' Clio summoned her lines. 'When I woke up on the beach I was freezing and still drunk. I just wanted to get back to bed, but then I walked back and Gary was there outside my caravan. And he was angry. Really angry.' She had to keep to the truth as much as she could – then it would be easier to maintain the lie. She kept her eyes open, barely blinking, keen to avoid the memory of Gary's body lying on her step. She had to tell the story she had come up with on the way here – the one that made her the killer.

'Angry with who?'

'Me, of course.'

'OK.' Marco looked at her, nodding. 'And what did you do?'

'Well, I was pretty pissed off, to be honest. He was... well. He was invading my home. And we don't get on very well. I mean, we didn't get on...' She was still processing the fact that Gary was gone. 'Since we separated, I mean.'

'I'm aware.'

'He was drunk and he was in my face, blaming me for everything.' She described a scene that had happened so many times for real that it felt true. 'He kept asking me for money – as if I have any now.' A tear rolled down her cheek. It was the little touches that mattered. She inhaled the stale air of the interview room, the picture of a wronged woman.

'And I got angry. I couldn't help it. I was drunk, it was early in the morning, it was my birthday, and he kept coming at me. Saying everything was my fault, saying that I'd ruined his life, when in fact he had ruined mine. Saying that I was a bitch and I'd turned everyone against him. You know? And it was too much.'

Anger smouldered inside her. She was replaying years of arguments, of fights, each one making her feel a little bit smaller, a little less worth loving.

She was shaking for real now, but still made sure she got the words right. Here was where she had to be consistent. Marco would never know she was quoting from the script of a fringe production of a play about domestic violence. She transported herself back to that stage, raising her face to the light. 'He was really drunk. Really scary. And he wouldn't leave.'

'Go on.' Even Silent Cop was mesmerised. Her pale eyes were trained on Clio's, her pen paused above the page.

'And I was drunk too and I didn't understand why he was there. I didn't understand why he thought I was in the wrong, when he was the one who had blown up my life. And then...' Clio took her time, giving the words fresh impact. 'He just went for me. Like – lunged – and grabbed my arm. And I thought – maybe this time. Maybe he's going to hurt me.' She let tears fill her eyes. Thank goodness for that handsome director at the Edinburgh Festival who had shown her how to summon tears every single time.

Marco noted something down. 'Had Gary done that before? Tried to hurt you physically?'

'No.' Clio shook her head. 'Never. I mean, verbally yes. But not physically. And it was terrifying.'

'I see.' Marco nodded and made a note in his pad.

'And then I felt scared, just so scared, and I just wanted him to go away. But he wouldn't and he started screaming all this stuff, saying all these things about Nina, and I – I'll do anything for my girl – and I don't know how really – I can't remember – but I just grabbed a rock and hit him. And...' Clio looked down. 'I somehow hit his head. And I only meant to get him to go away. I just wanted him to stop saying those things about Nina. Not...' She executed the perfect dramatic pause. She dabbed her eyes. 'Not all that blood.' She forced herself to think back and found she was actually crying. 'It was everywhere.'

Silent Cop was writing so fast she had practically made a hole in the paper. Marco sat back, head on one side. 'And what did you do then?'

Clio blinked. 'I panicked, of course. Isn't that what anyone would do?'

'I don't know. I've never hit anyone on the head with a rock.'

Amber had frequently complained that Marco was a sarcastic arse. Spot on, as usual.

'Well, he fell and lay there. And I panicked. I had no idea what to do, and I didn't want to get my friends involved.'

'And the weapon? The rock?'

'I went to the beach and threw it into the sea. The rain must have washed my footprints away, I guess.'

Marco frowned. 'I see. And you only hit him once?'

Clio nodded. 'Yes. Once. From behind. I was scared he would attack me. He was so angry. I did it in self-defence.' She swallowed. 'I didn't mean to kill him. But I was drunk. And angry. And he kept going for me and I was scared of what he might do.' She forced the words out, hoping that she might feel better once it was over. 'I wouldn't have wished dying on anyone, not even him. I didn't mean to kill him. I'm not like that. I just wanted him to go away.'

'So you say.' Marco smiled in a way that told her he didn't believe her. 'Well, interestingly what you tell me is tallying with the evidence so far. We found one of your fingerprints on the chain he wore around his neck.'

'What?' Memories swirled and clouded around her. Then, the light pierced through. Of course, she must have touched it when she had taken his pulse.

Marco sighed. 'Well, thank you, Clio. Are you still sure you don't want a lawyer?'

'Positive.' A lawyer might help her get off. A lawyer might land Nina in the frame.

He shrugged. 'OK. But I'd recommend you get one. Now we'll put you back in the cells until a space becomes available at HMP Whitworth.'

Whitworth? Oh God. That had been on the news only a few weeks before. Rioting. Grievous bodily harm. Burning mattresses raining from the rooftops. Clio dug her nails into her palms, panic rising.

Better her than Nina, though. This was the choice she had made.

Marco pushed his chair back. 'OK, well that seems to be everything. We'll prepare your statement for you to sign, Clio.'

His expression was stern as he carried on. 'Clio Lawrence, I am formally charging you with the murder of Gary Goode. You do not have to say anything, but it may harm your defence if you do not mention, when questioned, something which you later rely on in court. Anything you do say may be given in evidence.'

And that was it. She had done it. Clio's legs wobbled as she stood up. She didn't feel like a hero now. She felt old and scared and lost – as if she had walked into the wrong scene in the wrong play and any second now someone would start booing.

But she had protected her daughter. She was made of fear and sweat and terror, but she had protected Nina.

Once, aged seventeen, she had done an excerpt from *The Ballad of Reading Gaol* for a drama school audition. She hadn't got in. But she would have to hope that now she could play the role she needed to play for the rest of her life. Now, to give her daughter a future, it was time to produce her greatest performance yet: Clio Lawrence – killer.

31

@SUNSHINESANDSONLINE
Followers: 3200
NEWS BLAST: Clifftop Killer

A local woman confessed today to the murder of Gary Goode and has been formally charged. She can now be named as Clio Lawrence, the wife of the deceased. She claims that she acted in self-defence and will be arraigned on Monday at Southampton Magistrates' Court. At a press conference today Detective Chief Inspector Marco Santini stated that they were not looking for anyone else in connection with the killing. Ms Lawrence has been remanded in custody pending a bail hearing on Monday morning, a huge relief for the town, which can finally focus on the February fair that starts on the pier next week. Get your skates on, folks. We'll see you there!

Shares: 2200
Likes: 3000

32

GARY

7.30 p.m.: Death minus eight hours

'Is this your idea of paying your debts then, Gary?'

Gary opened his eyes. His head was killing him and he appeared to be face-to-face with a fishing net. His stomach turned and he sat up, looking for something to be sick into.

'Gary.'

He ignored the voice as memories started to return: Nina, looking exactly like her mum as she shouted at him; him turning away, and then something heavy landing on his head. He gingerly felt the back of his scalp, and his hand came away with blood on it. 'Shit.'

'Don't ignore me, Gary. I've maimed people for less.'

Gary groaned.

The speaker exhaled in frustration. 'Let's get a light on? I think he's forgotten who he's talking to.'

A torch illuminated a woman staring down at him. Short grey hair, navy coat with golden buttons.

She waved. 'Cooeeee.'

Oh God.

She smiled, a snake about to swallow him whole. 'That's right, Gary. Remember me?'

Gary realised that his evening could actually get worse as the woman straightened the string of pearls at her throat. Marg had found him.

Gary's brain was running in slow motion, struggling to fit things together. She clearly wanted something. What was it? He had done her extension last year – top-drawer designs as he recalled. Had her kitchen counter come loose? Had the archway collapsed?

And then he remembered. Ten grand. He owed her ten grand which he didn't have. And God knew he was in no fit state to run.

She was shaking her head now, lips tight. Behind her the lone street light flickered. 'Get him up.'

'Gary.' Chunky fingers waggled in his face. Marg's sidekick had a broad nose and a neck as wide as the English Channel. 'Time to get up.'

'I don't know if I can.'

'Oh Gary. Silly Gary.' Marg shook her head. 'You know you'd have been my type back in the day.' She reached a hand towards him.

She fancied him. Of course she did. He was going to have to sleep with her in lieu of payment. Gary swallowed. Could he do it? Could he get past the wrinkly neck and the varicose veins?

She slapped him, hard. 'But you're too old for me now. I like them young.' She pulled her sidekick towards her and kissed him.

Gary wondered if now might be a good time to escape. He tried to stand, but his legs wobbled and he fell back down on the path.

Marg's tone was regretful as she wiped lipstick off her lover's mouth with her thumb. 'There's no escaping, you know. I know you're stupid, but surely you're not that bloody stupid. I made my terms very clear. And I don't appreciate having to track you down like this.' She indicated her outfit. 'I was on my way to a show, and instead I am here. With you. And that, Gary, is a problem. And I don't like problems.' She tapped her pocket, and Gary was sure he heard the sound of metal.

To a passer-by, Marg was a classic nana, a sprightly seventy-something out for her evening constitutional. But Gary knew better. His jaw ached where she had hit him and he was sure there was more to come. Normally, Gary would be able to figure out a plan, but with his head bleeding and his mouth tasting of death even he was struggling. Bloody Nina. He would make her pay, just see if he didn't.

Marg pulled something out of her pocket. A knife. His insides dissolved.

She leant down and pressed it against his neck. He needed to get up, to fight back, to save himself but he couldn't move.

His tongue felt thick and swollen. 'Look, Marg. I'm sorry the money's late. I ran into a spot of bother.' The ring. That was what he had been doing – he had been finding the ring. 'But I've got something for you.'

'If it's not cash, I'm not interested.' Marg was enjoying herself. Of course she was. She was the kind of woman who removed people's fingernails for fun. 'You just need to give me the money and then you can get yourself to A&E to sort out that head injury of yours.'

'I...' Fuck, his head hurt. Gary wanted to cry. Reasoning with her was as futile as persuading a bullet to make its way back up a gun barrel, but what else could he do?

'Look. I had the money. I did. But then my wife – soon to be ex-wife – took it. Clio. She's got it.'

'She does, does she?' Marg removed the knife and folded her arms. 'Clio? She took the money, did she? Really?'

'Yes.' Gary felt absolutely no guilt as he said this. It was Clio's fault Nina had attacked him. Her terrible parenting had made this mess. If Nina hadn't hit him, he would have found the ring, and would have been under the covers with Denise by now. Yes. He felt his old confidence flooding back, despite the blood trickling down his neck. Here it was – his second coming. The bloody resurrection.

'And when was that?' Marg was crouching down now. She used the same perfume his granny had worn. Violets. It made him think of bingo and those pink wafer biscuits she had always kept in the tin on the mantelpiece.

Focus, Gary. 'When was what, Marg?'

'When did she take the money, eh?'

The pain in his head was like a knife. 'Earlier. When she came to my house.'

'Oh yes. And what time was that?'

'I don't know. I wasn't there.'

Gary was quite proud of this answer.

Marg folded her arms. 'Very funny. Strange though, because she has been nowhere near your house, has she? She had a go at you in the Copper Kettle, to be sure.' She spoke with a discomfiting mildness. 'Is that what you mean? Did she take the money from you there?'

'Yes.' Gary grabbed the lifeline. 'I got confused. It's the head injury.' He rubbed his scalp again, wondering if he was going to bleed to death during this conversation. Given Marg's expression that might be no bad thing.

'Oh Gary.' Marg shook her head but her grey bob barely moved. 'You still think you can lie to me, don't you? Silly boy.' Her hand disappeared into her pocket again. The knife reappeared. 'I don't like liars, Gary. And I don't like people who don't pay their debts.

So…' She put her head on one side, a tiny bird with a very dark heart. 'You need to bring that money to me tonight.'

'Tonight?' Gary had suddenly realised how cold it was. And how dark. What time was it? Where was his phone?

'Midnight. To the multi-storey.' Marg's voice was calm. 'Or you'll be dead by dawn.' That smell of violets again as the tip of the knife pressed against his skin. 'Got that?'

Gary took a breath. 'Yes.'

'Only joking.' Her face barely moved. 'I'll torture you first.'

'Right. Great.' Gary didn't know if he could stand, let alone find ten grand by morning. Maybe he could escape. Find a canoe, like that bloke a few years back. John Darwin, was it? Gary wouldn't screw up like him though. He would get to Panama and never come back to this dump. 'I'll get it to you, I promise.'

'You'd better.' Marg wagged a finger. 'So, be sensible Gary. Be sensible.' She tapped the knife against her hand, before sliding it away into her Chanel handbag and smiling benignly at an evening dog walker making his way along the shore. 'He's had a few too many.' She indicated Gary, sharing a laugh with the man.

If only he had. If only he bloody had. Gary staggered up, nearly falling back into the speckles of his own blood, clinging to the railing next to the path.

'See you soon, Gary.' Marg walked away.

Gary stood, hanging on to the railing, hanging on to life. He had no idea where to go. No idea what he was doing. But he would find a plan. He always did.

Didn't he?

33

Amber:– Got anything for me?

Freya:– What happened to waiting?

Amber:– I have waited! Got anything for me?

Freya:– 😶

Amber:– Please?

Freya:– Didn't know you knew that word.

Amber:– Hahaha.

Freya:–…

Amber:– ???

Amber:–???

Amber:– And you say I'm the one who holds a grudge.

34

AMBER

During Amber's time on the force, she had prided herself on her ability to pivot. Give her a dead end and she would find a hidden entrance around the corner. Give her a firm alibi and she would identify a new suspect before the end of the day. And so, after another night of sweating into her duvet, she had realised at 4 a.m. that Marg Redfearn was the woman she needed.

When Nina had mentioned that Gary had borrowed money from a loan shark, Amber had known that it would be Marg. She was queen of the Sunshine Sands criminal scene and all roads involving illegal money inevitably led back to her. She and Amber were old acquaintances – in fact Amber had been the officer who had first realised that the woman with grey hair and a neatly tied neck scarf was in fact a serious criminal player.

Marg had stepped into the shoes of her father, Tommy Redfearn, a drug dealer with a sideline in GBH and theft. Now, after multiple encounters, Amber could see that Marg was very much her father's daughter. For years she had fooled the police that her husband Tyler had been the kingpin, but when he died she had no one to hide behind any more. She moved her operations around various lock-ups and deserted pool halls around the town, never staying for long, presiding over operations wearing a benign expression and a variety of pearls inherited from her beloved mum. She wasn't exactly the ideal collaborator, but Amber needed information. If Freya wouldn't give it to her then Amber had no choice – Marg was the only answer.

She tried to justify it to herself as she approached the house. Who cared if Marg was rumoured to be importing firearms from the continent hidden in shipments of ice lollies, or that she had recently invested in a chain of kebab shops which were showing every sign of being a front for the family firm? She had even used sweet shops to sell cocaine once upon a time, linking in with her elder brothers' efforts in London and beyond.

Marg kept herself out of the frame, of course – to all intents and purposes a well-heeled pensioner still living in her mum's old home at seventy-two. As Amber approached the white-walled cottage set back above the beach, she could see that the pansies in the hanging baskets were freshly watered and that daffodils stood tall in glazed blue pots on either side of the red front door. Amber raised her hand to knock, only for the door to open before her knuckle had made contact.

'What do you want?' Marg peered out, gold half-moon glasses resting on the end of her nose. Her steely blue eyes were as unwavering as ever. 'You've been fired. Go away.'

'And hello Marg.' Amber smiled.

'Don't smile. It doesn't suit you.' Marg ran a beady eye over her flowers, reaching down to snap off a lone dead head. She was an RHS member – a regular at the Chelsea Flower Show. 'I'm about to go kayaking and you're in my way. What do you want?'

Amber followed her lead, not beating about the bush. 'I want you to tell me Gary Goode's movements over the last week of his life. He borrowed money from you, which means you've been having him followed, so I know you have all the information I need.'

'Interesting.' Marg tapped ringed fingers against the immaculate white door jamb.

'Is it?'

'Trying to prove the force wrong, are you?' Marg's gaze was an X-ray, cutting through lies to the reality that lay beneath.

'I'm trying to prove my friend innocent, yes.'

'But she's just confessed. I saw it on the news.'

Amber nodded. 'Yes. But she was confused. She doesn't really remember. Bloody menopause.'

Marg swore under her breath. 'Oh, I remember that. Hell. Pure hell.' It was the most confiding Amber had ever seen her. 'HRT, that's the answer. Sorted me out a treat.' She smiled. 'Helped my libido make a comeback too.'

Amber didn't want to think about Marg's libido. 'Um. That's good. But...'

'And acupuncture too. That helped.' Marg opened her door wider, revealing the collection of guns she kept in a glass cabinet on the wall behind her. All licensed, of course. No fool, Marg. She placed a hand affectionately on the glass. Behind her, her current protection guy with benefits, Sam, lurked in the kitchen doorway, his shoulders as wide as the hallway itself.

The threat was clear but Amber was going to have to ignore it for Clio's sake.

'Gary's movements? Can you help me?'

Marg sucked air through her teeth. 'What's in it for me?'

Amber raised an eyebrow. 'A halo?'

Marg flicked a hand dismissively. 'Who cares about those?'

Amber smiled. 'Fair point. The chance to do the right thing?'

'Not interested.' Marg narrowed her eyes. 'Unless you're offering to pay me what Gary owed me?'

Amber shrugged. 'I'm unemployed. So no.'

'There are other ways of paying.'

Amber shook her head. 'No.'

'Then no dice.' Marg shrugged.

'Shame.' Amber steeled herself. 'Because if you don't help, I might have to tell people about your car parking racket.'

'I don't know what you mean.' Marg showed not one flicker of recognition. No wonder she won so much at poker.

'The one you run out of the promenade multi-storey?'

Marg folded her arms. 'You're delusional. No wonder you were fired.'

'No, I'm not.' Amber shrugged. 'And you wouldn't want me blabbing, would you?'

Marg watched her, frowning. 'I've helped you before and it didn't end well for me. That business with Freya's fellow.'

Amber prickled at the mention of her old friend. 'I protected you, like I said I would. And it didn't end well for me either, did it? I'm the one who's out of a job.'

'I like you, Amber.' Marg looked like she was about to close the door. 'But I can't help you, unless you'd like a job?'

'No thank you.'

'Then, goodbye.' She swung the door, trying to shut it.

But Amber already had her foot in place. She flinched as the door slammed against it, but held firm. She could hear Sam's heavy footsteps heading down the hall. He pulled the door open, almost growling, but Amber spoke as if he wasn't there.

'Marg, please. Just listen for a minute. Gary Goode was an arsehole and he assumed he could just shit on you like he did on everyone else. He's left you out of pocket – like he did with pretty much anyone he ever had dealings with. So... Give me the information I know you have, so I can catch his killer. They can pay you.

Because really, they're the reason he hasn't given you the money, aren't they?'

Marg considered this. Sam waited, fist poised.

'I just need to help my friend, Marg. Please?'

Marg arched an eyebrow. 'Saving your friend again? Like last time?'

Amber nodded. 'Just like last time, Marg. Only a million times more important.'

Marg gave a slow nod. 'Just so we're clear. If I help, you will owe me one, Amber Nagra. There will be a debt to be paid. Yes?'

'OK.'

'Then I'll do it.' Marg nodded. 'I'll help you. A package will arrive later. And I'll give you some extra information now too, just to show willing. The post mortem. He was killed by two blows to the head, not one.'

'I knew it!' Amber didn't ask how Marg had found this out. She didn't want to know. But two blows meant that Nina was in the clear. Someone else had killed Gary Goode – someone Amber was going to hunt down.

'Thank you, Marg. Thank you.' She turned and walked back to her car.

She had just made a pact with the local devil but it was worth it. Any price was worth paying to save Clio.

35

CLIO

Clio found she was spending increasing amounts of time pretending that she was starring in a movie. It was preferable playing someone facing a lifetime behind bars than actually *being* the person who was never going to taste freedom again. She lay on the thin mattress and pulled the scratchy blanket up to her chin. The top of it was damp with tears.

She turned over onto her side, only for her left hip to remind her that this wasn't a good idea. Rolling to the right would involve putting her nose too close to the brown patch on the wall and so she settled onto her back again, hoping her pelvis would forgive her. In the cell next door a man was alternately screaming and banging something against the door – a hand or a head, she couldn't tell. He spoke in a flurry of swear words, some of which Clio was definitely going to try out on Nina when she got home.

Except she wouldn't be going home, would she? She would remain here in the holding cells until she was transferred to prison. And then she would remain there until all her teeth fell out and no one remembered her name.

Clio was about to succumb to tears again when the door slammed open.

'Clio, come with us please.'

Clio dragged herself to her feet. Much as she didn't like it here, she liked the interview room even less. Besides, she had confessed, hadn't she? What else was there to talk about? Reluctantly, she walked along the dingy corridor, past grey metallic doors presumably containing people who had actually committed crimes. She wondered if they felt better or worse than she did. What they had done. Whether they were going to prison too.

Prison. She sagged as she entered the interview room, conscious of the camera trained on her face, her feet dragging. She slid reluctantly into the plastic chair, which appeared to have been deliberately designed to give her a slipped disc.

'Smile for the camera' she muttered under her breath.

She looked up and there was Marco entering the room. She had no idea what time it was but she was becoming pretty convinced that he lived here. And that he must own at least ten of those boring white shirts.

She waited, hands clasped in front of her, an old hand now. *For Nina*, she told herself quietly.

Marco sat down, digging in his pocket for a notebook and pen. Silent Cop passed them to him and clicked her own pen expectantly.

Marco looked at Clio, his eyes tired. 'Clio. We meet again.'

'We do.' She looked up at the camera. 'I'm Clio Lawrence, I live at number 15 in the Sunshine Sands Caravan Park.' She stretched. 'Anything else?'

'No. That covers it.' His hair really did need a cut. 'Clio, before we start, are you sure you don't want a solicitor present?'

Not this again. 'Yes, I am totally sure that I do not want a solicitor.'

'Really?' He drummed his fingers on the table. 'We could call one of the duty team?'

For Nina. 'I'm sure.' Clio shook her head. 'No solicitor.'

'OK, then.' Marco clicked his biro into action. 'Well, some new evidence has come to light.'

'What is it?' Clio's mind leapt to the trophy. What if Bez hadn't got rid of it? What if it had been found by the police and everything she was doing was for nothing? There it was again – the showreel of torment: Nina in handcuffs; Nina in a cell; Nina's life over.

No. Clio lifted her chin. She exhaled, casting off the exhaustion that was weighing her down. She checked the time, surprised to see that it was apparently morning again. Outside, presumably, the world was still turning. People were getting up, washing tired faces, making coffee, scrolling through the news. At the caravan site, Bez would be frying bacon for Nina, who would emerge, fuzzy and taciturn, rubbing the sleep from her eyes.

How Clio wished she could be there with them. She hoped her girl would have more luck building a future than Clio had enjoyed – that she would become a doctor and make the world a better place. All Clio had really achieved was Nina. Her one gift to the world was the girl she was protecting now.

She shifted in her seat and waited for the next curveball to land.

Marco looked through his notes. 'You told us that you only hit Gary once. On the head. Is that right?' His eyebrows rose.

'Yes.' Clio's stomach was churning again.

'And then you threw the rock into the sea?'

'Yes.' She was so tense she thought her jaw might crack.

'And then...?'

'And then nothing. I pretended to find the body. The End.'

'And nothing else?'

'Nothing.' She held his eyes. Do not look away first, Clio. The first rule of lying. Gary had taught her that, laughing on one of their first dates. *The first sign of lying is losing eye contact*, he had said. *The second sign is looking up and to the left.* At the time it hadn't occurred to her to wonder why he knew.

Silly Clio. If she ever dated again she would choose a man with a savings account. That would make him reliable, wouldn't it?

As if anyone would have her after twenty years in prison.

Marco was talking again. 'Well, it's very strange. Because the post mortem found something else.'

'That's impossible.' Everything in her was tight. Fists, neck and – miracle of miracles – her pelvic floor too. She hadn't known she had it in her.

Concentrate, Clio.

'Yes.' Marco sat back, flexing his hairy hands. Silent Cop scribbled away. 'The post mortem found that Gary didn't die of a head wound.'

'What?' Clio hadn't been expecting that. 'Of course he did. Like I said, I...'

Marco continued. 'He died of *two* head wounds. Or rather he had two head wounds when he died. Which rather gives the lie to your story about self-defence, doesn't it?'

Clio's mouth was hanging open. 'What do you mean?'

'Well, you'd have to be really angry to hit him twice. The first blow must have knocked him to the floor. Why did you need a second? Unless you intended to kill him?'

Two head wounds? Clio wanted to get up – to pace, to think. Nina had only hit Gary once – she had been totally clear about that. One blow. He had fallen. Clio had confessed to protect her girl, but now... She shivered. Was she, in fact, protecting someone else? She could feel uncertainty rising. Here was yet another example of life raising its middle finger and watching her drown.

She wished Jeanie and Amber were here. She wanted Nutella and a spoon. She wanted their arms around her. But for now, Clio had no option but to stick to her story. 'Look, Marco, I hit him once. That's all I know. He came, he argued with me, he lunged and I hit him. OK? And he didn't look like he already had an injury.'

'Well, it was dark, you said.'

'Yes, but, I mean... I would have noticed, wouldn't I?' Clio made herself breathe.

'I don't know.' Marco put his head on one side. 'There is another explanation, isn't there? Maybe you hit him twice, Clio. Maybe it wasn't self-defence. Maybe it was in fact a deliberate, aggressive attack by you on your husband. You hated him, that much is clear. He had taken your home, your business and your money and now he was coming for even more – he was coming for you.'

Clio couldn't answer. If she spoke the truth they might find out about Nina.

Marco frowned. 'Now, if you did hit him twice, then you'll be up on a murder charge, Clio. Not self-defence. Murder.'

Clio swallowed. Her girl. She couldn't risk saying anything that might incriminate her. The words were out before she knew they were coming. 'Maybe I did. I don't know. Like I said I've got brain fog. So maybe. Maybe I did? Hit him twice? I don't know. I just don't know.'

'You don't know.' Marco rolled his eyes, leaning even closer. 'You were very clear before, Clio. Be careful now. What you say really matters. Did you, or did you not, hit Gary Goode twice in the head on the morning of the fifth of February 2023?'

'I...' Clio hesitated. She wanted to save Nina. But she didn't want to save somebody else.

'I don't know.' It was the best she could do.

'You don't know?' Marco shook his head. 'You are seriously telling me you don't know if you hit your husband twice on the head or once?'

'Yes.' Clio felt the flutter in her chest, the panic rising.

A muscle flickered in Marco's cheek. 'Then I'm afraid we're going to stay here until you tell me everything you really know. And I mean everything, OK?'

'But you know it all now.' She dug her fingernails into her palms. She would not cry.

'I'm not sure I do. So we'll start again. At the very beginning.'

Heat was prickling up her spine now. It was quite possible she would burst into flames.

'Do you want tea?' Christ, she must be looking bad. Silent Cop had actually spoken.

Clio shook her head. 'No thanks. A cocktail would be good though.'

Marco shook his head. 'Hahaha.'

'Not a joke.' Clio steadied herself. 'Water would be great, if that's OK?'

Clio started to tell her story again, wondering who had dealt the second blow. She could only hope that her friends were well on their way to finding the killer, because it was pretty obvious that Marco Santini was going to take Clio's word for it that she was the sole culprit.

But Clio didn't want to save anyone who wasn't Nina. And increasingly, now the charge of murder was in the room, she found that she really wanted to save herself.

36

3.30 A.M.: 8 FEBRUARY 2023.

@SaveClio

Jeanie:– Got something. Call me in the morning.

Amber:– So you're awake too? FUN, isn't it?!

Jeanie:– Yumi on one boob, Jack punching me in the face, Tan in spare room. Time of my life.

Amber:– And here's me all alone in my sweaty PJs.

Jeanie:– Heaven.

Amber:– What have you got?

Jeanie:– Not sure. Vivienne has an alibi – in London that night. Many many Insta pics.

Amber:– OK.

Jeanie:– Johnny though – meant to be in London but never made it.

Amber:– How do you know?

Jeanie:– No pics. And J always posts. Vivienne there, but not him.

Amber:– Loving your work. So where was he?

Jeanie:– Dunno. And something else. Probably being stupid, but…

Amber:– Spill. And dear God work on your self-esteem.

Jeanie:– I told you I worked on the Fernandez Tech account till I went on mat leave?

Amber:– Yes.

Jeanie:– Something is off – can't find his co-founder anywhere on social media. Called Rajiv. Lead designer and co-CEO. Used to be inseparable but now nothing. Why?

Amber:– 🫥

Jeanie:– Now Johnny's getting all the credit – sole inventor of the chip etc.

Amber:– Why would that make Johnny kill Gary?

Jeanie:– Not sure. But maybe Gary found something out? Started doing something stupid? Blackmail…? I don't know. Probably being silly.

Amber:– Not silly. Great work. Knew you were an Agatha.

Jeanie:– 😌

Amber:– What did you do on Fernandez Tech account?

Jeanie:– Made teas, took minutes, that kind of thing.

Amber:– So…Can you take your kids back to work for a morning? Have a look around? See if you can track down Rajiv – it's a good lead.

Jeanie:– Take my babies? To glossy London? My trouble-magnet babies?

Amber:– Perfect distraction while you get Rajiv's contact details, no?

Jeanie:– I'm not allowed to say no, am I?

Amber:– 😊

Jeanie:– Then… 👍😅
Amber:– Look for anything that might show what happened. Board minutes. Old headshots. A news story? Anything that your firm might have on file about getting rid of Rajiv – draft press releases etc. No way he went without a fight – that chip is worth billions.

Jeanie:– 🤞🐝⚽🗻

Amber:– Hello, Yumi and Jack.

Jeanie:– ddddddjjjjjjffffffdanceremojitttttttaaaaaaawineemoji

37

AMBER

At half past nine the next morning Amber was on her third coffee, engrossed in the notes that Marg had sent over last night. Marg did things properly, Amber had to give her that, and whoever she had terrified into following Gary was a pro. Everything was here: filling up the car, going to the gym, visiting clients – even his liaison with Cherie at the Gloriana Hotel was here in black and white.

But there was nothing conclusive – no clues to make Amber pursue any particular suspect over another. There was nothing unusual in that, but still Amber felt her traditional kick of disappointment. Her back was aching and she realised she was in danger of becoming welded to her chair, so she set her mug down and stood up, stretching. Her morning ritual was overdue: Annie Lennox blasting from the speakers, one hundred crunches, one hundred press ups and two kilometres on her exercise bike.

As she reached crunch number forty-nine her doorbell rang. Swearing, Amber padded across to the front door only for it to ring again before she could reach it.

'For God's sake, give me a chance.' She swung the door open. 'Oh God. It's you.'

'Charming.' DCI Marco Santini raised an eyebrow. 'Especially when I've brought your favourite breakfast with me.' He held out a McDonald's bag. 'Egg McMuffin?'

'Oh fuck off.' She slammed the door, resting her burning face against the wood. How dare he turn up here unannounced, surprising her in her sports gear, unshowered, unprepared.

She opened the door again, just to tell him what a bastard he was.

He held up his hands. 'I know. You hate me. But can I come in?'

'No.'

'Even if I share information from the case with you?' He put his head on one side.

'Why would you do that?'

His eyes darted around the house. 'I...'

'Yes?'

The penny dropped. He needed her.

Amber's mind ticked and whirred. On the one hand she didn't want to do him any favours. On the other Marco's information might be useful – not that he needed to know that yet.

She watched him, unsmiling. 'Did you get hash browns too?'

He nodded. 'You know I did. Three.'

Amber stood aside. 'Come in, then. But remember I have a panic alarm and I'm not afraid to use it.'

He came into the living room, his wide shoulders barely fitting through the door. He looked as if he had slept in a bin, his hair sticking up and a large white stain on the sleeve of his black woollen coat. Once, Amber would have cared enough about the state of him to feed him fruit or ask what was wrong, but now she just folded her arms and stared at him.

He sat down on her sofa with a sigh, instantly making the red fabric look as crumpled as he was. He had once joked that his style icon was Columbo, but today Amber thought that was doing the shambolic TV detective a disservice. Whatever Marco touched turned to wrinkles and Amber knew she would be getting the hoover out as soon as he left.

She remained standing. 'Are you missing me, then?'

'No.' He ran a hand through his shaggy dark curls. The lines on his face were so deep they could have been carved out with a skewer.

'So why are you here?'

'Because I know you'll be investigating too. And I wondered if we could help each other out.' He leant back and made as if to rest his filthy black shoes on Amber's dark Japanese-style coffee table.

'NO.'

Marco put them down again. 'I forgot about your clean freak tendencies. Sorry, I've been on surveillance all night.'

'Don't you have juniors to do that for you nowadays, boss man?'

He laughed, a warm rumble that had once made her think he was her friend. 'Funny. With the cuts they're making at the moment, it's all hands on deck. And I like to keep my eye in, anyway.'

'How the mighty have fallen.' She plumped a cushion, turning back to see that Marco was watching her, his brown eyes suddenly shrewd.

'What, Marco?'

He shrugged. 'Nothing. It's just that you don't seem very upset that your best friend is a killer.'

Amber chose her words carefully. 'Well, Gary had it coming, didn't he?'

He raised an eyebrow. 'Still, your best friend is going to prison. For years, if she's convicted. How come you're so calm?'

So that was why he was here. Not because he needed her, but because he wanted to interview her.

Well, good luck to him. She sat down in her favourite leather armchair, tucking her feet up underneath her, settling in.

'There's no point in me getting upset, is there Marco? No point getting "emotional."' Her fingers made quotes in the air. 'Wasn't it you who taught me that?'

Marco let this one hang. Too difficult, too direct. He was the kind of man who ghosted girlfriends, a boss who hid in the office until he could have a difficult conversation via email rather than in person.

He sipped his tea. 'The post mortem's interesting. Gary died of a blow to the head, administered between 3 and 3.30 a.m., but there was a second head wound too.'

Amber held her breath, thinking of Nina.

Marco put his cup down, ignoring the coaster that Amber had placed on the table. She leant forward and slid it into place. 'So, with two blows, it couldn't have been self-defence, could it? As Clio claims?'

'Why not? She could have hit him once and he kept coming, so she hit him again.'

He picked up a pink squeezy anti-stress ball that had resolutely failed to live up to its name. Then he put it down again. 'But in her early interviews and in her confession, Clio was adamant she only hit him once.' Marco's eyes raked her face. 'Now she says she isn't sure.'

Poor Clio. She must be going through hell. Amber opened the McMuffin bag. 'Marco, she was pissed, of course she can't remember.'

'So you think she could have hit him twice?'

Oh fuck off. As if she was going to answer that. Instead, Amber was going to get what *she* wanted out of this. She was going to fill in some of the many blanks that surrounded this case.

'Was the body moved at all?'

'No. A blood spatter indicates that the step was where he died.'

'Uh-huh.' Amber chewed for a moment. Hash browns really

were the unacknowledged stars of the breakfast table. 'Any witnesses?'

'None on the night. The weather really was terrible. Winds from the north, you know? There was no one out. The gale was so strong...'

Oh God. Once Marco got going on the weather Amber's entire day would disappear.

She took a wet wipe from the packet on the table and scrupulously cleaned her greasy fingers. 'Is there any CCTV of him? Or of the killer?'

'No.' Marco shifted in his seat. 'There are no cameras down that side of the beach, so we haven't got any eyes on the killer. Everyone in town had their hoods up against the rain, just to make things even less clear. And the killer knew the area – it might have been luck, but I'm guessing they knew what they were doing. Clio temped for the CCTV head office recently, did you know that?'

'Yes.' Actually, Amber had forgotten this. Clio had endured so many terrible temping jobs since being kicked out of Looking Goode. There had been a methadone clinic, a toilet roll factory, and a Botox clinic where the owner had sent Clio home within the hour for refusing to have treatment herself 'to fit in with our clientele.'

'How about his phone, Marco?'

'It's gone. Divers can't find it. The fish are probably feasting on it by now.' He brushed crumbs off his lap onto her sofa. Amber gritted her teeth. Then he stood up, banging into the coffee table, too ungainly for her neatly arranged living room. 'And how about you? Anything to share with me?'

'Nope.' Amber shook her head.

He stared at the empty wall above her fireplace. 'You took it all down then? All your... research?'

Amber's skin prickled. 'Yeah.' Suddenly she couldn't meet his eyes. She didn't want to think back to the day he and Freya had arrived here unannounced and found what Amber had been up to. 'Yeah. I took it all down.'

'Good.' He looked at her sideways, blinking from beneath his fringe. He really should get a damn haircut. 'I wish you'd forgive me, Amber.'

'You fired me, Marco. How can I forgive you?'

'I had to fire you, given what you had done. It wasn't personal.'

Shame roiled inside her. Shame and rage. 'It felt personal, Marco.'

'I wish you didn't see it that way.' He turned. 'But I can see you're not going to tell me anything, even though it's your friend who'll end up in jail. But I'm here. If you think of anything – anything that might help.'

'Sure.' She knew she would never call him.

'And Amber.' He pressed his lips together. 'I really didn't have a choice about firing you. You broke the rules – not once but over and over. You can't pursue personal projects in police time. Especially against a colleague's wishes. You know that.'

Amber didn't want to hear all this again. She understood that she had broken a rule or two, but her motives had been nothing but good. That was what Marco had never acknowledged – that was what hurt.

'Goodbye, Marco.' Amber needed to spend some time with the new punchbag in her garage.

'Bye.'

Amber felt a bolt of pure anger as she slammed the door behind him. He was so stupid. She should be in charge, not him. She remembered the way that he had emptied the contents of her desk drawers into a cardboard box – those sad Rich Teas and the lucky rainbow pen that had clearly had its time. All her colleagues, watching silently as she left. Jerry Maguire had looked like the bloody Pied Piper compared to her. Sod Marco. She would solve this first. They would be begging her to come back.

She got down on the floor again and had made it to crunch number seventy when the doorbell rang again. Amber stomped down the hall and pulled it open, assuming it was Marco back for more. She was ready to be rude this time.

Instead, she was met by a wild-eyed Denise, hair flying, cheeks red. Before Amber could stop her she had stalked into the hallway, oozing the kind of aggression normally in evidence in a four-hour motorway tailback.

Amber blinked. 'What the hell?'

Denise was already in the living room.

Amber followed her. 'How did you find my address?'

'I'm a journalist. It's easy.' Denise's voice shook with rage. She held out her hands, palms raised, and Amber saw three mobile phones. 'My only problem was escaping the family liaison officer who insists on trying to share my pain every bloody day.'

'Why...?'

'Gary was a bloody bastard.' Denise took a shuddering breath. 'He was shagging around.'

'Yeah. He does that.'

'Marshall told me. When I went over there trying to get the money he owed Gary.'

Amber feigned ignorance, remembering the rose thorns in her ear.

Denise picked up the McDonald's bag and started twisting it in her fingers, as if it was Gary's neck. 'Only it turned out Gary had made up the figures. And that Marshall had actual videos of Gary and his wife Cherie going at it. The BASTARD.'

Amber wondered what her neighbours were making of all this. Denise's voice spiralled even higher. 'So I got home, and I remembered what Clio said at the café, about burners, and I turned everything upside down trying to find them. And here they bloody well are. He kept them in the car. The footwell, believe it or not, under the carpet in a little gap. Just like Clio said he would.'

The McDonald's bag wasn't long for this world. Little pieces were flying everywhere. Amber itched to pick them up.

Denise turned, eyes flashing. 'And you're going to help me to unlock the damn things, so I can find out who else he was shagging, and make their lives hell. I don't share men.'

Amber swallowed. 'I don't know that I can help—'

Denise pointed a shaking finger at her. 'Oh yes you can. Because my contacts on the force told me two things. One: you're a cow, but you're brilliant.'

'Um...'

'And two: they told me why you got fired – what you did to your friend's fiancé. And I don't think you want your besties finding out about that, do you?'

Amber stiffened. 'I don't know what you mean.'

Denise shook her head. 'Don't even try it. You're just embarrassing yourself. I'll tell them, unless you help me.'

Amber chewed on her lip. She had meant to tell Clio and Jeanie all about what she had done, but somehow she had never found the right moment. It was easier to pretend that she was wronged – that she had been unjustly fired, than to tell the truth. If they knew that she had broken regulations and stalked someone, then whatever her motives, they might not want to be her friends any more. And they were her family – had always been her family.

She couldn't lose them. 'OK, let me have a look.'

'Good.' Denise made herself at home on the sofa. 'Off you go then.'

Amber looked at the phones.

They could contain the key. The missing piece. Adrenaline fired inside her. These phones might help them find the killer.

38

JEANIE

Taking a deep breath, Jeanie stared at the door of the building which had been her second home until the twins were born. It had been over twelve months since she had last entered the light glass foyer, crossed the marble floor and swiped her way through the sleek entry gates leading to the lifts that rose to the floor above. Back then she had been about eight months' pregnant with the twins, her proud belly entering the building several seconds before the rest of her, her hair bright with pregnancy shine.

Today she was with her actual babies, who had spent most of the train journey to London catching up on all the sleep they hadn't had last night. Jeanie wished she had been able to join them – she had been up since three, when they had started crying and Jeanie had wearily brought them into bed with her. Jeanie and Tan had enjoyed their normal whispered 'it's my turn to sleep' argument, before Tan had decided the matter by citing work the next day and staggering blearily off to the spare room. Jeanie had wept into her pillow for a whole ten seconds until Jack had puked and she had spent the next hour attempting to find a sleepsuit that was clean, while terrified that he would die of pneumonia.

All in all, she reflected as she steeled herself to go inside, she had never felt less like a detective, or even like a human being for that matter. She felt her chances of succeeding on this secret mission were low, even without wingmen as unpredictable as Jack and Yumi, especially as she couldn't actually get the double buggy through the revolving door.

She pushed harder, sweat prickling on her brow, even though it was minus two outside. Before having children, she had never thought much about doors – they were simply things that opened and closed, allowing her to access the places she wanted to reach. Now they were too narrow, too heavy, too fragile – never quite designed for the baby juggernaut that was effectively her third leg. She looked up to see Mark the receptionist staring at her through the glass. Relief washed over her. She had bought him a hot chocolate every Friday morning back when she had worked here. Any minute now he would come and help.

But his tanned face remained blank. She smiled, but got nothing in return. And then the penny dropped – he didn't recognise her. She wanted to cry. Ten years she had worked for this company, ten years of walking in and out past Mark and his team, of waving and asking how their holidays had been and what they had got for Christmas. And now she was a mum, he had no idea who she was, even though she had put make-up on and had brushed at least half of her hair. She sagged, leaning on the handlebars as Yumi started her tired whine, which generally spiralled as quickly as a boiling kettle. Jack rubbed his nose with a tiny hand and started to whimper.

Jeanie took a breath. Maybe she should just go home. The chances of her finding out anything useful were minimal, whereas the likelihood of her still having a job to go back to after the twins had wreaked havoc in the office were next to none. Her phone buzzed. She leant against the huge windows of her former office and read the message.

Got anything yet? Denise here with G's burner phones – we're trying to unlock them.

Jeanie typed back.

Why is Denise helping us?

Amber replied quickly.

She found out G was cheating on her. Raging.

Jeanie tried to jiggle the buggy as she typed.

Watch out world. You in yet?

Amber sent a short response.

Nearly.

Jeanie straightened.

On the case.

Before she could talk herself out of it, she knocked on the window, gesturing to Mark to help her get inside.

'Sorry, madam, I didn't realise you were coming in here.' Mark used his key to open the other door so the buggy could come through. His light blue uniform was as crisp and spotless as ever.

Jeanie forced herself to meet his gaze. 'Madam?' She tried to smile. 'Really?'

He put a hand to his mouth. 'Oh my goodness, Jeanie? Is that you?'

'Hi Mark.' Jeanie gestured to the twins, looking impossibly gorgeous in their matching Winnie the Pooh snowsuits. 'Meet the twins. That's Yumi on the right and Jack on the left.'

He crouched down beside them, tickling Yumi under the chin. 'But they're so big!'

'Not really.' Since they were born Jeanie had spent hours obsessing over height and weight charts, worrying about why they weren't growing faster – fearing that what she was feeding them wasn't enough, that her milk was somehow defective. The two of them ate well but still remained stubbornly small, consistently skimming the lowest centile when she weighed them weekly at baby clinic. 'They're nearly one now. They should be a lot bigger.'

'Do you mean you haven't been back to see us for a whole year?' Mark scratched his sandy hair. 'Why on earth not? We've all missed you so much.'

'Have you?' Jeanie could vaguely remember a time when she had been worth missing, an era when her WhatsApp chats were full of invitations to nights out and movies and Sunday lunches. A time when Tan had found her sexy and she had more to talk about than which twin had or hadn't done a poo today.

'Of course.' Mark straightened up and wheeled the buggy over to the reception desk, which was as immaculate as ever. The big silver sign-in book was at right angles to the large black phone and Mark's cherished black pen holder was still in its traditional position at the front. 'Now, let's get you signed in. You're heading up to Miracle, I take it?'

'Yes.' Jeanie's stomach dropped. Miracle Marketing: a company she had fallen into when a temp job turned permanent and had somehow never found the drive to leave, despite the insane hours and mediocre pay. Her old boss, Lianne, had been badgering her for weeks about returning from maternity leave – *I think it's time now, Jeanie, don't you?* – and now Jeanie was going to have to meet her face-to-face.

She was not looking forward to it.

Mark handed her a laminated visitor lanyard, and she signed in.

'Are you coming back soon, then?' Mark was easily the biggest gossip in the building. 'Because the girl covering your job is a disaster.' His eyes sparkled. There was nothing he liked more than a disaster. 'Can you guess what she did?'

Jeanie didn't want to know. 'I'm sure she's doing her best.'

'Well, the sooner you're back the better.'

Jeanie didn't agree. She didn't have the energy for spreadsheets and the endless stress of coordinating meetings with clients and managing budgets that always spiralled out of control. Most of all she had no idea how she could balance that job, that five days a week job, with being a mum. Even the idea of it made her want to start breathing slowly into a paper bag.

'Thanks Mark. I'll...' She tried to turn away, but Mark had more gems to share.

'Last week she forgot to book a room for the board meeting! The CEO was here and everything.' He laughed, showing perfect white teeth. 'Such drama.' He spread his hands wide. 'And then...' He leant forwards conspiratorially. Jeanie might never escape – she didn't have time for this. Then, out of the corner of her eye she saw a movement. Yumi was raising her little hand and...

Instinctively, Jeanie tried to stop her but it was too late. There was a splattering of pens at her feet and Mark's pen holder fell to the floor. Yumi looked up and Jeanie felt a tug of connection, of conspiracy, even. It was almost as if her daughter had seen what was going on and helped Jeanie out of a conversation she didn't want to have.

Teamwork. That was new.

Jeanie surprised herself – and the twins no doubt – by giving them a huge smile. She turned to Mark with renewed confidence. 'I'm sorry.' She bent to pick up the pens and then made a decisive move for the barriers. 'I'd better get going. Can't keep people waiting now, can I?'

'Great.' Mark was now focused on reorganising his pens. 'Enjoy yourselves.'

'Bye then!' Jeanie pushed the twins through the barriers, inwardly thanking whoever designed it for making it wide enough for both obese businessmen and buggies.

As she pressed the button on the lift she steeled herself. This was for Clio.

She thought of her friend, bright hair flying, arms outstretched for the hugs that she loved so much. Jeanie missed her. She missed the text that Clio sent every morning, checking that Jeanie was OK – always with a bad joke or an animal meme included. Clio hadn't missed a day since the twins were born, no matter what. Since Clio had been under lock and key Jeanie had felt the lack of it – a painful reminder that her friend was out of reach.

Jeanie clenched her fists as the lift opened to reveal the mono-chrome reception desk bearing the Miracle Marketing logo. She could do this. She would do this. She would be the friend Clio needed and find out where Rajiv had gone and why.

39

AMBER

Amber tried another code, but still the phone refused to unlock. Denise was lying back on the sofa, a cushion over her face.

Annoying.

Amber tapped in more numbers. 'Why did you bring the phones here, Denise? Instead of taking them to the police?'

Denise groaned and turned onto her side, tucking her long legs up into the foetal position.

Wakey wakey. 'Denise?'

Denise rose reluctantly onto one elbow. 'I don't want everyone knowing my business. I mean, Gary shagging around – it's, like, so humiliating. Telling you is just about OK – I mean, who are *you* going to share it with?'

Amber swallowed the insult. 'Look, Denise, Gary was an arsehole. Even if he had been married to Cindy Crawford he would still have slept around, in case that makes you feel any better.'

Denise flicked through the magazines on Amber's coffee table, piles of unread *Economists* that Amber was hoping to absorb by osmosis. 'Who's Cindy Crawford?'

Amber rolled her eyes. 'A supermodel.'

'No. I'd have heard of her.'

Great. Now Amber got to feel ancient as well as irritated. 'Fine. It doesn't matter.'

She walked through to the kitchen and flicked the kettle on. She stared at the *Breathe in, Breathe out* poster that Clio had got her for Christmas, and singularly failed to do either. She reached for the coffee canister and spooned several heaped teaspoons into her cafetière.

Denise appeared behind her, staring around the small space, judgement stamped across her face. 'Don't you even have a Nespresso machine?'

'No I bloody don't.'

Denise flounced over to the kitchen table, flopping down, all teeth and drama. It was like having Clio in the room minus any of the fun. Amber's heart twisted. Clio – still inside. Clio – alone.

'Have you got any chocolate?'

'Nope.' Amber poured in the boiling water, tempted for a moment to turn and tip it over Denise's head. Still, she had brought the burner phones, and they were the best lead Amber had. She picked one up while the coffee brewed.

'Are you sure you don't know what his code was?'

'Of course I'm sure.' Denise twirled a strand of her hair. 'I just can't believe he was cheating on me. He had hair plugs, for God's sake. He was lucky to have me.'

Amber nodded, wanting to get on with the task in hand. 'Yes. Now...'

'His Insta is full of me. All these shots of me with him, saying how gorgeous his girlfriend is, and then he goes and shags around.' A tear rolled down her cheek. When the sobs started, Amber knew she had to say something, if only to make them stop.

'There, there.' She patted Denise half-heartedly on the shoulder. 'At least he never tried to sleep with me.'

'Well, of course he didn't.' Denise's derisive tone did not improve Amber's mood. 'Why would he?'

Amber returned to the cafetière as Denise ranted on. 'I even said to him, I did, I said that I'd kill him if he was unfaithful. If he wasn't dead already, I swear I'd have a go myself.'

'Really?' Amber poured the coffee into two mugs. She was getting tired of this now – tired of listening to the woman who had replaced her best friend and shown absolutely no remorse. She tried another combination of numbers and got sod all for her trouble.

Denise was on her feet again now, fists clenched. 'I've never had a man doing anything behind my back before.'

Amber thought this was unlikely, but decided not to share as Denise was now standing dangerously close to the knife rack.

Amber stared at the first phone as intently as if it was going to tell her all its secrets. What would Gary have used? She had tried 0000. And 1111. Maybe...

His birthday? The same as Amber's, as it happened. 1177.

Nope.

She tried Clio's birthday. Nothing.

She had to get in.

An image flashed into her mind. Gary tipping a beer bottle back outside the beach hut. His arm was around Clio in her tight scarlet dress, his suit pressed, his hair dark next to her blonde dip dye. The hope on Clio's face – the faith. He had said something about how he loved beer nearly as much as his new wife. They had all laughed at the time – not so bloody funny now, was it?

What brand had it been?

She looked at Denise. 'What was his favourite beer?'

'Kronenbourg.'

'Of course!' Amber tapped in 1664.

The screen glowed into life.

'Got it!'

Denise came and leant over her, her perfume nearly choking Amber. Too much. Too strong. Denise in a nutshell, really.

'Why is there nothing on it?' Amber was systematically trying all the icons – no messages, no emails, no...

'There. Texts. Loads of them.' Denise tapped the screen impatiently. 'He hasn't even password-protected them.'

Amber scanned the messages, her breath catching. Gary really had been having his cake and eating it. This phone was full of messages to a woman who might be Cherie or might not – the nickname she was saved under was 'Cleaner.' But the messages suggested that Gary wanted a lot more than cleaning from her; he wanted role play, he wanted hotel rooms, he wanted considerably more than fifty shades of grey.

'BASTARD.' Denise was about to blow. More than familiar with this sensation herself, Amber took her by the hand and led her through to the garage, where she pointed her towards the punch bag that had been having a rough time of it ever since Amber was fired. Denise ran towards it as eagerly as a thief with the crown jewels in her sights. Amber left her to it, hearing the thump and thwack and hoping that it helped.

She returned to the phone and called 'The Cleaner'. She held her breath as it rang out. Amber wasn't surprised – she wouldn't pick up the phone to a dead man either. There was a beep and then a voice spoke. *Hi, this is Cherie.*

Amber's brain fizzed with questions. She sipped her coffee, pacing the small kitchen, past photos of Clio and Jeanie and of Rooney, the rescue lurcher from her third foster placement, who had felt like the first real family Amber had ever had.

Cherie. And Marshall. She needed to know more about them. Could one of them have killed him? Maybe things had got too intense between Gary and Cherie? Did Cherie kill him to stop him pursuing her? Amber put her mug down, wondering. Who had taken the video of Gary and Cherie together? She was no closer to finding out.

She hoped the next burner phone would help. Gary had used the same code, of course. He had always thought he was smarter than everyone else and he had always been wrong. Amber flicked through the messages. This time they were addressed to The Devil and Gary's moniker was the epically uninspired 'X'.

Amber scrolled downwards, her heart quickening as she read in black and white what Gary had been up to. She started with the oldest messages, seeing that he had extracted two payments of twenty-five grand from 'The Devil'. It was all here: the demand, the begrudging capitulation, the transfer arrangements.

But not the secret itself. Amber called The Devil's number, but it had been disconnected. Frustration seethed inside her. Time was ticking on. Clio would be charged soon, and once that happened Amber knew that her friend would never escape this allegation – people in the town would always remember her as the killer who walked free.

Amber opened up burner phone number three, as Denise slugged away in the garage. She scrolled through the messages, inwardly thanking Gary for finally giving her something to laugh about.

One phone for Gary the blackmailer. One for Gary the adulterer. And one for... Gary the serial beauty addict. It contained arrangements for acid peels, a mobile fake tanning service and a hair 'technician.' Amber snorted as she remembered the number of times Gary had proclaimed how lucky he was to look so young, how he couldn't understand why he never got wrinkles no matter how much he went in the sun. The five grand he had spent on Botox last year might provide the answer to that.

Bloody Gary. He was the reason Clio was in a holding cell, that

Nina couldn't stop crying no matter how much DJ tried to cheer her up, that Jeanie was back in the office she hated and that Amber was here, unexercised, listening to a woman she loathed pummelling the hell out of her punchbag.

Amber put her empty mug in the sink. Whoever had killed Gary had been clever. They had apparently left no tracks – nothing found in the fingertip search of the area, no CCTV, no licence plates, no nothing. But Amber was getting closer, she could feel it. 'The Devil' may have murdered to protect their secret. And then there was Marshall, who might not be as relaxed about Cherie's infidelity as he had made out to Denise. He might even be The Devil himself.

She would dig deeper. Had Marshall arranged for the footage of Gary and Cherie to be taken? Was he was using it as a cover to implicate someone else? Amber dropped to the floor and started her seventy-first crunch.

As soon as she had finished, it was time to go and see Marshall and find out more.

40

JEANIE

'Jeanie!' Olivia's eyes opened wide, the flick of eyeliner at the corners as precise as it had always been. 'It's so good to see you.'

'You too.' Jeanie kissed her old colleague on both cheeks, feeling the sweat pooling beneath her bra. Confidence came off Olivia in waves and Jeanie instantly felt dowdy – the Nokia to Olivia's iPhone. Even back in her working days, standing next to Olivia had never exactly made Jeanie feel good about herself. Now after two kids and a new commitment to elasticated waistbands it really wasn't doing her ego any favours at all. Her red dress felt overdone, her carefully swept up hair ridiculous. How could she have been naïve enough to assume that she could just step back into her old self, when she was minus any shred of her old confidence or self-belief?

'How are you?' She looked around the office, trying to compute actually being here again, seeing the huge glass meeting rooms, the water cooler with its emerald-green eco-cups, the red beanbags clustered around the break-out area. When she had left for maternity leave, she had felt so much a part of this place that she had worried she would go to pieces without it. Now, she felt out of place, jittery, someone with a handful of coins in a card-only boutique.

'I'm well, thank you.' Olivia smoothed her already flawless fringe.

'That's good.' Jeanie searched for more conversation but came up empty. Panic was rising but she pushed it down. All she had to do was to get Rajiv's contact details, have a quick look through the files, and get out of here. Easy. She took a deep breath and looked down at her children. They were hungry. Letting them loose would be as unpredictable as releasing a puppy at a children's birthday party.

She unclipped the first strap.

'How long has it been, now? Since we've seen you?' Olivia rested one glossy red nail on her chin. Jeanie remembered manicures. Now it was a self-care moment if she managed to brush her teeth. Last year Tan had asked her what she wanted for her birthday and had found it hysterical when she asked for a bath in which nobody burst in wanting a snack.

She unclipped the second strap and Yumi stretched her pudgy arms to the ceiling, starting her warm-up. 'Just over a year.'

'Awwww. They're so cute!' Olivia's expression belied her words. She took a step backwards. 'Time must fly when you're having fun with these two, eh?' She peered at Yumi, thin brows raised. 'Are her cheeks normally that colour?'

'No.' Jeanie licked her finger and made an attempt to wipe off the purple marker that Yumi had applied herself that very morning when Jeanie's back was turned.

'And Jack. Is he always that energetic?' Jack was fighting his way out of his straps already. Olivia leant down to wipe an invisible stain from her vertiginous heels. 'He's very lively, isn't he?'

Once, Jeanie and Olivia had been close, leaving together, buying each other lattes, advising each other about men and perfume and how to handle their mums.

Now they were worlds apart.

Jeanie unzipped Jack's snowsuit. 'He has his moments, like they all do.'

'My niece doesn't. She just sits there playing quietly with her toys. She barely moves!' Olivia laughed.

'My two are more the sporty types.' Jack let out a yell of protest as Jeanie rested a hand on his head, trying to make him stay where he was.

Olivia's expression was reminiscent of Jeanie's mum when she had once had the twins for a sleepover and called at 10 p.m. saying they needed to *Go. Home. Now.*

'Well, I can't believe how much time has gone by.' Olivia smiled. 'We've been so busy here.' Her trill set Jeanie's teeth on edge. 'What brings you back today?'

'I just wanted to say hello.' Jeanie felt the inadequacy of her words. 'I've missed you all.' Jack ruined the moment by doing his best to bite her hand. 'Argh!' She shook her head, trying to smile. 'He's such a joker.'

'Um. Yes.' Olivia took another step backwards. 'Now, it's so lovely to have you here, but we do have a big meeting coming up at 11 a.m. A new client. They're one of the biggest producers of wet wipes in the country. As you can imagine, we've gone to town.'

'I bet.' Jeanie could vaguely remember once feeling a thrill at the start of a new campaign. The whiteboards. The coffees. The camaraderie. Maybe that was what confounded her most about motherhood – the sense that she was so very alone.

Olivia clapped her hands together. 'So, who would you like me to find for you? Most of the old gang are still here. Can't get jobs anywhere else, can we?' That trill again. 'Emily, your maternity cover is off today, but...'

'I don't know – I'm happy to see anyone and everyone.' Jeanie kept moving, towards her old office, tucked away around the corner next to the stationery cupboard. She had shared it with Olivia – two desks pushed together with a heady view of a brick wall outside. As they walked, colleagues started to look up, drawn from their presentations and spreadsheets to watch her children not behaving in the buggy at all. *For Clio.* Jeanie tried to smile, sweat prickling down her back. Even her hair seemed to be sweating, which was a bloody cheek given how much of it was falling out. Middle age and motherhood just kept on giving.

'Jeanie!'

Oh God. Lianne. Her old boss. Just seeing her made Jeanie want to run. All those years as her assistant, juggling multiple tasks across multiple projects, with the only constant being Lianne's endless expectations. Lianne was both a brilliant and a terrible boss: brilliant because she was kind and supportive, but terrible because she had the highest standards of anyone Jeanie had ever met. A 'well done' from Lianne was the Miracle Marketing equivalent of an MBE and was so rare that Jeanie had always noted them down in her diary. Yet when Jeanie had been going through IVF Lianne had been exemplary – giving Jeanie the time off she needed and covering for her when she was ninety-nine per cent IVF drugs, mixing up meetings or quoting the wrong figures in negotiations. She owed Lianne a lot and hated being in front of her like this – all sweat and wrongness and flailing children.

'Well thank goodness you've finally decided to come and see us.' Jeanie had forgotten the warmth of Lianne's smile – the way it erased her wrinkles until there was nothing but the curve of her lips and the belief in her green eyes. Jeanie had also forgotten the way it had made her feel: efficient, capable, a woman with something to contribute. She hadn't felt like that in months and it jolted her. Had she accidentally turned into her mum since having the twins? Staying at home; scared of the world; growing thinner and sadder. Unseen, disappointed, frustrated.

Maybe she had. But not today. She lifted Jack out and placed him on the floor. Yumi followed. 'Go play.'

They both looked at her, faces at matching angles. Then Jack turned his head, finding nothing but wide-open office space – the thrill of the open road. He turned it the other way to see a tempting selection of cupboards and drawers. He gave Jeanie one more glance.

'Aren't they little sweeties?' Lianne bent down, in a position that Jeanie knew was dangerous. Any second now Jack would grab her chiffon scarf and try to garrotte her with it.

And there it was. Jeanie gulped as Jack closed his tiny fist around the material, before starting to use Lianne as a human climbing frame. Next Yumi made a bid for freedom and was crawling towards what used to be the stationery cupboard. Nothing was safe. No one was safe. It was the perfect diversion. And for once Jeanie didn't try to fix it. She pressed Olivia's arm as she tried to sidle away.

'Could you keep an eye on them for a minute?'

'Well, I am rather busy.' Olivia gave a small squeal as Yumi reached the stationery cupboard and gleefully started to pull plastic wallet folders off the bottom shelf. Good girl, Jeanie thought fiercely. And then she was off, scattering vague apologies liberally to left and right as only a mother with baby twins can. She found her old office. She found her old computer. And she left the chaos raging outside while she tried to log in.

Inevitably, she had forgotten her password.

She drummed her fingers on the desk. Was it Icarried8watermelon?!

No, apparently it was not.

How about 1UpTheDuff@|*?

No.

Sod it. She looked around. Olivia's computer in the other

corner of the office was up and running and the screen was unlocked. Jeanie walked to the door, peering along the corridor. No one was approaching and she could hear the delirious squeals of her children, clearly having the time of their lives. Swearing under her breath she approached the computer, a picture of Olivia and a predictably hot boyfriend in the middle of the screen.

Time to do some digging. Jeanie worked as fast as she could, fingertips light across the keyboard, everything so familiar and yet so new. She clicked into the client files, finding the Fernandez Tech folder, scrolling through client contact databases, desperately trying to find Rajiv's name. She started on the oldest files, beginning her search there. Miracle Marketing had run several campaigns for Fernandez Tech. Jeanie remembered the late nights, the pizzas, the endless bloody coffee runs.

In the files Jeanie found images of Rajiv and Johnny standing together, up until 2015 when suddenly Rajiv disappeared. Now all the campaign materials were full of Johnny, with his 'visionary leadership' and 'technological genius'.

Jeanie was going to find out why – in the hope it might lead to a motive for Gary Goode's murder. She scrolled the database again but there was no mention of Rajiv. Biting her lip in frustration, she scrolled through one last time. And that was when she noticed it – a number on a contact list from the first campaign. A mobile number for Rajiv Francis. She tapped it into her phone and prayed that it would work, taking the email as well just for good measure. She would contact him on her way home – no point in waiting now she had come this far.

She shut down the files, sat back and looked around the office for a moment. It was as if she was seeing the broad oak desk, the ergonomic metallic chairs and the cream walls through a stranger's eyes. Once, it had been home – but now it felt cold. There were no toys, no clothes piled up, no brightly coloured books featuring Postman Bears or Alien Teas.

She missed home.

'What are you doing at my desk?' Olivia appeared at the door, and Jeanie noticed that her hair was a little less immaculate than before. Yumi was in her arms, making a grab for her ponytail, which was working loose.

Jeanie held her arms out for her girl. 'I just needed to find somewhere to breastfeed.'

Olivia paled and she handed Yumi over and backed out rapidly. 'Well. I'll leave you to it. Jack made it to the filing cabinets but Lianne's with him now.'

'Thanks.' Jeanie was surprised to find she wasn't worried. Jack would be OK, just as Yumi had been. She pressed her lips to Yumi's soft cheek.

'Thank you, baby girl. Thank you.' She gave her a quick feed and then carried her out of the office.

Lianne was sitting on a beanbag playing peekaboo with Jack.

Jeanie smiled. 'It's hard to say which of you is enjoying themselves more.'

'I know.' Lianne rose to her feet. 'I'd forgotten how much fun they are at this age.'

Fun? Really? Jeanie picked her son up in her spare arm, cuddling both children to her. Maybe they were fun. Maybe it was time she remembered that.

Lianne chucked Yumi under the chin, her green eyes dancing. 'Good to meet them both at last. And you just let me know when you're ready to come back, Jeanie, OK? No rush. You'll know when you're ready.'

Jeanie was surprised to find tears in her eyes. For months she had been avoiding Lianne's emails – archiving them before she had replied so she could pretend they didn't exist. But maybe that had only made her anxiety loom larger. She placed Jack in the buggy, relieved when he didn't fight her. Yumi plugged a thumb in her mouth as she was strapped in next to him.

'Are you off then? What a shame.' Olivia radiated relief. 'Did you see everyone you wanted?' She was practically frogmarching them out.

'I did, thanks.' Jeanie kissed her old colleague goodbye and pressed the button to call the lift. It had been a good morning, against all the odds. Jeanie pushed the buggy inside and hit the button for the ground floor. Maybe that was how things were once you were a mum. Maybe you took the joy where you could, she thought as the lift swept downwards, taking her back to her normal life – to feeding and naps and to trying to clear her best friend of murder.

41

@SUNSHINESANDSONLINE
Followers: 5000
NEWS BLAST: Clifftop Killer: are there two murderers on the loose?

The plot thickens in the terrible story of the death of Gary Goode, as it appears that not one, but TWO killers are out there. Our source on the force has revealed that the victim died from two blows to the head rather than one, indicating that more than one person is involved. A local woman, Clio Lawrence, wife of the deceased, is still in custody having confessed to the killing – but who else should also be inside? Keep your eyes peeled and help us all to protect our town.

Shares: 2680
Likes: 3200

42

JEANIE

'Why is there a list of suspects on the twins' blackboard?'

'What?' Jeanie looked up from her phone where she was trying to call Rajiv for the millionth time. Tan was in the doorway, pointing at Amber's writing beneath Tinky Winky's purple feet. She exhaled in frustration as the number rang out yet again.

Tan came and crouched next to her, brow furrowed. His black hair was neatly brushed, his blue T-shirt spotless, his jeans pressed. He took pride in his clothes, pride in his neatness, pride in the way he lined up his shoes when he got in from work. He was the only tidy thing in their house nowadays. He put a hand on her shoulder.

'Jeanie? Are you OK?'

'No.' She put her hands to her temples. 'I've got about two minutes till the kids wake up from their nap, and my one lead in this whole mess is going nowhere because he won't answer his phone.' She shook her head, wondering why she had ever thought she could help. 'And I miss Clio.'

Tan nodded, and she thought maybe he had finally understood. Maybe he had finally seen how much was on her plate. Maybe he would take a day off and actually help, for once. She looked back down at her phone, trying to sweep the curls out of her eyes with her left hand. As usual, they failed to obey her.

'That's a lot, Jeanie.' He hovered for a second. 'A lot.' She looked up at him expectantly, waiting for whatever solution he was about to propose. A beat passed.

'Do you know where my laptop is?'

It took her a second to register. Here she was, trying to save her friend, and Tan was worried about his bloody laptop.

'Your laptop? Seriously?'

'Yes.' His brisk tone irritated her. Once, she had always known he was there for her – had loved the certainty of being listened to after a childhood spent with four sisters, all of whom were louder than her. Back then even the goldfish got more attention than Jeanie, with her large ankles and even larger confidence issues.

'I can't find it.' His face was sombre, as if the end of the world was nigh. 'And today I have to—'

'Are you seriously asking me to find it? Did you hear what's been going on in my life recently?' He flinched. Even Jeanie was surprised by the ferocity of her voice. 'I'm not only looking after our children while you're heading to work, but I'm also trying to stop my friend going to prison. I really don't understand why I should be running around finding your laptop as well.'

Tan roamed the room, lifting piles of books and digging into the tub of plastic toys that spilled out onto the carpet.

'But Clio confessed, didn't she?'

His tone irritated her. His wrinkle-free T-shirt irritated her.

Tan irritated her.

'Yes.' She nodded. 'But it's not as simple as that.'

'Why not?' He was now picking up Lamaze sunflowers and pieces of Duplo, before replacing them exactly where they had been before when the tubs were *right there*.

'Stop searching for a moment and talk to me, Tan.' She was

seeing why Amber got angry now. It was quite liberating now she was giving it a try.

'I am talking to you.' He paused. 'But I need to find my laptop. I have a big—'

Jeanie exhaled. 'What's the point? You never listen.'

'Well, you're not listening to me either.'

'Yes I am.' She looked down at her phone and refreshed the screen. A message from Amber.

Off to get down with the kidz at Printz store opening in Brighton with Marshall and Cherie. Checking in with Nina first. Good luck with Rajiv x

Jeanie was now officially panicking. Amber was out there making things happen, while Jeanie was just – drifting. Useless, as always. If Clio got locked away it would all be her fault.

'You're not, Jeanie. You're not listening.' Tan's voice was clipped. 'You're on your phone.'

'I'm busy.' Jeanie lifted her mug of tea but it was cold.

'Busy? With your friends?'

'No. Busy trying to *save* my friend, Tan.'

He was lifting the sofa cushions now. 'I know you love Clio. But sometimes you – and I – we need time too. You know? Just – us?'

'Why?' She checked her email just in case Rajiv had got back to her. Nothing. 'I look after the kids and never sleep. You work and get your eight hours a night. That's it, isn't it? That's our marriage, end of.'

'No, it's not.' Tan's voice was a gunshot. Jeanie looked up. Tan didn't do angry. 'That's not all, Jeanie. It's all you are choosing to see.'

Jeanie took another biscuit from the pack of chocolate digestives at her side. She didn't offer him one. That would show him.

He stepped towards her and now she only wanted him to go away. She refreshed her inbox again. Nothing.

'Jeanie, you're so preoccupied all the time.'

'I've got a lot on.' Jeanie winced as she heard a bleat through the baby monitor. 'Like I just explained, if you'd been listening.'

Another bleat. Jeanie's shoulders were so taut they might crack.

Tan knelt by her side. 'Jeanie, I was listening. But I've got things happening too.'

'What have you got happening?' She looked at him. 'You go to work, you come home, you sleep. That's not exactly difficult, is it?' She knew she was being unfair but couldn't stop. 'Meanwhile this morning I had to take our children to my office as cover, while I'm trying to access information to help Clio. I'm...'

'You've used our kids as decoys?' Now Tan was regarding her with absolute horror.

'Yes.' She took another biscuit and bit it in two. 'I was looking something up to try to solve Gary's murder.' OK, that sounded bad. 'They were with my colleagues, and I was...'

'They were with your colleagues?' His voice was quiet again now. Saddened. It infuriated her even more. 'You barely take them anywhere with me.'

'This was different.'

'Was it?' He got back on his feet and moved away. Normally she would go up to him, put her arms round him, try to fix it, but today she was too tired and too worried. She had nothing left for him.

'Things need to change, Jeanie. I want to start taking them out with you: not just to nursery, but to the park. To the seaside. I want us to be a family, like we dreamt about. All four of us. You always make us stay here.'

'That's because—'

'Because you don't trust me?'

'No, Tan. Of course I trust you. But I—'

'Look.' He paced to the window, staring out at the deserted street. 'I know you're scared of the water after what happened when you were younger. I get it, I do. But that doesn't mean our kids need to be scared of it too. We don't want to make them scared of everything like you are.'

She looked away, shaking at his betrayal. They didn't talk about what had happened when she was sixteen, just like they didn't talk about his mum walking out or the way they both hated his dad.

Actually, that was a lie. They often talked about how much they hated his dad.

He took her hand. 'Jeanie, what's going on with you?'

The sympathy in his voice made her insides curdle. She had heard that tone before, back before Tan, decades ago, when she was carried out of the pool that day. She had brought a whole swimming gala to a halt when she hit her head on the diving board attempting a reverse somersault with tuck before falling unconscious into the water. Apparently she had plunged to the bottom, bleeding copiously, and lifeguards had dived in to drag her to the surface.

Sympathetic murmurs had filled the stands as she came round, horrified to find that she was receiving CPR from her teacher Mr Moss with his yellow teeth and terrible breath. *Jeanie and Mr Moss kissing in a tree.* Jeanie could feel her cheeks burning even now. Was that when it had started? The fear? The sense that disaster lay around every corner? That she couldn't trust herself? Or was that day the seed, which had grown ever larger from the moment she held Yumi and Jack in her arms and realised how vulnerable they were?

Tan took her hand. 'Jeanie. We need to talk. After work? Today?'

'I can't. Not today. I need to help find Gary's killer.'

'Fine!' Tan was losing control. 'Well, let me know when you can fit me in. The other night I woke up and you were on your phone.

No wonder the kids weren't sleeping with that blue light in their faces.'

Jeanie started to laugh – a wild, hyena sound. 'You think my phone is the reason they're not sleeping, Tan? You think my phone in our room is the reason they wake up at 1 a.m. every sodding night in their room down the hall and scream until I bring them into our bed?'

'Well, they might sleep better if...'

Fury pulsed through her. 'They're never asleep, Tan. Not unless I am too. Jack needs his tummy stroking as he drops off, Yumi won't sleep without her Bunny and yet persists in hurling it out of the cot. You may not have noticed, but they're awake all day with me, especially now nursery is closed due to a chicken pox outbreak.' Jeanie blinked back tears. How had they got this far apart? 'So, this is the only time I have for me. Now. And I need it for Clio.'

'For Clio. Of course. Always, Clio.' This seemed to take the fight out of Tan. His shoulders slumped. 'Well, when I finally find my laptop I'm off to work. Work which I hate, for your information. Away from the kids, who I adore, in case you care. Good to chat, I'll see you tonight.'

He only adored them because he didn't have to deal with them.

'Bye.' He didn't kiss her. She didn't care.

Tears stung her eyes. She was reaching for another biscuit when her screen lit up.

Her heart accelerated. Rajiv was calling her back at last.

43

AMBER

'I'm coming too.' Nina nodded decisively. 'I can't sit just sit around like this. I want to come and help.' She looked at DJ, who was sitting in the corner of the caravan, feet up against the windowsill, hunched over his iPad. He was tangling a strand of his long brown hair between his fingers, face furrowed, his normal smile noticeably absent.

Nina raised her voice. 'You could come too, couldn't you?'

He didn't answer, thumbs typing furiously.

'DJ?'

'Just give me a second.' He frowned. 'Can't you see I'm busy?'

Nina looked away, hurt.

DJ finished typing, saw Nina's stricken face, and realised what he had done.

'I'm sorry, love.' He stood up and crossed the room towards her, only for his phone to fall out of the back pocket of his shorts. As she picked it up Amber noticed it was the latest iPhone. Even teenagers had better phones than her nowadays. He dropped a kiss on Nina's lips, all bashful contrition. 'Work's a bit mad and my boss won't leave me alone.' He rolled his eyes, seeking sympathy, but Nina just looked down, pleating her pink top between her fingers, her lips pressed into a line. She was going to make him work for it.

Good for you, Amber thought, sharing a glance with Bez, who was stirring yet another vat of chilli in his kitchen. Tupperware was stacked up all over the counter, pot after pot of Bez's favourite comfort food. She held out the phone to DJ and he thanked her and tucked it away.

DJ got down on his knees beside Nina and reached for her hand. 'Where do you want me to go with you?' He kissed her fingers, once, twice, big brown eyes never leaving her face.

Nina relented. 'To get the lowdown on Marshall and Cherie Fernandez. Amber thinks they may have been involved in Gary's death.'

'Do you?' DJ turned his head. 'I can see that.'

'Really?' Amber sat down on the edge of the sofa. 'Do you know them, then?'

'Yes, I...' He hesitated. 'Just a bit. From the marina. They've got an Oyster 885.'

Amber leant forward, her chin in her hands. 'I have no idea what that is.'

'Sorry. It's a yacht.'

She smiled. 'That explains why I've never heard of it. Have you ever seen them doing anything suspicious?'

'No.' He shook his head. 'Not suspicious. Just...'

'Just...?'

'I crewed them a while ago and overheard them having a row.' He put his arm around Nina. 'About – you know – Cherie...'

This was useful. Amber nodded. 'Recently?'

'Last month, I think. They had a bit of a set-to. Marshall waving his arms about, complaining that she'd missed some event or other, saying that it was time she finished this affair and moved on.'

Amber felt her pulse quicken. 'And what did she say?'

DJ kissed the top of Nina's head. 'Cherie was having none of it.'

'How did it end?'

DJ sighed. 'Like rows normally do. They kissed and made up. You could see the boat rocking.'

Nina giggled for the first time since Gary's death. Amber wished Clio was there to hear it.

'Have you told the police this?'

'Yes.' DJ pulled Nina close. 'Can't wait till we go out on my boat again.' He gently kissed Nina's cheek and her arms folded around him. He was clearly forgiven. 'And I'd love to come with you today, but I've got to get back to the marina. A bugger of a client's just moored and the boss wants me there, even if it's only to make a brew and smile.'

'But you said it was your day off.' Nina pouted.

Something like impatience flickered across DJ's face before he smiled. 'I know, love. I'm sorry. But it's just for a bit, while we sort him out. He's a big spender and I need the cash. OK? For our big trip.'

Amber took a step forward. 'What big trip?'

DJ grinned. 'Nina's agreed to come away with me, haven't you?'

'No.' Nina shook her head. 'You know I haven't. I can't – not with Mum—' She swallowed. 'Not with things how they are. And I need to revise, too, somehow.'

His face darkened. 'But you promised.'

'No, DJ, you must have got the wrong idea. I never—'

Amber didn't have time for this. She got her keys out of her bag. 'Are you coming, Nina?'

Nina thought for all of a nanosecond. 'No. I'll stay here. It looks like we need to talk. I can just come along to the marina with you, can't I, babe?'

For a second DJ's brow furrowed. Then he wound an arm around Nina. 'It's alright. You don't have to. Go with Amber. It'd do you good to get out of here for a bit.' He checked his phone again, preparing to leave.

'No.' Nina cuddled into him, pulling him back. 'I want to stay with you.'

Amber heard a bang and stuck her head around the flimsy kitchen door. Bez was stirring the chilli with more force than was strictly necessary.

'Are you alright?'

Bez shook his head.

'No.' He lowered his voice to a whisper. 'I'm worried about her. She won't go anywhere without him.' Even Bez's glasses somehow looked tired – Amber could see spots of sauce on the right lens. 'I need Clio. She always knows how to bring Nina out of herself.'

Amber grinned. 'She'll be back soon, Bez.'

'Really?'

'Really.'

He smiled, visibly relaxing. 'OK.'

Amber leant against the door jamb, head on one side. 'Bez, Nina's a teenager and she's going through a lot. You're doing well. Really well.'

'Am I?' His glasses steamed up as the kettle boiled.

'Yes.' Amber smiled. 'You are.'

He wiped his glasses against his shirt. 'And how do you think Clio's doing?'

'God knows.' Amber sighed. Clio had just spent her third night in custody – as a woman who always took a variety of pillow sprays on holiday it was unlikely she was exactly flourishing.

Bez tasted the chilli and threw in more salt. 'I miss her.'

'Me too.' Amber nodded. 'But don't worry, we're working on it.'

* * *

The drive to Brighton in her Mazda was just the tonic Amber needed. Foot down, top down – the dream. By the time she reached the seafront, she couldn't feel her fingers but her spirits were on the rise. She parked up around the back of a big hotel and walked past bright café awnings, inhaling the sugary scent of a roast chestnut stall before arriving at the huge Printz store that was opening today.

A crowd of teenagers wearing the latest Printz range thronged outside – their lime green and neon orange hoodies even brighter than the logo glazed onto the big glass doors, the signature Printz thumbprint picked out in pink. Amber automatically made herself smaller as she approached, tucking her hands into her pockets and lowering her head. She was here to see, not be seen. She made her way through the crowd, seeking the owners who had told the world that they would be here. It was a different world – one of selfies and posting and overpriced trainers. Marshall and Cherie had done well to keep these teenagers hooked for so long.

Amber rounded the corner and came to an abrupt halt, sliding down behind a postbox to tie her non-existent shoelaces.

'I'm so sorry, baby. It all got so out of hand.' Amber recognised Cherie's silky tones from their encounter in the garden.

'Why did you let him?' A gruff voice. Marshall. 'You know Johnny and I don't get on. Why did you let him manipulate you like that?'

Amber peered around the postbox and spotted the two of them in a doorway, Marshall facing inwards, Cherie facing out onto the street. They were so close together Amber could barely make out which one was which. She stayed low, listening, willing the seagull keening above her to shut the hell up.

Cherie spoke, fast and low. 'I'm sorry, Marshall. Johnny came to me asking for help – said Gary was demanding money, that he knew I was sleeping with him, all that.' She ran a finger down Marshall's cheek. 'And I said no, of course. But he must have worked out where I was staying with Gary – the hotel staff are so indiscreet – and next thing somehow you had got the video. Johnny must have had me followed or something.'

Amber punched the air. So Johnny must be The Devil on Gary's burner phone. Jeanie had been right – Gary had been blackmailing him and Johnny must have taken a video of Gary and Cherie to try to get him to stop.

But Gary hadn't stopped, had he? And so maybe Johnny had gone one step further.

All Amber needed was proof.

Marshall's face was set. 'You don't think Johnny was trying to frame us for killing him?'

Cherie shook her head. 'Good luck to him if he was, darling. We both know where we were that night and God knows we've got enough witnesses. How many people saw us at Dolce? Two hundred?'

'Good point.' Marshall stroked Cherie's cheek. 'At least the police won't be coming after us.' He kissed her, long and hard. 'Now, let's open this store, shall we? Then can I take you for lunch?'

Cherie laughed. 'I'd rather you took me to a hotel...'

'I can do that too.' A husky laugh before they turned and disappeared through the door behind them into the store.

Amber stayed where she was, thinking hard. Johnny had cancelled his trip to London to stay in town. Johnny had a secret he had paid thousands of pounds to keep quiet. A secret worth killing to keep.

Johnny Fernandez was now their prime suspect.

44

JEANIE

Jeanie hadn't hesitated. Not for a minute. After putting down the phone to Rajiv, without even pausing to see if she had enough snacks, she had bundled the kids into the buggy and got out of the house, leaving Tan to find his laptop on his own. As she unlocked the car she paused for a moment – wondering if this was how other parents lived their lives. Not performing risk assessments before a trip to the shops, not panicking if they didn't have wellies or sun cream – just getting out there and living.

Tan's words rang in her ears as she drove and she put on her favourite playlist to try to drown them out. 1990s classics blasted out of the speaker, and both children were unusually quiet, mesmerised by the movement of the car. Jeanie sang along to 'Smells Like Teen Spirit' as she turned off the ring road onto an industrial estate, passing a storage facility and a soft play centre before pulling up outside Rajiv's shop, 'Figure It Out'.

It had a shambolic air: the front window was full of mobile phones, cables and charger packs, jumbled together as if someone had dropped them from a great height and never bothered to untangle the result. The shop sign was hanging at an angle and as she got the twins out of the car and manoeuvred them into the buggy Jeanie could see a patch of mould blooming on the roof. She tucked the twins in tight as the wind whistled through the car park, bustling them past an ancient red Mini and into the shop as fast as she could.

Inside, it was busy, much busier than the outside had led Jeanie to expect. A long line of people were queuing up, various items of electrical equipment tucked under arms or held in eager hands, all waiting to speak to the dark-haired man behind the counter.

Rajiv. Seeing him, Jeanie was back in those early campaign meetings again, listening to his calm voice as he talked Johnny down from whatever impulsive position he had adopted. She remembered his short black hair, clipped beard and the way he had always made a point of thanking her for her help. His voice had lost none of its patience, and he was busy explaining to an elderly customer that no, his phone was not deliberately forgetting his password.

The man sighed heavily, rubbing worried fingers across his navy cable neck jumper.

'Go on, Charles.' Rajiv held out the man's phone. 'Try your code. I promise you, it won't bite.'

The man hesitated in a way that reminded Jeanie of her mum when confronted with a new remote control. Then he tapped the screen four times.

'See?' Rajiv's face lit up. 'You can do it.'

'So I can.' Charles beamed. 'So I bloody can. Thank you, Rajiv, you're a diamond.' He picked up the phone and tucked it away in his pocket, shuffling his way back towards the exit.

Naturally Jack chose this golden moment to stick out a tiny hand from the buggy and dislodge a stack of headphones at the end of an aisle. They clattered to the floor and everyone turned to stare. Blushing, Jeanie dropped to her knees, dispensing rice cakes to the twins in a bid to keep them quiet. Her anxiety was back, the *Jaws* music that would never end, and her palms were sweating despite the chill in the store. She waited, pretending to browse, as Rajiv patiently worked his way through the queue. He was the town helpdesk, it seemed, unfreezing iPads, fixing keyboards, a warrior doing battle against the spinning wheel of internet doom.

'Jeanie? Thank you for coming.' Rajiv appeared in front of her, having rapidly made his way through the last customers. 'I'll just close up the shop for a bit, so we can talk.'

He shut the door of the store as the last shopper left. His serious expression melted away as he looked at the twins. 'And who are these bubbas?' He balanced on his haunches, pulling faces so silly that they cackled with laughter.

'Yumi and Jack.' Jeanie loved this flowering of pride in her little ones. 'They're nearly one now.'

Rajiv reached out a finger and tickled Yumi under the chin. She erupted into giggles, throwing her head back and kicking her legs in delight.

'They are gorgeous.' As he squidged Jack's toes she could see that the collar of his shirt was threadbare.

'Thank you.' Jeanie wondered how he had ended up here. Back when they had worked together he had always worn brightly coloured T-shirts under dark suits, Converse on his feet. He had looked expensive, smelling of woody cologne, arriving at meetings with the latest gadget in his pocket.

She stroked Yumi's hair. 'Thanks for seeing me, Rajiv.'

He stood up. 'Of course. I remember you from the campaign.'

'You do? It was years ago.'

'Of course!' He smiled. 'You were the reason we went with our logo. You came up with it, didn't you?'

'Did I?' She had always thought Lianne had dreamt up the

Fernandez Fox. Jeanie had just been the one who put everything in place, ready for other people to be brilliant.

'Yes. I remember it well.' He walked across the shop, past shelves of adaptors and flash drives, gesturing to a couple of battered plastic chairs in the corner. He sat down opposite her, and Jeanie gave the twins some cloth books to play with. 'Now.' He scratched his beard and pulled a packet of sandwiches from a rucksack hanging from a shelf. 'How can I help you? I've got a few minutes before my weekly Samsung troubleshooting workshop begins. We generally get a good crowd.'

'You like helping people.'

He nodded. 'I do. And it was all I had left, after...'

'After you and Johnny broke up?' Jeanie put her hand to her mouth. 'I'm sorry. I meant since you left Fernandez Tech.'

He grinned. 'That's OK. I guess we were a work couple. Once.' His face darkened.

'What happened?'

'Johnny happened.' Rajiv's mouth twisted. 'I'm not allowed to say much more than that – he made sure of that. Why do you want to know?'

'I...' Jeanie had prepared a cover story on the way here but it felt flimsy now. She decided to tell the truth instead. 'We think Johnny is linked to the death of Gary Goode.' She thought of what Amber had called to tell her as she was driving here – that Johnny had taken the photos of Gary and Cherie. 'We think Gary was blackmailing him, and that Johnny might have killed him to shut him up.'

'Johnny?' Rajiv shook his head. 'I doubt it. I don't like the guy, given what he did to me, but I don't think he's a killer.'

Jeanie stopped, surprised. 'I...'

Rajiv's eyes were dark. 'Look. I worked with Johnny for a

decade, developing the chip. I did the tech, he did the selling, and he secured our funding from investors.'

'But Johnny was the sole heir to his dad's fortune. Surely you didn't need investors?'

'He lost it all.' Rajiv tickled Yumi's palm, eliciting a giggle. 'Every penny. Bad investments, debts – it all got out of control. Back when he was with Lola, his first wife. He was broke for a while, then I came along.' His mouth twisted bitterly. 'And he saw a way back.'

'I had no idea.' Jeanie shook her head, reaching over to wipe some dribble from Jack's chin.

Rajiv nodded. 'He definitely had to raise the money for our company. I watched him do it. He has the gift of the gab. He makes people trust him, like I trusted him.'

'And then what happened?'

'And then he screwed me over.' Rajiv finished his sandwich and sat back, his eyes far away. 'Look, I'm not meant to talk about it. I signed an NDA without realising what it was. Stupid, hey?'

Jeanie thought of Clio, signing away her inheritance. 'No. *Trusting*. Not stupid.'

A wry laugh. 'You're very kind. And between us? I can tell you that he took my name off everything, had me kicked off the board, gave me a few thousand pounds of "severance" and then disappeared with the tech that I had developed.'

'No.'

'Yes.' Rajiv ran a hand through his hair. 'Believe me, I still have sleepless nights about how dumb I was.'

Jeanie saw the pain on his face. 'And you couldn't – prove it was you? Who designed it?'

'No. My word against his. He took me out of every single document, deleted my picture, relabelled the designs. And our investors didn't care – they just wanted to start making their money.' Rajiv hung his head. 'He had all my prototypes, designs, etc. He absolutely shafted me.'

'Oh God, I'm sorry.' Jeanie put a hand on his arm. 'That happened to my friend Clio too.'

Rajiv raised an eyebrow. 'Well, I hope she's better off than me right now.'

'Not really. She's in a holding cell on trial for Gary's murder.'

Rajiv's eyes widened. 'Oh no.'

'That's why I'm here.' Jeanie had another question to ask. 'But how did Gary find out about all this? Because I'm guessing he did?'

Rajiv nodded. 'Gary did my extension a while back. And he said he came across documents when he had to move them to knock a wall down. But, in truth, I think he must have been nosing around.'

'Sounds like Gary.'

'It does, doesn't it?' Rajiv shrugged. 'Anyway, he found a load of letters I had sent to Johnny, laying out what he'd done, how the tech for the chip was mine, you know – the whole story. I tried for years to get what I was owed but Johnny just took out injunction after injunction, swamping my lawyers in paperwork. He stalled me until I had no money left to keep going.' He shook his head. 'He destroyed me.'

'And Gary worked out what he'd done?'

'Yeah.' Rajiv nodded. 'But only after he spiked my drinks – I'm teetotal. There's no way I would have said anything otherwise.'

'No!' Jeanie's hand flew to her mouth. This was low, even for Gary.

'Yes.' Rajiv nodded. 'So I must have told him the whole story, and for a while nothing happened, and then the next thing I know – in December last year, so a couple of months ago now – I get this message from Johnny telling me to stop blackmailing him. I told him I wasn't – I even tried to see him the other day to clear it all up – I didn't want the police on my case on top of everything else.'

'And...?'

Rajiv started on his second sandwich. 'And by the time I turned up at the house Johnny said he knew it wasn't me and he had a plan and I should just piss off.'

'Charming.' Jeanie's voice was a squeak. 'Do you think he wanted to kill Gary?'

'No.' Rajiv shook his head. 'Like I said, Johnny's too clean to be a killer. He'd be afraid of getting blood on his shoes.'

Jeanie thought back to the pool around Gary's body. So much blood. Her stomach curdled. 'Maybe he got angry. Maybe he just did it on impulse.'

Rajiv sighed. 'Maybe. I mean, you never know. I just...'

'What?'

'I'd just be surprised. He'd have got someone else to do it for him. That's much more Johnny. Look at how he developed the chip.' He gave a mirthless laugh.

Jeanie nodded, looking out of the window, seeing a new line forming. 'Thank you, Rajiv. You've been so helpful.' She stood up. 'Just tell me, how did you arrive here? Start the shop?'

He crumpled up the sandwich bag and threw it into the bin. 'I bought it with the last of my money. It's not much, but it's a start. I've got regulars. I'm going to launch a home tech support service for all the locals who need it too. Get a bike. Get fit.' A twinkle had returned to his eye. 'And I'm cooking up something new as well. Another industry game-changer, I hope. I'm not going to tell you about it though.' He mimed a zip across his lips. 'I'm not going to tell anyone at all, until it's patented and protected and officially mine-all-mine.'

'Good idea.' Jeanie got to her feet. 'Good luck. And thank you for talking to me.'

'I hope you get whoever did it.' Rajiv went back to the door and turned the sign to *Open*. Instantly a small child ran in, a Samsung tablet tucked under his arm. 'Rajiv, Roblox won't work and I need to get online NOW!'

Rajiv bent down to him. 'OK. Well, let's see what's going on, shall we?'

Jeanie looked back at him as she left. A brilliant man, surrounded by gamers and forgotten passwords. Whether or not he had killed Gary, there was no question that Johnny was already a guilty man. Guilty of taking credit for something he hadn't done – guilty of taking the life that Rajiv could have known.

45

2.00 P.M.: 8 FEBRUARY 2023.

@SaveClio

Jeanie:– We were right. Gary blackmailing Johnny over cutting Rajiv out of Fernandez Tech chip.

Amber:– The multibillion selling chip?

Jeanie:– Yep. So do you think Johnny's our man?

Amber:– He has motive. He has opportunity. He has means. Which is good. Because I'm just outside his front door.

Jeanie:– Amber! Never go in alone, isn't that a thing in the police?

Amber:– I'm not in the police.

Jeanie:– 👀 Be careful.

Amber:– Always.

Jeanie:– You're crossing your fingers behind your back, aren't you?

Amber:– No comment.

46

AMBER

Amber reached down to stroke the tabby cat that was winding its way in and out of her legs. She suspected she would be under surveillance from someone deep inside the sprawling house in front of her, and paying some attention to the family pet always went down a treat. If she was going to commit fraud by impersonating a police officer, then she might as well do it in style.

She stood up, got her fake warrant card from the car, and walked up the wide stone steps. Gary must have climbed them too. The thought sent a shiver down Amber's spine, making her hesitate, wondering if she was unwise to have come here alone.

She decided to ignore herself and ring the doorbell. Johnny had a major motive to kill Gary and Amber had no choice but to dig further. Maybe things had escalated – maybe Johnny had shown Gary the video and he had refused to stop demanding money. The only way to get any clarity was to talk to Johnny now and to analyse every movement of his hands and twist of his face. To push him, hard, towards whatever truth he was withholding. To find the missing clue that would identify him as Gary's killer.

'Yes?' Johnny himself answered the door, rubbing his hair dry with a thick white towel. A packed bag was at his feet and he smelt as if he had recently taken a walk in a pine forest.

'Mr Fernandez?' Amber flashed her card. 'I'm DI Nagra, from Hampshire Police. I'm here to ask you some questions about your relationship with Gary Goode.'

Johnny frowned. His pale blue polo shirt had a predictable Ralph Lauren logo on the chest. His cream chinos were spotless, his loafers neatly tied – he was probably about to get on a yacht or a helicopter, heading to somewhere annoyingly exotic. But there was an energy to him – a restlessness – that told Amber that it wasn't so simple. His eyes darted around, as if expecting an unpleasant surprise.

He was already shaking his head. 'But you've already interviewed me. That big guy – Santini. With the hair. He came here with another officer.'

Marco.

'Well, we have some supplementary questions now.' Amber nodded authoritatively and set one foot inside. 'It shouldn't take too long to clear everything up.'

He blocked her and she realised he was taller than he had first appeared. His bare arms were sinewy beneath his tan. He could definitely do some damage if he wanted to.

She smiled up at him. 'It'll take five minutes, tops. And then I'll be out of your hair. OK?'

'Three.' He stepped aside. 'I have calls to make and I'm heading away on business soon.'

Business? Or escape?

He continued. 'My wife's away working and the nanny's at the dentist so I really am at full stretch here.'

Amber stepped into the long hallway, adorned with vases of fresh-cut flowers. From behind a closed door came the roar and gunfire of a game in full swing. *Call of Duty*, if she wasn't mistaken.

She had played it herself a few times, with Nina and her friends before they had become teenage enough to find her socially unacceptable. She had enjoyed it far more than she had let on, grinning as she racked up points and kills, thumbs hammering on the controller.

'My son, Christian.' Johnny gestured towards the closed door with his thumb. 'Rarely comes out in daylight. Still seems to live here despite having a place of his own.'

'Is he a daddy's boy, then?'

'Hardly.' A sideways glance. 'Barely listens to a word I say.'

'Classic teenager, then?'

'I suppose so.' Johnny led her rapidly along the corridor towards a door at the end.

The reason for his haste became apparent when they entered a huge kitchen to see a child, the same size as Jack and Yumi, chewing on some plastic keys in a play pen by the big oak table. A diamond tiara was perched in her golden hair. The air smelt of cinnamon and lilies, and piles of documents were spread across the hulking sideboard by the window. Amber longed to read them.

'Come here, Bear.' Johnny scooped his daughter up, burying his face in her hair, his whole face softening.

Amber took the chance to examine the tiara more closely. They couldn't be real diamonds, could they? On a one-year-old's tiara? Dear God. She looked around the kitchen and then back into the playpen. Yes, that really was a Dolce and Gabbana rattle lying on top of a Pucci cushion. Amber folded her arms. Good luck, Bear. Good luck having any kind of perspective in a house like this.

Johnny settled Bear down again and sat in a chair next to the play pen. He didn't offer Amber a chair or a drink, meaning she had to stand awkwardly in the middle of the kitchen like a courier waiting for a signature.

He flicked through the messages on his phone, making it very clear he had many better things to do than talking to her. 'So what else do you need to ask?'

She leant against the counter, pulling out a notebook from her pocket and clicking her pen into action. 'Can you tell me more about your relationship with Gary Goode?'

Johnny swore under his breath. He stood up as if to leave, and then sat down again. 'I've already talked about this. I barely knew the guy. He did a bid for our renovation – and we went with someone else. The End.'

Amber nodded, keeping her face impassive. 'You didn't know him in any other way?'

'No.'

'Not at all?'

'No.' Johnny shook his head, his voice rising a note. 'As I've already told your colleagues.'

'So...' Amber took her time. 'He wasn't blackmailing you?'

There it was. A glint of shock in Johnny's eyes.

'No. No one is blackmailing me.'

'Really?' Amber watched him.

'Really.'

'Interesting.' She tapped her pen against her chin. 'Because we have found evidence that Gary Goode was in fact doing just that. We have found messages to you from his burner phone over the past three months, and it's my guess that when we get into his accounts we'll find some sizeable payments from you too. Ringing any bells?'

Johnny didn't answer. A muscle twitched in his cheek.

'Far from being unknown to you, Gary Goode was extorting money from you in return for guarding your secret.'

'I don't have any secrets.' He leant down and kissed his little girl's hair. The message could not be clearer – I'm a family man, upright, trustworthy. Leave me alone.

Whatever.

Amber persisted. 'You don't have any secrets? Not even about the chip that's at the heart of your firm's success? The one that is the reason you are one of the richest men in the country?'

'Nope.' Johnny checked his watch again.

'How about Rajiv? Does that name ring any bells?'

Johnny rolled his eyes, but not before Amber saw a flicker of anxiety. 'I fired him. Years ago. What's he got to do with anything?'

'He says you stole the chip from him – that the tech was all his. That you took his designs and pretended they were your own. What do you have to say to that?'

'He's a liar.' That arrogant snarl. He put his Aviator shades on, clearly keen to hide. Frustration was building inside her. Why did this man believe he was better than everybody else? Why did he think it was OK to kill a man and let Amber's friend, her beautiful innocent friend, take the blame?

Well, Amber was here to make sure that he didn't get away with it.

'If he's a liar,' she said, savouring every word, 'then why did you pay Gary to keep it quiet?' She stood over him, staring right into those bloody sunglasses, seeing her own reflection, the veins on her neck taut, her lips tight. 'How do you explain that?'

Johnny gave one small shake of his head. 'I don't know what you're talking about.'

Amber wasn't surprised. A man like Johnny wouldn't cave after one interview. He hadn't got away with stealing another man's IP without being made of steel.

She dropped her voice. 'So... can I ask you one more question?'

He pushed his chair back and stood up. 'What?'

'Where were you at 3.30 a.m. on the third of February?'

'Here. Asleep.'

She exhaled. 'But you were meant to be in London, weren't you?'

'Yes.'

'But then you stayed here?'

'Yes.'

'Why?'

'I felt unwell.' His knuckles were white around his phone. Amber stepped back as he stood up. 'Which I have already told your colleagues. If they are your colleagues, that is. Can I see your ID again, DI Nagra?'

Amber smiled. Time to make her exit. To find proof of what he had done. 'You've seen it once. That's enough. And thank you for the information you have shared today – it's helped to clear up a few key issues. Now, I'll get out of your way and let you enjoy those calls you talked about.'

She walked briskly down the hall. At the top of the steps he stopped her, his hand on her arm. He put his face close to hers. 'Whoever you are, you're not police.'

She tipped her chin upwards. 'Yes I am.'

'No. Police always come in twos.' He gripped her arm just a little too tight. 'So I suggest you piss off and don't come back. I didn't kill Gary Goode and I didn't get blackmailed. I'm not that stupid. So get the hell out of here.'

A footstep sounded in the hall. Johnny turned, hand up. 'Christian! Not now.'

'But Dad, you promised that we could go together.' Amber saw a figure appear behind Johnny, face in shadow. 'And now that I've—'

'Not now, Christian!' Johnny blocked the doorway. 'Go away. Don't screw this up too.'

The arm and leg paused and then disappeared, footsteps slapping angrily along the hall. A door slammed.

It was pretty clear who the favourite child was.

'Teenagers.' Johnny's face was dark. 'Now piss off.' Amber descended the steps, feeling the chill of his eyes on her back every step of the way.

She was close now. Close to the truth.

She just needed to talk to Denise. She needed to get proof that Johnny had been paying Gary. Then she could make her move.

47

GARY

2.30 a.m.: Death minus one hour

Gary woke up with his feet in freezing sea water. For a moment he thought that Marg had got hold of him, that he was already tied up in a remote lock-up being water-boarded by one of her multitude of thugs. But instead, he was face down on the beach, sand in every possible orifice, sporting the mother of all headaches.

He must have passed out again. Memories fragmented and rearranged themselves: Marg's knife, Nina's yelling, Johnny's laughter. He shuddered. Maybe he was dead. Maybe this was hell – a never-ending showreel of the most humiliating moments of his life. He flexed an arm and saw a clump of seaweed encircling his wrist. He wasn't dead. He was just lying face down on the beach. Wet. Sandy. But alive.

Of course he was. He was Gary Goode. He would always live to fight another day. All he had to do was get up. He raised his head, his neck aching, only for a wave to come in and soak his face. He spluttered and coughed and pushed his way up to a sitting position of sorts, his head nearly resting on his knees.

He wondered how much time had passed. The lights from the pier were off, so it must be late. He wondered why he was here. His brain groped for answers and he had a vague feeling that he had been trying to get to Clio. Why? His head was as thick as that God-awful minestrone soup she used to make. You could cut that stuff with a knife.

Concentrate, Gary. He pressed his temples with his hands and realised how cold they were. What time was it? Denise would go nuts when he got home. Why had he been heading to Clio? A wave washed onto his shoes and he pushed his way up the beach, swearing as the pebbles grazed his backside. The ring. Of course. That was it. The ring.

Well, Gary was never one to give up. He had set out for the ring, and he was going to get it. And then he would go to the police and tell them exactly what Nina had done – how she had tried to kill him. That would show Clio. That would serve her right.

But then there was Marg and her midnight deadline, which no doubt he had missed. The thought of her accelerated Gary's attempts to move. He was wide open out here – dark beach, howling wind, not a soul in sight. He just had to get on his feet.

He tried once and fell. A second time and staggered. On his third attempt he stood,

head swimming, swaying slightly as the wind tried its best to push him back down. But he could not be stopped – not this time.

As he wove his way across the sand, he heard voices from the dunes over the waves roaring behind him. He marched on, realising with greater clarity than ever that absolutely everything was Clio's fault. If it wasn't for her, he wouldn't have had to fight so hard to keep the company afloat. If it wasn't for her, he would have the ring and Marg wouldn't be on his case.

If it wasn't for Clio he would be a happy man.

He walked forward, a man possessed. The ring. Clio. Nina. The ring. Clio. Clio. CLIO. He was going to bang on her door and bloody well have this out once and for all. He was going to tell her what he thought of her, make no mistake about it.

He made it to the bottom of the cliff path and started to climb, hauling himself up on the metal handrail, ignoring the tiredness and the pain.

He didn't see that someone was watching him. Someone hidden in the shadows, hoodie pulled up, eyes focused only on Gary.

He didn't see the person who would become his killer.

48

CLIO

Clio lay on the hard mattress, counting the bricks on the wall. After spending so much time here she knew that the fifth brick from the top had a brown stain that was shaped like a heart, while third from the bottom someone had scratched the words 'Get me out of here'.

Clio could see why. She knew now that she wasn't playing a role – instead the future stretched out, relentless and real as she lay trapped in a prison of her own making. It had been bad enough when she had believed she was saving Nina, but now it was even worse. Who had hit him a second time? Who was she accidentally protecting?

It was as hopeless as that time Nina had spilt Ribena all over Clio's wedding dress the day before she had walked down the aisle with Gary. Talk about a sign, if only Clio had been clever enough to understand it. Her tummy rumbled and she glanced at the tray on the floor, hoping it might have morphed from lumpy mash and gristle into real chips with vinegar and a bottle of ketchup. The food lay there, unappetising. Her hunger died. So this was how to diet.

She turned her face to the wall, running her fingers through her greasy hair. Half of her was desperate to retract her confession, but the half telling her to keep Nina's secret was stronger. She sighed, scratching at the rash that always flared up when she was away from her aqueous cream. She wondered what Amber and Jeanie were doing now. She hoped they were moving in now, ready to catch the killer. Clio was due in court soon. They were running out of time.

It was time to tell herself the story again – the one that had been comforting her every day and night in here. The story of Nina's life: of how her little girl would go on to glory, living a life of happiness doing what she loved to do. But now it didn't work. All it did was to remind Clio of how much she missed her daughter. She wanted to cuddle her girl, to hold her, to tell her how much she loved her. Clio let the tears roll down her face and onto her neck. She turned her head only to encounter yet another bump in the mattress and she wept even more.

She was never getting out of here, that much was clear. She sat up, and started to pace. Three steps. Turn. Three steps. Turn. Sweat prickled beneath her top. The heat was starting – beginning in her chest and radiating outwards, taking everything in its wake. She drank the little water that remained in her cup but knew that it was nowhere near enough. A dribble on a forest fire.

Her face was burning now and all she could think about was banging on the door and demanding that someone should let her out NOW. She wanted a shower. She wanted to run. She wanted to get a poster of Tom Cruise in *Cocktail*, stick it on the wall and 'Shawshank' her way out of here. She wanted to be free.

Just as she was leaning her head against the wall, seeking a cool that wasn't there, the door opened. For one miraculous second she thought it might be Amber and Jeanie.

But of course, it was Marco.

'Clio, you need to come with me.'

'OK.' She wiped her eyes and walked down the corridor,

hearing the click of her knee, wondering how her tummy was still pushing against her waistband even after three days of eating nothing. The only material advantage of being incarcerated appeared to be piles. Fantastic.

She entered the interview room, disturbed to find that it felt like home.

'You look rough.' Marco sipped a coffee, closing bloodshot eyes against the steam.

Clio snapped back, 'You don't look so good yourself.'

'Thanks.' He folded his meaty hands on the table, nostrils flaring. Clio wondered how science had come far enough to be able to get Richard Branson into space and yet still hadn't solved the problem of nasal hair.

Marco shifted in his seat. 'We're letting you go.'

Clio didn't know whether this was good or bad. Was Nina being arrested instead? 'What? Why?'

Silent Cop predictably said nothing.

Marco continued. 'Some new evidence has come to light.'

Nina. No. The trophy?

She must stay calm. 'What evidence?'

'That doesn't concern you. And it doesn't mean that you're off the hook – we're bailing you home while we follow up our new lead.'

Clio bit down her panic, looking around her, catching sight of something on the table in front of Marco. It was a plastic bag containing a necklace – a silver shark's tooth on a black plaited string. She had seen the necklace before, at the caravan.

And now it was here, inside an evidence bag.

'What is that doing here?' The words were out of her mouth before she could stop them.

'What?' Marco had been looking down at his notes.

Nina had been wearing it, Clio was almost sure of it.

She must protect her girl. 'My necklace.' Clio felt panic rising as she told the lie. 'Why is it here?'

'It's yours, is it?' Marco raised an eyebrow. 'Are you sure about that?'

'Yes.'

'Really?' He glanced at it, lying next to the evidence file for Gary's murder. She had seen him take papers and objects from this file and read them or show them to Clio during their previous interviews. The fact that Nina's necklace was now in it was bad news. Maybe Bez hadn't spotted it. Maybe the police had checked the beach hut. Maybe her daughter was about to get brought in. Clio would do anything – anything to stop it.

Marco's eyes were bright, appraising.

'It was found at the crime scene. It has Gary's DNA on it.'

Clio's stomach swooped. Why would Nina's necklace be there? With Gary's DNA?

'I must have dropped it.' Was it Nina's? Or was her mind playing yet more tricks on her? Her memory raced, trying to catch the image that was eluding her. 'It's always falling off. The catch is faulty.'

'Is it?' Marco folded his arms. 'Well, it was found earlier in a second fingertip search – wedged under a stone by the top of the cliff path.'

Clio's sluggish brain struggled to find the answers. Had someone planted it there to frame Nina? The thought was a bucket of ice down her back. Who would have done that?

Hang on. It wasn't Nina's. Clio caught her breath. It belonged to someone else.

DJ.

She looked at Marco, opening her mouth to tell him. She closed it again. If she told Marco about who really owned the necklace, then surely DJ would tell Marco about what Nina had done to Gary. Clio had to find another way.

'Um. How long will it take? To get me out of here?'

'A while yet.' He was already standing up. 'We'll put you back in the cells until we can process your release. And once you're allowed home, you have to stay there. And you're not allowed to leave town, OK? This doesn't mean you're off the hook.' He stared her full in the face. 'And I know it's not your necklace, Clio.'

'What?' She swallowed, her mind still preoccupied with DJ. 'What do you mean?'

'There's no catch on it, Clio. It ties. Now, I don't know why you lied, but maybe try telling the truth next time. OK?'

She dropped her eyes to the floor. 'OK.'

DJ. Something wasn't stacking up here. She remembered that iPad screen. The northern slang. Why had he been looking at that? Clio frowned, her brain retracing all the things Nina had told her about DJ. That he lived at the marina. That his parents' home was a terraced house in Moss Side and they didn't have enough money to visit him down here. That his friends were all back at home, so he mainly hung out with hers.

Who was this boy who had made her girl light up? And what was his real name? Nobody was actually called DJ. Why hadn't she noticed that before? Fear simmered inside her. She needed to be out there finding out more about him. Finding out if he was a threat to her daughter.

She couldn't tell the police anything without potentially implicating Nina. And so, as she was led back to her cell she started to pray, hoping that Bez could keep their daughter safe until Clio could get home and save her.

49

8 P.M.: 8 FEBRUARY 2023.

@SaveClio

Amber:– Checked Gary's bank accounts with Denise. Two payments landed since December from an offshore account. Am sure they're from Johnny. Am going back.

Amber:– Jeanie?

Amber:– Am going to find him. Address is The Magisterium, Granmore Road, South Sands, just in case.

Amber:– Now's the time to tell me not to.

Amber: OK, then. See you on the other side.

50

GARY

3.15 a.m.: Death minus fifteen minutes

As he trudged up the cliff path, Gary faltered. He looked around, his head aching, his mouth dry. It had taken him ages to get this far, not helped by the fact that he seemed to be permanently heading into the wind. He was exhausted, but his hatred of Clio drove him on. She wasn't going to hold him back any more. This time he was going to stop her.

This path was tough going, though. His feet kept slipping on the rocks and his legs felt as heavy as his spirits. He would never get there. He came to a halt again, breathing heavily. He heard a sound behind him and turned, peering through the darkness.

A tree branch snapped, bent double by the wind. Gary exhaled. Of course there was no one following him. It was mad o'clock and stormy – everyone sensible was in bed. Including Clio, blissfully sleeping, unaware of his approach.

That brought a smile to his face. How he would surprise her. He started to move again, with more energy now, making steady progress towards the top of the cliff and the caravan she now called home.

A figure was following him, moving lightly on trainered feet. They were in no hurry. They had all night and he was heading exactly to the perfect spot. A few more minutes wouldn't hurt.

Gary climbed upwards, stopping now and then to put a hand to his head, steadying himself before being propelled forward by hatred of his ex. It was amazing what rage could do, he thought. He went to pull out his phone, only to remember it wasn't there. Shit. Denise would give him hell when he got home.

But he could handle all that when he was good and ready. As he reached the top, his chest heaving, he was only metres away from Clio and her shabby little caravan home. The handrail ended and he took a faltering step alone.

One more step. Two. What time was it? He didn't know. What day was it? It didn't matter. He was Gary Goode. And...

'Hello.'

He whirled around. It took him a second to recognise the face grinning at him through the darkness. He blinked and looked again.

'What the hell are you doing here? What do you want?'

The person smiled slowly, and walked towards him. Gary saw the huge rock in their right hand and reached and pushed them, as hard as he could, his fingers brushing against metal and falling away. Then he turned and tried to run.

51

AMBER

Johnny didn't answer the door, but Amber was at the point where housebreaking appeared a mere trifle given the other things she had got up to this week. Lying, taking on a fake identity, impersonating a police officer, liaising with a known criminal – these activities had become as normal to her as investing in sleep apps that still saw her wide-eyed at 3 a.m. or trying to make her finances add up now that she didn't have a salary.

Her heart thudded as she crept over the thick carpet in what appeared to be a guest bedroom, ears trained for any sound or movement. She brushed wisteria leaves from her hair, stretching out her fingers after climbing up a drainpipe to a first-floor window that had been left ajar. She stopped to listen. Nothing. She pushed open the door, pressing herself against the wall as she eased out onto the landing, moving as quietly as she could. On her right she saw a huge bedroom, complete with a pink chandelier, fluffy cream rugs and a four-poster bed that was as wide as Amber's front room. A teal silk blouse lay on the pillow, a pair of Levi's at its side and on the floor she saw several colourful V-necks and polo shirts that must surely belong to Johnny. It looked like he had left in a hurry. No surprise there.

Amber crept past two more closed doors, stopping when she heard a creak on the stairs. She froze, barely breathing. Vivienne's Insta feed showed that she was up in London catching up with her absurdly expensive-looking friends, but of course that wasn't necessarily the truth. Amber waited, pulse spiralling, but no one appeared. She exhaled again, cautiously pushing open a door, only to see a toilet with a gleaming golden seat.

She exited hastily and kept looking. Door after door opened onto yet more bedrooms until at last Amber found what she was looking for, padding into a room with wooden shelves along one side, and red wallpaper flecked with gold on the other. A huge poster of the Fernandez Tech Fox dominated the back wall and by the bay window was a wide oak desk, covered in piles of paper. She tiptoed towards it, seeking information – hunting for proof that Johnny was Gary's killer. Bank statements, company accounts – anything that would demonstrate conclusively that the money paid to Gary had come from him. If Amber could find that then she had his motive nailed, right there in black and white. With his weak alibi it would be easy to make the case that Johnny had killed Gary to keep his secret quiet.

Amber surveyed the desk. For a tech entrepreneur Johnny seemed surprisingly reliant on old-school stationery. A stapler waited patiently behind a teetering pile of lever arch files. A red pot packed with highlighters had fallen onto its side, spilling its contents onto stacks of Post-its in green, orange and pink. Amber ran a finger over Sellotape, rulers and Bics, knowing that something was here – knowing that she must be close. She started leafing through everything, working systematically through the piles. She found restaurant invoices, scribbled notes, a bank statement showing an eye-watering overdraft, a memory stick.

Her heart was racing, every fibre of her alive. She was so absorbed that she didn't hear the car pulling up in the driveway. She read and searched on, so intent on her task that she missed the slam of the front door, the creak on the stairs, the footstep in the hall outside. It was only the squeak of hinges that brought her to life. She leapt forwards, crawling into the gap beneath the desk, folding herself small, hoping that whoever it was wouldn't know she was there.

She heard breathing, footsteps coming towards her.

And that was when she saw it, sticking out from beneath a pair of old slippers wedged between the back of the desk and the wall. A rental guarantee agreement for a marina apartment; typed, but with a note scrawled across the bottom in looping handwriting. Handwriting she had seen before.

She held her breath as the footsteps came to a halt in the middle of the room. Her brain was whirling as the pieces slammed together, clashing, cancelling one another out. A secret. A blackmailer. A lover. A daughter. A dream. An empire. A dark night. An opportunity.

She read the note again.

Dad – this is the place. Can't wait for you to see it. We could go sailing again, like we did with mum?

The footsteps began again, coming closer and closer to where she was hiding.

Dad. Johnny's dad was dead, so this must be from Christian. But the handwriting. Where had she seen it before?

And then she remembered. Her hand flew to her mouth and she gasped despite herself.

Bad move.

The feet were right in front of her now.

'What the hell are you doing here?'

She looked up and saw the burning eyes of a killer.

52

JEANIE

Tan was cooking a romantic dinner. Jeanie knew this because he wasn't wearing a hoodie. She knew this because he had swapped his slippers for trainers. And she knew this because absolutely every pan they owned was full of the collateral damage that happened every time he started to cook.

'It won't be long now.' He had a tea towel thrown over his shoulder which was smeared in the remains of a jar of chopped tomatoes. She spotted that his T-shirt had a green blob on the collar, but decided not to tell him.

She sat down at the kitchen table, rubbing her eyes, tired after the day's adventures and the conversation with Rajiv. She wanted to message Amber and find out what was going to happen next, but her phone was currently face down in a bag of rice after an unexpected swim at bath time.

She watched Tan, stirring and tasting with an expression of intense concentration on his face. He made cooking look as hard as the school science experiments Amber had always had to step in to save, just before Jeanie set her hair alight or inhaled a noxious gas. He was trying, she could see that. But there was no excitement fluttering in her belly, no anticipation spiralling inside. She was so tired after getting the twins down that all she wanted was to put her feet up and eat baked beans out of the can until she heard from Amber again.

She must make an effort. She must try to talk to him. She forced herself to her feet and walked over. She began to put her arms around him only for him to move to stir a pan, leaving her trying to cuddle the air. She sat down again, folding her arms.

'What's this all about, Tan?' She knew she sounded irritable. Terse. Ungrateful.

'I thought I'd make an effort.' He was grating cheese and inevitably one of his fingertips got involved.

'Damn.' He stuck it under the kitchen tap. The water rebounded off a stray chopping board and splashed up onto his lenses. Wordlessly, Jeanie held out a tea towel and he dabbed at his glasses.

Maybe romance really was dead. She wrinkled her nose. 'What's that smell? Didn't you empty the bin today?'

Instantly his shoulders stiffened and she kicked herself. Here he was preparing a lovely meal and all she could do was criticise him. She really had turned into her mum.

She must try again. For the first time in forever it was just the two of them. No children demanding attention with sticky fingers, smiles or tears. No workmates peering out of Zoom screens in the kitchen, or blaring out bleak homeless statistics while the twins ignored Tan's pleas for them to be quiet.

Just the two of them. Tan and Jeanie. The way it used to be.

She opened her mouth and closed it again. They had forgotten how to talk to each other, that was the truth of it. Everything had changed and she didn't understand why. She just knew she missed him.

'Jeanie?' Tan took her hand in his. 'I'm sorry.'

She tipped her chin towards him, really looking at him for the first time in weeks: his thick dark hair, his wide mouth, the smell of his cologne. She loved that smell. She took a chance and leant in and kissed him, her heart leaping at the softness of his lips, so familiar and yet so new.

'What are you sorry for, Tan?'

'For not seeing how difficult it is for you. With Clio gone. With the kids. Everything.'

Jeanie looked down at their fingers. She was going to say it was OK – to smooth things over as she usually did. But something stopped her. She wanted to tell the truth. She wanted not to be the wife she thought he wanted, but to be herself.

'I've been so lonely.' She couldn't look him in the eye.

'I know.' His thumb stroked the back of her hand. 'I...' He sighed. 'I thought the twins were all you wanted. More than me. More than – us.'

'No, it's not like that.' She glanced at him, regret rushing through her. 'I...'

'I always feel like I'm getting things wrong – when I bathe them and use the wrong pyjamas or when I change their nappies and they scream.' He was gathering momentum now. 'And sometimes you look so – so disappointed in me. And then with Amber and Clio you're different. Like they're your family rather than me.'

'They are my family, Tan. But...'

'And I know I've locked myself away in my study, or stayed late at work. But I didn't know what else to do, really. Work was the one thing I had going for me. Until today.'

'Today?'

'Yeah.' He hung his head, his handsome, kind head. 'That's why I was so worried about my laptop.' He was playing with her fingers now, anxiety stamped across his face. 'I had to give this presentation to a potential donor. And if they don't come on board the boss is going to have to cut jobs. Including...'

'Yes?'

'Including mine, Jeanie.' Two spots burned in his cheeks and Jeanie realised how much he had been keeping from her.

'But you're brilliant at what you do.' He had been shielding her, protecting her. She understood now. 'They're not going to fire you.'

'It's a small charity, Jeanie. And times are tough. The cost of living crisis, grants getting smaller. It costs twice as much to shelter a family of four for a week as it did two years ago. So they'll have to cut down on caseworkers like me, won't they?' His words were pouring out now, bubbling as much as the sauce he was cooking on the stove. He reached out and stirred it, still talking.

'Because the families have to come first – of course they do. I know that. But I don't know what I'll do instead. I don't know how I'll feed us all. I...'

Jeanie had forgotten how big his heart was.

She reached out her arms and drew him close. 'We're a team, Tan. It's not down to you to feed the family. It's down to *us*.' She leant back, putting her hand on his cheek, her heart quickening when he turned his head and kissed it.

'So I thought I'd make a big gesture tonight.' Tan indicated the pans. He grinned. Maybe he was still in there. Maybe she could find her way back to him. They were still Jeanie and Tan, weren't they? The couple who had met in a Tokyo cinema and somehow made it all the way to Sunshine Sands.

The bag of rice started to vibrate. She turned to Tan.

'Sounds like my phone is back. Is it OK if I check it?'

'Sure.' He kissed her gently on the lips. 'It might be about Clio.'

'Thank you.' She pulled the phone out and looked at the screen.

'Oh God, no.' She shook her head, suddenly cold. 'No, Amber. NO.' She dialled Amber's number, pacing frantically as she waited for her friend to pick up. Why had Amber gone to Johnny's alone? Why couldn't she ever wait for help like a normal human being?

'It's nearly ready.' Tan spoke over his shoulder while prodding a blackened piece of meat.

'Tan.' Amber's number rang out. Every instinct Jeanie had was telling her this was bad – as bad as the night Amber had come over with a bottle of whisky and told Jeanie that she had been fired. She remembered tucking her comatose friend up on the sofa, wiping the tears from her cheeks.

Jeanie knew what she had to do. 'Tan, I'm sorry. I know you've gone to so much trouble, but I've got to go.'

'What?' He turned.

'I'm sorry.' Jeanie looped her arms around him. 'Amber needs me. She's gone alone to Johnny Fernandez's place, to try to get proof he killed Gary. She left well over an hour ago and I can't get hold of her. I've got to go after her and check that she's OK. Do you see?'

His face was set. 'You're setting out to meet a potential killer? On your own?'

'Yes, Tan. It's what I have to do.' Jeanie thought of Amber bravely heading into danger, of Clio taking the blame for her daughter's mistake. It was Jeanie's turn now.

'But...'

She held up her hands, stopping his words. It was her time to talk. 'You know, if I don't go, they'll forgive me.' Her eyes stung with tears. 'I know that. They've done it before, they've been doing it for years. Clio and Amber are always there for me – ever since we made friends in PE. Whether I'm splitting my shorts on a trampoline aged sixteen or whether I'm desperate for babies my body won't let me have. They are always there for me – they rescue me. And now I'm going to rescue them.'

She kept her head up, holding his eyes. 'And you might think I'm crazy, but you know what? I hope the twins have friends like Clio and Amber. And I hope they run to help them without a second thought.'

Tan didn't move.

Now Jeanie's tears were falling. 'Tan. Please. Try to understand. Amber and Clio are my family. But you are too. And I'm scared you might not love me – like they do. Forever. I'm scared I might have lost you.'

The words hung in the air as big as a skywritten banner.

'Right.' Tan started untying his apron.

'Right?'

'OK.'

'OK?' She stared at him, her heart beating wildly. 'OK, what?'

He walked to the table and picked up his car keys. 'I do love you. I love you so much that I'm coming with you. We can't have you going on your own, can we?' He turned off the hob. 'It would probably have tasted crap anyway.'

Her smile started in her heart and spread all over her body. 'This one might have been the game changer. You never know.'

He nodded. 'I'll choose to believe you.' He held out her phone. 'Thousands wouldn't. I'll get the twins in the car, OK? And yes, I will park miles away from the house and no, I won't let them out of my sight. And I'm calling the police while I'm at it. We need back-up.'

'OK.' Jeanie started dialling Amber again.

The number rang and rang and rang.

53

GARY: DEATH O'CLOCK

Gary had got away. Somehow, he had escaped his killer.

So he was invincible, after all.

He had made it to Clio's bottom step, and man, was he about to give her what for. He would take everything. Not just the ring. But everything.

And then he felt it. The slam of rock into bone. His vision was blurring. Blood was rushing through him and out of him, spattering onto the steps he was trying to climb. He turned, wanting to laugh at his assailant, wanting to prove his immortality. No one could keep him down. No one...

He was Gary Goode and he would live forever.

Just as he thought it, he fell, heavily, loudly, onto Clio's step.

Because Gary Goode was far from immortal. Gary Goode was dead. And the person who had killed him stood over his body and laughed, before pulling their hood up and walking away into the night.

54

AMBER

Amber stared at the figure looming above her.

'DJ?' He looked so different. No baggy shorts, for starters. Instead, he was in jeans, hair pulled back into a ponytail, dark red T-shirt stretched tight across his chest. His slouching ease was gone and he was bouncing on his toes like a ninja, all muscle and energy.

Amber could still take him down though, and she started to unfold herself from underneath the desk in readiness.

He pushed her to the ground again, more roughly than she had anticipated.

'DJ, what's going on?' She noticed the way his hand rested on the pocket of his jeans. A knife? A gun? She felt strangely calm, her mind trying to find the answers. DJ was here, but he didn't look like DJ any more. His accent was different – more Eton than Manchester now. And the writing – last seen on a note in Clio's caravan. A note addressed to Nina.

And it clicked.

'Oh my God, you're *Christian*. You're Johnny's son. You're Christian AND you're DJ.' She gave a low whistle. Now the pieces were falling into place. Christian didn't want his father's secret getting out – for financial reasons? Maybe he had his own plans? Either way, when Nina had run back to tell DJ/Christian that she had hurt Gary, it had presented him with the perfect opportunity to finish Gary off. Christian was DJ. DJ was Christian. Nina's boyfriend was a killer.

Oh, poor Nina.

Christian stared at her, his hands moving in a slow clap. 'Well, give the detective a medal.' He stared at her, nose wrinkled, as if she was a piece of rubbish that had just missed the bin. 'Why are you under my dad's desk? Nosing around, are you?'

Amber wanted DJ back again. DJ with his baggy T-shirts and his kind smile, his hair flopping over his face.

She decided to try to blag her way out.

'I got a bit lost trying to find the loo. Your dad invited me over.'

He folded his arms, leaning down so close she could smell the spearmint on his breath. 'Liar. Dad left about thirty minutes ago, driving like a madman, all the way to London, if I'm not much mistaken. Doesn't want to be anywhere near me, apparently, even though I've done him a favour.' He rolled back and forth on the balls of his feet, a grenade with its pin pulled out. 'Well, screw him.' Anger flared in his eyes.

Amber needed a weapon but there was nothing but thick carpet down here. Not a paperclip, not a staple.

'So…' She smiled up at him. 'Can I come out?' She snuck a hand into her pocket, reaching for her phone.

'I'll have that, thank you.' He grabbed it and threw it out of the window. 'Oh, and while I think about it…'

He walked towards the door, reaching for the key. She had to force her way out of here before he locked them in. She got up, starting to sprint only to come to a halt as he pulled out a gun, turned, and pointed it right at her heart.

No.

Amber had been at gunpoint before, but only in training, facing a weapon firing blanks. She waited, her heart thumping. She had drunk tea with this boy – or this man? – but she hadn't known him. She had laughed at his jokes, bought him drinks and yet never sensed the evil that lay inside.

'I'm sorry about your dad, Christian.'

He shook his head. 'Don't you dare pity me.'

She held up her hands. 'No, no, I'm not. I don't pity you.' Her mind whirred. 'Why would I – you're clever, aren't you?'

'I think so.' The barrel never wavered, even as he sat down in his father's green leather office chair. 'Not that anyone around here noticed.'

'So, let's see.' She stared him straight in the eye. 'You knew Gary was a problem. Maybe your dad told you about him?'

Christian sneered. 'No. But uncovering the blackmailer was one of the little projects Dad liked to give me. After I left my last shit-hole of a school and got the job at the marina, he rented a flat for me, in return for a few "favours". One of them was tracing the blackmailer's IP. After I'd got the name I did some investigation, found out more about Gary, checking out his weak spots. I went to his house, talked to his team – you know.'

'And... Nina?'

Christian smiled, his eyes suddenly alight. 'Nina. Yes. That was luck. Or fate. One day, when I was staking out Gary's office, I saw her, waiting for him. She wanted to get him to release some of the money Clio had put into the company, apparently. She was just trying to help her mum – she never sees how bloody useless Clio is...'

Amber bit her tongue so hard it hurt.

'And she was all sad and teary, so I put on an accent, made up a name, and comforted her. I thought she might be useful.'

Amber clenched her fists but knew she had to keep him talking.

'So you got together with her? Not because you actually liked her, but as a source? Very smart.' She feigned admiration while wanting to rip his head off with her bare hands.

'Wrong.' His gaze was unnerving, a cat observing a mouse before the kill. 'No wonder the police fired you. I love Nina – everything I'm doing is for the two of us. She's my life, and I'm going to give her an amazing future. I'm going to show her how much I love her, starting tonight.'

'But...' The zeal in his eyes scared her. 'She doesn't know who you really are. She doesn't know what you've done.'

He shook his head. 'She would love me even more if she knew.'

'But you let her think she had killed Gary.' Amber knew she should be careful, should weigh her words, but she was so angry she couldn't hold them back. 'There's no way she'll ever trust you again.'

'You don't know her like I do.' He walked towards her, holding the gun steady in his right hand. 'Now, lovely though it is to chat, I have to go. Nina and I are going away.' His smile knifed her. 'And we're never coming back.'

NO.

Amber launched herself at him, wrestling and scratching. She had surprise on her side and she wrenched at the fingers holding the gun, her legs kicking out. He let out a roar as the gun fell to the floor. Amber kicked it away, going for another punch. She missed and he grabbed her arm, twisting so hard she screamed. She started a desperate list of resolutions. If she got out of here, she would be a better person: she would say yes to one of her foster brother's frequent invitations; she would even be honest with her friends about the reason she was fired.

If only she got the chance.

'Don't you dare get in my way.' Christian's voice was a hiss. He was making for the gun, holding her so tight now she could barely breathe. 'No one is going to stop me.'

'Don't bet on it.' All Amber had left were her teeth and she sank them into his hand as hard as she possibly could. He let go of her, howling, and she lurched for the gun. His hands closed around her ankles, trying to pull her away, dragging her across the carpet.

But she was nearly there. The gun was inches away and she pulled even harder to free herself, breath rasping, fingers straining.

'Don't you dare, bitch.' He let go of her ankles and leapt forward. Their heads collided in mid-air and for a moment all Amber could see was stars.

'Fuck!' The pain was unbelievable. She tried to shake it away, and tasted blood in her mouth. But the gun was still there. Waiting. All she had to do was get to it.

With a final dizzying lunge she reached it, her fingers closing over the barrel. But his were there too.

'Get off!' She scratched at his arms. 'You don't get to do this.'

Christian snarled. 'I'll do what the hell I want. Now let go.'

'No way.' She tried to headbutt him. He tried to knee her in the groin. Nobody was winning, but she had to keep on fighting. Nina wasn't going to be taken away – not while Amber drew breath. She planted herself as squarely as she could on both knees, leaning backwards and pulling with all her might.

'That's it!' Christian screamed so loudly her ears were ringing. 'You've wasted enough of my time now! I'm going to kill you, with my bare hands if I have to.'

Amber closed her eyes and clung on to the gun, hoping for victory, hoping for rescue, hoping for a miracle.

Hoping she wasn't going to be the next person to die.

55

JEANIE

Jeanie had forgotten that Tan was a seriously good driver. For a while they had been stuck in second gear, navigating the snarl of the town on match night, but soon they were speeding towards Johnny's house, the twins asleep in the back, Tan's eyes checking the satnav as he screeched round corners with pinpoint precision. If Jeanie weren't so terrified about Amber, she would ask him to pull into a gateway and kiss the hell out of him.

But she was terrified. As they got closer to the Fernandez house she kept picturing her friend, beaten, bruised, dead. Her stomach clutched. If only she hadn't let her phone get wet her best friend might not be in mortal danger right now.

'Can we go any faster?'

'Not really.' Tan spoke through gritted teeth. 'The car's starting to judder. I think it's in shock.'

'Me too.' Jeanie's brain unhelpfully summoned an image of Amber's lifeless corpse.

Tan squeezed her hand before turning through the open gates into Johnny's driveway. Tan rocketed up the gravel drive and braked sharply. Jeanie was out before he had switched the engine off, stumbling over her own feet in her eagerness to get towards the house and find her friend.

Tan put a hand on her arm. 'Jeanie, I don't think you should go in there alone.'

Suddenly she was sixteen again, standing on the edge of the diving board.

He pulled her to him. 'The police will be here soon. We should wait for them.'

'No.' Every second counted. She looked up at the vast house. Somewhere inside all those windows and doors, behind the pillars and the heavy front door was her friend. And her friend needed her.

No more hiding. She was going to dive in.

'I'm going in, Tan.' She kissed him on the lips. 'You stay with the twins.' She cupped his cheek. 'I'll see you soon.'

'But Jeanie...'

'I have to go.' She pressed his fingers in hers and sprinted towards the house, running up the steps and throwing herself at the front door. It remained shut, impassive, impossible.

'Come on, Jeanie.' She turned and ran around the side of the house, past the columns, past the over-trimmed hedges, past the rows of flowers as neat as any army on parade, and round to the back. Her feet crunched on gravel, her breath ripped through her. There must be an open window somewhere, a ledge she could climb onto, a door with a broken lock.

She charged at the huge bi-fold doors that spanned the width of the terrace, but only succeeded in bruising her shoulder. Then she heard a scream. Panicking, she redoubled her efforts to find a way in. How could they have so many bloody windows and scrupulously remember to lock every single one? Seriously?

She jumped over a low wall that ran around the side of the kitchen and tried one of the back doors. There it was. The magical squeak of rusty hinges opening. She was in. It was pitch dark and smelt of mud and wellies. Jeanie bumped into a bucket, a bench and what appeared to be a statue before remembering she could use her phone to light her way.

She made it through to the kitchen and ran towards another scream. She flicked her curls out of her face as she sprinted past a long table, nearly tripping over an indignant cat and hurtling out into the hall. That scream again – it chilled her bones. It was coming from above her. She looked around, chest heaving, wishing she put on a decent bra.

Another scream, this one even louder. Stairs. She had to find the stairs. She ran down the hall, past door after door, attacking the steps as ferociously as a *Gladiators* competitor facing the final Eliminator. At the top, she heard another scream, a little to her right. Amber was guiding her in, as clear as an air traffic controller at Heathrow.

Jeanie accelerated towards the sound. It was definitely Amber. It reminded her of that awful dance class where Amber had been forced to wear a swirling pink dress and had shrieked so loudly that their teacher had given her detention for a week.

Jeanie stopped outside a heavy wooden door. She pushed it. It didn't budge. She kicked it. And hurt her foot.

She had to get in there. A run up. That should do it.

She tried again, bouncing back, her head hitting the floor as she fell.

'Shit!' Her hands went to her head in agony. 'That bloody hurts!'

'Jeanie?'

Jeanie crawled towards the door. 'Amber?'

'Can you untie me please? When you've finished doing whatever the hell you're doing out there?'

Relief flooded in. Amber was being sarcastic. She must be feeling OK.

'Untie you?' Jeanie leant against the door, feeling useless. 'But I can't open the door.'

'Try turning the handle? He got a call as he was leaving and I didn't hear him lock it.'

'But...' Jeanie tried it and the door swung open. 'Oh.' She flicked on the light and winced as she saw Amber. Her friend was on the floor, her back to the leg of a heavy oak desk, her hands tied behind her back, blood running down her face.

'Oh my God.' Jeanie ran over and hugged her close. 'Are you OK?'

'I'm fine. Don't worry. He had a gun, but...'

'A gun?' Jeanie's hand flew to her mouth. 'Oh my God, I...'

'Jeanie. Just untie me. I got hold of it and threw it out of the window.'

'A gun?'

'Yes. We had a fight, he was about to shoot me, then I threw the gun out of the window, he punched me and tied me up, and here we are.'

'But...' Jeanie's brain appeared to have shut down. She sat back on her heels. 'Are you OK? Did he hurt you? Did Johnny hurt you?'

'Not Johnny, no.'

'What? Then who...?' Jeanie looked around, wildly.

'Christian. His son.'

'His son?' Jeanie frowned. 'Why would he...?'

'Please untie me.'

Jeanie tried as best she could, given her trembling fingers. 'I don't understand.'

'There's more I'm afraid. Christian is DJ.'

'DJ? Nina's DJ?'

'Yep.' Amber nodded. 'Nina's boyfriend is Johnny's son, who was pretending to be DJ. And I think he killed Gary.'

Jeanie reeled. 'DJ?'

'Yes, DJ.'

'But...' Jeanie thought of Nina's face when she looked at DJ. What a horrible surprise she had in store. 'Why...?'

'Unclear. But I blame daddy issues. Or money.'

'Shit.' Jeanie became aware her mouth was hanging open. 'Where did he go?' She found some scissors on the desk and bent down.

Amber gasped in relief as Jeanie snipped through the ties. She stood up, flexing her fingers. 'He's gone to get Nina. And he has probably picked up the gun. So we need to get over there. Now.'

'OK.' Jeanie didn't hesitate. 'Let's go.'

56

CLIO

Clio ran all the way back to the caravan park, past groups of men shouting at each other about referees and goals and fouls after some kind of local cup match, past couples on dates and workers walking home. She didn't really take any of it in – all she could see was her girl and the man who might not be what he seemed. As she ran, she tried to call Amber and Jeanie to ask them to get to the caravan site, to see if Nina was OK. Neither of them picked up. And then there she was at her own front door, chest heaving, mouth dry.

There was Nina sitting on the sofa, feet tucked up beneath her, textbooks piled to her left. Clio could see her through the window, looking up at DJ. Relief flooded through her. Her girl was OK.

But then she looked again. Was that DJ? His hair was tied back ruthlessly into a ponytail, and where were his shorts? Clio peered more closely, seeing Nina's arms arcing wildly through the air, as if she was defending herself. Adrenaline spiked and before she knew what she was doing, Clio was on the move.

She burst through the front door. 'Nina. Are you OK?'

'Mum.' Her daughter's face was stained with tears. 'Mum. Help me. Please.' Her voice was so tiny, just as it had been all those years ago when Clio had decided to leave Bez and Nina had asked her why.

Clio clenched her fists. Whatever DJ was doing he could piss off and do it somewhere else.

'I think it's time for you to go, DJ.' He turned, and she saw this wasn't the DJ who loved her daughter, who wrote her notes, who lay patiently at her side as she studied. This version had a chill in his eyes, his mouth set, a muscle flickering in his cheek. Behind him the TV was on mute, contestants in a game show mouthing answers while Lee Mack shook his head in mock despair.

'Get out.' Clio was right next to him now. He stared at her, unblinking, DJ recast in marble. His T-shirt was so tight she could practically count his ribs.

He spoke in a cut glass drawl. 'I'm not going anywhere. Not without Nina.'

Clio blinked. 'Why are you talking like that?'

'Like what?' He folded his arms. 'I can talk like a Texan too. Would that be better?' He grinned. 'Oh ma Lord I just love this cute little itty-bitty van of yours.'

His face reset as he held his hand out to Nina. 'Now. Let's go.'

Clio put a hand protectively on Nina's shoulder. She had no idea what his sudden transformation meant, but she knew that Nina wasn't going anywhere with him. 'Nina is staying here.'

He folded his arms. 'Really? You too?

'What do you mean?'

'Your bloody friend was trying to stop me too. Until I put a stop to her.'

Clio flinched. 'What? Who? How...?'

'You'll find out soon enough.' He sighed. 'It's getting late. We have to go now. Come on, Nina.'

'No.' Nina shook her head, burying her face in her hands.

'I was trying to do this the nice way, but now you've given me no choice.' He pulled out a gun.

An actual bloody gun.

Clio didn't hesitate, clenching her fists and stepping in between him and her girl. She was back in the delivery room, cradling her baby, swearing she would do anything she could to protect her. She looked around, searching for the kettle, for any kind of weapon that she could aim at this devil who was trying to harm her daughter.

'No, no, no.' Un-DJ shook his head. He pressed the gun against Clio's forehead.

'Mum.' Nina lunged forwards only for DJ to push her away. He spoke to her through clenched teeth. 'No, Nina. No. Don't be so stupid. We're going away – just like we planned.'

'You're hurting me, DJ.'

He didn't seem to care. He turned back to Clio, gun steady.

'Move a muscle and I'll kill you.'

This couldn't be happening. Clio had made this boy peanut butter on toast and listened to him banging on about boats and about how much he missed his mum. Had everything been a lie? 'What are you doing? Why are you talking like that, DJ?'

'My name is Christian. And this *is* my voice.' Un-DJ's face oozed contempt. 'My real voice. Can't you recognise a fake Manchester accent when you hear one? Being an actress, and all?'

Clio bridled. All these weeks of welcoming him in – of embracing him as Nina's beloved boyfriend. Amber was right. Clio's radar needed work.

'DJ? Please.' Nina's voice made Clio want to weep. Her daughter was a little girl again, lost in the supermarket, asking strangers where her mum had gone. Somewhere deep inside Clio, steel glinted. She didn't care what happened to her – all that mattered was getting Nina out. Every limb tingled with the need to hurt this intruder, this liar, this fake.

She had her fingers on her phone.

'No.' He grabbed it, throwing it into the sink.

Nina whimpered, a dog kicked by its master. 'Why are you doing this?'

'I told you, love.' The word was a lash. 'I'm going away.' His voice was flat, as if he was choosing bathroom tiles from a catalogue. 'And you're coming with me, Nina.'

Nina shook her head.

'But DJ, I—'

'Christian. My name is Christian. Christian Fernandez.'

'What?'

'And we're going to go to the marina and sail away. Just like we planned.'

'You planned, not me.' Nina pleated a cushion between trembling fingers. 'I want to do my A levels, to be a doctor.' Clio ached to hold her. 'And you can't just leave your job, can you? Your family?'

DJ/Christian snorted derisively. 'I don't have a family since Mum died – Dad's made that very clear. I'm done with him. I'm done here. It's time to go.'

'But I'm not done, DJ. I mean, Christian.' Nina fought to get her words out between sobs. 'I want to stay here.'

Christian tightened his finger around the trigger. 'You don't mean that.'

Clio kept her voice low, trying to calm him. 'Why do you need Nina with you?'

He put his finger on the trigger. 'Because I love her.'

'If you loved her, you'd give her a choice.'

'Shut up.' He raised the barrel until it pointed at her head. 'Shut the hell up.'

'Don't kill her!' Nina's courage pierced Clio's heart. 'I'll come with you, OK?' She took his hand. 'But can you let Mum go? She's got nothing to do with this.'

Christian gave a decisive shake of his head. 'No. She knows my plan. It's too risky.' He took Nina's hand and jerked her onto her feet.

Nina stood, her eyes glistening with tears. 'Why are you doing this to me?'

He shook his head impatiently. 'I told you. Because I love you. You killed Gary – I'm trying to help you.'

'No, *you* killed him.' Clio knew this with a fierce certainty. 'It was you. Your necklace was found at the scene with Gary's DNA on it – that silver shark's tooth one. I knew I recognised it when I saw it at the station. So stop blaming Nina.' For once Clio welcomed the fire that was growing inside her. It made her bigger, braver. She ran at him, head down, aiming every inch of her five-foot-one frame squarely at his chest.

'Oh Clio.' Christian neatly stepped to the side so Clio dropped to the floor, head banging against a can of paint. 'Always so dramatic.' He pulled some cable ties from his pocket, tying her wrists behind her.

'Why are you doing this?'

'Insurance policy, now I know the police are after me. That bloody necklace – I knew I'd dropped it somewhere. Having a hostage might help us get away.' He took Clio and shoved the gun barrel into her back, pushing her towards the door.

'Get a move on. And no noise or you're dead.'

Clio walked on jelly legs, down the steps and towards the blue sedan that was parked outside. Please let someone be around. Anyone. Bez. Where the hell was Bez?

Christian prodded her and she staggered forward. 'Get in the back.' His eyes narrowed. 'Nina? You drive.'

Clio slid into the back seat and he slammed the door. Nina slumped heavily into the driver's seat, gripping the steering wheel in shaking fingers. Clio wanted to tell her that everything would be alright. She wanted to hug her, to kiss her, to reassure her.

But Christian was in the passenger seat, his gun on his lap. 'The marina. Drive.'

Nina shakily put the key into the ignition and turned it.

As the car moved forwards, Clio found herself praying for a miracle, even though she knew it wouldn't come.

57

AMBER

Amber was used to racing along dark roads in pursuit of criminals, but she wasn't accustomed to singing nursery rhymes at the same time. She had wanted to drive but Tan had been unusually insistent, so now here she was in the middle, squeezed in between the car seats, the twins either side of her with little thumbs plugged into little mouths. Yumi's ponytail was sticking up like a radio antenna while Jack was apparently trying to eat his own hand. Amber came to the end of a resounding rendition of 'Baa Baa Black Sheep' and eyed them hopefully, searching for signs of sleep. All she got was a burp from Yumi.

She shifted uncomfortably, abandoned rice cakes crackling beneath her, and wished they could drive even faster. Every second mattered. She thought of the madness she had seen in Christian's eyes and fear pulsed through her: fear for Nina, fear for what he might do to her if she didn't play along.

They screeched into the caravan park to see that Clio's caravan was in darkness. Bez had just pulled up and was opening the door of his pick-up. Amber leant over Yumi and opened the window. 'Where is she?'

His head turned infuriatingly slowly. 'Who? Clio?'

'No. Not Clio. She's at the station. I'm talking about Nina.'

'No. Clio's been let out on bail.' Bez frowned. 'The police called me because she forgot her wallet, apparently. Very Clio. Do you know, once she managed to—'

Amber cut in. 'Where is she, then?' Dread began to creep. 'Is she in your van, Bez?'

He peered across the site. 'I don't think so. No lights on.'

'Shit.' Amber had thought that Clio would be safe at the station at least. She edged past Yumi and ran to the caravan, pressing her face against the windows, wanting to see red hair with blue tips, to hear singing, to feel the noise and energy of her friend.

Bez came and stood next to her. 'Where's Nina gone?'

Jeanie was at Amber's side. 'We think DJ has taken her.'

'Taken them where? For some food, do you think? The Codfather, maybe. I...'

Amber held up a hand. 'No, Bez. He hasn't taken them for fish and chips. He's taken them at gunpoint.'

'DJ?' Bez's face was a question mark. 'Nina's DJ? Nah.' He took his glasses off, polishing them against his jumper. 'This is a wind-up, yeah?'

'No, Bez.' Jeanie set him straight. 'His real name is Christian. And he killed Gary.'

'What?' Bez's smile froze on his face. 'But...'

'And we think he might have Clio and Nina.' Jeanie laid a hand on his arm.

'No.' Bez ran a hand over his hair. 'What do we do?'

Amber exhaled. 'We go and find them. Now.'

Bez puffed out his cheeks. 'Please tell me this is a joke?'

'No, it's not.' Amber wished he would catch up. 'I think the marina is our best bet. He kept talking about sailing away with Nina.'

Bez's hands became fists. 'Over my dead body.'

'Great minds, Bez, great minds.' Amber was moving already. 'Johnny has a boat moored there. Once Christian's on it, he could take Clio and Nina anywhere.'

They didn't have much time. Jeanie was already back at the car. 'We need to go after them.' She turned to Tan, pushing her unruly curls out of her eyes. 'I'll go with Amber, OK? You call the police again and keep the kids away – I don't want them to get hurt.'

'No way.' He shook his head. 'I'm not letting you go alone.'

Jeanie's voice was firm. 'No, Tan. Keep them safe. I'll be OK. I promise.'

They shared a long look.

'OK.' Tan kissed her. 'Stay safe.'

'I will.' Jeanie turned away.

'I love you, Jeanie.'

Jeanie's face lit up. 'I love you too.'

Bez revved his engine and Jeanie and Amber climbed up into his pick-up, slamming the door behind them as they bumped along the clifftop road that wound its way down towards the marina. Towards whatever might happen there. Towards whatever came next.

58

JEANIE

'Oh God, I forgot how huge this place is.' Jeanie pressed her hands to her cheeks, staring out at the ranks of boats moored along endless pontoons. 'We'll never find them.'

'Why not?' Amber stalked up and down outside the marina office, which was unhelpfully empty. 'We just have to split up. We can do it. And besides...' She gestured out towards the water. 'It's February so there's not as much going on, is there? We just have to check the few that have lights on. He must be in one of them.'

'Maybe the police will get here?' Jeanie looked hopefully towards the main road, but Amber took her by the shoulders, her eyes gleaming in the half-light from the marina lights.

'Until they do, we are all there is. And we have to find them, OK?'

'OK.' Jeanie swallowed her fears and scanned the sleeping boats, their masts reaching up towards the sky, sails furled. It was eerily quiet. It was decades since Jeanie had been here – trying not to puke during endless childhood Sundays on her dad's beloved schooner: aged eight, ten, twelve, freezing her bits off as they ploughed through choppy grey seas; gritting her teeth for the sheer joy of his smile and of his company.

'Where is he?' Bez thundered down the path towards them, holding something long and orange in his hand.

Amber gestured towards it. 'What's that?'

He shrugged. 'A plastic golf club. It was all I could find in the pick-up.'

'Great.' Amber strode on. 'That should really help defend us against a loaded gun.'

Bez loped along beside her. 'I was thinking I could clout him on the head?'

Jeanie followed them. Her attempt to ignore the water wasn't going very well. It was everywhere. Lapping, dark, a threat. She set foot on a pontoon, jumping back when she felt it sway beneath her. Oh God.

Amber continued, moving at speed, staring into the window of a small motorboat as she passed. 'Nope. They're not in there.' She carried on, moving fast, hands in her pockets. Jeanie followed, breathing slowly, carefully. She closed her eyes, forcing the panic away.

And as she opened them, she saw it – the Fernandez Fox logo on the side of the hulking motorboat at the end of the pontoon, tied to the hammerhead berth.

'They're over there.' Jeanie started running. 'Look, there's a light on.' Through the darkness she could see a dark figure, bent over, grappling with a rope. 'He's taking the line up.' Jeanie was in the lead now, her feet skittering along the path, trying to get to there in time. The figure leapt back onto the boat and Jeanie heard the chug of the engine.

'Shit.' Amber streaked past her. The figure on the prow aimed something in her direction.

He fired.

All the breath left Jeanie's body. 'Oh God. Amber!'

Her friend was still moving. She didn't stagger. She didn't fall. Instead, she leapt across the narrow gap that was opening up between the pontoon and the boat, and landed on the low bathing platform at the back, dropping down onto her knees.

Jeanie froze, expecting another shot. But someone had appeared behind Christian from the doors leading below deck, and was trying to grab his legs. Jeanie could see curls and long limbs and a sob escaped her. Nina. Nina was still alive. Thank God.

Christian turned, yelling, clearly trying to get Nina to let go. He wobbled but then regained his balance, raising a hand to knock Nina to the floor. Jeanie heard a scream.

And all the while the gap was getting wider.

But, as Jeanie ran towards them, she realised Christian had forgotten something. The long black power cable was still plugged in, pegging the boat to the pontoon. It gave Jeanie a chance, if only she could dare to take it.

Even as she thought this, he spotted the problem. Nina was on him again, and he whacked her across the face with the gun. She fell and this time didn't move again. Jeanie was there now, at the edge of the pontoon, the water frothing beneath her. Christian was revving the engine, trying to jerk the power cable out of its socket so he could get away.

Bez grabbed the end. 'I'll hold on.' His face was set. 'For as long as I can.'

'Jeanie!' Amber held out a hand to her, the other clinging to the rail at the back of the boat's diving platform. 'Come on!'

Jeanie stood paralysed, her heart pounding. The engine grew louder and the boat bucked against Bez and the cable. The water below was a threat, everything she was scared of, promising to swallow her up again. She trembled. She couldn't do this. She would drop again – drop to the bottom and never return.

'Jeanie?' The belief on Amber's face broke Jeanie's heart. She couldn't live up to it.

The gap was one metre now, maybe more. Bez was holding on to the cable for all his might but the boat was about to escape his clutches. Amber stood, her hand outstretched.

Jeanie felt failure seeping through her again. She had screwed this up, just like she screwed up motherhood every single day. Like...

Oh, sod it. She was bored of herself now. It was time to leave that bloody dive behind once and for all.

She took a few steps backwards. A good run up always helped, didn't it? And then she launched herself forwards. She progressed to the closest thing she got to a sprint and jumped into the unknown.

Oh but it was a long way. The sea roiled below her as she flailed through the air and she knew she was going to drop, knew she was going to drown and then...

She landed.

Or rather, her arms landed. Her legs were still very much at sea.

'Oh God.' She kicked wildly, only succeeding in dislodging her shoes. She heard a ripping noise from behind her and the boat jerked forwards, released from its mooring.

'Noooooooo.' She was slipping, her hands grasping for purchase, her legs dangling.

'Help!' The sea was so cold.

But then a hand grasped hers. A strong hand. A hand that would never let her go.

'Up you come.' Amber somehow dragged her onto the bathing platform, her arms and legs splayed out in a soggy starfish impression. A shot rang out and Jeanie was up on her feet again, checking for Nina, seeing if anyone was hurt. She had bloody done it and now she was made of adrenaline, fired with all the courage she had lacked for so long.

They peered up to the deck above them, to see Nina on her feet again, grabbing Christian. Amber and Jeanie climbed up the steps from the bathing platform and crept across the deck behind them, midlife ninjas. They were close now. Nina's teeth were set, her eyes savage.

'Drop the gun, Christian.'

'No.' He shouted. 'Don't make me hurt you, Nina. I love you.'

'No you bloody don't.' Nina laughed derisively. 'This isn't love. This is kidnap.'

Christian glanced behind him and saw Amber and Jeanie staggering as the boat bumped over the waves. Without him steering they were going nowhere, rotating back towards the marina, in danger of clipping the other boats moored on the pontoon.

'Stay back or I'll kill her!' His hair was wild as he waved the weapon around like it was a bubble gun at a children's party.

Jeanie's eyes were everywhere. Where was Clio? Still below? Still alive?

She looked at Amber. 'Ready?' She mouthed.

'Born ready.'

'Then let's go.'

They were about to rush him when he turned again, Nina's hair now held in one hand, his grip tightening. She whimpered, pain etched across her face.

'Don't get any bloody ideas.' Christian's other hand was steady around the gun. 'You two aren't exactly in your prime. You wouldn't want to do yourselves an injury, now, would you?'

He pointed the gun at them but Jeanie stepped forward anyway, raising her voice above the engine. The deck bucked and dropped beneath them.

'Why are you doing this, Christian?'

He pointed the gun at her chest but she could only think about Nina. She would make him talk – give Nina time to get away.

His voice rose high above the breeze, tinged with madness. 'What's the point of asking questions? You'll be dead in a minute.'

'DJ, no.' Nina's face was wet with tears.

Jeanie persisted. 'I just want to understand, Christian. Why did you kill Gary?'

'He was threatening to ruin Dad – so I stopped him.' He laughed. 'I need Dad's money too, you see. To get away – to leave this dump and see the world. There was no way I was losing the chance of getting that money. Dad was in a state – he had cancelled his trip to London that night, stayed here, because he was trying to find someone to stop Gary talking. And then Nina turned up at mine and she made it so easy – telling me how she had hit him – it was the perfect opportunity. It was luck – me being late to meet her, Gary being at the hut. Or maybe not luck – maybe just meant to be. Once she had told me I just waited till she was asleep, found him and finished the job.' He laughed. 'It was so perfect – the way he headed to Clio's van – the perfect chance to frame her.'

The boat was rocking now. Big though it was, without someone at the helm it was lost. But Christian's grip on the gun never wavered. His smile was manic, deranged.

'I thought Dad would be pleased, you know.' Sadness flickered across his face for a second, before anger replaced it. 'But as usual he chose to see the worst in me. Yelled, said I'd ruined the family name, that the police would think it was him. Then he buggered off. So now...' His thumb was playing with the trigger. 'I've got nothing to lose, have I? I'm taking his boat and my beautiful girl and off I go.'

Jeanie struggled to keep her balance as the deck undulated beneath her feet. 'And then what, Christian?'

A sidelong glance. 'What do you mean?'

'Well, what happens next?'

'Nina and I travel around the world.' He stumbled but regained his footing. 'For ever.'

Nina groaned as he threw back his head and laughed. He had let go of her hair now. Jeanie watched him, waiting for her chance. 'Clio was so easy to manipulate – I knew she would step in to save Nina. But I covered all the bases, just in case. I even sent Marshall the video I took of Gary and Cherie to put him in the firing line.' His face was alight. 'It was fun, seeing everyone running in the wrong direction, knowing I was cleverer than all of you. Especially Dad. He thought I was a loser who kept getting expelled, who kept giving up. He never knew what I was capable of. Mum would have known. Mum would have been proud of me, taking control and getting the girl I love and disappearing with her across the sea.'

Nina's voice was so low Jeanie could barely hear it. 'Oh no she wouldn't.'

He swivelled. 'What?'

'She wouldn't be proud. And you haven't got the girl you love. You haven't got her at all.'

'Oh yes I have.' He bent and kissed her, staggering against the deck, losing his footing. 'I love you, Nina. We're meant to be.'

'Yeah?' Nina caressed his face and something in Jeanie died. 'Well, the feeling's not bloody mutual. Fuck off.'

She shoved him hard in the chest. Amber ran forwards with a warrior's battle cry, knocking Christian sideways and pushing the gun out of his hands. He swore and fought her off, landing a slap across her face that cracked like a gunshot. She groaned and fell. Nina was next, only to be punched in the stomach, landing heavily on the deck.

Jeanie steeled herself. The boat was rotating round and round and nausea was rising. But Amber and Nina were down and there was only Jeanie left. She would do this. For Clio. For all of them.

Christian was reaching for the gun. It was now or never.

Jeanie closed her eyes, imagined she was standing high above that swimming pool, head raised to the sky, took one last breath, and dived towards Christian.

59

AMBER

The gun went off as Jeanie was in mid-air.

'Jeanie!'

Curls flying behind her, Jeanie landed on top of Christian, knocking the gun out of his hand. Amber heard the breath being expelled from his body but he was already trying to force his way up again. Amber grabbed the weapon and tucked it into her back pocket.

Jeanie didn't move. She just lay there, still and silent as Christian fought beneath her.

Amber's whole world was a scream.

Not Jeanie. Please. She couldn't lose her: not kind-hearted, chaotic Jeanie who was so much bigger than she knew, so much braver than she believed herself to be. Amber looked for blood as she sank down on her knees, stroking her friend's curls.

Christian was trying to escape, but Nina took the gun from Amber's pocket and trained it on his face. He wisely decided to stop.

Jeanie's eyes fluttered open. 'Am I dead?'

'Oh, thank God.' Amber pulled her off Christian and hugged her close. 'He missed.'

Nina pulled the handcuffs from Amber's back pocket. 'Can you do the honours?'

'Anything for you.' Amber handcuffed him to the railing that led down below deck. Then she ran back to Jeanie, dropping down to her knees and pulling her close.

'I must be dead. You're hugging me.' Jeanie clung on tight.

Relief brought tears to Amber's eyes. 'You were so brave.'

'I was?' Jeanie sat up. 'Ouch.'

'What?'

'I've clicked my back out.'

Christian started scraping his handcuffs against the rail, swearing loudly. Jeanie looked at him with the closest she came to a sneer. 'Oh stop it.' She shook her head. 'You're pathetic.'

'Go to hell. How dare you take everything away from me?'

Amber stared at him. DJ. Christian. Whatever his name was. There was no point in replying – he was far beyond the point of listening. He would become famous, but not for racing around the world. Everyone in Sunshine Sands would know his name, but only because he was about to go on a very long visit at His Majesty's pleasure.

'Clio.' She and Jeanie looked at each other, as panic started to swirl. 'CLIO.'

Amber ran across the deck and slid down the ladder into the cabin below. She looked around, seeing a leather sofa, a dining table. No Clio. She opened a door but only found a broom. She tried another. It was locked.

Screw that. Amber broke her second lock in a week.

And there was Clio, tied to the toilet, head in hands.

Alive. Gloriously, wonderfully alive.

She looked up, her red hair glowing in the electric light. 'Where's Nina? Is she OK?'

Nina barrelled in, curls flying. 'Here I am, Mum. Right here.' She threw her arms around Clio, the two of them competing to see who could cry the most. Then Nina turned her head, half-laughing, wiping her eyes.

'I can't believe you all just did that. You three are proper bad girls.'

'What do you mean?'

Nina ticked a list off on her fingers. 'Jumping onto boats, taking on gunmen, fighting killers. You slayed it.' She walked towards the steps. 'I'm going back to keep an eye on whatever he's called up there. I don't trust him.'

Amber nudged Clio, as she knelt down to untie her. 'Slaying it is good, right?'

'Right.' Clio stretched her arms out in front of her with a sigh. 'It's very good.' She frowned. 'You lot took your bloody time, didn't you?'

'There were a few things in our way.'

'Clio!' Jeanie hobbled in behind her and the three of them put their arms around each other, tears mingling with relief mingling with love.

Amber was first to pull away. 'That's quite enough of that.' She stood up, feeling the boat starting to shudder. 'Shall we go home, bad girls?'

'Yes.' She and Clio helped Jeanie up the ladder, and they stood staring at the marina, which apparently they had never quite managed to leave. Two police cars had finally arrived to help. Go, Marco.

The boat rocked and continued its relentless spinning.

Clio hugged Nina tight. 'Does anyone know how to drive this thing?'

'Absolutely not.' Amber shook her head. 'I wish Bez was on board. Wasn't he a deckhand after you brutally dumped him, Clio?'

Clio grinned. 'Which time?'

Amber thought of what Bez had told her about the night of Gary's murder, of the way he had gripped onto the cable, trying to save his girls. His candle for Clio had burned for a very long time.

Jeanie limped forwards. 'I can do it.' She smiled. 'My dad taught me.'

And Amber and Clio smiled at each other as Jeanie took the tiller and steered them all home.

60

@SUNSHINESANDSONLINE

Followers: 6000

NEWS BLAST: Local 'Bad Girls' outwit the police to find the Clifftop Killer by @DeniseMillsom

The murderer of Gary Goode has at last been identified and a local teenager, Christian Fernandez, is now safely under lock and key. He is the son of business magnate Johnny Fernandez, and our source revealed that he killed to protect his father's secret: that the family business was based on a tech idea stolen from Rajiv Francis, who is now back at the helm of the company his ideas helped to found.

In a killer twist, the murderer was identified not by local police, but by a trio of local women, one of whom was the police's prime suspect after finding the body on her doorstep. All in their forties, these bad girls broke into houses, spied at the spa and took on false identities to save their friend. Clio Lawrence, Amber Nagra and Jeanie Martin used their common sense and courage to track down the killer, never giving up until they had found their man. All hail a new crimefighting team!

Read more in our paper this week – this correspondent's last piece before moving to London to work on The Sun's social pages. Take care, Sunshine Sands – it's been a blast.

Shares: 4000

Likes: 6280

61

AMBER

Amber was face-to-face with the man who had fired her. He looked embarrassed. He looked humble. He looked everything she could wish him to look.

She kept quiet. She was damned if she was going to make this easy for him.

Marco coughed. 'I wanted to say...' Amber arched an eyebrow. 'Well done on the case.' The words came fast, as if being propelled out by sheer force of will. 'Great result. I mean...' She could almost see his ego squirming. It was delicious. 'We would have got him in the end. Obviously.'

Amber didn't comment. The press didn't think so. Denise had done her job well. They had met yesterday when Amber had texted her to let her know who had killed Gary. Why not give Denise a scoop? Without the burner phones they wouldn't have found out about the blackmail. And without seeing the bank deposits they wouldn't have known that Johnny had complied and found their way to Christian.

'And Christian Fernandez.' Marco's arms were folded so tightly over his chest that Amber was surprised he could breathe. 'Such a shame. He'll be locked away for a very long time indeed.'

'Yes.' She felt no sympathy for Christian. It didn't matter if his father had been a fraud – Amber had never even known her parents at all. It didn't mean you had to go around killing people. It just meant you had to build your own family, like she had.

Marco kicked the ground with his shoe. 'He's still asking to see Nina.'

Amber shook her head. 'Not going to happen. She never wants to see him again.'

Silence thickened between them. Amber looked at the framed certificates on his wall. His commendations, his graduation, the various courses he had done.

They didn't seem to have made him happy.

He tapped a pen on his desk, taking a breath, visibly bracing himself as he addressed a spot just behind her left ear.

'Amber... I'm very – sorry – about how you've been treated over the past few weeks. Although you did break the rules, it wasn't necessarily fair of me to – to proceed so vigorously.'

'No, it wasn't.' She remembered her vow. If she got out of Johnny's house, she would tell her friends the truth.

He steepled his fingers. 'You made it very difficult for me, Amber. Especially when Freya made a formal complaint. And I tried to tell you that tailing Freya's fiancé like that was a no-no – that you had to stop. He nearly took out a restraining order. I had to talk him out of it.' Amber opened her mouth but he carried on. 'And I know you thought you were doing the right thing – looking out for your friend...'

'You're not that good at apologies, are you? This is turning into a lecture.' Amber fanned her face. His office was boiling. Either that or she was blushing. Blushing at the memory of Freya's face when she had come to Amber's house and seen the wall of evidence that

Amber was collating about her fiancé and his various infidelities. Amber hadn't foreseen that, rather than being grateful, Freya would be angry with her; that Freya would tell her to get out of her life for ever. 'Well, maybe I should have listened, Marco.' The words didn't feel as bad as she had anticipated. 'Freya might still be my friend if I had.'

'Are you saying I was right?' Marco's tired eyes widened in surprise.

'Let's just accept we both screwed up, Marco. Deal?' She held out her hand.

'Deal.' He reached out and shook it.

'I'll be getting on then.' Her chair scraped against the floor as she pushed it back.

He leapt to his feet. 'There is something else, actually.'

'What?' She picked up her bag.

He straightened a photograph on his desk. 'Well, we were hoping...'

She waited.

'That you might come back and join us again?'

One beat of silence. Two.

'Interesting.' She folded her arms. 'And how are you going to square that? Given the public nature of the accusations made against me?'

'Well...' He sipped his tea. 'Those accusations have now been withdrawn, so—'

'Freya withdrew them?' A smile tugged at the corner of her lips.

'Yes.' He nodded. 'After we'd had a little – chat.'

Amber frowned. 'You made her withdraw them?'

'No.' The change in his pockets jangled as he moved. 'As if I could ever make her do anything.'

Freya must have forgiven her. Deep inside Amber a light began to shine.

He toyed with his paper cup. 'So, what do you think? About coming back?'

She shook her head. 'No thank you.'

'Pardon?' Of all the answers he had expected, it had clearly not been this.

'I said no thank you.' She rose to her feet. 'But I'm glad you asked – it means the world.'

And she left him, staring at the chair she had just vacated, scratching his head and wondering what on earth had just happened. But Amber didn't need to explain. She just needed to live her life, her way. And she was done with this. The drab corridors, the paperwork, the shitty shifts, the lack of control. She had tasted freedom now and she wanted more. She wanted to operate outside the rules – to be a bad girl doing good things.

She walked with her head high along familiar dingy corridors, past the water machine that was constantly empty, the snack machine that only ever dispensed Snickers and the kitchen that always smelt of tuna sandwiches.

Would she miss it? Her old job? As she spotted Freya in the kitchen she realised that the only thing she would miss was her friend.

Amber took a teabag and plopped it into the mermaid mug next to Freya's.

'Got enough for one more?' She gestured at the kettle.

Freya rolled her eyes. 'Go on then – it's your lucky day.' She poured hot water into Amber's mug – Freya's equivalent of a white flag. 'Who on earth let you in here?'

Amber smiled. 'I have my ways.'

'Don't you just.' Freya squeezed her teabag with a spoon. 'Well done on the case.'

Amber nodded. 'Thanks.'

'And you did it all without me. Had a feeling you might.' Freya spooned her traditional three sugars into her tea, before leaning against the kitchen counter to take her first sip. She watched Amber, her brown eyes still guarded. 'Marg, was it?'

Amber nodded. 'She helped.'

'Good luck owing that one a favour.' Freya rolled her eyes. 'So are you coming back, then?'

'Well...' Amber put her mug down, facing her old colleague head on. 'I said no. Time for new things, I think.'

'Oh yeah?'

'Yeah.' Amber found she was nervous now. Freya's dark eyes on hers, the tilt of her head. It had always been Freya, for Amber. Ever since Hendon, ever since they had shared their first Twix in a squad car, ever since Freya had said hello.

She knew Freya would never feel the same. But it didn't matter. Amber would carry on, their one drunken New Year's snog a golden memory that she would lock away as carefully as the letter her birth mum had tucked beneath her when she left baby Amber on a bus and never came back.

She took a deep breath. 'I just wanted to say I'm sorry.'

Freya stilled, her hand halfway to the biscuit tin. 'You're sorry?'

'Yes.' Amber nodded. 'Sorry for everything. For putting Dev under surveillance by myself, without asking. For not listening to you, for not backing off.' Amber sighed. 'I thought I was helping, but...'

Freya shook her head. 'No. You weren't. I love him, Amber and all that stuff you made up – it nearly broke us.'

'I didn't make it up!'

'Stop.' Freya held up her hands. 'Not again, Amber.' Amber pressed her lips together, remembering the day Freya had seen Amber's wall covered with images of Dev, papered with maps, assignations, clues. All the evidence was there – only Freya didn't want to see it. That was love for you.

'Well...' Amber tipped the rest of her tea into the sink. 'I really am sorry – for hurting you. All the best, yeah?' The words felt woefully inadequate to mark the end of a friendship as long as theirs, but they were all she had. Words were Clio's thing. Amber was all about action.

She stepped out of the kitchen, looking round the open plan office she would never be part of again. Her desk was already covered in files, a young officer intent on the screen of her PC.

She turned back. 'Goodbye.' She raised a hand in farewell to Freya and walked away, her own woman, holding her head high.

62

JEANIE

Tan got in from the shops and she was waiting for him.

'OK.' She didn't even say hello. 'I've been thinking...'

It took her a second to realise that he was talking in time with her. 'We need to make some changes.'

They both laughed. 'Great minds, no?' Tan looked around at the unusually tidy living room. No toys strewn all over the floor. No crumbs spattered over the carpet. 'What have you done with the children? Have you tidied them up, too?'

'Don't panic.' She smiled. 'They're not here.' She gestured around the house. 'They're at the new childminder's. Three mornings a week. Starting today.'

'What happened to nursery?'

'Too posh.' Jeanie grimaced. 'So I moved them. I hope you don't mind. You've been working so hard, I just did it. I want Yumi and Jack with kids like them. Kids with working parents and mess, parents who argue and then make up again. Real parents. Not ones with nannies and castles.' She smiled. 'Houses with Playdough in the carpet and toys all over the stairs.'

'Oh, thank God.' Tan put a bottle of milk in the fridge and

turned back to her. 'I hated dropping off at that nursery – I always felt like a peasant because our two didn't have Cartier hats.'

'Well, dropping them off at the childminder's is a game-changer. She makes me feel like I might be doing something right.' Jeanie grinned. 'Which as you know is worth its weight in gold.'

Tan smiled, taking his glasses off and rubbing his eyes.

She put her hand on his. 'Are you working at home today?'

'Yes.' He nodded. 'I've got a new project so I need to concentrate.' He put his glasses back on. 'Now that we've won that funding I'm heading up the team, working with the council on improving social housing provision.'

'That's great, Tan!' She kissed him, trying not to mind when he looked surprised. Maybe her breath smelt bad. Maybe he hated this dress. She pulled back. 'So you're not being fired then? Like you thought?'

'Um. No.' His cheeks were flushed. 'More of a promotion, actually. I feel a bit silly now for being worried.' He picked up the mug his best friend had given him for his fortieth – Tan and Jeanie's faces beaming beneath a bright red rim. He threw a teabag in. 'Do you want one?'

'Sure.' She stood next to him, leaning against the counter.

He spoke without looking. 'So is it OK for me to talk about your work stuff now?'

Guilt seeped through her. 'Of course. I'm so sorry for making you feel you couldn't.'

He shook his head. 'You didn't. Not really. I just didn't know whether – whether you were missing your job, or not missing it. Whether you want to be with the kids full time, or don't? So it just felt easier to leave it. To not talk about it.' He splashed boiling water into the mugs. 'In case you resented being with them.'

Jeanie put her head against his shoulder. 'I never resent them, Tan.'

'Really?'

'Not much, anyway.' She giggled. 'But I do miss – me. Not the old me who worked all the time and peed on sticks every ten minutes and obsessed over getting pregnant, but the one who knew who she was.'

'OK.' He played with her fingers, turning them over in his. 'So how do we get that Jeanie back? How can I help?'

Jeanie nudged him. 'I don't know. But I am sure that I don't want to go back to my old job.' She remembered her conversation with Lianne and smiled. 'It's too full-on. Too much with the kids as well.'

He nodded. 'So?'

'So I'll have a look. See what's out there. Is that OK?'

He stayed silent.

Jeanie felt a twinge of concern. 'Tan?'

Silence.

'Tan?' She felt a rush of panic. 'I need to do this. I can't go on just – washing and cleaning and never using my brain except to make up bedtime stories. You know?'

'I know.'

'So I need to do this. To find something I can do. OK?' Her heart was beating fast.

'Absolutely.' He ran his fingers gently down her cheek. 'I'm just happy to have my Jean Jeanie back.'

She had opened her mouth to make her point again, but closed it rapidly.

'You are?'

He smiled. 'I've missed her a lot.'

'You have?' She looked at him – this kind man. Father of the twins. Maker of elaborate and messy meals. Race driver in times of crisis.

Her Tan.

He grinned. 'Now can we talk about something important?'

'Like how none of your socks ever match?'

'No.' He pulled her close. 'More important even than that.'

A kiss. So light it made her want more.

'Yes?' Her breath caught.

He suddenly dropped down to the floor.

'Are you OK? Has your ankle gone again?'

'My ankle's fine.'

'Your toe?'

'It's not my toe. And please stop listing every injury I have ever had. I'm trying to do something romantic here.'

'Romantic...?' She blinked. His hand was reaching into his back pocket.

'Jeanie...' His voice was husky, his face wide open as he tipped it up towards her. 'Jeanie. My beautiful girl. Will you...' His hand shook as he opened the red velvet box. 'Will you marry me?'

For a moment the question hung in the air. Jeanie's hand flew to her mouth. He had the ring now – the aquamarine stone gleaming, the platinum gold band shining. His grandmother's ring. And he wanted her to wear it.

'Jeanie?' The need on his face took her breath away. This man knew all of her and he wanted her anyway. This man was her heart, her happy place.

'Yes please. Yes please, I'd love to marry you!' And she was down on the floor with him, kissing him, laughing, crying, knowing that this was where she belonged, knowing that he was her home.

'My Jeanie.' Tan's voice was a whisper as he slid the ring onto her finger. She held it up, love rushing through her, understanding at last that she had found her forever.

They pressed together, hands in hair, arms around each other, breath quickening, until the inevitable ring of the phone interrupted them.

'Leave it.' He was unbuttoning her blouse.

'I can't.'

Another button. 'But this is our one chance, Jeanie. No children.'

'But it might be the childminder.'

'But...'

'I'm picking up, just in case.'

'I hate it when you're right.' He let her go and walked to the window.

It was the childminder. Ten minutes later they were on their way to pick up a vomiting Yumi, Dettol and a bucket in tow. They held hands all the way, the ring safe on her finger, a guarantee of the future to come.

63

Amber Admin @SaveClio NAME CHANGE to @BadGirls

Amber:– Ladies. We have things to discuss. Get over here. Now.

Clio:– I'm in the next caravan. Would it kill you to get off your bum and come and talk to me?!

Jeanie:– Childminder a-go-go. Am on my way.

Amber:– Clio, yes it would. Jeanie, no one says 'a-go-go.' FFS. See you in ten.

64

CLIO

'I've got something for you.' Bez dug into his pocket and pulled out a stick of chewing gum.

'Erm. Thanks?' Clio grimaced. 'That's nice of you. I'll be sure to brush my teeth better. Apologies.'

'Oh shit. Not that.' Bez patted another pocket of his thick black hoodie. 'Here it is. Ta da.'

He brought out a small box. 'Your ring.'

Relief flooded through her. 'Thank you.' She opened the box, running her fingertip over the tiny diamonds. It was back with her, right where it should be. She held it up to the light, smiling. 'There's most of Nina's university fund, right there.'

She looked through Bez's window to where their daughter was busy slapping fresh green paint onto one of the caravans. 'How do you think she's doing?'

Bez shrugged, resting his long legs on his coffee table. 'Up and down. Some days raging angry, some days weeping into the duvet. But she's not giving up. Not our Nina.'

Clio nodded. 'Agreed.' She sipped her coffee. Nina caught her staring and pulled an AirPod out of her ear. She walked over, addressing them through the open window.

'Stop worrying, you two.' She brandished her brush. 'I'm not about to kill myself. Or self-harm. I'm just a teenager dancing and painting a MILLION CARAVANS because my horrible parents want to teach me that violence isn't the answer.' She pouted. 'Get over it.' She blew them both a kiss and got back to her work.

Clio looked at Bez and smiled. 'She's OK.'

Bez reached for another biscuit. 'Yes. A tough lesson for her, though. First love isn't all it's cracked up to be, is it?'

Clio nudged him. 'I dunno. We did OK, didn't we?'

'I suppose we did.' Bez smiled. 'Apart from all the rows.'

Clio blushed, knowing that she had caused most of them. She tucked her now pink hair behind her ears. 'Well, OK, apart from those.'

Bez chuckled. 'Let's change the subject, shall we?'

Clio smiled. 'Nice idea about her painting the vans.'

Bez shrugged. 'She needs to understand that violence is never the answer.'

Clio gave a dramatic gasp, placing her hand on her breastbone. 'You're doing discipline now?'

'It's never too late to learn.' He looked down, kicking the carpet with the toe of his boot. 'I mean, look at you, starting over at forty-five.'

'Like I have a choice.'

'I was just wondering...'

'Yes?'

'Have you remembered yet?' His voice was a note higher.

'Remembered what?'

He spoke in a rush. 'Anything about what happened the night Gary was killed?'

'No.' She shook her head. 'Nothing.'

His face clouded. 'Ah. OK.' He shrugged. 'Doesn't matter. They're not prosecuting you, are they? For giving false testimony?'

She shook her head. 'The charges were dropped. My GP wrote an amazing letter confirming that I am officially incapable of remembering things at the moment due to my wildly fluctuating hormones.' She kept her voice light but in truth the letter had depressed her. Perimenopause made her feel so bloody *old*. 'So they decided not to prosecute.' She twisted the belt of her jumpsuit between her fingers.

'Well, you did an amazing thing for Nina, lying like that.'

'I did my best.'

There was a sharp tap on the window and Amber's face appeared.

'I said ten minutes. Get in here.'

She disappeared into the nearest static caravan, which she had hired out of the blue at the weekend, after putting her house on the market and refusing to say why. Since Christian had been arrested she had gone underground, appearing only to steal Clio's coffee or to punch the hell out of the bag that now hung in the laundry block.

'I'd better go.' Clio stood up. 'But – see you later, maybe?'

Bez nodded. 'I'd like that.'

As Clio walked down the steps Jeanie pulled up in her car. She looked flushed and happy, her hair drawn back in a ponytail, her curls soft around her face.

'Pink hair!' Jeanie hugged Clio. 'I love it.'

'I needed a change.' Clio did a twirl. 'Time to move on, don't you think?'

'Definitely.' Clio noticed that Jeanie was steadfastly avoiding looking towards Clio's caravan. Clio understood – the memories of Gary's body were just too strong. Clio and Nina had been staying at

Bez's since the murder and Clio would move into a new van as soon as she could find the energy.

Arms around each other, they entered Amber's caravan, to find that their friend had already painted it a severe grey and had accessorised it with two desks, a huge whiteboard, a laptop and a filing cabinet.

'Wow, you've made the place really homely.' Clio dropped into one of the two black leather chairs in front of the desk. 'It's just like the dentist.'

Amber leant against the desk and folded her arms. 'Thanks.'

'What's going on, then?' Clio waited expectantly.

'I'm setting up a detective agency.' Amber picked up a pen and put it down again at exact right angles to the black phone in the corner of the desk.

'What?' Jeanie was leaning against the window sill, exuding the kind of glow that could only mean that she and Tan were finally having sex again. And. Hang on...

'Jeanie. Is that a ring?' Clio was on her feet now. 'Are you...?

Jeanie's cheeks flushed. 'Yes!' She held out her hand. 'He proposed!'

'Oh my God.' Clio threw her arms around her friend. 'This is great. A wedding! We can dance. We can drink. I love a wedding.'

Jeanie's face fell. 'Oh God. A wedding. I'll have to invite my mum.'

Clio squeezed her harder. 'I'll protect you. Besides, she'll love it. Hasn't she wanted you to get married for years?'

'Yes, but...'

Amber coughed. Loudly. 'Jeanie, I am bloody delighted for you, you know that. But please can we concentrate?'

'On what?' Clio clapped her hands. 'She's getting married. What could be more important than that?'

'I'm setting up a detective agency, that's what. And I want you two to work for me.'

Clio and Jeanie stared at her.

'Pardon?'

'You heard me.' Amber wiped her already spotless desk. 'I just incorporated the name today. The Bad Girls Detective Agency. I got the idea from what Nina said at the marina, and from the *Sunshine Sands Online* posts. It's good, don't you think?'

Clio glanced at Jeanie, indicating Amber with her thumb. 'Did I hear her right?'

'I think so.' Jeanie faltered towards a chair and sank down. 'I'm not ready for this.'

Amber tutted under her breath. 'I want you two to work for me. Did you hear that part?'

'Yes.' Clio pushed her chair back so it teetered on two legs. 'But I'm not sure it's a good idea.'

Amber sighed. 'Clio, now Gary's dead, it's pretty obvious he's run Looking Goode into the ground. So, you need a paying job, don't you?'

She turned to Jeanie. 'And you don't want to go back to Miracle Marketing, and you need flexibility, and this will be perfect. You'll be doing the internet research side – you know, trawling social media, online histories, that kind of thing. You can fit it around the kids.'

Jeanie's neck was going blotchy. Bad sign. 'Amber, you don't need to do this. I don't need you feeling sorry for me, giving me a job out of pity.'

'I'm not.' Amber tapped her notebook with one of the twenty Bic biros she had stored in the *Murder, She Wrote* mug on the top left corner of the desk. 'You're going to make a brilliant detective – that's why I'm hiring you. You're sharp, you're determined and you miss nothing. Not to mention you'll go the extra mile to get a result.'

Jeanie's face glowed.

'And you, Clio...' Amber leant forwards. 'You can play all the roles – all the undercover roles we need to crack our cases.'

Clio's chair slammed back into position. 'Me? Paid? To act?'

'Yep.' Amber nodded. 'You'll be brilliant.'

'Maybe.' Clio was trying her hardest not to look impressed. She must put up a bit of a fight, or Amber would pay her a pittance, the skinflint. Clio and Jeanie had seen Amber negotiating in the souks of Morocco on Clio's hen weekend – she would have both of them on the minimum wage given half a chance.

'I've sold the house to fund this, that's how much faith I have in the idea. And in us.' Amber was on her feet now. 'So what do you say? Are you in?'

Clio looked at Jeanie. Jeanie looked at Clio.

'Oh shit, I forgot.' Amber was blushing. That never happened. 'There's something I need to tell you first. About why I was fired. You see...'

Clio waved a hand dismissively. 'That's old news, Amber.'

'No.' Amber shook her head. 'You have to listen. You see I did do something wrong – that's why they fired me. I – kind of – stalked someone. Dev. Freya's fiancé. I thought he was up to something, and he was, and I was trying to look out for Freya, but...' She stopped. 'I promised myself I'd be honest.' Her eyes were glued to the floor. 'Because I've never lied to you before and it felt horrible.'

Clio's heart twisted. She opened her mouth, but it was Jeanie who spoke first.

'I don't care,' she said simply. 'If you thought something was wrong in my life, I hope you'd do the same for me. Isn't that right, Clio?'

Clio nodded. 'I couldn't put it better myself.'

'Really?' Amber raised her head. A tear rolled down her cheek.

'Oh no.' Clio stood up. 'This isn't a time for crying. You've just

started a detective agency. This is a day for wine and bad dancing.'
She gestured at her jumpsuit. 'Naturally I have come dressed for the
occasion.'

Amber wiped her cheeks. 'But is it my agency, or our agency?'

Clio smiled at Jeanie. Jeanie smiled at Clio.

Amber watched them, as she had always watched them, as she
had always looked out for them.

'I'd love to say yes...' Jeanie took a step towards Amber, giving
Clio a conspiratorial wink.

Clio moved too. 'But there's just one thing we'd like first.'

'To seal the deal.'

'To cement our new start.'

'What?' Amber's eyes flicked from one to the other. 'What do
you want?'

Jeanie held out her arms. 'Give us a hug and we're all yours.'

Clio echoed her. 'Just one little hug.'

'I...' Panic was etched across Amber's face.

Jeanie was right next to her now. 'You hugged us the night Gary
died. And on the boat.'

'Because you nearly died!'

'Because you love us.' Clio smiled, arms wide. 'Come to
mamma.'

'Oh God, if I have to.' Amber spread her arms and drew them in.

'It's a yes from me.' Jeanie spoke into Amber's shoulder.

'And it's a golden bloody buzzer from me.' Clio snuggled close
to both of them, these two friends, these two loyal and messy
women who had saved her life.

Amber extracted herself, retreating to the safety of her desk.

'So, do you want to hear about our first case?'

Clio sat down. 'Hell, yes.'

Amber turned her iPad round for them to see. 'A lover who isn't
playing ball. Marg, the moneylender who helped me – you'll meet

her soon enough – is convinced her twenty-five-year-old boyfriend Sam is seeing someone else. I owe her one so I said we'd check it out. And... a new one, straight in as soon as I set up the website this morning. Let's have a look.' She clicked the email open. 'A wedding singer – a very handsome one, by the look of it – who's under suspicion of theft. A groom wants us to investigate.'

'I'm a very good wedding guest.' Clio sat back down again. 'I'll go undercover and keep an eye on him.'

'Sure you will. Until you have a prosecco or four.'

Clio bridled. 'Well, I'd have to blend in, wouldn't I?'

Amber rolled her eyes. 'You'd have to do your job.'

Clio held her hand up dramatically. 'Don't rein me in, boss. Not on my first day.'

Amber put her mug down. 'I'm not reining you in. And please don't call me boss.'

Clio's eyes lit up. 'This is going to be so much fun.' She clapped her hands. 'Isn't it?'

'It really is.' Jeanie nodded happily. 'So, what do you want us to do?' She waited a beat. 'Boss?'

Amber rolled her eyes despairingly, but she was grinning too.

'Well...'

And so, full of excitement and hope, the Bad Girls Detective Agency got to work.

ACKNOWLEDGMENTS

Firstly, a huge thank you to my husband Max who is a) not dead and b) nothing like Gary. Big thanks too to Evie and Aidan for being the best children in the world (not biased at all, obviously), and to Mum, Dad and Richard for being the most faithful cheerleaders ever. Sarah Turner – thank you for telling me to go for it; Tamara Bathgate thanks for listening, listening and then listening some more; Cressida McLaughlin, Jenny Ashcroft, Kim Curran and Freya Sampson – thanks for your early enthusiasm; Cesca Major – I wouldn't have written this book without THAT phone call, and Ali Lippiett you are the greatest sounding board – let us walkies together for ever.

I am so grateful to Claire Pollard and Stuart Gibbon for helping with the police background to this book and to Ben Lippiett for your marina insights. A big thank you to Anna Barrett at the-writers-space.com for initial feedback and encouragement. To anyone writing a book – GET HER ON YOUR TEAM.

I am indebted to my agent Charlie Campbell, for such kindness, humour and determination while making things happen and to my editor Isobel Akenhead for being such a brilliant mix of wisdom, insight and FUN. I love working with you both. Thank you to Sam Edenborough and everyone at Greyhound Literary, to eagle-eyed copy editor Debra Newhouse, to proofreader Gary Jukes and to the mighty team at Boldwood Books, especially Amanda Ridout, Nia Beynon, Claire Fenby-Warren, Jenna Houston, Marcela Torres, Sue Lamprell, Ben Wilson and Leila Mauger.

Last, but not least, I am so grateful to you, lovely reader. Thank you for choosing this book and I hope you loved reading it as much as I loved writing it. If you did, feel free to tell everyone you know. Spare no one. Katie x

ABOUT THE AUTHOR

Katie Marsh wrote romantic fiction before turning to crime. Her debut novel was a World Book Night pick and her books are published in ten languages. She lives in the countryside and loves strong coffee and pretending she is in charge of her children.

Sign up to Katie Marsh's mailing list for news, competitions and updates on future books.

Visit Katie's website: https://katie-marsh.com/

Follow Katie on social media here:

Poison
& Pens

POISON & PENS IS THE HOME OF
COZY MYSTERIES SO POUR YOURSELF
A CUP OF TEA & GET SLEUTHING!

DISCOVER PAGE-TURNING NOVELS FROM
YOUR FAVOURITE AUTHORS &
MEET NEW FRIENDS

JOIN OUR
FACEBOOK GROUP

BIT.LYPOISONANDPENSFB

SIGN UP TO OUR
NEWSLETTER

BIT.LY/POISONANDPENSNEWS

Boldw∞d

Boldwood Books is an award-winning fiction publishing company seeking out the best stories from around the world.

Find out more at www.boldwoodbooks.com

Join our reader community for brilliant books, competitions and offers!

Follow us
@BoldwoodBooks
@TheBoldBookClub

Sign up to our weekly
deals newsletter

https://bit.ly/BoldwoodBNewsletter

Printed in Great Britain
by Amazon

34240648R00195